THE LOG HOUSE ON THE RIGHT

A Novel

HOLLY JO RADTKE

Print Edition
ISBN: 979-8-218-56328-8

This is a self-published book. Published by Holly Jo Radtke.

Cover design by INK Book Designs

Printed in the United States of America

This book is dedicated to:
My amazing husband.
Thank you for all of your support and patience
while I begin to navigate the writing world.
I love you!

PART ONE

ALDER DAUGHTLER

Chapter One

WHILE I'M PROUD to say that I'm officially a University of Nevada graduate, I can't be a Las Vegas Rebel forever. It's time for me to move back home: to Montana. I'm far from a rebel, anyway. I never missed a class, I went above and beyond for my studies, and I cried when my grades weren't perfect enough. My classes were challenging, but they also served as a distraction from my struggles with my social life. I rarely had the urge to party, which is ironic given the city I was in, but studying Early Childhood Education and Psychology with a career goal of family therapy and trauma therapy for children tends to keep one busy. I didn't have the time to have regular night-outs, nor did I make the time.

I was no stranger to Vegas. Growing up there for the first eight years of my childhood drew me back for my college years, but after experiencing heartbreak at its finest, I no longer wanted to be associated with the place. My boyfriend throughout college, Harrison, was all I could dream of until the relationship became a nightmare. I was caught up in unwanted miscommunications and pure immaturity. Being the other woman and a second choice isn't quite my style when it comes to relationships. My poor choices in men led me to give up on the dating life altogether. Maybe it was because I was shy and allowed just about anyone into my life, or perhaps it was my ability to trust everyone around me. As a reserved and introverted person, I've always felt the need to change myself to fit in with friend groups and attract certain guys. I never really felt like I could live my life as Jaemes. Sadly, I no longer know who Jaemes truly is because of that. I do know I can't continue to quietly sit in a corner for the rest of my life. It's time to show who Jaemes really is, whoever that may be.

I'm honestly not sure how it's going to go in Montana. I have my parents and friends here, but what about me? Can I really be myself here? I'm about to find out. I scheduled a few house showings in my hometown, and I start both a new job and internship soon. I always told myself that I should branch out and live somewhere I've never been and start a new life, but I couldn't pass up the amazing career opportunities that led me back here. My long train of thought gets interrupted when my best friend, Ember Ellis, sweeps me away with a giant hug inside the airport, reminding me that there are even more positives about my decision to move back home.

"Hey, Jaemes!" she squeals. "I fricken missed you so much."

"You're crazy. I just saw you a few weeks ago," I laugh as she lets me go.

Ember helped me with packing most of my belongings back in Vegas. I met Ember when I moved here in fifth grade, and we've been inseparable ever since. Going through my school years with Ember was always an adventure. In high school, I was determined to follow in my mom's performing footsteps and join the dance team alongside Ember. As a shy teenager, being on the dance team and befriending Ember helped break me out of my shell, giving me the confidence to meet new people. We maintained our strong friendship throughout our college years, despite the long distance. She stayed here in Montana and was accepted into a nursing program. We visited each other numerous times, making sure to meet during holiday breaks. Like many close friendships, we always continued right where we left off.

"Yeah, well, so? Can't I still miss my best friend?"

"I missed you, too, you freak of the week," I tell her and return the hug.

Ember hooks arms with me, and we head outside with my neon yellow hardshell suitcase following behind us. As we near her vehicle, I see her boyfriend, Bennett Tanner, and her younger brother, Eric, waiting for us.

Ember and Eric could pass as twins with their perfect porcelain skin and deep red, curly hair. Ember's lengthy hair reaches just past the middle of her back. I have always been envious of her natural beauty. Many people are surprised that she doesn't wear colored contact lenses, given that her eyes are different colors. Her right eye is green, and her left eye is blue.

"As you can see, I needed company. Plus, I thought maybe you would like to see these guys, too," she says close to my ear as if she wanted to keep that a secret.

"Of course I do. It's been so long since I've seen either of them," I tell her, taking in a breath of fresh Montana air.

"Welcome home," Bennett says as soon as we reach the vehicle.

"Thank you. I'm glad to be back," I reply.

"Can we please stop to get something to eat?" Eric asks without looking up from his phone. Ember takes my luggage and gives it to Bennett to place in the trunk.

"No. I'm sure Jaemes wants to get home," Ember assumes.

She assumes correctly.

Eric scoffs and opens the car door to get in. "Are your parents even home?" he asks me.

"I spoke with my mom before my flight departed. They won't be home for a few days. With me being out of the house for the last few years, they've been working a lot more, so no surprise there."

"You're coming to my house with us, then," Ember says. "We have a lot to catch up on."

My hometown is approximately forty minutes away from

the airport. The whole drive home, I admire the mountains surrounding us, the cows and horses spread out in the fields, and all the natural beauty Montana has to offer. It's nothing like the artificial beauty from the loud city and bright lights of Las Vegas.

The afternoon sun is warm, but nothing like the desert heat I was accustomed to. I'm craving this fresher air and can't wait to sit outside and relax in it. Maybe returning home won't be so bad. I almost forgot how authentic the nature and scenery are around here.

We turn onto a gravel road, indicating we are almost at the Ellis household. This road evokes a range of memories and a sense of joy. I see the left turn up ahead, and I can't help but notice the log house on the right. The Ellis' have always lived down the road from this log house, which has never looked this elegant and well cared for.

"Whoa, someone actually cleaned this place up?" I ask.

"My buddy from work bought it a few years back and fixed it up," Bennett mentions.

"Whoever it is did a phenomenal job. It looks amazing," I say, trying to quickly glance at the log house and the property around it as we drive by.

"Alder Daughtler," Bennett says, clarifying his name.

"You should have seen the amount of work and hours they put into that house," Ember adds. "If they weren't working, they were working on that house."

Bennett looks back at me from the passenger seat. "We got it finished up about a month ago." He turns to Ember. "He's probably getting things ready for his housewarming bonfire tonight."

Bennett works as a construction electrician. He explains that he and Alder want to start their own business soon. They have been good friends for years and have always worked well together. Ember expresses her interest in going to Alder's bonfire, and Bennett states that he told Alder they'd attend but had to pick up a friend from the airport first. I'm hoping they don't expect me to join. All I want to do after a long day of traveling is relax with my best friend and catch up on whatever needs catching up on. We are due for some much-needed one-on-one time.

Ember pulls into their driveway and parks the car.

"Alright, Bennett, I think it's time for that basketball rematch," Eric says.

"You're just asking for more embarrassment, dude," Bennett replies as he goes into the garage to grab a ball.

The boys start their one-on-one basketball game in the driveway, and Ember and I walk down the road. The sun is about to set, but thankfully, it's still giving off some warmth.

"How's everything going with your nursing career? I know you were looking for the right position, but are there any updates?" I ask her.

"Actually, I recently accepted a travel nurse position. I'll get to meet new people and see some pretty neat places," she tells me. "Although I've just started, I know it's going to be the job for me. My coworkers seem awesome, which makes it even better."

"Great. I moved back home just in time for my partner in crime to leave me. You were one of the only reasons why I was semi-okay moving back to Montana," I admit to her.

"Oh, please. Spare me. You'll get over it just like I had to when you moved back to Vegas for college. Besides, it's not like I won't ever be home."

"Oh, I see how it is. You're trying to get back at me," I tease, trying to find the light in this news. "Will that affect your relationship with Bennett? I'm sure it can't be easy."

"We'll make it work. It will be like having a typical relationship and a long-distance relationship at the same time," she laughs.

"I guess distance makes the heart grow fonder."

"Are you happy to finally be back home?" she asks, then engulfs me in a bear hug, causing me to nearly tip over onto the gravel road.

"You know, I love you and the love you have for me, but one of these days, you're actually going to hurt me."

"Don't be a baby. Just take it," she chuckles. "On a serious note, how are you holding up with the whole Harrison situation?"

I knew he would be brought up at some point, but I still had high hopes of avoiding the subject altogether. I need to move on, and talking about him will only slow down that process.

"I'm doing okay. I was hurt at first, but now I'm pissed more than anything."

It took a long time for me to come to terms with the fact that my three-and-a-half-year relationship with Harrison had ended for good. He was my everything for the duration of my college years. I couldn't have asked for a better person to be by my side throughout all of my college experiences. He understood me and was patient, despite our personalities being polar opposites. He saved me from all of the assholes I seemed to attract when I started freshman year.

Halfway through my senior year, I discovered from my roommate that a rumor was circulating about Harrison still being involved with his high school girlfriend. When I brought it up to him, he never denied it. Apparently, he thought he could live two separate lives, as he is originally from Colorado, and she never planned to accompany him to the University of Nevada. Harrison was undecided about whether he was going to stay in Las Vegas after graduation or move back home. I made his decision easier when I told him that I wasn't staying and he wasn't coming with me.

"I can't believe he turned out to be another asshole. You

two were so cute together—it made my heart melt," she pouts.

"How do you think I feel, Em? I thought I was going to marry him, and we would start a family together. It's hard to get over someone who was really important to you. Especially when he wasn't who I thought he was." My mood turns even more depressed as I recall my past with Harrison and what our future *should* have looked like. Now, we are states away and living our own lives separately as if our relationship never existed.

"Please tell me you're going to the town's party next weekend. We need to find you a man who will help get you over this hump."

The mayor is hosting a party to celebrate the town's one hundredth anniversary. Otherwise, this small town isn't known for putting on any celebrations or events, so it's a big deal. I roll my eyes at her before responding.

"Ember, the last thing that's on my mind right now is going to the town's party for a man, let alone a housewarming party at *this* man's house," I say while gesturing with my hand to the log house we are nearing.

"Come on…it should be fun…if you go, too!"

"We'll see. I already agreed to help at one of the booths. The therapy office I'm interning at asked if I wanted to help," I inform her.

Our walking route has taken us to the front of the log house, and I'm now able to take a better look at it. Before we turn around to go back, I examine everything in front of me. The barn features brand-new siding, the lawn has been freshly mowed, the logs on the house have been refinished, and there is a fire pit with concrete edging for outdoor seating.

I see a man on the porch working on the wood paneling. Three large dogs are roaming around the yard. They look like Labrador Retrievers—one white, one chocolate, and one black. After the dogs start barking our way, he looks up and sees us and waves us down, which makes Ember nudge my arm with her elbow before walking toward the property entrance. He walks down the porch steps and meets us halfway down the driveway. He's tall and fit, wearing ripped blue jeans that are dirt-stained, and a gray Coors Light t-shirt. His white ballcap is on backward, and he's wearing black sunglasses. As I look at him a little closer, I notice he has some facial hair. It's longer than a five o'clock shadow but shorter than what I would consider a full-on beard.

"You're still not done with this place?" Ember asks him.

He shakes his head and then removes his sunglasses from his face. "I can't seem to catch a break."

I can tell he's trying to figure out who I am when he finally looks at me. His eyes are hazel, and they sparkle in the setting sunlight. Ember takes this opportunity to introduce us. "Alder, this is my best friend in the whole world, Jaemes." She turns to Alder. "Jaemes, this is Alder."

He holds his hand out to shake mine but doesn't say any-thing. However, I don't say anything either. I've been known to be socially awkward, and I don't want to chance saying anything stupid. His hands are calloused and dirty, but he holds a tight grip during our handshake. He seems to be the type of man who isn't afraid to get his hands dirty with a project. Someone who would take matters into his own hands if it came down to it. Someone who doesn't take shit from anyone. A man who is entirely different from the egotistical, preppy, party boys I was into in college. But these are only assumptions, like judging a book by its cover.

An extremely handsome, manly book cover.

"Hi, it's… really lovely to meet you," I blurt out loud. My face instantly feels numb. *Really lovely to meet you?* Could I sound any more eager? Although I'm trying to be a more talkative and outgoing person, I still come across as awkward and embarrassing. I have a lot of work to do if I want to change who Jaemes is. It's a constant battle within myself—getting rid of the old that's been alive for over twenty years and building a new self with a different personality that you're proud to show everyone, in and out of your life. Starting a new life in your hometown isn't easy. I want people who know me not to recognize me, and for new acquaintances to know exactly who this new version of me is. So far, I'm not doing a great job.

I look at Ember, waiting for her to say something since I seem to be having a hard time.

"So, are you good to go for tonight?" she finally asks.

"Just about. Once I'm done with this bullshit," he says, gesturing toward the area of the porch he is working on. "You guys are more than welcome to come. I told Bennett about it a few days ago."

"We just might. I think Jaemes needs a fun night out," she says, tilting her head my way with a smirk on her face. Again, I roll my eyes at her and shake my head. She knows I would much rather sit at home and sleep in what was once my bed.

"Cool, see you later, then," Alder says before looking at me one last time and then returning to his porch, while we slowly make our way back down the road to Ember's house.

"You are so awkward," Ember laughs.

"I'm totally no way, not going," I tell her, then glance back at Alder, making his way back to the house.

My comment causes her to stop in her tracks. "And why not?"

"Ember, I know when I'm not wanted. Did you see the way he looked at me?"

She scoffs and continues walking again. "No, you're being ridiculous."

"I'm not stupid. He didn't say one word to me. That wasn't a good first impression. There's no way I'm going back to that house."

"You'll be fine. Give him a break. He's probably tired from

constantly working on house repairs. You always get this way when you meet new people. Have a few drinks, loosen up a little, and have fun. Try to overcome your awkwardness."

She's right. I don't do well with large gatherings, especially with people I'm not familiar with. It's not enjoyable being the shy one. I was content and comfortable in high school because I could spend many years with the same people. It was the same experience during my college years. Now that I am back home, I feel out of my comfort zone as I comprehend starting all over again. But is there a better way to start a new life than going to a stranger's housewarming party on your first night home?

I guess there's only one way to find out.

Chapter Two

HERE WE ARE on walk number two toward the log house. This time, Bennett accompanies us. Ember and Eric spent the last half hour arguing about whether or not he could also attend Alder's bonfire. As much as we all love Eric and his unique sense of humor, these people seem more mature and might not want to spend their evening with an eighteen-year-old.

By the time we arrive, it's completely dark outside, and many people are already gathered near the fire pit. The log house glows from the lights shining through all the windows from inside. As we approach the patio doors, the music can be heard before we open them. Once we step inside, I look at the downstairs level. I have always wondered what the inside of this house looked like. A bar is located immediately to the right of the patio doors, with people surrounding it. Straight ahead of the patio doors is a nice living room with a sectional couch and a TV mounted on the wall. The layout is open and spacious, with a few bedrooms, a bathroom, and a laundry room. Surrounding the walls are assortments of animals that are also mounted, lending the log house a more outdoorsy atmosphere.

Ember engages with someone she seems to know and takes off, leaving me alone. Once again, I feel awkward and find myself looking for someone to talk to without feeling the need to hide behind Ember the entire time.

"You want a drink?" one of the guys behind the bar asks me.

"I could go for a Jack Daniel's and Coke if you don't mind. And make it a double," I immediately respond.

"Ah, a whiskey girl. My kind of lady."

Of course, I am.

It's about what every other guy says when I mention that I have the balls to drink whiskey. I have my stepdad, Rian, to thank for that. My mom met Rian when we briefly lived in Los Angeles when I was eight. He works as a pilot and flies commercial planes. He introduced my mom to the airline industry, and she began working as a flight attendant when fame didn't work out in her favor. After my mom married Rian, we moved here to his hometown in Montana. Rian never had any children of his own, nor had he ever been previously married. They were happy with me as an only child, and I was pleased with the parents God gave me. Every day, no matter what kind of day Rian has, he will make a Jack and Coke to end his day. If it weren't for him introducing me to the savory taste of whiskey, I'd probably be a damn vodka drinker like most girls.

The guy hands me a tall glass, and I thank him for the drink. After he winks at me, I turn around and see Ember talking with a small group of people near the couch. As I attempt to get to know new people, I find that the guy who made my drink is already conversing with a group of people who just arrived. I walk over and join Ember to see if this will be any easier with her around.

"Hey, thanks so much for leaving me," I say to her sarcastically.

"Oh, good, you have a drink!" she says ecstatically. "I went to search the house for some beer, but apparently, everything is down here." She heads toward the bar and helps herself. Many people who were at the bar earlier are now sitting outside by the fire.

As we walk across the lawn and onto the cement slab surrounding the fire pit, we notice that all of the white wooden chairs are taken. Since we didn't bring any chairs of our own, we remain standing with the rest of the group.

I try my best to incorporate myself into Ember's conversations. I chime in when I can; otherwise, I listen, nod, and drink. Music is playing on a portable speaker in the background. With the combination of the music and all the chatter from everyone here, it's somewhat difficult to make out what people are saying at times.

"Hey, Whiskey Girl." When I turn around, I see the guy who made my drink standing behind me. "Looks like it's almost time for another one." I'm not ashamed of how fast I drank my cocktail. He's the only one who would know my pace anyway, since he was the one who made it.

"Well, I will say you made it pretty damn good," I tell him.

As I finish off my drink, he grins and holds out his hand, indicating that he will refill it. I smile back and give him my glass. The liquid courage will kick in at some point.

My eyes scan around the fire pit, and when I get to the other side, I surprisingly catch Alder's eyes on me. He no longer has a hat on, so now I can see his hair. It's short and chestnut brown. A shorter cut on the sides and it's slightly longer on top, which shows a subtle shaggy style.

A blond girl is sitting on his lap, giggling at a different conversation. He doesn't seem phased by me catching him staring. He slowly looks away and turns his attention back to her conversation. I almost feel relieved to be noticed by him. Maybe I didn't completely blow it with my first impression. I keep my eyes steady on him just for fun, and then he makes eye contact with me again. This time, he gestures for me to accompany him with a two-finger beckoning sign.

I take a slow, deep breath through my nose and then start to filter through everyone and their diverse conversations.

When I reach him, he appears more intimidating than before.

"What's up?" I ask him, trying to conceal my nerves.

He turns his head to me and slowly eyes me up and down. My brows narrow with confusion as I impatiently wait for his answer. What could he possibly want from me when there are so many other people here for him? I turn to walk away just as he finally responds.

"He's only trying to get in your pants."

"Excuse me?" I say, turning back to face him.

"Tate. He has his sights set on you; I can tell. I'd be careful."

"Who is Tate?" I wait for him to answer, but instead, he gulps his beer and then shakes the can to see how much is left. Who does he think he is? I don't need to be looked after. Not anymore, anyway. I'm done seeking out guys who only care about the bedroom. "Okay, well, thanks for the heads up, but I think I can handle whoever Tate is."

"Like I said, just be careful. He gravitates toward people who are new to town."

"I'm not new. I just moved—" I become distracted when I suddenly feel a hand on my back. The guy who has been making my drinks is now standing beside me again.

"So, what are we talking about?" he asks us eagerly as he hands me my drink. By this time, the blond girl sitting on Alder's lap ends her separate conversation.

"Oh my God, I have to pee," she says, finally noticing we are standing here. Her face turns from friendly to sour when she sees me. I think it's time to remove myself from this conversation between the guy who thinks he knows me and his unpleasant girlfriend. With her eyes still locked on me, she gives Alder a playful peck on the cheek before grabbing another girl and going inside. I suddenly don't feel very welcome here.

"Wanna go for a walk? See the property?" Alder asks me, standing up from his chair now that his lap is finally free.

"Nah, bro, she's good," Whiskey Maker says and then puts his arm around me, pulling me closer to him as if I'm his.

Ah, this must be Tate.

I shrug my shoulders and go with it. I know how to handle guys like Tate. After he walks me back to the other side of the fire pit, I throw his arm off of me. He confirms my assumption as he introduces himself as Tate.

"Good to know," I tell him frankly. "I'm Jaemes."

"I wanted to make sure you knew my name before you started calling me Whiskey Guy or something," he confesses.

I laugh at that. "Awe, you're my little whiskey boy," I say while pinching his cheek.

Oh boy. Either the liquor is kicking in, or I'm doing a fabulous job of my new version of flirting.

He flirtatiously nudges me with his elbow in response. I feel his fingers lightly graze my hand in an attempt to hold it, but he immediately lets go when Alder grabs hold of his arm and snatches him away from me.

What the hell?

Alder takes him back to the other side of the cement slab as I tap on Ember's shoulder. Something doesn't seem right.

"What's up with that?" I ask, showing her the intense conversation that's being had between the two guys.

"They have always butted heads. He must have done something to piss Alder off because he doesn't take any shit, especially from Tate. You'll understand once you get to know him better."

"Who, Alder or Tate?"

"Both."

I try to ignore the situation and stick with Ember, but it's hard to avoid the two men who seem to be bickering back and forth. I try to make out what the issue is, but reading lips isn't my forte. Tate shakes his head and throws his hands up defensively. He eventually storms away from Alder before approaching the patio doors and meeting the blonde girl, who is coming back from the bathroom. As those two talk, I walk back over to Alder, now knowing who he was referring to earlier. Is he sure it's Tate who has his sights set on me, or could it be that he does?

"How about that walk?" I ask him. He seems a little heated from his conversation with Tate, but I'm hoping a stroll around the property will help him cool off.

"Sure. Follow me," he says, leading the way to the barn.

When he turns on the lights, I notice the horse stables to our right. It looks well taken care of, as if horses could be boarded here. To our left is an entryway to a more open area.

"Do you plan on training horses?" I ask.

He chuckles. "No. I have no idea how to train horses." He immediately seems more at ease, as if he needed this time away from everyone. If I'm being honest with myself, I could say I needed the time away, too.

"This is a perfect place to board and train horses, Alder. Why did you fix it up this way?"

He shrugs. "This is how it was. All I did was restore its appearance and reinforce its structure. Who knows, I might sell it one day if the right offer comes along." He walks over to another entryway, and I take in all of his hard work. I'm surprised to hear that he would sell this place after everything he's done to it. He made this house and barn his own. Based on how it looked before the renovations, he basically rebuilt everything from the ground up.

After a moment, he whistles to get my attention and smiles when I turn to him. "Come over here."

"Did you just whistle at me?" I chuckle, slightly taken aback.

"Sorry, it's a habit. I have three dogs, remember?" His smile becomes fuller. It's the first time I've seen his face like this. I'd be lying if I said it didn't make me feel a little warm inside. His smile enhances all of his features beautifully.

I join him in the last part of the barn. It's a garage that looks like it was turned into an office space or an extra living quarter. It has a desk and a filing cabinet in the far corner. A large couch is up against the wall to our left. A TV hangs on the opposite wall, and repurposed cabinets surround a small kitchenette. Much cleaner and more amusing than a garage.

"This is nice. Do you ever park anything in here?" I ask him.

"No, not normally. This is more of a guest house. I just park my truck outside. I guess if I had to park something in here, I would; but so far, I haven't needed to." He pats the seat next to him on the couch, signaling for me to sit. I slowly walk over to join him. I'm starting to wonder where the blond girl is and if she has any affiliation with Alder. What was the reason for wanting to show me around and be alone with me?

"So, what's up with you and Tate?" I ask, sitting beside him on the couch.

"There's nothing to talk about when it comes to Tate. He's just..." He takes a drink of his cocktail, and I do the same to silence the awkwardness. "What's up with you? Are you from here?"

I get the hint that he wants to change the subject and nod. I'll find out at some point, I'm sure. "Kind of. I've lived in a few different places, but I'm mostly from here, yes."

"And what does that mean?" he questions.

"Um..." I freeze up a little inside, as if I've just realized we're in a building alone, making it hard to have a conversation with him. I take another sip of my cocktail and swirl the ice around the glass.

When I don't answer his question, he asks, "Okay, well... when did you move here initially?"

Come on, Jaemes, stop acting weird and just talk to the guy.

"When I was nine. That's when I met Ember, and we've

been best friends ever since."

"Makes sense," he responds.

"When did you buy this place? I don't ever remember seeing you around."

He thinks for a moment. "Three years ago. Almost four. I moved here from South Dakota shortly after Bennett. We've been good friends for most of our lives as well. After trade school, we found jobs at the same place and eventually want to start our own electrical business. What do you do for work?"

"I just graduated from the University of Nevada, Las Vegas with a degree in Early Childhood Development and Psychology. My end career goal is to counsel children who experience childhood trauma or families with children who need guidance getting through traumas. That's sort of why I moved back here. I accepted a job position at an elementary school that will help me get my foot in the door. I'll be working with children who typically express their feelings through negative and aggressive behaviors, and help navigate them back to more appropriate behavior for a school environment."

"Good for you," he tells me. "You've got a lot of patience."

He places his arm on top of the couch. His hand is nearly touching my shoulder. Even though we are at arm's length from each other, I can't help but feel a sense of closeness between us. This conversation and alone time must be fueled by alcohol consumption. When we were introduced earlier today, his demeanor was as if he couldn't care less about who I am and where I came from. Now he's sitting close to me as we remain the only two together, separated from everyone else, in a room that's located in a different building. How did this happen?

"I think I'm going to make one more and then head out," I tell him as our drinks near empty. "Plus, I'm sure your girlfriend is wondering where you are."

"Girlfriend? Who said I had a girlfriend?" he asks, genuinely curious as to who I'm referring to.

"The blonde who was sitting on your lap earlier. Isn't she your…" I trail off now, thinking my assumption may be wrong.

Alder lets out a deep chuckle and shakes his head slightly. "She wishes."

I say no more about the blond or Tate, and he follows me out of the barn, but then separates from me and rejoins everyone back at the fire. Ember accompanies me to the bar inside the house after we meet halfway in the yard.

"Where the heck did you go?" she asks me.

"You'll never believe it," I tell her matter-of-factly.

"Try me."

"I was sort of in the barn talking with Alder."

"Shut up! Tell me everything," she demands as we walk back into the house. We each grab one more drink before calling it a night, and I fill her in on my conversation with Alder.

Well, that was *supposed* to be the plan.

Chapter Three

M Y HEAD IS pounding, my throat aches, my eyes burn, and my face is… *wet?* I get the strength to open my heavy eyes. Staring back at me just inches from my face are two adorable brown eyes, a wet nose, and a wagging tail. I look over at the nightstand, hoping to see my phone sitting there. Instead of my phone, there's an open package of half-eaten Pop-Tarts and a bottle of water. I sit up and realize I don't recognize where I'm at. Another dog is lying at the end of the bed. My surroundings are reminding me that I slept at Alder's last night.

I get out of bed slowly, ensuring I don't make any noise. I walk into the Hollywood-style bathroom and lock both doors. Of course, my hair is messy, and the little amount of makeup I had on is all over my face. I pull my long, bronze hair up into a messy bun and then wash my face with water from the sink. I'm forced to accept that this is as good as it will get as I painfully look at my reflection in the mirror.

I walk out of the bathroom and toward the closed bedroom door. I hear a man's voice who seems to be talking on the phone. I chicken out and sit back on the bed. I suppose now would be a perfect time to eat the rest of the Pop-Tarts and finish the water. My stomach feels nauseous, and my head is throbbing. I rummage through the blankets on the bed and finally find my phone. I bring up Ember's name and send her a text message.

Me: *Where are you?*

I wait for a response for ten minutes, but there's no reply.

It's time to rip the band-aid off and open that door. Immediately, the sun blinds me when I walk out of the bedroom. When my eyes finally adjust, I see that I am standing in the dining room with the kitchen to my right and a living room straight ahead next to the porch doors. The main door to the house is just past the dining room area to the left. I glance out of the window and see the fire pit still smoldering. I indeed spent the night at Alder's house.

"There she is. Alive and well."

I turn slightly to the right toward the same voice I heard talking on the phone earlier. Alder is sitting on the couch with his phone next to his ear. He abruptly ends the conversation and turns his attention to me, the random woman who just walked out of his bedroom.

"I'm alive, but definitely not well," I correct him.

He lets out a light laugh and points to the kitchen counter. "That bottle of Advil is for you."

Without hesitation, I walk to the counter and take three capsules from the bottle. "I'm sorry I made you sleep on the couch last night. I do not normally drink that much. I'm more of a social drinker and not the 'drink to get drunk' type."

"I didn't mind sleeping on the couch. It's all good," he says.

The last thing I wanted to do was to attend his bonfire, regardless of the occasion. However, I did start to enjoy myself as the drinks kept flowing. Something about Alder makes me a little nervous, not in a scary way, but rather in a bashful manner. I should be able to do and say what I want without worrying about looking or sounding pathetic. That's one of the things I need to work on the most about myself. I need to have more self-confidence and the courage to be *me*. But I shouldn't care what Alder thinks of me. It's not like I'll be seeing much of him after this.

"Do you have any idea where Ember is?" I ask him. "I tried texting her this morning."

"She and Bennett slept in one of the bedrooms downstairs," he says, folding a blanket and draping it over the back of the couch. "She got a little tuned up last night, too. There was no way we were trusting you two to walk home."

"You underestimate her, then."

Ember has always been known to be the life of the party. One time, when she came to visit me in college, she stayed awake for over twenty-four hours with a constant buzz and never became incredibly intoxicated. Her ability to drink and remain somewhat normal is incredible. And the hangovers? They are nonexistent for her. She is a wild one, but I love her.

"What's the address here? I should call for a ride if Ember is still sleeping. I'd love to go home and cure this cute little hangover."

"I can drive you," he says.

"You don't have to do that. You gave up your bed, food, water, booze, and Advil for me. I couldn't ask you to drive me home after all that."

"I insist," he says, nearly cutting me off.

"You may have to clean out vomit in your truck," I warn him.

"I'll take my chances. I'll even stop on the way and get you breakfast."

Maybe I'll be more up for food after I clean myself up a bit more.

WHEN ALDER SAID he would stop and get me breakfast, I didn't think that meant he'd stop at a sit-down joint. A drive-thru or a gas station would have sufficed. Sassy Stacy's is a popular bar and grill open for breakfast, lunch, and supper. It has an old-time saloon vibe to it. Although I love the food here, I'd much rather go home and sleep the day away.

I exit his truck, leaving my used clothes in a bag in the back seat, and enter the restaurant, practically drowning in Alder's clothes. However, I'm more comfortable than I was when I first woke up. He was kind enough to let me use his shower and lend me some of his clothes. Even though his body wash smells fantastic on me, the high octane of the scent is making my uneasy stomach turn.

"What can I get you two for drinks right away?" the waitress asks as we take our seats in a booth by the window. I pull the shade so the sun doesn't create a glare off the table and blind me. My head hurts way too much for that.

"Chocolate milk and water, please," I tell her.

"Irish coffee for me," Alder orders.

I almost puke hearing him order a coffee with whiskey in it. Apparently, he didn't get enough to drink last night. Either that, or he is just like Ember and can drink whatever, whenever, and not be bothered by it. When the waitress returns with our drinks, I immediately chug half my chocolate milk with an amused Alder watching.

"Don't judge me. Believe it or not, chocolate milk has more electrolytes than water and most sports drinks. I always drink it when I'm hungover," I say before proceeding to drink the rest of it.

"No judgment on my end," he says.

Usually, the heaping amount of food Alder orders would sound good to me, but I'm on the verge of dying. I'm still dehydrated, and my whole body feels sore. I end up ordering pancakes and a side of buttered toast.

"Are you from around here?" I ask, finally thinking of something to talk about.

"No…I grew up in South Dakota."

"What brought you to Montana?"

"My family vacationed here a lot growing up. One day, my parents bought a ski resort, and the rest is history," he says, continuing to eat.

"We never went on any extravagant family trips. Just camping mainly," I tell him.

Alder laughs to himself and takes another bite.

"What?" I ask, wondering what could be so funny.

"Nothing. It's just..." He finishes chewing and wipes his mouth with a napkin, "you've said all this already. Last night, you asked the same questions and said the same things."

"Oh, sorry."

"It's fine. It's cute how you can't handle your alcohol," he teases.

I throw a napkin at him. "Like I said, I don't normally drink that much."

I can only eat a few bites of my food. If I eat any more, it will unfortunately come back up after it hits my stomach. I sit back and watch him. I watch him eat, I watch him drink, I watch him look around the place like he has never been here before. His eyes will catch mine occasionally, but I can't look away. I'm trying harder to figure him out rather than focusing on what he might be thinking of me.

"I can pay," I tell him right after the waitress lays our bill at our table. I reach for it, but he quickly snatches the paper bill from me and lays his credit card down on the table, all while maintaining eye contact with me. I look at him pointedly. "Come on, it's the least I can do. I've been a nuisance, and because of that, I owe you."

"You owe me nothing, Jaemes."

"Why didn't Ember take care of me last night?" I ask.

"Ember is my best friend's girl. You are best friends with Ember. She was off doing only God knows what most of the night, and I couldn't find her. No one else knew you, so I stepped up to the plate. Plus, you were...entertaining."

"Well, I'm glad I could entertain you and your party," I say with sarcasm.

"Remember when you tried to break up a fight between Tate and Preston?" he asks with a chuckle. "You held your ground, but I stepped in before you almost got your ass kicked." He takes a sip of his whiskey-infused coffee and then continues. "Plus, I wanted to see Tate get his shit handed to him."

"Yeah, I remember. Things are a tad fuzzy, but I remember. I still don't understand why you don't care for him."

His shoulders rise and then back down again while a sigh escapes from his lips. "I don't like the way he treats women," he tells me. "And I didn't like his encounter with you. I know him well enough to know his true intentions."

"Why do you care so much about what he does?" I ask genuinely, wanting to know his answer.

"That's a conversation for a different time," he says as he moves the plates to the end of the table for the waitress. "Ready to go?"

I don't understand what the issue is between Tate and Alder. Although I know why Alder doesn't like him, I still don't get why he's concerned about what he does with me. Or anyone for that matter. Ultimately, it's none of his business. No one is getting hurt, right?

When we reach his black Chevy, I give him directions to my house. The house I lived in for thirteen years before moving off to college. "I bet you're excited to see your family," he says.

"I'm not sure when I'll get to see them. My parents are working this weekend."

Alder smiles. "Oh, I know."

"Ha. I bet you do. Drunk me can't keep anything to herself, apparently."

"Any siblings home?" he asks.

"Nope, I'm an only child. I'm surprised I didn't tell you that last night."

"Me, too," he laughs.

We pull into my driveway and notice how empty it looks. There are no cars parked in it, and the shades attached to the windows are closed. Rian always insisted that everything be locked and closed whenever no one was home. Alder puts his truck in park.

"Thank you again for everything, and I sincerely apologize for making you take care of me last night. I feel bad you had to sleep on the couch in your own home."

Alder turns his head to me. "I would say, 'Don't worry about it,' but I think we both know you will."

"It's like you know me so well," I say in a monotone voice.

Alder smiles, making that warm feeling return. I've enjoyed his presence. I still feel like a complete loser for relying solely on liquid courage to get through the night. I end up smiling back at him and not wanting to leave the truck, but then I remember that the most comfortable bed in the world awaits me inside that house.

Chapter Four

"SURPRISE!" I HEAR from multiple people the second I walk through the door. It takes me a minute to realize what the hell is going on. I look to my right; no one is in the living room. I look to my left; no one is in the dining room. However, my mom, Rian, and Ember are standing in the kitchen straight ahead. On the counter is a colorful cake, and a "Welcome Home" sign hangs above the patio doors to the right, behind the living room.

"Well, well, well. Look who doesn't have to work after all," I say as I hug Rian and my mom. My parents tried to keep their distance from me when I was at college. My mom wanted me to have a chance to explore and discover who I am, without any influence from them. Rian, on the other hand, would call and text me more often. I was the child he never had, which meant a lot to him. It meant a lot to me, too. Someone who isn't biologically related to me by blood or obligation steps up and takes me in like I am his world.

I look over at Ember, knowing she can tell I am immediately annoyed with her. "How are we feeling this morning, lovely?" she asks me while she brings me in for a hug. I grunt for an answer.

"Yeah, you best believe Ember filled us in on your home-coming evening," Rian says.

"Oh, I'm sure she did. After all, it was her fault I got to the level I ended up in."

"Excuses, excuses," my mom says as we all catch her wink

at Ember with her striking eyes.

My mom has always had the look of fame. Olive skin tone, light freckles, deep blue eyes, and long, thick, wavy chocolate hair that reaches her lower back. I remember seeing her face on billboards and taxi cabs around the city of Las Vegas, advertising events and shows. She was an incredible dancer who performed at many concerts and various shows. She'd come home after all her auditions so happy and confident. Everyone loved her and noticed her exceptional talent for dance. While I was at school, she would perform in the matinée shows. During the evenings and weekends, she would pick up a few bartending shifts just down the road from where we lived. That's if she knew I would have a babysitter. I've always looked up to my mom. She worked hard, stayed humble, enjoyed life, and looked good doing it.

"Alder said you and Bennett were asleep downstairs when I woke up. I'm so confused. When the hell did you get here?" I ask her, still annoyed that she never texted me back.

"Your lovely parents contacted me and said they wanted to surprise you by coming home early. However, they got caught in traffic and asked me to distract you until they could get here. I helped set up the welcome home decorations and picked up your cake. Right before I left Alder's house, I asked him if he could help us by giving you a ride home, but to take his time. I told him when it was safe for you to come home, and everything worked out."

I thought maybe Alder was turning into some gentleman by offering to take me home so I didn't have to pay for a ride and taking me out for breakfast so I could potentially avoid the worst hangover ever. He only did that to help Ember and my parents with this surprise. Why does that annoy me? Maybe I thought he was starting to like me, and I liked the idea of that.

I feel stupid.

I head downstairs to my bedroom to drop off my bag of

clothes. I could definitely go for a long nap. My room has always been set up perfectly for sleeping. The air is cold downstairs, but my bed is soft and warm. No light can seep through the window shades, and my fan has the perfect amount of noise. However, the people upstairs in that kitchen went through a lot of hassle to set up this welcome-home surprise for me. They love and miss me, and I can't blame them for wanting to spend every minute catching up.

All three of them are seated at the dining room table when I walk back upstairs. Alder's blanket-like sweatpants and long-sleeve T-shirt make it hard to stay awake. I join them at the table and listen to the end of their conversation after grabbing myself some cake. I take a big corner slice with the most frosting; but if it's whipped frosting, I might puke and head straight to bed disappointed. Anyone who knows me should know that buttercream frosting is the only frosting that should ever be on a cake, in my opinion. Even though my stomach is still full from Alder's forced breakfast, I could use something sweet to assist my hangover cure.

Drink water, *check.*

Take Advil, *check.*

Shower, *check.*

Eat breakfast, *check.*

Indulge in more food, *check.*

Nap. *Ugh, when will anyone let me nap?*

"How are you and Bennett?" my mom asks Ember from across the table.

"Great. He and Alder plan to start their own electrical business soon. I hope it will be soon, anyway. It would be good for both of them. They work very well together and deserve to see their hard work pay off at a successful business they can call their own." Ember takes a sip of her water.

"That sounds amazing. I hope it will work out for them," my mom says.

"Who's this Alder guy?" Rian asks in between chews of another slice of cake. "You both keep bringing him up, and apparently, he had quite the housewarming party last night."

Ember and I laugh when we realize we never explained who Alder is. Ember takes the lead on this one since I barely know who he is.

"Alder works with Bennett, and they have been best friends for a long time. He's from South Dakota, same area as Bennett." Ember takes another sip of her water and then continues. "He's the one who bought and flipped that log house down the road from us."

"I'm surprised he bought that place. From what I remember, it needed a lot of work," Rian says, then turns to my mom. "We should drive by one of these days and take a look at it."

My mom gives him a *yeah-right* look as she gets up from the table to put away the leftover cake. "And when do you think we will have time to do that, Rian? We are constantly on the move."

"We can drive by there when we are out and about," Rian tells her.

He joins her in the kitchen, and she playfully rolls her eyes at him with a half-smile.

"Hey guys, I love that you all did this for me. It was a huge surprise that I did not see coming, and I love you for that. But would anyone be mad if I went to take a nap?" I ask.

"Yeah, I would!" Rian shouts from the kitchen.

My mom slaps his shoulder and shakes her head. "Of course, you can go get some rest, honey. I get it, hangovers suck. Oh, and aren't you going to look at that house tomorrow? I can go with if you want me to."

How did I forget about that? Buying my first house should be one of the only things on my mind right now. My mom is right, hangovers suck.

"We'll see. I'll let you know after I wake up," I tell her.

"I have to run anyway," Ember says. "I'll talk to you later, Jae."

I happily remove myself from upstairs and head for my room. After I close my bedroom door, I slide right into my soft bed, which makes me comfy in the dark and cold room. I try to zone out peacefully while listening to the buzzing noise from my fan. My hangover starts to subside as I continue to think about my future. Tomorrow could be a big day for me.

Could.

Chapter Five

*T*HIS IS IT.

I scan the house once more, absorbing all its details. All I need right now is a house big enough for just me. The outside of this house reminds me of an elongated cabin. It stands near a cliff, overlooking a river. The inside is laid out nicely. There's an exterior side door that goes into the kitchen on one end of the house. The kitchen leads to the living room, and the living room in turn leads to the only bedroom, located on the other side of the house. The bathroom and laundry room are located adjacent to each other, situated between the kitchen and the living room, which creates a wider hallway. The front door is located near the living room and is connected to a small outside porch. The bedroom also has an exterior door that leads to an identical-looking porch.

The good news is, I can close on this house within the next month. I'm excited for this new chapter in my life. I've completed my schooling, and now it's time to prove that I can live independently and be a successful adult. I decided to help one of the therapists work at the booth during the town party today, so I could learn more about the office and the job itself. I couldn't be more thrilled to say that I get to start my career so soon after graduation. Everything is coming together perfectly.

After examining my future home many times, I head straight to my parents' house to pack my belongings. Since I won't be able to move in for another month, I can only pack items that I don't use daily. But I would rather get a head start since I have the free time. On my way, my phone dings, indicating I have an incoming text message.

Unknown: *Are you going to the party downtown tonight?*

I don't answer the random text I just received until I get home. I try to think of who it could be since everyone I know should already be saved in my phone. I pull into the driveway and park my car before picking up my phone again. I closely examine the unrecognizable phone number that texted me once more before sending a response.

Me: *Who is this?*

Unknown: *Alder. You put your number in my phone last weekend.*

I instantly roll my eyes at my stupidity. I feel dumb and disappointed in my actions. I hope I didn't make a complete fool of myself at that bonfire. Without hesitation, I save his number in my contacts.

Me: *Ugh, sorry…*

Alder: *For what?*

Me: *Oh, I don't know, maybe for invading your privacy by violating your personal belongings. I swear I'm not that annoying. I barely ate anything the day I traveled home, so those few strong drinks I had didn't do me any good.*

Alder: *You were having a good time, like everyone else. You need to stop apologizing so much. It's unattractive, you know.*

Me: *What makes you think I'm trying to impress you? If I feel like I should apologize to someone, I will apologize.*

Alder: *Alright, fair enough.*

I lock my phone, leaving the conversation in a lull, and head inside my parents' house to gather some of my belongings. I'm too excited to chat right now. I want to rummage through my items and hopefully find enough boxes to put everything in. In the garage, I only see a few boxes big enough to haul my heavy items. I'm searching high and low for more when my phone dings again.

> **Alder:** *So, are you going?*

I'm curious as to why he wants to know so badly. Do I leave him hanging so I can continue to focus on me and my move? I should. But I don't.

> **Me:** *I'll be there, but I'll be working at a booth. I don't plan on staying long, as I have a lot of packing to do.*
>
> **Alder:** *What are you packing for? If you don't mind me asking.*
>
> **Me:** *I found a house not too far from here. I'm closing on it next month.*
>
> **Alder:** *Need any help?*
>
> **Me:** *That's very nice of you to offer, but I think I'm okay. Thanks, though.*
>
> **Alder:** *Well, if you change your mind, you know how to reach me.*

I set my phone down and catch myself smiling. I don't know why I enjoy the thought of him reaching out to me so much. I need to snap out of this feeling and focus solely on myself. I just bought a house, and I start my new job at the end of the summer, as well as my internship, in the next few days. I shouldn't be caught up in anything else. I won't have the spare time, and I can't be distracted.

The sun is about to set, and I have been on the move all day. I take a break to watch the sun move beneath the mountain range in the distance. After I sit on one of the patio chairs out back, I hear my mom open the door behind me.

"Mind if I join you?" she asks.

I shake my head. "Not at all." I thank her for the seltzer she hands me, and we crack our tabs. I always loved how my parents would occasionally let me have an alcoholic beverage underage. Since I was sixteen, they agreed that only one drink at home would be okay. We would unwind from our day on the patio and enjoy a delicious cocktail. That's when my love for whiskey came into play. Wrong or not, they knew what teenagers were like anyway.

"I see you started packing," she says after sipping her drink. "How's that going?"

"Good. I found some boxes in the garage and started stashing things away. I guess I'm as ready as I can be at this point."

"Do you have anyone helping with your bed and furniture? We can check with Marnie to see if Greg is available to help, if you'd like. We *would* help, but our work schedule looks hectic around that time."

"No need. Alder offered to help, so I might actually take him up on that," I cautiously inform her.

She starts to take a sip of her drink but stops halfway. "Alder…" she thinks for a moment. "Bennett's friend, right?"

I nod my head.

"He seems like a nice guy," she admits.

I scoff slightly as I play with the tab of my can. "How would you know?"

"Well, let's see here…first, he took care of 'drunk you' when 'sober you' couldn't. And second, he helped distract you while we set up your welcome-home surprise. So, I would consider him to be a nice guy."

"I guess he's alright," I say in response with a smile I can't fight away.

I glance up at the sky. The sun is now tucked behind the mountain range, making it look like the mountains are glowing. When I look back down at my phone, I notice a few notifications I haven't opened yet. One of them is a Facebook notification.

Alder Daughtler accepted your friend request.

"Oh, my lord!" I toss my phone on the patio couch next to me.

"What now?" my mom asks.

I lean back and shake my head with my hands over my face. "Just 'sober me' finding out more things 'drunk me' has done."

She laughs at me, and we both turn our heads when we hear Rian opening the patio door. He has just returned home from work and is still wearing his pilot uniform. "What are you two doing out here without the fire table on? It's a perfect evening for it," he says.

"Just busy chatting, babe," my mom answers.

"I'm making a whiskey cocktail," he states and then turns to point at me as if he's silently asking if he should make me one, too. I finish my seltzer before answering him.

"Sure, why not? Maybe I can answer a few of my own questions if I drink something a little stronger."

Rian proceeds to the kitchen, and my mom continues to sip on her seltzer next to me. She goes on to tell me how proud she is of everything I've already accomplished in life and gives me the "I told you so" speech. I know I have to give myself more credit. It's not every day you get your own house, a job offer, and an internship right after finishing school.

When Rian returns, he hands me my cocktail and sits beside my mom.

"I say we finish up with these drinks and head downtown to the party to celebrate," he says to us regarding my recent successes. "You're finally back home, bought a home yourself, and are opening many doors toward your career. We couldn't be more proud of you, Jae Jae."

"I'll be there but won't be doing much to celebrate. I

offered to help one of the therapists work their booth," I tell him.

"Look at her," Rian says to my mom, "taking initiative right away. However, be sure to take time for yourself, too. It's important to keep a healthy balance."

"Aye aye, Captain," I salute.

The party doesn't start for a few more hours, but I want to arrive early enough to find the booth I'll be working at. So, I agree to go right after my drink, like my parents. At least we should find decent parking. Ember won't be super thrilled when she finds out I won't have time for her tonight. She was looking forward to another evening with me, and the party was the perfect excuse. However, I'm excited to keep my mind going in the path it's supposed to go. That is, if I can get Ember to leave me alone long enough. I laugh at that thought.

Here goes nothing.

THE MAYOR AND townspeople did a spectacular job planning this party. I'm amazed by the setup. Downtown has never looked so beautiful. We live in a small town, so all the booths are set up along the outskirts of downtown, with a variety of food trucks at the end. In the middle are a few bouncy houses for kids, and at the other end is a stage for the band. It almost reminds me of a miniature county fair.

I meet with one of the therapists who is working the booth with me, and I've never felt more welcome. We discuss my educational background, primary career goals, and current career standing in more detail. He tells me he's had a ton of successful interns go on and live their career dreams after spending a few years working and shadowing at their office. It makes me feel incredibly excited knowing that I'm walking down the right path.

"Here are the brochures we can give out to people who want more information about our services. If anyone has any questions, feel free to turn them over to me. Over here are all of our business cards with our contact information." He hands me one of his to look at.

Jerry Shaw, LMFT.

This office is staffed by a combination of licensed family therapists, psychiatric medical doctors, social workers, and counselors. It's the perfect place to explore a wide range of specific careers that I could potentially choose from. Our booth is located between the school district's booth and the local medical clinic's booth.

Talk about the perfect location.

After a few hours of meeting people and listening to Jerry's conversations, I'm surprised that Ember hasn't shown up yet. She's a busy energizer bunny, so I'm sure she hasn't gotten around to this part of the party yet. She can get distracted easily, and the vendor booths aren't really her thing. My mom and Rian finally walk by and stop to introduce themselves to Jerry once we are free of people.

"Dr. Kerry Wimer is scheduled to work the last shift. You are free to join the rest of the party if you'd like, or you can stay as long as you please. I heard the Mexican food truck has amazing food," Jerry informs me.

"I think I'll stay and hang around for a little longer. I've had a lot of fun here so far." Jerry smiles and exits the booth while Dr. Wimer enters. She introduces herself and tells me to call her Kerry. It'll be nice to hear her part of the job and what she has to say to people.

"Look who I finally found," Ember says, approaching the booth. "I thought I'd never find you. When do you get to leave?"

"I can leave whenever, but I'm going to stay for a little longer."

Her facial expression quickly changes from excitement to annoyance. "What? Why? Your mom said that you've been here since it started. The next band is setting up, and I want to have fun with my best friend." Her bottom lip turns into a pout.

Kerry overhears our conversation and chimes in. "You can definitely go, honey. I greatly appreciate your dedication, but you should go and enjoy yourself." She playfully rubs my shoulder with a friendly smile.

"Ember, I'll be sure to catch up with you soon, I promise," I reassure her.

"Okay, fine. Although I'm impatient, I'm still proud of you." She gives me a quick hug and hops back over to Bennett, who is talking with someone at another booth just a few down from mine.

"I'm sorry about her," I chuckle.

Kerry smiles. "Don't be. It's nice to have a close friend like that."

After another hour goes by, I think about possibly leaving the booth to enjoy the final hour of the party. The day is nearing dusk, and the string lights near the stage are lit up, hanging above the closed-off road that's being used for the dance floor. Some booths are already closing down early, and most people are gathered in front of the stage as the band continues to play classic country hits.

When I look to my left, I see a man and a child at the school district booth.

"Dad, can I please go on the bouncy house one more time? *Please?*" I hear the child beg. His dad lets him go one more time and then looks up to notice me watching. He smiles and shakes his head.

"Kids, huh? They always want just one more," he laughs.

"I can't blame him. Those bouncy houses look like a lot of fun," I tell him.

He walks to our booth. He must work for the clinic, as he is wearing the same shirt as everyone else at the clinic booth on the other side of us, which features the clinic logo in the upper right-hand corner. His dirty-blond hair is tousled on top and has a wave to it. He appears too sophisticated and sexy for a doctor, but who am I to judge?

He holds out his hand and introduces himself as Ledger Yearwood.

"Jaemes," I tell him, shaking his hand.

"Kerry, how's everything going over here?" he asks the doctor next to me.

"Can't complain. I have a great intern helping me out." She turns to me and says, "Dr. Yearwood occasionally refers patients to our practice."

"Nice to meet you, Dr. Yearwood," I smile.

"Likewise," he says with a smile in return. "If you're still around a little later, I'd love to continue our conversation, Jaemes. My son, Archie, will be leaving with his mom in the next half hour."

"I'd like that." I blush as he smiles at me before retrieving his son from the bouncy houses. Although I promised myself not to get involved with a man so soon, I can't help but gush over Ledger. He's a doctor, a dad, and very handsome. But how do I know our conversation will get close and personal? He's a doctor who works with the staff at the therapy office where I'm interning. I'm sure our conversation will remain professional, as it should.

Just as I'm about to tell Kerry I'm heading out, someone else catches my eye. He looks over and sees me, then does a double-take once he recognizes me. He says something to someone in his group and then walks in my direction.

"Hey, long time no see," Alder says once he approaches my booth. His tall, muscular build immediately becomes a distraction as I remember our last interaction. And just like our few other encounters, I become nervous even when he doesn't try to intimidate me with his presence.

"Yeah, it's been a while," I unnaturally joke back.

"How's it going? Are you able to get away yet?"

Kerry is busy talking with a couple who have a few young kids playing nearby, so she isn't able to intervene and tell me to "go have fun" like she could when Ember was around.

"Um, I think I have to stay just a little longer, but I'm planning on joining Ember if I can."

"Damn. I was hoping I'd get you out for a dance," he admits.

I scrunch my face and tell him maybe next time.

He smiles and taps on the booth table I'm standing behind. "Alright, well, I'll let Ember know you'll eventually be looking for her." He starts to walk away, as well as the couple that Kerry was talking to. The band begins another song, and I recognize it right away by the instrumental introduction— "Two Dozen Roses", one of my favorites.

"I love this song," I tell Kerry. Alder must have heard me say that because he immediately turns around to face me again.

"If you can name who sings this song, I'll keep walking, but if you get it wrong, I expect that dance," he challenges me.

"Easy. Shenandoah," I tell him confidently.

Ha, sucker.

He continues to stare at me while I keep a smug smile on my face, knowing damn well I won. However, he doesn't accept his loss and takes my hand, pulling me away from the booth and toward the stage. I look back, and Kerry encourages me to keep going.

I can't help but giggle as I try to keep up with him. My nerves are still there, but easy to ignore as the music gets louder and we get closer to everyone else who is also enjoying the song.

Alder starts by twirling me and then grabs my waist with

his other hand. I feel more comfortable when I start to notice how good of a dancer he really is. He has no problem leading, and I have no issues with guiding my body to the music alongside him. He makes my smile enormous when he starts singing with the chorus and sways his hips to the beat while leaning inward closer to me. I mimic his moves and start singing with him. The only thing I feel right now is that I'm having the time of my life. How does he do this to me?

We find ourselves in the middle of everyone, and when I turn to my right, I see Ember and Bennett dancing as well.

"Yes, girl!" she shouts ecstatically with wide eyes when she notices Alder and me dancing together. I laugh at her excitement and shake my head at Bennett as he tries to steal my dancing partner away from me.

"No, no," Alder says, shaking his finger at Bennett with a mischievous smile, then joins his hands with mine. I feel butterflies flutter in my stomach when he touches me and moves my body with his. All four of us belt out the chorus of the song once it comes along again, and Ember and I can't help but laugh at the silly boys enjoying the music to the fullest.

Eventually, Alder and I lock eyes and sing along with the song as if we are telling the story of the lyrics to each other. When the instrumental part of the song approaches, he pulls me in closer, and our movements slow down. The smell of his cologne puts me in a trance, and I get chills on my arms being so close to him. My smile never leaves my face the entirety of the song. His hands push me out and then pull me back in once the bridge of the song ends.

I don't want this moment to end.

The band transitions into the next song as "Two Dozen Roses" finishes. Ember reaches for me with her sweaty hand. "Come get a beer with me. I'm so thirsty." She pulls me along with her. My other hand is still in Alder's, and I look back at him. He keeps a hold of my hand until I'm no longer in reach.

I could use a drink myself, but I also don't want to leave him. I'm worn out by all the feelings that I felt out on the dance floor. The connection that was created while looking into Alder's eyes and having the best time was sensational. I wonder how he felt and if it's anything similar to how I'm feeling.

Was it just as magical for him, or was that just a fun, spontaneous gesture that he'd do with anyone? Perhaps he chose me because I was his only option at the time. The thoughts become overwhelming.

Ember buys us a beer, and I chug my first few sips. I'm trying to cool off my body and calm the high I'm on. Alder and Bennett followed suit, and we all take a seat at one of the picnic tables while watching the party wrap up. Ember is next to me on my right. Naturally, Bennett is sitting across from Ember, and Alder is sitting across from me. The bouncy houses deflate, the booths are being dismantled, the food trucks are closing their windows, and the band says "thank you and goodnight" to the crowd at the end of their last set.

What I didn't expect was to be approached by Ledger again. What all happened within the last half hour made me forget all about Ledger.

Whoops.

"I'm sorry we didn't get any more time to chat, but here's my number. Hopefully, we can get that chance again soon." He hands me one of his cards with his personal phone number written on the back. "Have a good night." He smiles at everyone I'm seated with and leaves the party. I glance at Alder, and his jaw clenches up while he watches Ledger disappear.

Maybe that moment *was* just as magical for him, after all.

Chapter Six

M Y SLEEP IS interrupted by the sound of fast and heavy footsteps coming from upstairs. I turn over to my nightstand and check the time on my phone. It is just past six o'clock in the morning. The footsteps grow louder as I hear them approaching my room. The door swings open, and in comes Ember. She runs toward me and jumps onto my bed.

"Happy freaking birthday, bitch!" she yells as she climbs on top of me. I try to hide under all my blankets, but this girl seems like she already took a crazy pill this morning.

"Aren't you supposed to be working?" I ask in a muffled voice from being buried beneath the blankets.

"Jae, we haven't celebrated our birthdays together in forever. I took today through the end of the weekend off from work to celebrate with you," she states.

"Okay, but can I please sleep in? No celebrations should start at six in the morning." By this time, I know I sound annoyed. I am not a morning person whatsoever. It doesn't matter if it's my birthday or not, I need my sleep. Ember gets off of me and starts jumping on my bed.

"No, the sun is rising, so that means we must rise."

She is so weird.

She hops off my bed and throws the blankets off me. "I will make you a coffee with Bailey's, and then we can sit and watch the sunrise on the patio with some blankets."

"And how many cups of coffee and Bailey's have you had already?" I immediately regret asking her this. I'm not sure I want to know the answer. She stops in the doorway to my bedroom and tells me not to worry about that and to meet her on the patio.

After I get out of bed, I open the shades to my window. As always, it's freezing in my room, so I put on sweatpants and a sweatshirt. My hair gets tossed up in a bun, and I slip on my slippers before going upstairs.

Good enough.

I'm still half asleep as I make my way up the stairs. Rian is watching the news in the living room and sipping his coffee like usual.

"She sure is chipper this morning," he says as he brings his lips to the steaming mug to take a sip. "I wish I had that much energy."

I slowly shuffle my way to the patio doors. "That might be because she has already had one or two birthday coffees without me." He chuckles at my comment as if that wouldn't surprise him.

"Happy birthday, Jae Jae," he tells me.

"Thanks, Ri guy."

I walk outside to join Ember. She is on the patio couch, wrapped in blankets with her coffee. There are a few blankets for me lying beside her, and my coffee is waiting for me on the end table. She looks as if she has been awake for hours. Her long red curls are settled neatly on her head in a beautiful bun. Her make-up is fresh, and she's dressed to impress. I immediately sit, grab the blankets, and pick up my coffee. After I took a sip, I thanked her for making it perfectly. It's not too hot and has an excellent coffee-to-Bailey's ratio. She even gave it a birthday twist by adding whipped cream and rainbow sprinkles.

"So, whatcha wanna do today? Anything you want," she insists. She might be more eager for today than I am. However, it's still early in the day.

"I don't know. I haven't been awake long enough to think about it," I tell her.

"What are you talking about? You've had weeks to think about it."

"Ember, I've been a little busy doing adult stuff. And now I'm starting to focus on packing," I sigh.

"Oh, so you ended up finding a house?" she asks.

I nod. "It's a small house over by Boulder River."

"Boulder River? I didn't know there were any affordable houses over there."

"It's just a small, one-person house. I can show you sometime if you want."

"Of course, I want to see it. We can drive by it on our way to the festivities."

I look at her, more scared than confused. "What festivities?" I ask.

"Jae, if you're not going to make any plans for your birthday, what kind of friend would I be if I didn't surprise you with a bunch of fun festivities?"

I'm going into today with caution. It literally could be anything. Ember doesn't mess around when it comes to birthdays, holidays, or trips, especially if it's for someone she loves and cares for, like lucky me. "Start getting ready so we can start your birthday. And take your coffee with you," she demands.

I make my way back inside with my blankets and coffee. I wonder if she would be mad if I crawled back into bed and slept for just one more hour. I wish I had a door handle with a lock. Although that still wouldn't stop her from banging on my door until I got up. That's typical Ember, though. She gets more excited about others than she does about herself. I love that about her. She has never once shown that she isn't the greatest friend of all time.

You don't want to be on Ember's bad side, though. That

girl knows how to fight. Her broader body build isn't something to mess with. In high school, she sent a boy to the hospital for bullying. I remember her being in a lot of trouble for that, but she didn't care. It was for a good reason. If she can't keep the peace, she will find a way to get it back one way or another. All of the girls wanted to be her friend. Some girls would try to be just like her in every way. She would constantly have boys swooning over her, too. But somehow, Ember and I just clicked, and all we needed was each other.

My mom is now awake and sitting in the living room with Rian. "Happy twenty-third, baby!" she shouts as she quickly walks toward me, nearly spilling her coffee.

"Thanks, Mom," I say, laughing at her as she throws her arms around me and squeezes. Sometimes, she can be just as crazy as Ember. What is it about me that makes everyone so extreme? I can't imagine I'm *that* lovable. It will always be something I won't fully understand. I'm just your average-looking twenty-three-year-old who lives an ordinary life and has run-of-the-mill things. I certainly wouldn't say that there is anything unique or spectacular about me, but whatever.

"What's on the agenda for today? Are you going to hang out with that Alder guy?" my mom asks me as she releases her hold on me.

"What?" I ask, confused as to why she would think that. "No, Ember has the day all planned out, apparently."

"Oh, Ember is here? Already?" Her eyes scan around. "Where is she?"

Rian chimes in, in the background. "Didn't you hear her this morning? She was all over the place," he laughs.

"She's waiting for me out on the patio," I say, gesturing to the doors. "Why did you think I was doing something with Alder?"

"Oh, I thought you saw," she gestures to the small table near the front door. "He sent you those."

I look over and see a beautiful arrangement of roses. When I approach them, I pick up the attached card.

"I brought flowers to your door last night.
I couldn't help but wonder what it might be like
If I had 'Two Dozen Roses' and an older bottle of wine.
If I really could've hung the moon, would it change your
mind?"
Happy Birthday, Jaemes.
I hope it's one you'll never forget.
—Alder

Now it's impossible to hide my smile. He gifted me two dozen roses with the lyrics of my favorite song attached. The patio doors open, and I realize why Ember woke me up early and rushed me outside. "He must like you," Ember says, approaching me with a smile. "He wanted to drop off a little surprise for you."

Alder's generous gesture was highly thoughtful. I can't wrap my head around him thinking about me like this and making this bold of a move. I reach for my phone and pull up our text message conversation.

Me: *Thank you for the roses. It's one of the sweetest things anyone has done for me.*

I don't wait for a response. I couldn't even if I wanted to. Ember shoves me downstairs so we can start the day.
Here we go.

AFTER AN EXTENSIVE and eventful day, I feel exhausted. It was a great day, but we spent a lot of time running around. We went out for a lovely brunch in the city. Before venturing off for the day, I wanted some good food and a Tequila Sunrise. Ember had her typical Bloody Mary. Afterward, we spent a few hours at a spa getting facials, massages, manicures, and pedicures. The usual activities girls typically do. And then, of course, we went shopping. No outing with Ember goes without shopping. Toward the end of the day, I felt this was more about her. She's lucky I love her. However, I did find a few new outfits and a new pair of shoes.

"Sassy Stacy's is having a band tonight. Do you want to go? We can have supper and a few drinks there if you want," Ember inquires as she drives us back home. During this time of year, places like to schedule live entertainment. Many people enjoy spending time outside, listening to music on a beautiful summer evening. It helps keep the regulars and out-of-towners coming, as this is a busy camping season. The drive is a good thirty to forty minutes, depending on traffic and the time of day. I'm tired, but that plan does sound like a great way to end the night.

"I'm down, but I don't want to stay for very long. My energy is running low from my early morning and busy day," I say as I side-eye her.

"Shut up, you know you love me. The band starts at seven o'clock. Want to head straight there, or do you want to stop home first?" she asks me.

"If I go home first, I'm not leaving. I will be a magnet to my bed."

"You are so lame. We'll head straight there, then. I'm not going to chance losing you to your bed."

I laugh at her and shake my head. Sometimes, that's all you can do. "Probably a good idea," I tell her.

My phone dings, and I see that it's a response from Alder.

Alder: *You're welcome. Try not to drink too much this time. You seriously don't want to forget your birthday like the card said.*

Me: *Funny!*

I can finally see Sassy Stacy's just down the road. The parking lot is packed with all sorts of vehicles, so we have no choice but to park on the side of the road. It's only five-thirty in the afternoon, and there is already a crowd. Fortunately, we have plenty of time to eat and enjoy a drink before the band starts.

We considered ourselves lucky when we saw one of the booths become available right as we walked in. Otherwise, there wasn't any other place to sit. I was surprised when our waitress only took a few minutes to take our drink order. Ember and I ordered a beer on tap and then glanced at the menu.

"Tonight's special is a club sandwich with chicken noodle soup on the side, and the drink of the month is a 'Stac-orita,' which is Sassy Stacy's famous spicy margarita. You can make it extra spicy for a dollar more, or you can make it extra sassy for two dollars more," the waitress explains as she points to those items on the menu. I thanked her for the information, and she left our table to grab our beverages.

"Oh, there's Bennett! Let's go up to the bar," Ember says as she bolts up with excitement. He's with a small group of guys, but it's hard to tell who he's with exactly since people are shoulder to shoulder here. The waitress notices that we have relocated and gives us our beers at the bar.

The band is setting up their equipment and testing the instruments. I keep looking at Ember, hoping to include myself in her conversations when a semi-recognizable voice turns my attention away. "Don't tell me Jaemes is drinking alone?"

Does it really look like I'm here by myself?

To my surprise, I see that same handsome blond doctor I met at the town's party standing beside me. His baby blue eyes stare into my soul as I try to respond.

"Hi…Dr. Ledger Yearwood, right?"

"Hey, you remembered." He smiles. "But I typically go by just Ledger."

"I'm actually here with a few friends." I gesture to Ember next to me and the group she's talking with.

"What brings you guys here tonight? The band, I'm guessing?" he asks me.

"Sort of. It's my birthday, so we're just finishing out the day here."

"Well, happy birthday," he says and holds up his glass to cheers.

"Thank you," I tell him after our sips.

"I never caught your last name when we met."

"Dovaughn."

"Wow, even a beautiful last name. I thought there was no way your name would be as beautiful as the way you look tonight."

I laugh and ask, "Are you always this cheesy?"

He sighs. "Lord, I hope not. But it *is* true. You have a beautiful name and are a gorgeous woman if I do say so myself."

I thank him with a smile and finish my beer.

"Looks like you could use another."

Ember notices my absence due to my lack of communication. She looks at Ledger and then at me. "Hey, why are you ignoring me?"

"I'm not—relax," I say, giving her a sympathetic hug. "Are you finished with your beer yet? I can get the next round."

"Allow me," Ledger interrupts.

"And you are?" Ember looks at him, puzzled.

"Ledger Yearwood." He reaches his hand out to her.

"Ember Ellis," she tells him, shaking his hand.

"Sorry, Ember, to me it looked like Jaemes was here alone and thought I'd come over and see if she wanted a drinking buddy. Come to find out, it's her birthday."

"Yeah, well, I'm the birthday girl's drinking buddy to-night. Sorry," she says playfully.

"Very nice to meet you, Ember," Ledger tells her, and then heads to the other end of the bar for more drinks.

"Is he the same guy who gave you his number at the par-ty?" Ember asks me.

"Sure is."

"He's a looker," she smirks, glancing at him again.

"Easy, your boyfriend is right next to you," I kindly re-mind her. "But you aren't wrong. He's a sight for sore eyes, that's for sure." I join her in watching him do his thing at the other end of the bar.

My phone vibrates, interrupting our thoughts about Ledg-er.

Alder: *You'd better slow down. Remember what happened last time?*

I look up from my phone and slowly look around. I'm more focused on how the hell he knows what I'm doing versus reacting to his message. I let Ember know that Alder texted me again. She adores how well things went with us at the party downtown. She keeps telling me that if I didn't drink as much as I did the night of *his* party, I wouldn't have had the confidence to dance with him at the *town's* party, nor make the first move by putting my number in his phone. And she's right. "Sober me" and "drunk me" are entirely different entities, but I'm not necessarily thanking "drunk me" just yet.

"He said I should 'slow down.' How does he know—"

"He's standing at the bar with Bennett and everyone," she says, pointing him out. "He just got here, like, five minutes ago."

I look in that direction, and of course, there he is, with his eyes on me and a smirk on his face. I shake my head at him, and again, I can't seem to avoid this stupid smile that appears, knowing that he is here, too.

Me: *Mind your own business, Alder. I don't plan on getting carried away tonight.*

I watch him as he reads my message. I see his shoulders move slightly as he subtly laughs at what I said.

Alder: *Sure. I'll believe it when I see it.*

Alder: *Oh, and tell Ember it's her turn to take care of you this time.*

I laugh at his message before looking over at him. He smiles and winks at me, then puts his phone back in his pocket and continues his conversation with someone at the bar. I feel myself blush.

"Happy birthday," Ledger says, approaching us again. He sets a tall glass of beer in front of me, and I feel my face get even redder. Then he sets one down for Ember.

What a gentleman.

"Awe, thanks. You didn't have to do that," I tell him.

"No, really, it's my pleasure. I'll be with that group over there if you get bored. We know how to have a good time."

I watch him walk to the group of people he's referring to. It hasn't been long since I returned home, and I'm already gushing over two men. I'm unsure of what's happening, and I don't know how I feel about it. It certainly isn't what I'm used to. I'm sure Ledger does this to many other women. However, he did seem genuine. Who am I kidding? He probably comes off that way to everyone. Either he's single, and something is wrong with him, or he's taken and is doing what all other scum bags do and hits on other women. There's no way he's *this* guy all the time.

"He seems into you," Ember states.

"I don't know how he could be. We just met."

"He must know what he wants. Props to him for going after it."

"There's nothing spectacular about me. If his type is average and available, you could be right. But I'm pretty sure he's just the kind of man who wants to see how many chicks he can pick up."

"Jaemes, you really don't think you're lovable, do you?" she asks with a sad look. "I can prove they are into you."

"*They?*" I ask in much need of clarification.

"Alder and Ledger," she clarifies.

I let out a vast laugh, indicating how delusional I think she is.

"Why do I keep catching *both* of them looking over here at you?" she asks.

"Oh, please. They're probably looking at you. You're the smoke show."

"*Honey, please*, I know when men are looking at me," she says with a sly and self-confident grin.

I carefully look over at Alder and then at Ledger, who both have their eyes on me until they see me lock eyes with them. They are making me feel self-conscious in everything I do. This might be an earlier night than I thought.

The band finally starts nearly thirty minutes after they were supposed to. After Ember and I finish eating, we move to a larger table closer to the band so Bennett and his friends can join us. That also includes Alder. Occasionally, I will catch myself watching Ledger and his group. Not because I'm interested in him necessarily, but because I'm curious to see what their good time looks like. So far, nothing too crazy is happening over there.

I see a few friends from high school who were also on the dance team with me. They wave me over, and I join them near the bar after squeezing my way through the thick sea of people. I haven't seen too many people from high school since graduation besides Ember, so it's nice to see these girls again. Our initial group conversation turns into small side conversations. Right now, it's me and a girl named Lexi. I'm half distracted while listening to her tell me how she's been doing. Alder is getting another drink at the bar, which is not too far away from us.

I hope it doesn't look too obvious that I'm checked out of this conversation with Lexi. I'm trying to stay engaged but can't keep my eyes off Alder. The way he stands, the way he leans up against the bar with his hands, waiting for his drink. I need to shift into a different mindset with him. I don't want to seem interested. When it comes to men, I need to analyze them a little bit more. Do they want a relationship or a one-night stand? Do I fall too fast for their charm? Alder dancing with me and sending me roses shouldn't get me this excited.

"Hello? Everything okay in there?" Lexi questions as she pokes my head to get my attention back to her. I can tell she has already had a few alcoholic beverages. Even if I were paying attention, I wouldn't be able to get a word in with Ms. Chattybox anyway.

Alder makes his way toward me to get back to the table. I keep my eyes on Lexi, but my peripheral vision is on him. I know he's right behind me when he is completely out of sight. I hold my breath, trying to remain natural. As he passes me, he lays his hand on the small of my back and doesn't release his touch until he's entirely past me and his hand can no longer reach me. I look toward him at the same time as those hazel eyes catch mine. It's impossible to look at this man and not smile, so I only give him a half smile. Enough to acknowledge him, but not enough to seem so eager from only a simple touch. My heart rate increases, and I can feel the beating in my chest intensify.

"Um, who is that?" Lexi asks me.

"What? Who?" I ask, playing dumb.

Lexi points to Alder with her drink in her hand while he sits back down at our table and says, "Him. The guy who just walked past you and is making your face all red."

"Oh, that's Alder."

"Are you guys a thing?" she asks. "Because if you don't hop on that, I sure will." She snickers at her comment, but I sense she isn't joking. Alder is a catch. I roll my eyes at her and avoid commenting back by taking a big sip of my beer. I told her it was good to see her again before returning to the table. She shouts, "Happy birthday!" as I walk away, and I hold up my glass in acknowledgment.

"Alder is buying a round of shots. You get to choose what it is, birthday girl," Ember sings. Deciding on shots is easy for me because I can handle anything. Whiskey, tequila, vodka, rum, gin, even those stupid girly shots where there's more of a fruity taste than the booze itself. I look around the table and glance at what everyone is drinking. Everyone has beer except a few random girls who have a mixed drink.

"Let's do tequila shots with salt and a lime," I say.

One of the guys at the table chimes in with his opinion regarding my choice. "Oh, man, tequila is rough. I'm not sure I'll be able to choke that down," he says.

Alder looks at him and tells him to stop being a child. "Besides," he adds, "I only get the top-shelf shit." He looks at me as he stands up from his chair. "You have to when it comes to tequila."

He's not wrong. Anything else would be like drinking gasoline.

IT'S ALMOST ELEVEN o'clock, and I'm feeling pretty good.

Between people buying me beer and shots, I'd say I'm about ready to go home. I'm starting to get hot sitting inside, and the door to cooler air looks inviting. I head out and lean my forearms against the railing of the porch as I hold what's left of my beer. The fresh air feels incredible. Tables on the porch are filled with people, and some smokers are standing in the parking lot. I don't smoke, but those cigarettes smell pretty good right now. The door swings open behind me, and I feel someone standing beside me. I can tell who it is by the smell of his cologne and how the touch of his arm feels against mine. We both stand silent for a minute and continue to casually drink our beverages.

"Can I ask you something?" I ask him.

"You just did," he jokes, prompting me to nudge his arm with mine. "Sure. What's your question?"

"That day when Ember introduced us at your house, when we were walking by, you acted like I was an inconvenience to you. You seemed distant and could barely even look at me."

"Is there supposed to be a question? I'm not sure what the point is here."

I turn around and rest my back against the porch. "I just want to know why you came off the way you did that day," I say with pure curiosity. "Why help with the surprise homecoming gathering with my family? Why bother dancing with me and sending the roses? Why care so much about my and Tate's interactions?"

He looks down at me and asks, "Were the roses too much?"

"The roses were a pleasant surprise. Especially coming from you." I tilt my head up toward his and speak directly to him. "I certainly didn't see that coming." I wait patiently for his response.

"Listen, I appreciate the people who are in my life. I have my friends, family, and coworkers, and that's it. I don't care to add anyone else to my life. I'm almost thirty, and I have everything and everyone I'll ever need. I don't care about meeting new people."

"That's understandable, I guess."

"But then I met you," he adds. "At first, I expected you to be just like any other girl I've met before. I did what I usually do during introductions. Make it clear and straightforward that you're nothing more than a stranger to me."

"Ouch. Way to make a girl feel special," I tease.

"Jaemes, it's tough for me to explain this," he continues in a serious tone. "I'm not so good with these kinds of subjects. Something just *drew* me to you. I felt something that I can't describe. It's anything but ordinary for me. It almost scared me, if I'm being honest. Hell, I didn't take in half of what Ember was saying when you two stopped at my place that afternoon. Whatever drew me to you initially made jealousy flare through my veins when I saw your interactions with Tate. Like I said before, I know how he is with women, and I wasn't going to let you get caught up in his asshole tactics. I couldn't help myself.

"Then, you made it so easy to strike up a conversation with you later that night. And our nice, flowing conversation made it that much easier for me to ask you to dance at the party, which I must admit was a lot of fun. You bring a sense of calmness and joyfulness wherever you go, and it makes me feel…I don't know…"

I remain silent and take a moment to absorb all of his words. It's a lot of information I wouldn't have ever envisioned him saying to me. But it feels good to hear him spew these thoughts out loud, especially if this sort of thing isn't easy for him.

"However, I'm typically good at ignoring those feelings, too," he adds. "I figured it wouldn't be hard to keep seeing you, but it turns out I was wrong."

We both take a drink to drown out the loudness of the silence between us.

"Well, I'm glad I made a good impression on you. So good, considering that you wanted to have a conversation with someone *new* like me and enjoyed my dance moves," I tell him while trying to hide my gushing smile.

He lets out a heavy sigh. "Jesus Christ, try not to flatter yourself too much," he jokes.

"Well, I didn't have much of a choice since I was practically dragged out there," I laugh.

The door behind us opens, and the muffled sound of the band grows louder and more evident. There is a large man with a black t-shirt that reads "SECURITY" in big, white letters across the front. "Hey, you guys can't take glass bottles outside. You'll need to bring them back inside or throw 'em," he informs us.

"Alright, no problem," Alder replies.

"Sorry," I say.

The bouncer goes back inside, and Alder starts to laugh. "*Sorry,*" he mocks me.

I push him, and a small amount of his beer spills out of his bottle. "Don't make fun of me," I tell him.

"Stop apologizing then," he continues, laughing. "You need to stop giving a fuck."

When we re-enter Sassy Stacy's, Alder gets pulled aside by someone standing near the entrance. It's the same blond girl who was all over him at his housewarming party. I mind my own business and squeeze my way to the bathroom. It's still hot in this place, so it's time to throw my hair up in a hair clip.

When I return to the table, I can't help but notice that Alder isn't back yet. I look over my shoulder to see that he is still talking with that girl. She seems giddy, but that's no surprise. It's hard not to be when talking to someone like Alder. I wonder how they know each other. Again, I try to mind my own business. It's not my place to worry about what he does or who he talks to. But I'd be fooling myself if I said I didn't care. After what he just said to me, I hope he doesn't talk like that to every woman, especially her. She makes it seem like they're a fling or something.

After a short while, I tell Ember I'm ready to leave. As I wait for her to chug the rest of her beer, I go to the bar to pay my tab.

"What's the name on the tab?" the bartender asks me.

"Jaemes Dovaughn," I tell her.

She walks to the POS system to print off my tab. When she approaches me again, there's nothing in her hand.

"Okay, honey, you're free to go," she says.

"What? How? I never gave you my credit card."

The bartender points behind me and says, "That gentleman gave me his card to put toward your tab." I look to see whom she is referring to. I sigh at yet another surprise I didn't expect. "He said it's for your birthday. Happy birthday."

"Thank you," I say without looking back at her.

I should probably thank him for covering my entire bill. I make my way over to him and tap on his shoulder to get his attention.

"I'm sorry; I don't mean to interrupt, but I'm heading out, and I wanted to make sure I got the chance to thank you for paying for my tab. You didn't have to do that, but thank you, Ledger. That was nice of you."

Ledger smiles back at me. "Don't worry about interrupting me. You shouldn't have to pay for your own drinks on your birthday. Consider it my gift to you."

"I should also thank you for keeping me company earlier. It was nice talking with you again."

"Are you sure you don't want to stay? I can give you a ride home later if you'd like."

I consider taking him up on his offer, but I know it would be a bad idea to stay any longer. "Thank you for the offer, but

I'd better go home now before I do anything I regret. Maybe another time?"

"Maybe another time," he agrees.

I walk past Alder and the blond to meet Ember outside—the girl glares at me as I walk by. I'm too tired to care, so I keep walking. Overall, my birthday was a success, and I had a great time with incredible people.

Ember pulls out of our parking spot and onto the road. "Alder wants you to let him know when you get home. He said he tried catching you before you left. But then I asked him, 'What about me?' and he just flipped me off. Which is fair, I guess."

"I'm surprised he was able to break away from his conversation long enough to tell you anything," I say back.

"Oh, I definitely got an evil look from her," Ember clarifies. "It's not our fault that Alder obviously likes *you*."

Alder obviously likes me?

I still don't understand that or believe it just yet. I'm forcing myself to keep my guard up. In past relationships, I have been all in, with nothing holding me back. I assume that when guys are in a relationship with me, they feel the same way. After getting heartbroken in relationship after relationship, I realized that wasn't ever the case. So, this time, it's going to be different. *I'm* going to be different.

Cheers to twenty-three.

Chapter Seven

THE SUN ISN'T up yet, and I've only been trying to get good sleep for a few hours. I try to clear my mind with reasonable effort. However, I'm not surprised I'm having trouble sleeping. I keep rummaging through *everything*—being back home and buying my own house, accepting a job offer that will advance my career, getting the opportunity to intern at a therapy office, Alder…

Oh, shoot, *Alder*.

I forgot to let him know when I got home last night. I didn't hesitate to go immediately to my bathroom to wash my face and brush my teeth when I got home. I was barely awake when I crawled into bed afterward. I had all intentions of texting him, but my brain shut down on me. I grab my phone and notice I have a missed call from him.

Do I call him back? *No, absolutely not.*

But what if he's worried? *He's not; otherwise, he'd call you more than just once and possibly send a text or two.*

Yeah, okay, but he's a guy and not just any other guy; he's Alder. He could be secretly wanting to know if I'm okay and doesn't want to show it.

Again, he's not.

I attempt to fall back asleep but find it difficult as I continue to have these back-and-forth conversations in my head. After failing for half an hour, I decide to give up.

Thanks a lot, Alder.

I smell fresh coffee as I head upstairs. My mom is already

awake and wearing her flight attendant uniform. Her makeup is always flawlessly applied, and her long, dark chocolate hair is always perfectly styled. She's sipping her coffee when she notices I am about to join her.

"You must not have had a crazy birthday if you're up already," she says.

"No, it wasn't too bad. Fun, but nothing crazy. Sorry that I didn't get to see you guys much yesterday."

She blows on her coffee to cool it down. "Oh, don't worry about that. I'm just glad you had a good time. You deserve it."

"I am tired, though. I only got five hours of sleep because Ember woke me up almost twenty-four hours ago, and Alder woke me up this morning," I tell her.

"Alder, huh? Are things looking serious between you two?" she asks.

"No, not at all. Well, maybe? I don't know. I wouldn't say it's *serious*. Just casual, I guess."

"I want to meet him," she tells me.

"Mom, we'll cross that bridge if we get there. And where is Rian? Don't you two normally go to work together?"

"Normally, yes, but he's covering for someone, so our schedules won't match up for a little while," she clarifies.

When I say my mom and Rian are inseparable, I mean it. They are always on the same flights unless one of them changes something in the schedule, as Rian did. They pretty much do everything together. How they don't get sick of each other is beyond me. I suppose if you're with the right person, there is no such thing as spending too much time together.

I go to the kitchen to pour myself some coffee and to fill up my mom's mug. On my way, I notice the floral scent of the roses Alder gave me. I observe them and absorb their beauty— all twenty-four of them. From the living room, my mom tells me she has something for me, which makes me jump since I was too distracted by the flowers. I spill some coffee on the counter and go to clean it while my mom goes into her bedroom. We meet back on the couch, and she mutes the TV. After a deep breath, she puts what looks like a photo album of some sort in front of me.

"What is this?" I ask her.

"Open it up. I'll explain along the way."

I do as she says and open it. It's a scrapbook with pictures and notes surrounding them.

"Did you make this?"

She nods her head and then points to one of the photos. In the photo, a man with shoulder-length blond hair and a woman who resembles my mom are sitting together on a motorcycle. The man is sitting in front with one hand on a handlebar. The woman is sitting behind him on the bike. Her arms are wrapped around his waist, and her head is resting against him. They are dressed in riding gear: black leather jackets, boot-cut blue jeans, and black boots.

"This is me about twenty-some years ago," she says, pointing to herself. And this is…" She moves her finger to the man pictured with her on the motorcycle. "This is your dad."

I glance at her for a second before returning to the photo. I look more closely at him and notice how similar we look. I have always wondered, since there isn't much of a resemblance between my mom and me. We had hardly ever talked about my biological dad. I remember when I was a young child, I would try asking questions about him, and my mom would always have the same answer.

"Trust me when I say I will tell you when you're old enough to understand. But for right now, it's nothing to worry about. All that matters is that we have each other, and until I can find someone worthy enough to be your dad, I'll take the role of both parents."

When Rian came into our lives, the subject of my actual dad became nonexistent because I had no reason to bring him up now that I had a great father figure in my life.

"His name is Jason Kellen. We were together for many years. He was a great guy. At that time, I thought he was the love of my life. He knew how to care for me and never let anything happen to me."

"So, what happened between you two?" I ask her. I know this is hard for her to talk about, so I try to be cautious. All the past feelings are being relived with this scrapbook of their history. I'm trying to be respectful and courteous in the kinds of questions I ask. She looks up at me with watery eyes. I can tell she's trying to be strong during this conversation, but I'm afraid that might be impossible.

"To be completely honest with you, Jaemes, I don't know. His whole demeanor and character changed almost instantly after I told him that I was pregnant with you. He became quiet, he started distancing himself from me, and I couldn't tell what was going through his head. He became disconnected from everything he loved, including staying in touch with his family, seeing his friends, going to work, and"—she trails off and wipes a tear that escaped from her eye—"and me. As much as I wanted him to talk to me about everything, he just couldn't. Maybe he needed space and more time to process the news of the pregnancy. He was acting so differently, and I felt myself starting to get afraid. Not of him, but of this person I didn't know anymore. Would he lash out at me if I begged him to talk to me? Would he leave me if I continued giving him more space? I kept coming up with more questions and *what-ifs* the more time I spent inside my head.

"One night, I woke up, and he wasn't there. I didn't think anything of it since that's what his new normal started to be like. Staying out late, coming home late, or not even coming home at all. He'd tell me he needed to work late or help out a friend. If that was the truth, I don't think I'll ever know, nor do I want to know. But that night, he vanished. He took everything he owned except for his favorite bandana and a note that he laid on the kitchen table of our apartment."

She flips through the scrapbook to the end. There is a piece of ripped notepad paper that reads *I'm sorry.* I stay calm and collected as I try to discuss this with her. I'm learning all this for the first time, and I'm starting to understand why she didn't want to explain this to younger Jaemes.

"This guy leaves his family behind with nothing, and all he has to say is 'I'm sorry'?"

"Trust me, I have tried to make sense of all this. I spoke with his friends and family and tried contacting his coworkers, but no one had seen or heard from him since the night he left. That remains the same to this day. I don't know if he's alive, dead, in jail, has a family with three kids—nothing. But I've never tried to find out either. I have had no need or want to."

I thoroughly examine the entire scrapbook. She explains who is in the photos and the stories behind them. Many of the images include motorcycles.

"You two looked so happy, Mom."

"I thought we were," she says.

"But you seem happier with Rian," I continue. "Everything happens for a reason. My dad couldn't give us the life we deserved, and Rian could. He's a better partner for you and a better dad for me."

"I wouldn't change anything about our lives, Jae. I came to terms with everything that had happened a long time ago. Your dad and I were young at that time. I was nineteen, and he was twenty. We were just kids with only a few years of adulthood under our belts. I see a lot of your dad in you, though. You remind me of him all the time."

"So, why did you pick this day out of all days to tell me about him? After I've asked you countless of times as a child."

"Well, I thought, now that you're done with school and getting ready to move out on your own, I thought this would be a good time to give you this scrapbook and talk about everything you've wanted to talk about regarding your biological dad. You're more mature now and able to understand things a bit better as an adult. There was no way I could tell a child your age about something like this."

"Does Rian know about my dad? Does he know you made this for me?" I ask her.

"Yes, he knows. We know everything about each other's past. You know how supportive Rian always is. He even helped me assemble the scrapbook."

I smile at that. It doesn't surprise me. It warms my heart that my mom got her happily ever after when, at one point, she thought she never would. After everything she has been through, she remains the strongest woman I know. I'm incredibly proud of her, and I let her know that.

"Thank you for making this for me, Mom. I'm truly grateful. It looks like you worked hard on this."

She smiles at me and finishes drying her face from a few more fallen tears. "It was the only thing I could think of that could show you who I was and the life we came from in great detail."

We stand up from the couch and come together for a lengthy hug. "Now, go stash that in one of your moving boxes. I need to fix myself up and get going, or I'll be late for my flight," she says.

I tell her thank you again before heading back downstairs. I look for a box that isn't packed full but end up sitting with it on my bed. I open it to the back and reread it, analyzing his handwriting more closely. This is the only personal item I have of his, and it's the bandana he is wearing in most photos. I stare at it until my vision becomes blurry.

I'm sorry.

I have a feeling there's more to this story, and I'm still not getting all the details that I'm looking for from my mom. But this will have to suffice...for now.

Chapter Eight

M Y MOM AND Rian were home for a little while after their last few flights. Over holidays and at any time during the summer, they get busy and seem to work months at a time, with only a few days in between for breaks. They don't mind their chaotic schedules since they still get to spend it together. There's nothing for them to come home to since I'm moving out soon. Plus, there's also that wonderful benefit of the paychecks that keep flying through.

Pun intended.

Alder recently told me about a Fourth of July gathering he's inviting me to at his house this afternoon. I'm excited to go back to that log house again. It will allow me to redeem myself and prove that what happened last time doesn't define me. The only thing that worries me is the potential conversations people may have regarding my previous visit.

I'm about to turn right into his driveway. The clock in my car reads three thirty-two in the afternoon. I purposely wanted to be late so I didn't appear too eager. However, the only vehicle I see is his truck, along with all three dogs running and jumping like they normally do when someone arrives. I feel stupid thinking I might have gotten the day or time wrong. I look back at his message, and he *did* say three o'clock on Saturday, July third. I call Ember to see where she is, but to no surprise, she doesn't answer. Maybe she will answer a text.

Me: *I'm at Alder's place. Where are you? I thought maybe you and Bennett would be here by now.*

I don't want to sit in his driveway, but I also don't want to drive away as if I'm afraid to be here. His dogs would make it much more obvious that I've been here and then left. I feel a sense of relief when my phone dings with an incoming text message. I'm assuming it's a response from Ember.

Alder: *You can come in, you know.*

Great, he's watching me. I'm glad I didn't end up driving away. I exit my car and walk up the porch stairs and to the front door. All three dogs follow me. I knock twice and then let myself in as the guard dogs follow suit. I see Alder leaning against the kitchen counter near the living room as I walk through the door. He's facing me, but his head is slightly tilted down, and his eyes are glued to his phone.

"You know it's rude to be late, right?" he asks, still focused on his phone.

"Where is everyone?"

He shrugs his shoulders, and his eyes lift to mine. "I don't know. I didn't invite anyone else," he says, his lips forming a guilty smirk. He finally locks his phone, places it on the counter, and gives me his full attention. I stay by the door, unsure of what I should do next.

"I'm confused. So, this gathering is just a gathering of me and you?"

"I guess you could say that," he replies.

My phone dings again, notifying me of another incoming text message. This time, it's Ember.

Ember: *What are you talking about? I'm with Bennett, and neither of us heard anything about Alder's.*

Of course, they didn't, and now I know why.

"If you wanted to hang out with me, you could have just asked me to come over," I mention.

He shakes his head and says, "I don't like rejection," then

heads into the kitchen and grabs two wine glasses. "You like wine?" he asks.

I let out a soft laugh. "First of all, yes, I do, but only red. Second of all, I'm sure no one likes to be rejected. And third, what makes you think I'd reject you?"

"Would you have?" he asks as he fills both glasses halfway with red wine.

"I guess you'll never know now," I say with a flirtatious tone in my voice, which makes him look up at me with a sexy grin in return.

I watch him as he places the wine in the fridge. He's wearing jeans and a black t-shirt, but he could be wearing anything and still be extremely attractive. He flashes the most perfect smile in my direction as he grabs the two glasses of wine. His eyes pierce through me as I stand in place.

"You don't have to stand by the door," he chuckles. "Come in and make yourself comfortable."

"Oh, right," I say with a titter. "Sorry."

As he walks past me and to the living room, he half smiles and shakes his head at my "sorry" comment. We end up sitting beside each other on the couch facing the fireplace. I thank him for the wine after he hands over the glass that's for me. I have to stop myself from chugging it. I'm more nervous now that I know it's just the two of us. I feel more comfortable leaning on someone else to help with conversations. Otherwise, my socially awkward self feels like she can come to the party and stay for a while.

"So, you don't normally do anything for the Fourth of July?" I ask, trying to break the ice.

"Yeah, every year my family gets together at my uncle's cabin for the weekend to celebrate."

"You didn't want to attend this year?" I ask.

"I guess I felt like there were better things to do this year," he says with a slight shrug of his shoulder.

"Like what? Hang out with me?" I laugh.

He goes to take a sip of the wine but ends up finishing his glass. "Wanna go for a walk or something?" he asks, ignoring my question.

I look down at my glass and then back at him. "If you want to attend things with your family, I can—"

"Jaemes," he cuts me off, "I do what I want, when I want. I'd be there if I wanted to be with my family this weekend. There is a reason why I bailed this year. You don't need to worry, you're not keeping me from anything."

I finish up my wine like I wanted to in the first place. "A walk sounds great. Can we take the dogs?"

He gives me a small smile and takes our empty glasses to the kitchen. Hanging up by the door are three harnesses and leashes. He puts them on one at a time. "You can take the white one. She's tamer than these two boys."

"Do they have names?" I ask.

He shakes his head, and then a grin appears as he puts the last harness and leash on the last dog. "No, not really. With three dogs, it's easier to call them 'dogs' so they all listen simultaneously."

"Makes sense, I guess," I say softly to myself.

He lets the dogs outside and locks the front door behind us. The dogs seem to know their boundaries since they eagerly wait near the end of the driveway. We are walking down the porch steps when my foot somehow gets caught up on my other foot, causing me to lose my balance.

Why am I so fucking clumsy?

My immediate reaction is to grab something to catch my fall. At the same time, I grab onto Alder, as he grabs onto me. Thankfully, I didn't completely fall down the rest of the stairs and roll onto the ground. For a moment, our faces are inches away. The more I take in his scent, the more I feel myself melt into his arms.

"Oh, wow, I'm so sorry," I tell him, trying to brush this moment off.

He leans in closer so we are mere inches from each other's faces. "Stop apologizing," he whispers and then slowly releases me. He grabs my hand and doesn't let it go until we reach the dogs at the end of the driveway. He takes the black and chocolate labs, while I take the white lab, and we start walking down the road.

"I'm going to have to start holding your hand everywhere to prevent you from falling, aren't I?" he asks.

"You might have to. Or be on standby so you can catch me. Either would work," I joke. I noticed his bandaged hand when he grabbed mine, so I ask him about it. His hand is wrapped up due to an electrical burn that happened at work yesterday.

"You should have Ember look at it," I suggest.

"I'll be fine. Most of the time, it's nothing to worry about. It *shocks* you more than anything."

"I see what you did there," I chuckle.

We are taking in the gorgeous scenery, and the dogs are joyfully trotting next to us. Occasionally, their leashes will tangle together, making us laugh as we constantly try to separate them.

"Tell me what your family is like," I finally say. It seems to be a secret or a sore subject that he doesn't wish to discuss. However, at some point, he has to mention *something*—his childhood, his parents, their journey from South Dakota to Montana—anything.

"There's not much to say. You already know most of the important stuff."

I can tell he's already not into this conversation, but maybe I can press my luck just a little more. "What was your childhood like?"

I end up waiting slightly longer than anticipated but remain patiently silent.

"When I was a kid, I was extremely pressured to be perfect. The expectation my parents had of me was…extravagant. I'm the only child, so the focus was always on me. My dad constantly compared me to my cousins. He wanted me to be better, stronger, more creative. It was as if he and his siblings were always competing to see who could raise the better child. I never had the opportunity to make many friends in school, despite participating in numerous extracurricular activities. If I wasn't at practices or events, I was in my room studying."

"What did you do on the weekends?"

He laughs lightly, glancing down at the ground as he recalls the memories. "Taking care of my mom. I never had a babysitter growing up. I *was* the babysitter…for my mom. She was a big drinker. Both of my parents were. My dad could handle the alcohol better, but he never cared for my mom when they were drinking, which was most of the time."

"I'm sorry, Alder. How's your relationship with them now?"

"What do you think? My parents had this vision of their only child being a huge, successful lawyer or someone who found the cure for cancer. But that wasn't me. I excelled phenomenally in school, achieving a GPA that any college would have accepted. However, when I turned eighteen and graduated from high school, I told them, *'That's it, it's time to finally be me and do what I want to do for once.'* And some other words mixed that they didn't like very much," he says, chuckling toward the end. "I attended community college and began working as an electrician because I wanted to work with my hands and see my work come to life. I partied a lot after I moved out, which got me into some trouble, but I finally felt free to do what I wanted, when I wanted. I made friends and built a life around what I wanted. It felt great, Jaemes."

In a way, I can relate to his story. But instead of battling with parents, I was battling with the unknown of my past and where I came from. I didn't have a typical childhood, and from the sounds of it, Alder really didn't either.

"I appreciate the fact that you didn't buckle under the pressure of their expectations. Sometimes you have to do what you have to do to make yourself happy. That's all that truly matters. If you're happy, they should be, too."

"What about you? What was the reasoning for college in Las Vegas?" he asks, changing the subject to me.

"I was born there and most of my family still lives there. After moving from Vegas to Los Angeles and then to Montana during my childhood, I wanted to return to where my story began. I missed it."

"So, why move back here? Vegas seems to make you happy; I can tell."

I embarrassingly laugh at that question, mostly because I don't want to answer it. But he answered the questions I had for him, so I guess I owe him. "Come on, the truth can't be that bad," he adds.

"Okay," I start, "I was in a relationship with a man that I cared so deeply for. I was under the impression that he felt the same way about me, given that we were happily together for three-and-a-half years or so. Almost halfway through my senior year, I discovered that he was still in a committed relationship with his high school girlfriend back home in Colorado. I was absolutely devastated, Alder. I tried to jump back into the dating game quickly, hoping to move on from the guy, but the men in Vegas were awful. My heart broke countless times, and I could never tell if someone was genuinely interested in me as a person or if they were just looking for a one-night stand.

"I happened to apply for many job positions and internships across the United States. I didn't care where I was going—all I knew was that I wanted out of Vegas. So, after accepting an amazing job opportunity and a perfect internship, here I am. Sure, Vegas was an amazing place to live during my college years. I could see my extended family and hang out with old friends, but if I want a husband or kids someday, Vegas won't make that happen for me."

"I get that. My role model parents didn't make marriage or having kids look like any walk in the park," he responds. "I'm sorry to hear about your relationship with your ex."

"Yeah, relationships aren't a walk in the park, either."

We release all three dogs when we enter the driveway again. I glance down at my hand, and a few blisters begin to form from holding the leash so tightly. When Alder notices, he takes my hand into his, and we continue to walk up the driveway.

"I want to show you something," he says.

We walk to the back of the house, where a small path weaves through all the trees. At the end of the path, there is an open grass area and a concrete bench. It's a beautiful and peaceful area located right in his backyard. We sit on the bench and watch the sun become heavy and slip behind the mountains.

"This is such a spectacular place. I can't believe you always get this view from your own home. And not to mention, you have a porch overlooking the sunrise on the other side. You're so lucky."

Alder casually puts his arm around me and grazes my shoulder with his fingertips. "Weird. It's like I'm having Deja Vu," he says. "It's the same reaction you had when you first saw this."

I side-eye him and thank him again for bringing up the fact that I, indeed, did get a little drunk that night of his bonfire. "Well, I'm sorry for repeating myself and for all the repeat conversations we may have in the future."

"I'm just giving you shit. Besides, I don't mind reliving these conversations with you." I get chills on my arms, and I'm not sure if it's because it's getting chilly outside or if it's a reaction to Alder's words. Either way, he notices and rubs my arm. Now it could be from his touch alone. "Let's go back to the front. I'll start a fire."

I agree without hesitation. Even though it's still beautiful with the glowing mountains back here, I prefer to be warm, and a fire sounds like the perfect solution. As we walk to the front, Alder pulls out his phone from his pants pocket. He sighs and shakes his head.

"I hate that I'm asking you this, but would you be okay if Bennett and Ember stopped by?" Before he gives me any chance to answer him, he continues. "You know what, I should just ignore him. Forget I even asked. That was stupid, and I shouldn't have said anything in the first place."

"Alder, it's okay if they swing by," I assure him.

But I do care if we're alone. I'm worried about doing or saying something embarrassing. I need someone to help ease the tension I feel within myself when I'm near Alder, and that perfect person is my best friend. I wasn't prepared to be alone with him at all today. With that catching me off guard, I didn't have the time to calm myself down or prep for possible conversations. What should we talk about? What questions should I ask? What would I do if our conversations didn't flow very well? I went into today without a plan and had no choice but to go with the flow.

I watch him start the fire while sitting comfortably in one of the chairs that surround the fire pit. He grabs logs from a pile stacked between two giant trees on the side of his property line. He goes back and forth between the log pile and the fire pit several times. When I ask him if I can help, he simply turns me down and smiles. He stacks a small pile of logs on the cement slab and builds a teepee with them in the pit. Afterwards, he stuffs newspapers and boxes inside it. I watch him the entire time. I focus on his every move and how he looks when he concentrates.

After he pours lighter fluid over the top, he lights a match from a matchbook. I watch his setup engulfed in flames. I can see his face so much clearer now that it's lit up by the fire. He stands there and watches it for a moment as I sit and watch him. He looks over at me and catches me staring at him. Surprisingly, I don't feel the need to look away. We seem so captivated by each other that we don't notice Bennett and Ember drive into the driveway. We both snap out of our trances when their car doors slam shut.

"Thanks for the invite, asshole," Bennett says sarcastically as they walk toward us. Alder looks at him with a smirk. "Technically, I did, but Jaemes was the only one who knew about it." He looks back at me and winks. I can feel my face becoming warm.

"Ha. Doesn't count, fucker," Bennett says as he hits Alder in the arm. "Hey, I know… you can make it up to me by getting me a drink."

"I'll get you a drink only because I was going to grab one for myself anyway," Alder states. He asks if anyone else wants anything but looks at me specifically.

"I'll take whatever you've got," I tell him.

"No, I probably shouldn't," Ember replies. "I have to work tomorrow, and I already have to drive this drunk idiot home."

Bennett looks at Ember, offended. "I'm not drunk," he says.

"Not yet," Ember clarifies.

"*Not yet*," Bennett says, mocking her.

Ember lets out a frustrated laugh like she's trying to keep her cool with him. "What the hell, one won't hurt. He's been nothing but annoying today."

"Sorry, I'm in a good mood, and you're crabby like you always are when you're on your period."

"*Okay!*" Alder says, trying to break up this conversation

before Bennett says anything else he will regret. "Bennett, come help me grab the drinks, yeah?" Alder grabs Bennett by the top of his shoulder and guides him toward the house.

Ember looks at me and rolls her eyes. "I swear, he's lucky I love him. And he *did* start drinking earlier today, so it won't take long until he's a goner."

I don't see them fight often, and whenever she talks about him, it's nothing but great things. I suppose when you mix feelings and alcohol, it can only go one of two ways. Feelings are either mutual, and everything is hunky-dory, or feelings are the opposite, and things get a little rocky, like how they are tonight with these two.

"So," she continues, "you and Alder, huh?"

"Ember, it's honestly nothing. We are just two people talking and enjoying each other's company," I correct her. I know I can answer that honestly because Alder and I don't even know what this is.

"Mhm," she says pointedly. "I know Bennett, and Bennett knows Alder, and from what I've heard, he's pretty interested in you."

"What do you mean? Like, he talks about me?"

"He must if Bennett knows things."

The guys come back with drinks, causing Ember and me to stop talking. I hate how I instantly feel nervous in Alder's presence. It's much easier now that Ember is here. I want to know more. Is he asking about me? What is he saying? Is he casually bringing me up, or is he begging to have a conversation? So much wonder in the air.

Most of the night, we all have separate conversations. My conversations with Ember snowball into other discussions, and the next thing we know, we don't remember what we were initially talking about. From what I can hear, Alder and Bennett mostly talk about work.

I look at my phone for the first time since I arrived here,

and just like that, it's already ten thirty at night. Ember says she has to use the bathroom, and I take that opportunity to tell everyone that I am going to head home. I get up to walk to my car, and Alder follows suit. When I reach my car, I turn around to see Alder approach slowly with his hands in his pockets. He gets about a foot away from me and stops.

"Thank you for inviting me to your Fourth of July party," I tell him with a smile. Even though this wasn't what I expected, I am glad he gave us the opportunity to be alone. I got to know him better as Alder rather than an acquaintance.

"I'm glad you stayed," he admits. Again, his eyes stare deep into mine while my body remains frozen, and my heart races with the unknown of what will happen next.

"Kiss her!" Bennett shouts from the fire pit. Immediately, Ember throws her empty beer can at him and tells him to shut up before calling him a dumbass.

Shortly afterwards, the tension is broken by fireworks going off nearby. We both look up only for a brief moment and then return to each other's gaze. Our faces turn colors from the illuminating fireworks flying in the sky. His index finger lightly slides underneath my chin, giving me reason to believe he might kiss me. So many mixed feelings and emotions are going through my head, but I remain still with my eyes glued to his as I try to figure out his next move.

"Don't forget to let me know when you get home this time," he says in a soft voice before returning to Bennett and Ember at the fire. That grin on his face indicates that he knows exactly what he just did.

Jerk.

I let out a shaky, deep breath and open my car door as best I can.

Driving home, I think about every detail of my day with Alder. We were both vulnerable, and I never imagined him to feel comfortable enough with me to talk about his past. I only hope that his holdbacks in life didn't make him the type of guy I'm trying to stay away from. I park my car in the driveway, and before I get out, I pick up my phone and text him.

> **Me:** *You don't have to worry anymore. I made it home just fine.*

It doesn't take him long to respond. As I close the car door, my phone vibrates with his reply.

> **Alder:** *Good. Sleep well. I have a feeling your dreams will be of me actually kissing you.*
>
> **Me:** *You wish. But you'll never know because I don't kiss and tell, even if it's only in my dreams.*

I did want him to kiss me, but I won't admit that to him. I'm sure he was testing me to see if I'd lean in and lock lips with him before he did. I won't give him that satisfaction. Until I know his true intentions, I don't want to start anything serious.

But I have a strange feeling that my heart won't let me have a choice.

Chapter Nine

I WOKE UP on Independence Day in the best mood. I don't remember the last time I was able to get a good night's rest without worrying about a single thing. Nothing could possibly ruin how amazing I feel right now. Life is good. Could this all stem from Alder? Does he make me feel this way? I haven't stopped thinking about him since I left his house last night. I don't remember going through my shower routine this morning due to my mind being ambushed with all sorts of thoughts.

It's only a little after eight o'clock in the morning, but I'm sure there will be Fourth of July festivities later to help distract me. Yet, I don't think I want a distraction from Alder. Perhaps just a distraction from the thought of having no idea when I'll see him again.

My phone lights up with a few notifications. I'm overly hopeful there's a text from him. Unfortunately, they are just emails and a text from Ember.

Ember: *Have any plans today? I get off work at 5:00 pm.*

I set my phone back down without responding to her. A part of me wants to see if Alder will get in touch with me first. In the meantime, I go for a walk to get out of the house and get some fresh air. It's a great way to pass the time.

When I decide to turn around to head back home, I get another text. Ember is so impatient.

Alder: *Meet me tonight?*

My heart skips a beat. I'm annoyed how my brain controls my body's reactions in this way. I go from calm to crazy when I see the text isn't from an eager Ember, but a drawn Alder.

Me: *Did someone finally get the courage to ask me out properly?*

Alder: *Maybe.*

Me: *Where am I meeting you?*

Alder: *I'll pick you up at 8:00 pm.*

Me: *See you then.*

I head back home with a little more pep in my step. Now I can text Ember back, letting her know that I, in fact, do have plans today. It's still early in the day, and Alder won't be here for a few hours, but I want to get ready for tonight sooner rather than later. I wear my white fringe shorts with my red and navy-blue striped shirt, and I curl my hair to create waves. Very rarely is my hair ever done this cute. It's usually stick straight or thrown up in a hair clip or a messy bun.

I'M GETTING ANTSY. I've been ready for a good six hours now. What better thing to do to help calm my nerves? Make a drink. I grab the bottle of Jack Daniel's and pour some of it into my cocktail glass filled with ice. I top it off with a bit of Coke and stir it well. It's time to relax on the patio and enjoy this wonderful evening with my friend Jack while I wait.

"No one answered the door, so I thought I might find you back here," Alder announces as he rounds the corner of the house and steps onto the patio. His unexpected appearance makes me jump and spill some of my drink. I had no idea he was here already.

"Well, you *are* early. I would have been ready to answer the door for you at eight o'clock, but it's only half past seven," I mention while cleaning off the side of my glass and wiping drops of my cocktail off my leg.

His cologne swiftly touches my face when he walks past, creating a comforting sensation. He sits on the patio chair next to me on my left. I catch his eyes scanning me over. He keeps his sight on my attire as he replies.

"I didn't have much going on today and became bored, so I got in my truck and drove around to waste some time." He looks down and clasps his hands between his knees while his forearms rest on his legs. "Next thing I know, I'm sitting in your driveway a half hour early."

He looks at me with only his eyes while I finish swallowing a large sip and then rest the glass on my lap. I don't take my eyes off the glass and remain silent, still trying to muster up a response. As much as I want to have a nicely flowing conversation, my brain isn't letting me admit my anxiousness and how badly I wanted to see him again. Not to mention how happy I was when he texted me again. So, I keep it close to the vest.

His lips form a small smile as he continues to hold my gaze.

"What's on your mind?" he asks.

"You," I shyly admit.

My lips start to mimic his smile—it's impossible not to with his eyes glued to mine. He suddenly gets up, takes my drink from me, puts the glass to his mouth, and chugs it until it's gone.

"Hey!" I giggle.

He pulls it away from his face and glances at it.

"Looks like you're finished. Let's go." He sets the glass on the end table and holds his hand out to help me up from the patio couch I'm sitting on. I gladly take it and don't let go until we get to his truck. "You make those drinks strong, by the way," he adds.

"You have to be able to taste the whiskey, Alder. Otherwise, what's the point? I only like Coke when it's mixed with whiskey. So, if I can't taste it, it's basically just Coke," I tell him.

He smiles and shakes his head at me. "I will say I'm impressed you can drink that."

"I'm impressed you could *chug* that. The way I make it, it's more of a sipping drink," I laugh.

After we pull out of my driveway, I ask him where we are going, but he fails to give me any details.

"Alder, we aren't doing anything illegal, are we?" I think he can sense the worry in my voice. I haven't been anything short of a "goody-goody" these past twenty-three years, and I've always played by the rules of the law. Getting into trouble never sounded worth it. It freaked me out, honestly. In our teens, Ember tried hard to get me to live on the edge with her. The only thing she ever did was pull me out of my shell, so I wasn't so shy and introverted. However, I will take credit for calming her down a bit. Over the years of our friendship, I steered her away from possible arrests and other destructive decisions many times.

"No, we aren't doing anything illegal," he says while grabbing my hand again and gently squeezing it for reassurance. "I wouldn't do anything like that. Especially with you. Plus, my parole officer would kill me if I did."

I look at him wide-eyed, which makes him laugh. "I'm kidding," he tells me. "Relax, I'll explain when we get there. And she wouldn't kill me. I've been on good behavior since I've been out of the slammer."

"Alder..." I say, side-eyeing him. "Be real with me because I don't know you well enough to know if you're lying or not."

He flashes a smile my way. "I'm sorry. I have a clean record, so nothing to worry about, I promise."

He holds my hand throughout the trip. An hour passes before we finally arrive at our destination. To my surprise, a good number of vehicles are parked in the parking lot, as well as a couple of luxurious RVs.

"So," he starts as we enter the parking lot, "this is the ski resort my parents own. It's not as extravagant as other resorts, but we still get a crowd in the winter. The top of the hill has a perfect view for watching fireworks."

"Alder, are you kidding? This is a beautiful resort. The fact that it's in the middle of nowhere and secluded by trees…I can't imagine what it looks like in the winter with the snow." The more we drive through the parking lot and the closer we get, the more beautiful it appears.

"Many people like it here because you don't have all the tourists. They tend to move toward the larger hills. We mainly get locals and their friends and families."

Alder parks the truck, and I immediately get out to look around. The property is surrounded by twinkling white lights. The landscaping consists of vibrant green plants in a sparkling rock bed. I sit on the edge of the stone wall and smell the neon-colored flowers.

"How have I never heard of this place?" I whisper to myself.

"Jaemes, smile," Alder says from a distance. As he walks closer to me, he pulls his phone up like he's about to take my picture.

I smile willingly.

After a few seconds, he walks up to me and shows me the photo he took on his phone. "Beautiful," he says.

"The scenery makes it," I tell him.

"I beg to differ." He's close to me, about the same distance as last night before I left his house. I look up at him and lose my breath when I lock eyes with his. I try to get myself out of these trances I seem to be in when he stands this close and looks into my soul.

"So, are all these vehicles your family's?" I ask him with a shaky voice.

The corners of his lips briefly form a slight smile, and then it slowly fades. His eyes continue to hold a steady focus on mine.

"Yeah, my family comes here to watch the fireworks."

His hand touches the top of my arm and then slowly ventures downward to my hand. He casually grabs it, and then we walk toward the hill.

"It's not just a one-day thing for us," he continues. "We start at my uncle's cabin and then work our way here for the fireworks on Independence Day."

"You have a big family? It looks like there are so many people here."

"There are around fifty of us who gather for the festivities. Give or take."

I think about his family and the possible reasons he brought me here. This makes me stop walking, let go of his hand, and cross my arms over my chest.

"Alder," I say his name with some frustration. He stops and looks back at me, confused.

"What?" he asks.

Quietly and through clenched teeth, I ask, "Am I meeting your family today?"

He laughs, relieved by the reality of my worry.

"Only if you want to. I was planning on secluding ourselves on the other side of the hill since privacy is always nice." I walk toward him, rejoining my hand with his. "Jaemes, relax. Why do you get so worried?"

"I don't know. I guess I feel the need to be perfect all the time. And I know I'm far from perfect, so it stresses me out. If I could change one thing about myself, it would be that. To stop worrying about what people may think of me."

"If you ask me, you don't have to try that hard. You can be yourself with me. At least, I hope you feel comfortable enough to do so."

He *does* make me feel comfortable, but I still feel like I need to impress him without embarrassing myself. I can't help but feel on edge knowing I could potentially run into any one of his fifty family members at some point. I don't want to ruin this amazing outing. The higher we get on the hill, the louder I can hear the laughter and shouting from everyone.

We finally reach the top, and the view is surreal. The sun is almost setting behind the mountains, and a few fireworks are already going off in the distance. We wouldn't be able to see them if we were on ground level. Alder sits on the ground and gestures for me to do the same. I can feel him watching me take all this in as he leans back on his forearms, his legs stretched out and crossed at the ankles. I'm sitting cross-legged and leaning back on my hands. We are quiet as we watch the fireworks get closer, and the sky becomes darker. I feel Alder nudge my leg with his.

"What's on your mind?" he asks me again.

I look back at him and smile softly. It isn't him this time. I've become distracted while also being able to be in Alder's presence at the same time, and it's a magnificent feeling—the feeling of being surrounded in awe.

I look back up to the sky.

"I just…it's so…" I sigh. "This view is breathtaking. The way the fireworks light up the black sky and showcase the mountains that have disappeared with the sunken sun." I slowly shake my head in admiration of it all.

Alder pulls on my arm slightly, motioning for me to lie flat on the ground as he does the same. "This is my favorite way to watch them. There's nothing else in sight except the paint splatter of the fireworks against the sky's midnight canvas."

"I love that," I say in a whisper. He turns his head to me, causing me to do the same. "Thank you for taking me here. I couldn't have asked for a better way to spend a holiday."

He sits up, bends one leg at the knee, and rests his arm on it.

"What's wrong?" I ask him, sitting up to join him.

I'm seated just behind his left shoulder. I hear him take a long, deep breath. I don't quite know what's going on or what happened, but I'm getting a little concerned when he isn't answering me. "Do you want to leave? It's okay if you do," I tell him, hoping to reassure him that he doesn't have to stay with me here if he doesn't want to.

He still refuses to say anything.

Instead, he turns his head toward me so our faces are closer than ever. He doesn't look into my eyes this time, but at my lips. Biting his lower lip, he places his left hand on my cheek. His thumb gently grazes me for a moment as his eyes go from my lips to my eyes. The next thing I know, our lips finally meet for the first time.

I lose my breath, and I can only hear my heart beating against my chest. Our first kiss is soft and gentle. He pulls away slightly, but I take the initiative to go in for a deeper kiss. His fingers travel upward and start to tangle in the waves of my hair. Our kiss turns fiercer and more desperate. A part of me can't believe we are doing this, and another part wants more of it. I feel weak, like I could fall down the hill if he lets me go. And for the first time in a long time, I forget the past and the feeling of despair, because my heart no longer feels broken.

"Alder!" a small and delicate voice calls out in the distance, making us separate from each other.

We stand up and attempt to act like nothing happened. The voice comes from a young girl who looks to be around five years old. Her long blond hair is slicked back in pigtails. They bounce up and down as she runs toward us. She's dressed in a red, white, and blue romper with white flip-flops. She's probably the cutest little girl I've ever seen. Alder kneels to her level as soon as she reaches us.

"Hey, little lady, what are you doing over here?" he asks her.

She hugs him, and he picks her up.

"Gruncle said he saw you over here, and I wanted to say 'hi' *so* bad," she tells him.

"Oh yeah?" he laughs.

The little girl, who is now in Alder's arms, points at me. "Who is she?" she asks.

He glances my way briefly and then introduces me. "This is my friend, Jaemes." She wiggles in his arms, indicating she wants to get out of his hold.

"Hi, Jaemes," she says to me. "My name is Annie!"

I crouch down to her level. "Hi, Annie. It's very nice to meet you."

"Annie is my cousin. Second cousin," Alder says.

"Actually, my name is Anniston, but everyone calls me Annie," she clarifies.

"Wow, so you're telling me you have not one, but *two* beautiful names?" I ask her.

She smiles and nods her head in response.

"How perfect for a beautiful girl like yourself," I say as I boop the tip of her nose with my index finger.

She giggles and says, "I'm going to roll down the hill now. Bye!" She runs off before we can say goodbye. I stand up straight beside Alder, and we watch her have the time of her life.

"Gruncle?" I ask, turning to Alder, curious as to what that means.

He smiles and looks over at Annie rolling down the hill. "Great Uncle. Since she was born, my uncle Dave has referred to himself as a 'Gruncle.' Now, that's all she ever calls him.

He's the nicest and goofiest guy you'll ever meet."

We both watch Annie run up the hill and roll back down several times. We can still hear people laughing in the distance, which causes me to turn my attention in that direction and see that a lady is approaching us.

"Have you seen Annie?" she says, walking up the hill breathless.

Alder points to the bottom of the hill, where the little girl has just finished her last roll and is now running back to the family gathering.

"Ugh, she's the only reason why I stay in shape," she jokes as she turns to head back the way she came. "Alder, stop being so antisocial and get your ass over here!" she shouts, walking backwards and then running the rest of the way. Alder looks at me for approval. I hold out my hand, motioning for him to lead the way.

I suppose I'll be meeting his family after all, and surprisingly, I'm feeling pretty good about it.

Chapter Ten

TODAY IS THE day I close on my house and finally become a homeowner. The feeling becomes real when I finish signing my life away, and the keys fall into my hands. I have all my belongings in boxes, and one by one, I carry them out of my old room, up the stairs, through the dining room, out the front door, and into the back of the moving truck. I wish I were in better shape for this. Every once in a while, I'll need a water break and time to catch my breath. I don't want to slow down, though. The faster I get everything out of here, the quicker I can get it all to my house. All I want is to get unpacked and settled so I can enjoy it.

I approach the box that contains the scrapbook. I look through it for the hundredth time. It still feels like I'm seeing it for the first time every time I look at it. Since receiving this gift from my mom and listening to her stories, I continue to wonder where my dad is today. I don't wish to have a relationship with him or even meet him, for that matter. I'm more curious as to what kind of man he eventually turned out to be. Is he the same man my mom described? Is he a completely different person to the point where my mom wouldn't even recognize him? Some part of me would like answers to these curiosities, but I'd also be okay if I never thought about him again.

Now that everything is in the moving truck, I can safely say my part is done.

For now.

I only have my bed, nightstand, and dresser to haul into the truck, but I will need more muscle for those items. Alder has been busy working and helping at the ski resort, so I'm banking on Bennett's help.

> **Me:** *Hey, do you think Bennett could help me move my bedroom furniture? I'm hoping to get everything moved out today.*
>
> **Ember:** *Of course! I don't think he's doing anything after work.*
>
> **Ember:** *Is Alder helping, too?*
>
> **Me:** *I didn't ask him. He's been preoccupied outside of work, so I don't want to bug him about this. Bennett, on the other hand, I don't care to bug.*
>
> **Ember:** *Yeah, you don't need to worry about Bennett. But OMG, Jae…just send Alder a text! You know he'd help you.*
>
> **Me:** *I don't want to add to his busy schedule. I'll find a different time to be a nuisance.*
>
> **Ember:** *You're being ridiculous, you know that?*
>
> **Me:** *Maybe. Tell Bennett thank you for me.*
>
> **Ember:** *I will. He just texted me back and gave me the go-ahead to tell you that he can help you out today. So, I'll see you later!*
>
> **Me:** *Great! I owe him. Can't wait to see you!*
>
> **Ember:** *Same, girl, same. Muah!*

It's early in the evening when Ember and Bennett arrive. I open the front door for them as Bennett parks his truck in the driveway next to the moving truck. However, I question what's going on when three doors open up. Bennett steps out of the driver's side, and Ember hops out of the back seat behind him. To my surprise, Alder walks to the front of the truck after closing the passenger side door.

Ember meets me first at the front door.

"Ember…" I complain. "What's he doing here?" She knew

damn well that I did not want to be added to his list of stressors. I know how hard he has been working in addition to helping with the remodeling at the ski resort. This time of the year is the only time they can update things if needed.

"You can't possibly believe that we can lift everything with just us three, Jae," she replies. "We're innocent here. All Bennett did was ask a friend to help. That friend just so happened to be Alder. He could have declined, but he didn't."

"That's all on a technicality, Ember." I give her a scowling look as she walks inside. She shoots me back a shit-eating grin. I know what she's doing. Bennett follows Ember, and I meet Alder halfway up the sidewalk that leads to the front door. I give him a defeated look.

"I'm sorry. I told them not to bother you," I tell him.

He grabs me by the waist and pulls me toward him, making me let out a light gasp. "Listen, don't ever think I'm too busy for you. If you need me, I'll be here, no questions asked. Alright?" he asks, making sure I understand.

"Alright," I say back. I smile and thank him for being so generous. "Thank you."

He walks toward the front door to meet Bennett downstairs but stops in the doorway and turns around to face me again. "Don't be afraid to talk to me, Jaemes. I'm not like those guys back in LV." He disappears inside, and I make my way toward Ember. We seem to get a little closer each time we're together. I'm still getting used to that. It's hard to wrap my head around the fact that this man genuinely *likes* me. It's something that I wouldn't have ever foreseen when I first met him.

After everything is officially packed, the guys drive the moving truck to my house while Ember and I lead the way in Bennett's truck.

"I told you," Ember blurts out.

I play dumb. "Told me what?"

"It's so obvious you two are a thing."

"How about you just worry about driving? Take the next left," I direct her. I sigh, indicating that I want to be done with this conversation, and then stare out the window.

"What's the problem?" she asks.

"Look, I'm just trying to play it cool with him. I'm starting to learn it's hard not to fall head over heels for this guy. I'm afraid I like him too much for where we are. I think the more I distance myself, the better."

"It's okay to like him, Jaemes," she reassures me.

We finally arrive at my new house, and all I want to do is keep myself busy and let everyone go home after the heavy items are taken care of.

BENNETT AND EMBER take off now that all that's left are the boxes, which I can handle myself, but Alder insists that he stay and help finish up. We go back and forth until everything is inside the house. It's half past eight in the evening, and I'm not sure how it got so late so fast. Alder and I are standing on the porch connected to the house's main door. Now that the truck is empty, a break is much needed.

"Alder, you didn't have to—"

"Stop, it's fine," he says, bringing me in for a hug. I hug him back, taking in his scent, touch, and the warmth of his embrace. I relax across his chest and close my eyes.

"I should probably return the moving truck before they close," I tell him.

Neither of us move for a while. I physically can't, as I remain like a magnet against him. He kisses the top of my head and then lets me go. Without hesitation, I grab his hand, and we head to the moving truck so we can return it.

I offer to give him a ride home afterward, as he initially

rode with Bennett and Ember. I hope he knows how much I appreciate everything he has done for me. I try to tell him, but he mainly cuts me off and says, "It's fine." Sometimes, we sound like a broken record.

After settling everything with the truck rental company, I return to my car, where Alder awaits me. It's been a long day, so I decide to leave the unpacking for tomorrow.

"I don't feel like going home just yet. Do you mind taking me somewhere else? I can put the address in the GPS," he states.

"Of course. I owe you for everything you've done for me."

I can feel him looking at me as we start driving to the address he entered.

"You don't *owe* me anything," he tells me. "Take a left here."

He lets me know when and where to turn as I drive. He has assured me that where he wants to go isn't too far out of town. Eventually, I figure out where I am taking him because it happens to be the same place I am going.

My new house.

"This looks oddly familiar," I tell him. I rest my elbow on the car's windowsill and attempt to hide my grin with the back of my hand.

"Everything okay over there? I can't help but notice someone is blushing," he says.

"Me? No, I'm just a little embarrassed for you. I think you put in my address by mistake."

"Shit, did I?"

I glance over at him, and he's looking at the GPS with a smile spread across his face. "If you don't want my company, it's fine. I won't take offense. I know how much you still have to do with unpacking. But really, the only place I want to be is wherever you are."

"I wouldn't mind your company," I tell him, turning into

my driveway.

"I like the property," he says as he gets out of the car.

"It's not much, but the river is nice," I say.

"Yeah, it gives you a place to skinny dip besides my nonexistent pond," he laughs.

"Oh, you think you're so funny?" I ask, pushing him. It's my try at flirting, I guess.

Lame, I know.

"Come on, I'll order some food," he says, taking my hand and pulling me toward the house. At this point, neither of us can hide our smiles. I'm really enjoying how things are going right now.

Alder orders us Chinese food for supper. He says it's his treat, and I can consider it a housewarming gift. He doesn't understand that I owe him, but he won't accept anything in return. Our super view is an empty floor with mountains of boxes surrounding us.

"I'm sorry that we have to eat on the floor," I tell him.

My apology makes him laugh. "Yeah, how dare you not have everything in order the day you move in?" he jokes, shaking his head. "Pathetic, if you ask me."

"But seriously, I can't thank you enough for helping me move today."

He takes another bite of his food and nods his head. "It was no problem. I was happy to help you out." His phone lights up with a notification, and the time shows ten o'clock at night. "Shit, it's getting late. I hate to run, but I have a lot to do tomorrow. Let me help clean up before I take off."

I do my best to hide my disappointment. I don't want him to leave, but I don't blame him for wanting sleep before getting up early tomorrow morning. It's even getting late for me. Time seems to go by faster when I'm with him.

"No, that's fine. I can handle it," I tell him. "I'll give you a ride home."

We walk through my bedroom and out to the other patio since my car is parked near that side of the house. I lean over the railing and sigh. It's incredibly dark, allowing us to see the moonlit sky and sparkling stars clearly. I feel Alder's hands land softly on my hips as he gently turns me around to face him. He picks me up, sets me on the porch ledge, and then separates my legs so he can stand closer to me. I can barely see him, but I can feel his breath against my lips. His hands slip under my shirt and venture slowly up my back. His touch is light and smooth. I wrap my arms around his neck, hoping to draw him in more. I feel like I'm malfunctioning due to being so calm yet so nervous at the same time.

Is this really happening?

ALDER DOESN'T HESITATE to unclamp my bra when his hands meet the back of it. I assist with removing it entirely, and then he swiftly throws it on the ground behind him. Our lips still haven't touched. His gentle hand ventures under my shirt once again, but this time, he starts at the bottom of my side and trails it up to my breast. My breathing becomes shaky as he rubs my nipple with his fingertips and firmly grips the top of my thigh with his other hand. When my breathing grows heavier and more rapid, he finally gives me permission to kiss him. We don't waste any time, and our tongues meet at the same time as our lips. I lift up on his shirt, urging him to take it off. Soon enough, it meets the ground next to my bra.

We stay connected as he picks me up and carries me back inside to my bedroom. He lays me down, and our lips still don't break away from each other. His breathing has now matched mine. I cross my arms, gripping the bottom of my shirt, and separate from him just long enough to slip it up and over my head. Alder stands up, leaving me lying on the bed, shirtless and breathless. The light shining in from the hallway gives just enough light for him to examine me. Before I can think about being shy, he unbuckles his belt, and his jeans fall to the floor. I gasp slightly when my eyes land on his boxers.

Whoa.

He steps out of his jeans and walks over to the button on mine. I lift my hips, making it easier for him to yank them off me. He hovers over me and slowly kisses me. I take this opportunity to control my breathing and prepare for what's about to happen. My mind won't stop racing. I'm worried about what he'll think afterwards. What if I don't do what he likes? What if I'm terrible? This isn't my first time doing this, but it is my first time doing this with someone I really like. It's overwhelming.

He breaks away from me to grab a condom out of his wallet. After removing his boxers, it doesn't take him long to apply it on himself. He leans down and whispers in my ear.

"Take 'em off."

His whole body is inches from mine. I carefully remove my underwear and toss them to the floor.

"Are you nervous?" he asks me.

I nod slightly but don't want him to think I don't want to do this. He brushes a piece of my hair away from my face. I place my hands on both sides of his face and press my lips to his. He separates my legs and eases himself inside of me, making us moan simultaneously. He moves slowly and is gentle, as he slides deeper with each thrust. Gradually, his pace becomes faster. The faster he moves, the better he feels, and the louder I get. I feel his moan against my lips.

His thrusts pause, but only for a second. He rolls over to his back, taking me with him as he is still inside me. I'm now on top of him, and I freeze. I don't like being in control because I don't know what to do. He senses my nervousness as I hesitate and starts to guide my hips in a circular motion while he pushes inside me, causing him to go deeper. Our moans continue, and now nothing about us is quiet. I've learned he doesn't like staying in one position for long. He sits up, and I wrap my arms around his neck *while he moves me up and down on him. At this point, we are moving at a pace so fast that we are practically begging each other for the end result. I place my head on his shoulder and whimper next to his ear. The louder I sound, the faster he goes. And the quicker he goes, the louder I become. I start to kiss his neck, and suddenly, his body shudders with a loud and pleasurable moan. We begin to slow our movements down, but our breathing stays rapid.*

Assuming we are done, I lift myself off of him, but he stops me.

"Oh, no. You haven't finished yet," he says breathlessly.

He throws me down to my back and reinserts himself in me. This time, he isn't so gentle. He starts to rub his hand between my legs, causing even more pleasure for me. I press my hips upward for more friction, and my body starts to tremble as I finally finish.

He kisses me deeply, then lies beside me. I feel him up against my back, and his arm wraps around me. I grab his hand, and we stay like this for the rest of the night.

I FELT SAD when I wake up alone the following day. Just me and my phone lying on the pillow next to me.

Alder: *How did you sleep?*

Me: *Good. Thanks for spending time with me during my first night here.*

Alder: *Of course. Thanks for giving me a ride back home.*

Me: *I would say it wasn't a problem, but that would be a lie. I sort of wanted you to spend the entire night with me.*

Alder: *Why didn't you tell me? I would've if you had asked.*

Me: *I don't know…*

Alder: *What can I do to make you feel more comfortable around me?*

Me: *It's nothing you need to do. I'm sorry.*

Alder: *I'm going to have to get used to you saying 'sorry' all the time, aren't I?*

Me: *If I'm someone you want to be around often, then…yeah.*

Alder: *Noted.*

Knowing what I had experienced last night was only a dream, I especially wanted Alder to be in my bed, lying next to me. My body is starting to crave him. It makes me wonder what our first time would be like, if there will be a first time at all. Will it be anything like my dream? I'm still trying to reconcile my dream with reality. It's messing with my head big time.

Alder: *So, it's my birthday in a few days. I'd love for you to join the party if you can.*

Me: *And you'll be turning…?*

Alder: *Dirty Thirty.*

Me: *Wow. Old man.*

Alder: *Easy…*

Me: *I'll see if I can make it work. I'll talk to you later.*

Alder: *Yes, you will.*

Even after everything he has said to me and done for me, I still feel hesitation when it comes to wanting to see him again. My walls are up and remaining sturdy when it comes to being with someone. I'm still trying to figure him out. It doesn't help when all of those feelings and concerns are muted when I am with him.

Whatever happens will happen, and I must let go and let God.

Chapter Eleven

'M STANDING BY my car, hesitant to go inside. The place is packed full of people. Either this is more of a popular bar than I remembered, or Alder is having quite the party. I was supposed to be here over an hour ago, but the delivery guys arrived at my house way later than they said. At least I finally have my furniture. I'm excited to see Alder, and I'd be lying if I said I wasn't missing him, but my first mission is to find Ember.

The band is playing outside, so the outdoor bar is open in addition to the regular operation of the inside bar. It will be hard to find anyone I know with the number of people here. There is a lot of ground to cover, and Ember could be anywhere. I see a space at the bar once I walk through the entrance. I grab the bartender's attention and order a drink. Out of nowhere, I recognize a familiar voice next to me.

"Wow, fancy seeing you here," he says.

I shake my head slowly and smile at him.

"How are you, Ledger?" I ask.

"I'm great. Thank you for asking."

I grab my drink and pay for it right away.

"What brings you here tonight?" I ask.

"I have a buddy in the band. I came here with a group of people to support him. He's the drummer."

"I've always wanted to play the drums, but I have no musical talent whatsoever," I admit.

"Really? Well, if you ever want to pursue your musical

dreams of becoming a drummer, I'll get you in touch with him."

I laugh at his offer. "Thanks, Ledger. That's very nice of you."

"Did you end up having a good birthday then?" he asks me.

"Yeah, I did. Thank you again for the birthday gift. I wish you'd let me repay you for my bar tab."

"No, no, no. It was the least I could do," he says.

"What do you mean? I don't think I did anything for you to owe me."

"It's not every day I get to chat with a beautiful lady like yourself," he says and then takes a swig of his drink.

"There's the cheesy pick-up line I was waiting for," I laugh.

"Jae!" Ember says as she reaches me at the bar. "Where have you been? I've been trying to get a hold of you."

"Sorry, I had furniture delivered, and it's a long story. But I'm here now," I tell her.

I feel Ledger's hand on my waist and his lips near my ear. "I'll be outside if you need me."

His hand swipes across my lower back, and the sensation of that gives me chills. Ember and I watch him walk away until he is out of sight. She turns and smacks my arm to snap me out of the spell Ledger seems to cast on me every time he's near me.

"Alder has been looking for you, ya know," she says matter-of-factly.

I start to comprehend what she is saying after it finally registers in my brain.

"Really? Where is he?" I ask her.

"He's outside with the guys." She grabs my hand and leads the way, plowing through people like she owns the place.

When we get outside, it's just as crowded as the inside, except the air feels cooler. The stage that the band is playing on is straight ahead. A log fence borders the property of the bar, creating a spacious environment for everyone who wants to be outside. Tables and chairs are positioned to the right and left, leaving a clear walking space in the middle. Waiters and waitresses are out here sporadically with their neon green shirts, along with the bartenders working the outdoor bar to the far left.

I casually look around for any sign of Alder.

Then, out of nowhere, two familiar arms wrap around me, lifting me off the ground. Those robust arms spin me around and then put me back down again. I immediately turn around to see Alder, but I don't get to look at him for very long. His lips plant down on mine, his hands placed on each side of my face. I take him all in and instantly feel secure. We are so lost in each other that we don't realize all the hooting and hollering from the group at Alder's table. After the band finishes their set, they give Alder a shout-out for his birthday, but that doesn't faze him in the slightest. He just keeps kissing me as if no one else is around.

We separate so I can wrap myself around him and tell him happy birthday. We are stuck together tightly, almost as if we are showing how much we have missed each other based on how tightly our holds are. When we ease away from each other, he grabs my hand and leads the way inside. I follow his guide toward a few empty chairs alongside the windows.

"How are you?" he asks me. I can tell by the half smile on his face that he has already had a few drinks, which is understandable, given that he's the birthday boy tonight. That would also explain his affectionate actions, which he just displayed in front of everyone. I don't think he would have gone to that extent if he were sober. But who knows, he continues to surprise me all the time.

"I'm fine," I tell him. "I'm glad I get to have a little fun with you tonight."

He takes my hand and rubs his thumb back and forth on the back of it. I'll never get used to the way his touch makes me feel. I don't ever want that feeling to subside in any way. "How's your birthday so far?"

"Better now. I've been waiting to see you all day." He intertwines his fingers with mine.

My mouth starts to open with a response, but we get interrupted by the blond, who can't seem to get enough of him. She shows up out of nowhere like it's her mission to find him whenever he's out and about.

"Alder!" she yells, and he lets go of my hand. "Come dance with me." She wraps her arms around him, and he doesn't seem to mind.

He chuckles at her and kindly declines.

"Come on…" she whines. Her hand grazes his arm. "Have I ever told you how sexy your sleeve tattoo is?" Everything about her demeanor is flirty, and he plays along. I'm having a hard time watching whatever *this* is. I take a much-needed long gulp of my drink and finally ask, "Should I leave you two alone?"

Her smiling face turns nasty when she looks at me. "If you would, that would be great," she snaps.

"Hey, be nice," Alder tells her lightheartedly.

Thankfully, Ember walks through the entryway to come back inside. "Hey, Em!" I shout at her. She sees me and starts walking in my direction. I get up to meet her, and Alder tells me to wait. I happily ignore him and give up my seat next to him since it looks like he is enjoying Blondy's company.

"Come to the bathroom with me," I demand. We quickly walk through another thick sea of people and enter the women's restroom. Ember goes into a stall since she actually needs to use the bathroom. I wait for her by the sink.

"Who's the girl who's always all over Alder?" I ask her calmly and collectively, even though on the inside I'm the complete opposite.

"Who?" she asks.

"The bitch—I mean, the blond," I clarify with slightly more frustration.

"Oh!" she laughs. "That's Riley. She has the biggest crush on Alder." She flushes the toilet and exits the stall to wash her hands. "I wouldn't worry about her, though," she says, pumping the soap onto her hands. "Everyone knows Alder isn't into her."

"Does Alder know Alder isn't into her?" I ask.

She gives me a look like I'm being ridiculous while drying her hands. "Don't let her get to you. She has always been a bitch. Just bite back if she barks at you."

"Since day one, she has never been friendly to me, and I've done nothing to aggravate her."

"Yes, you did. You took her dream man." She smiles devilishly.

The door to the women's restroom swings open.

Speaking of the devil.

Riley enters with two other girls. She's got a snarky smile splattered on her face. "I'm all done with Alder, honey. You can try to get with him if you want, but I have a good sense that he will be crawling back to me anyway, so it won't even matter."

That's it. If I wasn't already pissed off at her, I am now. I feel a surge of fury run through my entire body. If the human body showed color for moods, I'd be blood red.

I laugh at her in frustration. "It's cute that you actually think he likes you." I'd say more, but I'm not here for this shit.

I exit the restroom and find Alder with his back leaning against the opposite wall, arms crossed against his chest. He looks up at me as soon as I'm in his sight. I start walking away until I'm stopped by his hand on my arm.

"Jaemes," he says, trying to pull me toward him.

"Listen, Alder, I don't feel like hearing about your conversation with Riley or playing any stupid games with you." I make another reasonable effort to walk away, but he keeps pulling me back to him. His facial expression looks relaxed, and there isn't a single look in his eyes of desperation, which frustrates me even more.

"Jaemes, I told her to fuck off and that I have a girlfriend," he confesses.

I'm taken aback by what he just told me. He pulls me even closer to him with his hands wrapped around my waist, and I start to feel myself give in to him. "That is, if you're okay with that. I don't play games, and I don't just fool around. I know I—"

I shut him up by locking my lips to his, hoping this action would show him my answer. Just when I thought I was getting caught up in some petty high school-like drama, he showed me that he also wants a healthy and mature relationship, even after trying to convince himself he didn't need anyone else added to his life. He's someone I've been longing for even after trying to convince myself otherwise.

"Come outside," he says, grabbing my hand. "I need some Goddamn fresh air."

We returned to the table where he had been sitting when I arrived. There's a bunch of laughter coming from everyone.

"Alder, we were just talking about the time when you—"

"Be careful about what comes out of your mouth, Bennett. You know I'll kick your ass," Alder warns.

He sits on the only empty chair and slides me onto his lap. The band is beginning to play their last set. Classic rock music is being played while Alder's friends tell hilarious stories. I feel so happy right now. I'm starting to be introduced as Alder's girlfriend, and it feels *so* good. He makes me feel safe and calm enough to be myself.

The crowd is hushed by a flash of lightning and the rumbling of thunder that follows in the distance. This is the band's sign to stop and pack up their equipment. Everyone boos and complains, but when weather like this approaches, the band has no choice but to call it quits. The heavy air starts to churn, and thick raindrops begin to imprint themselves on the wooden tables. Everyone rushes inside all at once, squeezing their way through the doorway as the rain picks up. I start to get up with everyone else at our table, but Alder holds me down with his arms. I look him in the eyes, wondering what he's thinking since he's difficult to read tonight. He places a hand behind my neck and the other on my hip as he leans in to gently kiss me.

As the storm grows stronger, so does our kiss. At this point, we are now the only ones outside. Without separating from each other, Alder picks me up and sets me on top of the table. Both my arms and legs are tightly wrapped around him like I'm afraid he'll disappear if I don't hold on to him. I start to feel him through his jeans, which, to no surprise, begins to turn me on. It's starting to rain hard enough for us to break apart from each other, but not by much. He rests his forehead on mine.

"Come home with me?" he asks.

I nod against him, and we rush to his truck as if we have just now noticed that we've been sitting in the middle of a storm.

Chapter Twelve

"I'M SORRY I got the inside of your truck all wet," I tell Alder as he unlocks the front door to his house, and we rush inside. He turns the lights on and walks toward the fireplace to get it started.

"I think I've told you to relax on the apologies, Jaemes. It's hard to upset me. At some point, I hope you'll find that I'm a pretty reasonable guy."

I try to form a smile when he looks my way, but it's hard to do with how bad I'm shivering in the air conditioning. He laughs softly at me and tells me I can help myself to any of his clothes in the bedroom. Without hesitation, I take him up on his offer.

"I still need to return the other set of clothes I borrowed from you the morning after your housewarming party. Or I can just start a collection of your clothes at my house," I say as I start to close the door to his room.

"Yeah, at this rate, you're gonna run me out of clothes altogether," he teases.

It's not long until my sopping wet clothes are on the floor. I hang them in the bathroom so they can start to dry. When I rummage through his closet to see what he has, I notice the gray Coors Light t-shirt he wore the first time I saw him. I take it off the hanger and slip it on. This shirt is just long enough to hide the boxers I decided to wear along with it.

Before joining him again, I go into the bathroom to comb through my hair with my fingers and scrunch it up to make it look somewhat attractive. My makeup isn't running down my face, so that's a plus. I feel warm and cozy in his clothes, and I can smell his scent all over me. My boyfriend's scent. I'm going to have to get used to that.

Alder is my boyfriend, and I am Alder's girlfriend.

I exit his room and see that the fireplace is now lit. His clothes are off except for his boxers. He's scrolling through his phone until he notices I'm done changing and meets my gaze.

"I liked this shirt on you," I tell him.

He flashes a smile at me. "It looks better on you." He places his phone on the kitchen counter and goes to put on dry clothes. He kisses me on his way and then disappears into the bedroom. I make myself at home, cuddling with a blanket on the couch and staring ahead at the flames of the fire. I start to become sleepy once I warm up to a comfortable temperature, but I force myself to stay awake so I can spend more time with Alder.

When he's in my sight again, he's wearing dark gray sweatpants and a plain black t-shirt. He's walks to the kitchen and sees me lying on the couch.

"If I ask you something, will you please be completely honest with me?" he asks.

"Always," I say back. I sit up on the couch so he has my full attention.

He lets out a deep breath. "It's important that you are honest with me, Jaemes."

"You're scaring me. What is it?" I ask him.

"If I made a box of macaroni and cheese, would you share it with me?" he asks.

I grab a pillow from the couch and chuck it at him. He dodges it and laughs.

"Don't do that to me!" I yell. I laugh with him because of how ridiculous his question ended up being.

"What? It was a serious question to me," he says before

throwing the pillow back at me.

"I would never pass on a mac and cheese opportunity," I tell him.

"More and more reasons why I like you." He opens one of the cupboards and takes out a pan. He fills it with water and then proceeds to the stove. I watch him open another cupboard and take out two wine glasses. He pours the wine we had when I was here over the Fourth of July weekend. It doesn't look like it has been touched since then.

He walks over to join me on the couch and hands me one of the glasses of wine, then turns on some music to play softly in the background.

"Well, isn't this romantic? Drinking wine next to the fireplace," I say, grabbing my glass and bringing it to my lips.

"Don't forget the most romantic part is sitting on the stove."

"I like a man who can cook."

"I can cook. Not well, but I can. Are you warm enough?"

"Getting there," I tell him as I stay wrapped in his blanket.

"Let's get you closer to the fire."

We set our glasses on the end tables and sit together on the rug in front of the fireplace. I lean up against him, and he wraps his arms around me. We're quiet for a while—silent but content. If someone were to tell me this is where Alder and I would be just months after I moved back, I would have never believed it. At first, we were strangers, not wanting anything to do with each other. But fate brought us together because, for some reason, we were meant to be in God's plan. Alder doesn't compare to the other guys I've dated. He is more mature and knows what he wants. Those are just a few of the many qualities I like about him.

The next song that plays causes me to melt. He places a finger under my chin and tilts my head toward his as we listen to Shenandoah sing "Two Dozen Roses".

"Are you nervous?" he asks me in a whisper.

What in the coincidence…*my dream.*

Stunned, I shake my head slightly, assuming I know the reason for his question.

He nods, acknowledging me right before dipping down to my lips, but I don't let this cute make-out session last very long. I free my lips from his, unravel the blanket around me, and straddle his lap. I'm confident enough to start taking more control now. I can tell he likes it when his tongue enters my mouth at the same time as our lips rejoin. He places his hands softly on the bottom of my ass.

"Are you wearing my boxers?" he asks against my lips.

I bite my bottom lip guiltily and nod. "Sorry," I say.

"No, you're not," he tells me, and then flips me over so I'm lying on my back, and he's hovering over me. "I think it's hot."

I pull his shirt up and over his head. He bunches up my shirt near the base of my neck, exposing my chest as his hand glides up to my breast. His kiss departs from my lips and travels down to my neck. He adds his tongue and creates a sucking sensation on my skin. A gentle moan escapes my mouth as I run my fingers through his hair. He teases me by not staying in one place for long. His lips venture down to my left nipple, and the sucking sensation continues sending tingling vibes throughout my body, from my fingertips to my toes.

"Oh, God," I whisper.

He takes it a step further as his fingers trickle down my stomach and under the waistband of the boxers I have on. His hand moves in a circular motion right between my legs. The faster his hand moves, the more I moan, and the more I moan, the more he sucks on my breast. He takes my noises as a sign to go further once again. His fingers lower, and they slide inside me, making my hips thrust upward.

He leaves my breast and intensely covers my lips with his. I match his intensity as his fingers remain inside of me and go deeper as I continue to thrust my hips. I finally take the initiative to remove my shirt entirely. He removes his hand and tears the boxers I'm wearing off of me, ripping them down the middle. He grabs a condom and opens the wrapper with his teeth.

"Let me put it on you," I say breathlessly.

What am I doing? Where is this coming from?

He hands me the opened condom between his fingers, and I set it aside for the time being.

"Come here," I tell him.

He's standing before me while I'm still on the floor. I sit on my knees and slowly slide his sweatpants down. My head is telling me that I should be nervous as it's making my body shake, trying to remove his pants altogether. However, my heart is doing its job of trying to calm me down. Oddly enough, I feel comfortable in this moment between us. If you're with the right person, you should never feel uncomfortable. I pull down his boxers, and he steps out of them. I'm inches away from him.

All of him.

I wrap my left arm around him to his backside and cup my right hand underneath him. Before I know it, he is inside my mouth, and my tongue searches every part of him. Eventually, I feel him touch the back of my throat. Back and forth, in and out of my mouth. We both feel myself gag as he grabs the back of my head and moves faster and deeper down my throat.

"Holy fuck, Jaemes," he groans.

I release myself from him and roll the condom on. I don't want him to finish yet. He lays me down on my back and immediately pushes himself inside me. The feeling of his movements sends a rush of adrenaline throughout my entire body. Neither of us is gentle. We become sweaty as the glow of the fire projects onto our skin. The sexual tension between us is ignited, and I don't shy away from him.

"Alder," I say, winded.

He knows what's about to happen and continues harder and faster.

"*Alder...*" I shudder and whimper against him as he moans with final pleasure.

He slows down while his body trembles, and he releases himself. Our skin glistens with beads of sweat trickling down our bodies.

"I'm not cold anymore," I tell him.

"I'm not hungry anymore," he responds, "Plus, now that I think of it, I don't think I ever turned the burner on," he says glancing up at the stove.

I laugh at him, and he shuts me up with his lips one last time. I'm glad this time wasn't only a dream. It was better than a dream...much, much better.

I WAKE UP in a panic after the house shakes from the rumbling of the thunder. The constant lightning strikes light up the room. The storm was minimal for the majority of the evening until it recently intensified. I'm having a hard time relaxing, and my breathing is labored. I'm gasping for air and feel the need to sit up in bed. I feel Alder's touch on my back once I'm upright, gently rubbing it up and down.

"Relax, babe. It's just the storm," he says.

I struggle to speak, feeling frozen as my mind isn't functioning. Alder sits up next to me since I can't seem to calm myself down. His lips tenderly land on my shoulder for more comfort.

"I don't know what's going on, Alder. I have a strong feeling that something terrifying is going to happen," I say in between breaths. I check my phone with a shaky hand, and the time reads a few minutes before midnight.

"You're okay. I'm right here," he reassures me. "Take a deep breath. You're probably waking up from a bad dream."

His voice is soft and kind. I take a deep breath like he said, and he slowly guides me back down to lie with him. My head rests on his chest, and I try to relax, listening to his calm heartbeat and tranquil breathing. He shows he's there for me by wrapping his arms around me. My body relaxes against him, and I feel my heart grow. My mind is battling the anxiousness and the intense feelings for the man who is embracing me.

Chapter Thirteen

RIAN WILL OFTEN fly private planes out of a smaller airport for people to sightsee. He loves being a pilot and flying all sorts of planes. He's a people person who enjoys small talk and hearing people's stories. These people are primarily tourists wanting to see what the land of Montana has to offer. The beauty of the mountains, the hillsides, and the numerous parks are always a sight to see, especially at sunset. My mom and Rian mostly use the extra money he gets from private flying for vacations. They love to travel, hence the pilot and flight attendant careers. I've always thought my parents would be safe, prosperous, adventurous, and conversant doing their jobs.

Until now.

I'm lying awake in Alder's bed, staring at my phone while he sleeps. I get notifications from local news stations whenever there is breaking news. I see the headline titled *Sightseeing Aircraft Crashes in Smalltown Montana: Fatalities Unknown*. In addition to that news story, I have several missed calls from someone I was hoping I wouldn't have missed calls from.

My mom.

I'm abundantly awake after getting out of my tired daze and bolt out of Alder's room. I'm dreading making this call to my mom.

"Fuck, fuck, fuck," I whisper to myself as I wait for my mom to answer. I start pacing by the patio doors near the living room while I wait for her to answer.

"Jaemes, I'm freaking out," she says, panicky.

"So, Rian *did* go out flying this morning?" I ask her.

"Yes, and I have been trying to reach someone at the airport for answers, but no one is picking up the phone. Rian won't answer my calls either."

She starts hyperventilating.

"Mom, breathe. You don't know anything for sure. The airport could be busy, and Rian might have his phone on airplane mode for the flight. I'm sure that plane was from a different airport, and Rian is fine." I try to fight back the tears and ease my shaky voice because I know I could also be wrong. "I'm coming home. I'll be there soon." I hang up the phone and feel numb and weightless. My stomach starts to ache as it turns into knots.

"What's going on?" Alder asks from the doorway of the bedroom. His arms are crossed at his chest, and he is leaning against the doorframe with his shoulder. I'm sure he overheard my conversation with my mom after he felt me rush out of bed this morning.

Just the thought of having to explain something like this makes me want to vomit. Sure enough, I have to cover my mouth with my hand and try to run to the bathroom. Alder's eyes grow wide for a second as he watches me and then hurries to grab the garbage. He holds it in front of me as I spew out everything that's inside my stomach. When I know I'm in the clear, my knees buckle, and I drop to the floor. Alder, right beside me, catches me and gently lowers me to the floor. He brings me in as I start to sob in his arms and tell him that I have to go.

"Jaemes, tell me what's going on."

I search for my phone, which got lost in the shuffle of all this, and show him the breaking news headline.

"Jesus Christ," he says under his breath in disbelief. He holds me as he reads the article, which I know doesn't say much. The news knows nothing more since it just happened.

"Go do what you gotta do."

"I need to change back into my clothes, take out your garbage—"

"No, Jaemes. Your clothes are still wet, and I will take care of the garbage. You can borrow pants from me, and I can take you to your mom." He tilts my head up to his. "Okay?"

I close my eyes and nod as tears stream down my cheeks.

"Okay," he repeats. He kisses my head again and helps me to his room for pants.

I bury my head in my hands after I sit at the end of his bed. I can hear him open a drawer in his dresser. He hands me a pair of black sweatpants when he returns to me again. "They will be a little big on you, but there is a drawstring. Hopefully, you can tighten them enough so they stay on."

"Thank you."

I slip the sweatpants on and tighten them up. Alder is looking at me with great sympathy in his eyes. I'm drawn to his body, aching for him to hold me in his arms. He made me feel better last night, and I know he can ease my worry now. My arms are wrapped around him, and my face is now buried in his chest. I clench onto the back of his shirt, and he tightens his hold around me. I don't want to go home and face any of this. Regardless of the outcome, this isn't fun to go through. All the worry, panic, *the unknown* of it all. I just want to stay in his arms and ignore everything else. I don't want to feel anything else.

WE DON'T SAY a word to each other the whole way to my parents' house. I can feel him constantly looking at me as I stare out his truck's window. My fingers nervously tap on the window sill while my leg moves up and down even faster. My stomach drops to rock bottom when we pull into the driveway.

I don't move after Alder puts the truck in park. I remain staring straight ahead, unable to move yet again.

"I'm scared," I whisper. A few warm tears spill out of my wide eyes and run down my cheeks, dripping off my chin and onto my lap.

"I know," Alder says looking over at me like he has ever since he parked the truck. I can tell he doesn't know what else to say, and I don't blame him. I wouldn't know either, as this is not a situation anyone has to go through normally. He squeezes my hand to get my attention.

"Look at me, Jaemes."

I slowly turn his way. My eyes are tired from crying and worrying.

"I hope you know that I will always be here for you. Don't be afraid to let me know if you need me, okay?"

More tears fill my eyes. After how quiet he had been, I didn't expect to hear him say something like that. Granted, I've been just as silent. I applaud him for trying to think of the right thing to say.

"That means a lot. Thank you, Alder."

"Yeah, well, you mean a lot to me," he says back.

I try hard to give him at least a half smile. But it quickly fades as fast as it appeared.

I don't know how, but somehow, I exit his truck and find myself at my front door. This all seems like a dream. It's as if I'm floating, going from one place to another instantly and not remembering how I got there. My brain isn't registering anything to its fullest. I look behind me, and Alder is already driving down the road. Did I say bye to him? Was there even a goodbye kiss? I open the front door without even thinking. My mom is pacing in the living room while talking with someone on speakerphone, and the news is blaring on the TV with captions.

"Jaemes is here. Please call me if you hear anything," she

says, then hangs up the phone.

We both look at each other, and she lets out a vast sigh. She isn't crying, but her eyes and cheeks are red like she was. I walk over to her and hug her.

"I still don't know anything," she tells me. "I've called multiple places and everyone I can think of."

We take a seat on the couch together. I grab the remote to turn the TV down.

"Don't touch it," she demands.

I place the remote back down on the coffee table. My movements are slow, and I don't say anything. I don't know what to say, and I don't want to say the wrong thing. For now, I will let her do her thing and not stress her out even more. I said everything I could when I spoke with her earlier. I can smell Alder from wearing his shirt and pants. His clothes act like a constant hug from him and are the only things keeping me calm. I want to tell him I need his presence and that I never wanted him to leave me. But he has a life to live, too, and I can't let him drop everything for me all the time. Even though he told me not to be afraid to let him know when I needed him, I still feel selfish. I'm not going to be that needy girlfriend. I keep thinking about what he said in the truck when he dropped me off.

You mean a lot to me.

My heart feels full, but it's also breaking at the same time. It's the most confusing emotional combination I have ever experienced. It feels like a soothing heartbreak. My heart is trying to put itself back together while it breaks repeatedly. It's a rollercoaster I don't necessarily care to be on. It's a wild ride, and I might actually vomit again.

The front door opens, and my grandma walks in. My mom is a younger version of her mom, and due to my grandma's youthful appearance, the two of them look identical. She removes her shoes and puts her purse on the small decorative table near the door where Alder's flowers sat the morning of my birthday.

"Oh, you two," she says as she approaches us in the living room.

She gives us both a hug. My mom first and then me. After she lets me go, her hands stay on my shoulders, arms extended, while she eyes my appearance up and down.

"Oh my," she starts. "We need to take you shopping, dear."

I try not to roll my eyes. Instead, I smile and clarify that these are not my clothes.

"Grandma, these are Alder's clothes," I tell her.

Confused, she side-eyes my mom and asks her who Alder is.

"Her boyfriend, Mom," my mom says.

It's funny how my mom automatically assumes Alder is my boyfriend. It makes me wonder if anyone else has thought that even before we made ourselves an official couple. I don't say anything to my mom since she isn't wrong.

"Oh!" She turns her attention back to me. "Sweetheart, I didn't know you had a boyfriend, not to mention so soon after moving back home from college. Good for you," she says and then winks at me. "So, when do I get to meet this boy?" she asks as she sits on one of the chairs, and my mom and I sit back on the couch.

"Whenever the opportunity presents itself. I'd love for everyone to meet him, actually," I tell her.

"Khrystal, you haven't met him yet?" she asks.

My mom shakes her head no. "We've been busy with work this summer. When Jaemes wants to introduce us, she'll introduce us."

"Good lord, how loud do you need this TV?" she asks. "I'm old and don't need it this loud."

"Mom, please," she says defensively. "I can't miss anything. I still don't have answers to any of my questions. I don't know what to do," she cries.

"There's nothing *to* do, honey. Let the authorities do their job. I hear search and rescue is top-notch in Montana."

We end up watching the news for almost an hour. My mom has gone through nearly a whole bottle of Jack Daniels, and she doesn't even like whiskey. I think her nerves are evening out the alcohol because she doesn't seem drunk. We haven't heard from Rian, and we haven't received any answers.

All three of us jolt to a sudden knock at the front door. We don't move; we remain still, looking at each other.

"It's them," my mom whispers. "They are here to tell me they found him, and he's gone."

My grandma and I look at each other. She tells me to answer the door and then takes my spot on the couch next to my mom to console her. I don't want to be the one to answer that door, but I do anyway because I need to be the strong one out of the two of us. My mom needs her mom right now. I would want my mom at a time like this, too.

I slowly open the door and nearly fall to the ground. I scrunch down to catch my breath after holding it the whole time while walking to the door.

"Alder," I whisper with immediate relief and then stand back up. I could not be happier to see him right now as I go in for another one of his hugs. I wasn't sure when I'd see him next because of the uncertainty caused by this news circulating around us and the unresolved outcome.

"It's Alder," I say behind me, notifying my mom and grandma. "There's no need to panic."

"I'm sorry. I know this isn't a good time, but I just wanted to let you know that I picked up your car from the bar. I know you'll need it eventually, and I didn't want you to have to worry about anything else right now." He hands me my keys.

"Thank you," I tell him. "I forgot all about my car." I wrap my arms around him again, and he pulls me in with his. "I appreciate it. I appreciate *you*." His hand rubs against my back.

"Oh, he's a looker!" my grandma says from behind me.

"Mom…" my mom groans from a distance. I suppose I can now grant my grandma's wish and introduce her.

"Grandma, this is Alder. Alder, this is my grandma, Jeanie."

She walks up to him and hugs him. "Very nice to meet you, dear."

"Likewise," he says back.

"Alder dropped my car off for me. I left it at the bar last night," I inform her.

"Well, isn't that the nicest thing." She leans toward Alder's direction and puts her hand up to block what she is saying from me. "Someone has to keep tabs on ole drunky over here," she gestures my way with her thumb.

Alder laughs. "Tell me about it."

"Excuse me, you two. I'm right here!"

"Oh, goodness gracious honey, you know we're just goofin'," she says, tapping her hand on my arm and then winks at Alder.

"It was no problem at all. I was happy to do it," Alder says. "But I should probably get going. Bennett is waiting in the truck, and I still need to drop his ass back off."

"Tell him thank you for me, please." I send Bennett a wave.

Alder and I look at my grandma.

"Oh, please, I can take a hint. Alder, it was very nice to meet you. Please don't be a stranger," my grandma says before returning inside. Alder smiles back at her before turning his attention back to me.

"You doing okay?" he asks me sincerely. His eyes are planted on mine, and his hand is on my cheek. I grab ahold of his hand and lean my head into it.

"I wish you could stay," I whisper as tears fill my eyes again.

He leans down and kisses me long and hard. I know he doesn't want to leave me either, but life continues no matter what happens. I need to be here with my family, and Alder must resume his normal routine, even though I understand that it doesn't make it suck any less.

IT'S BEEN HOURS, but it feels like days. I saw the sun wake, and now I have seen it disappear, but it seems like I've seen it come and go a million different times. The more the sun dips behind the mountains, the worse my mom gets. She acts like the sun is an hourglass, and when it finally leaves the sky, Rian's time is up. My grandma and I have repeatedly told her that there is still the possibility that Rian could be with the authorities since this is an investigation and he was out flying at the same time as when the crash occurred. They might not let him talk to anyone until they are done questioning him. This only calms her momentarily, and then she's right back to square one.

I need a break from it all. I'm not out on the patio with her and my grandma for a reason. They are currently on the phone with my grandpa Cyrus. As I eavesdrop on their conversation, I notice an unfamiliar key attached to my car keys. I pick them up from the table in the dining room, and there are five keys instead of four.

My house.

My parents' house.

My car.

My office.

What the heck is this one for?

I went home to wash the clothes I borrowed from Alder, shower, brush my teeth, and change. How did I *just* notice this unfamiliarity after having them in my procession for a few hours already? I know it wasn't there when I arrived at the bar for Alder's birthday last night. At least, I don't think it was. I take a picture of the key and send it to Alder.

> **Me:** *This is new. Any chance you added this key?*
>
> **Alder:** *Yes.*

Mystery solved.

> **Me:** *Why? What's it for?*
>
> **Alder:** *The front door to my house.*
>
> **Me:** *You gave me a key to your house?*
>
> **Alder:** *I want you to be able to come over whenever you want. You can use it as much or as little as you'd like, even if you prefer never to use it; at least you have it, just in case.*

I place my phone back on the table. This is precisely what I need right now. I grab my keys and head to the patio's screen door.

"Mom, I'll be right back. Do you need anything while I'm out?"

"No, baby, I'm fine. Thank you, though," she responds.

"All right. Tell Grandpa I said hi," I tell her as I walk away and out the front door.

I hope he's home. I'm not fond of surprises myself, but I think he would like mine. All I know is that I need him, and nothing else is helping me get through the scare of the undivulged.

It's pitch-black outside. Alder's house is almost as dark as the sky. I was hesitant to go in, but he *did* give me a key and told me to come over whenever I wanted. I wonder if this is too much too soon regarding both him giving me a key to his house and me making myself at home even when he isn't. There is only one way to find out, I guess.

Typically, I park toward the end of the driveway to avoid having to back out a long distance. However, this time, I park my car farther up the driveway. When I get out of the driver's side, I notice that the stone pathway to the porch steps is located right next to the passenger side, making it a shorter walk to the front door of the house.

All three dogs greet me after I unlock the door and walk inside. I'm sure they think I am Alder until I turn the lights on. They get a whiff of my scent and realize I am not their owner. They seem more excited to see me, whereas they act more obedient and submissive with Alder. I kneel to pet them as they each push through one another to lick my face. They wouldn't do this with Alder. They would run up to him and sit nicely before him until he excuses them like a drill sergeant.

"Where's your dad, huh?" I ask them out loud.

I stand up and take my phone from my sweatshirt pocket.

Me: *I miss you.*

Alder: *I miss you too. How is everyone doing? Have you heard anything yet?*

Me: *No, nothing. The longer we wait with the unknown, the worse my mom gets.*

Alder: *Understandable. Are you still holding up okay?*

Me: *I'm hanging in there the best I can. Honestly, I could really use you right now. It's becoming one of the worst days...*

Alder: *Are you still with your mom? I'm getting a haircut right now, but I can stop over afterward if you want me to.*

Me: *Actually, I might have already taken advantage of the key you gave me...*

Alder: *Oh, no shit?*

Me: *I'm sitting on your couch right now. I hope that's okay.*

Alder: *Of course it is. That's why I gave it to you. Make yourself at home. I'll be there soon.*

I take the same blanket from his room and wrap myself in it. After plopping on the couch, I turn the TV on. The news channel pops on the screen from the last time it was turned on, indicating that Alder kept tabs on the crash while he was home. I sink myself lower on the couch to a lying position and sob into the blanket.

I DON'T REALIZE I have fallen asleep until I wake up to Alder walking through the door. It's true what they say. You can literally cry yourself to sleep. I gather all my energy to sit up and acknowledge him.

"Hi." My voice sounds pathetic right now.

He looks over my way and sets his keys down on the counter. "Jaemes, you look exhausted. Why don't you try and get some sleep?"

"I just woke up from dozing off. I should be okay for a little while." He joins me on the couch and pulls me to him. I can't fathom how my mood changes the moment he enters my presence. The second I touch him, all my fears seem to go away. Mentally, I'm still exhausted and overwhelmed with all the emotional pulls that have formed from today.

"Alder, I have no energy. I feel so drained and helpless," I say, sitting up to look at him. "I can't eat. I feel sick to my stomach, and I have no idea how I fell asleep just now."

"Because your body needs it. That is your body telling you that you need rest, babe."

I turn my attention to the TV again. It looks like nothing has been updated since the news came out. I would think someone would talk to the immediate family regardless of what they know. Anything to help ease the suffering from these dark and hidden actualities.

"Come here," he tells me. He stands up and holds out his

hand to help me up. Without hesitation, he scoops me up so that one arm is under my back and the other is under my legs like a cradle. He carries me to his bedroom and lays me down on what now seems to be my side of the bed.

"Thank you for making me feel so…cared for. Sometimes, I feel like you're too good to be true. I don't get how you can make the worst days seem not so bad, and you don't even try." Tears fill my eyes once more as I continue to show my vulnerability.

He sits at the edge of the bed next to where I'm lying. His thumb wipes away a tear that streams down my face. "I hate to see you like this," he says. "I miss your smile and that laugh of yours. All I ever want is to see you happy."

"Alder, *you* make me happy. These aren't sad tears any-more." I sit up so my face is adjacent to his. I look him in the eyes and say something I never thought I would say to him. "I think I might be falling in love with you," I admit to him.

He's silent. Almost too silent. He turns his head toward the window and rubs his jaw with his hand.

Oh my God, what did I just do?

"I'm sorry, I shouldn't have said that. I don't know what I was thinking. Forget I said anything. I know it's way too early to feel something like that. It's probably just my brain reacting to the emotional stress, and you *don't* have to say anything back. Honestly, I—"

"Jaemes," he says, making my rambling come to a halt. He's quiet again. I feel even more sick to my stomach as I know I just scared him off.

"I…I think I'm going to leave now," I tell him and start to make my exit. I get to the doorway of the bedroom when he stops me.

"Jaemes, don't leave."

I don't turn around. Instead, I remain standing in the doorway with my eyes glued to the front door. I don't want to hear what he has to say, but for some reason, I await the next words to come out of his mouth.

"Look at me," he says. His voice deep and masculine.

I don't. I remain standing with my back toward him, still eyeing the front door. As I try to move forward, I smell a whiff of his cologne, and he is suddenly behind me, grabbing the top of my shoulders to turn me around gently. I have no choice but to go with the movements that his hands are guiding me do and look him straight in the eyes. His lips start to move as if he is trying to gain courage for what he is about to say. And then he says it.

"I have been in love with you for quite some time now."

Chapter Fourteen

IT HAS ONLY been a week since the authorities found the victims of the aircraft wreck. Only a week since they identified all five bodies that were found, and received the news that there were no survivors, and Rian wasn't coming home. One week for my family to fall apart.

I haven't left my parents' house since the news first broke, and my grandma has been staying with us to help keep what's left of our family from shattering into even more broken pieces. She is the strong one, so we can feel free enough to be the weak ones. Ember and her family sent over a few meals that can be frozen and reheated easily. Alder has been stopping over daily to check on us and to see if we need anything. The Ellis and Daughtler families sent large, beautiful flower arrangements to Rian's funeral. I was supposed to start my new job already, but my start date was pushed back for bereavement leave.

My mom hasn't been able to sleep or eat. When my grandma tries to get her to eat any food, she vomits. The moment my mom notices that she has fallen asleep, she wakes herself up. She won't leave her bed or open the shades in her room. She has secluded herself from the rest of the world.

"How's she doing?" I ask my grandma, who is now exiting my mom's room.

She walks into the living room and joins me on the couch. "Oh, about the same. She's unable to keep anything down and isn't sleeping. I don't want her to end up sick. Hopefully, she will start to turn around with enough time."

I nod my head.

"What about you, sweetheart?" she asks with a hand tap on my knee. "How are you holding up? I don't want you to feel like you've been forgotten."

I know my mom needs the most care of the two of us right now. Rian was her knight in shining armor, her Prince Charming, her other half, her *person*. And she lost him completely. I don't know what that's like. What I do know is that I did lose a great dad and role model. He was a genuine man who stepped up to take the role of my dad and loved me like his own. Now, he is someone I will never see again. I have yet to grasp the reality of that. I don't feel like any part of this tragedy has fully sunk in. My mom, on the other hand, started her grieving process before we were notified of Rian's death.

"I'm hanging in there. It's hard to explain, Grandma. I should be feeling all this grief and sadness, but right now, I feel nothing. I don't feel *anything*. It's like there is an emptiness inside me." I get frustrated with the fact that I can't shed a tear when the father figure in my life is gone. I had no issues with crying when we were left with unanswered questions, but that's because the unknown is scary. Scarier than the truth.

"Everyone processes grief differently. Don't let it fool you. This is just how your brain is reacting to such severe heart-break. Whereas your mom is the opposite and is feeling everything so deeply and more powerfully," she explains.

"It's like my brain thinks this is a dream, and I'll soon wake up to my normal life. It refuses to accept that this is real life and won't allow my body to process this grief like it should." I turn my head to look at her. I can tell she is exhausted, too.

"Don't worry, honey. Time may not heal trauma entirely, but it will help." The muscles that form any sort of smile or facial expression are failing me right now. She stands up from the couch and holds my head in her hands while she plants a kiss near the top of my forehead. "I have to head home in the morning for a few days. I have to make sure your grandfather is taking care of himself. Lord knows what he's doing without me there." Her wink matches her half smile as she continues to talk, heading toward her room. The guest bedroom happens to be right across the hall from the master bedroom, where my mom is currently holding herself hostage. "He's probably eating junk food, not taking his medications, skipping his daily walks…" she trails off as she closes the door but opens it back up just moments after closing it. "And you should think about doing the same thing, sweet pea. It would be good for you to leave here and return to *your* home. Try to get your mind in a different place and resume your normal routine. It would be good for you. You know, to keep busy."

"But I—"

"Don't worry about your mom, honey. I've known her for forty-three years, and to this day, she is the strongest person I know. She bounced back when Jason left you two, and I'm very confident she will do the same this time. Your grandfather and I helped her get back on her feet at first, and then we let go of her hand so she could figure it out on her own. She needs to take care of herself, too."

"I understand that," I tell her. "But the difference between the first time with my biological dad and this time with Rian is me. I'm old enough to understand and go through all the same emotions with her versus just being in the background."

"Valid point, my sweet Jaemes. Goodnight, dear." She closes the door once again.

I decide to check on my mom again before going downstairs to my bedroom. I crack the door to her room and see that the TV is on, and she's finally asleep. I go inside and crawl into bed with her. She is lying on Rian's side, so I take her side. I grab the remote between the pillows and turn the TV off. I scoot closer to her and try to drift off to sleep, hoping to be the calm to yet another one of her storms.

"I love you, Mom," I whisper, and then there they come. All the grief, the tears, and the feeling of realization. I no longer feel numb. I feel fatherless.

Chapter Fifteen

MY FIRST MONTH of work is going much better than I thought. My grandma was right. I needed a distraction and trust that my mom could care for herself. After she left to go back home, I did the same. Eventually, my mom and I were able to talk to each other about Rian and get through our grief together. She hasn't returned to work yet because she feels she can't. The thought of working on the same type of transportation that killed her husband is painful to grasp. They worked together all the time and did everything together. Trying to navigate life without him will be tough for a while. I told her I'd be by her side whenever she needed me. I want to be there for her like she has been there for me my whole life.

Alder has been highly supportive, and he understands I must be with my mom as much as I can. I'll typically see her after work on weekdays and stay at her house until I go to bed. On weekends, I try to get her out of the house as much as possible. She still isn't herself, and it pains me to see her like this, but I know I have to give her time.

I'm missing every bit of how my life used to be. I miss my enthusiastic mom, Rian's witty humor and his presence, going out and being a twenty-three-year-old, and spontaneous outings with Alder.

Time. Give it time.

After a deep breath, I enter the coffee shop, where I told Ember I would meet her. I agreed to meet up with her since there is no school today or tomorrow, so that means a long weekend for me. The last time I saw her was at Rian's funeral. I haven't spoken much with her lately either since most of my time has been taken up by work and being with my mom. The only people I ever talk to besides my mom are Alder and my grandma, Jeanie. This will be the first time I have had a conversation with anyone else outside of work in a month.

Ember is sitting at a high-top table and sipping her coffee. There is another cup sitting next to her, which I assume is mine. She sets her coffee down when she sees me and gets off her chair. I smile at her, and we give each other a much-needed hug.

"I'm thrilled to see you. Can I ask how you're doing? I feel like it has been so long since I've heard a single word out of you," she says, sitting back in her chair. "Is your mom hanging in there?"

"Those are some loaded questions you got there," I tell her. I carefully unseal the lid of my coffee cup so it can cool off. "I'm sorry. I'm still trying to accept the new normal in my life while ensuring my mom is doing okay, too. Mixing all of that with starting my first job out of college and making sure my bills are getting paid after buying my first house is significantly overwhelming, to say the least."

She gives me an apologetic look. "Jae, if there is anything I can do, please let me know. I need you to know that it is okay to accept help when it's presented to you. No one is offering their help because they hope you don't take it," she says.

"I get that, Em. I really do appreciate you, but I want to try to navigate this on my own, though. I'm just glad I'm finally able to spend time with you again. And I could really use some Alder time as well. I haven't spent time with him in a while either. He comes over to see me and my mom when he can after work, but that's just for a few minutes."

"Well, here's a thought: maybe ask him to do something! I'm sure he's waiting for *you* to contact *him*. He's giving you the space you need during this hard time in your life and doesn't want to interfere with the grieving process that you and your mom are going through. Let him know you're ready to continue your relationship."

She makes a good point. It's harder for me to realize the obvious when everything happens simultaneously. I've been dealing with the unknown for a while now, so I'm glad I have her in my life to get me through the reality of what's actually known when I can't.

"You're right. You always seem to have the perfect advice, and I thank you for that," I tell her.

"What can I say? It's a gift," she says smiling.

After waiting for it to cool down, I bring my coffee to my mouth for a sip.

"*Fuck*, that's still hot." I wince.

When I agreed to meet Ember at this coffee shop, I wasn't expecting to see a certain someone I wish I didn't have to see, but here she comes.

"Excuse me, I couldn't help but overhear your conversation," Riley says as she walks up to our table.

Ember looks at her and laughs. "Of course, you couldn't help it. Someone says Alder's name, and you pop out of nowhere like a feral animal."

We wait for her to explain why she was eavesdropping on our private conversation and what she could possibly contribute to it. Her facial expression is full of smugness as if she can't wait to dig her nose into our business. I mean, her crush does happen to be my boyfriend after all. However, my mental energy has run out, and there is no more room to figure out anything else.

She sits down at the last chair that surrounds our table. "I don't mean to get involved—"

"Okay, stop right there," Ember interrupts with a slight chuckle. "You don't need to get involved in our shit, period.

Okay? Good-bye."

"Just hear me out," Riley then turns my way. "I'm over my thing for Alder. In fact, I'm seeing someone now."

"Good for you. What's your point?" Ember snaps.

"My point is…" Riley pauses and turns to me again. "Alder isn't exactly who you think he is. I mean, I should know. I know him better than you do."

Confused, I look at Ember, and she locks eyes with me, looking just as confused as I am.

"We've only been together for a short time," I tell her. "And why should I listen to anything you say? Let alone trust you?"

"Because I know I wouldn't want the same future as Alder if I were you." She looks at Ember and says, "You're her best friend. You should have warned her, but instead, you tunnel visioned on the fact that you wanted them together because you and Bennett are together." She laughs.

"Hey, watch it, bitch. You'd shut your mouth if you knew what was good for you. You don't know shit, and if you think you do, I'll easily change your mind with my fist against your skull," Ember says defensively.

"Easy now," Riley says with both hands up in surrender, but her evil grin never seems to leave her face.

"Warned me about what exactly?" My question now is for both Riley and Ember.

Ember seems like she wants to hear what she has to say just as much as I do as she glares her way. "Let's hear it," Ember says with a look that says *I can't wait to hear this one,* as she rests her chin on her hand and continues to stare in Riley's direction.

"The last conversation I had with Alder, he mentioned that he doesn't ever want to get married or have any kids," she admits.

This makes Ember burst out laughing, nearly spilling her

coffee. "Oh, please. He probably told you that so you'd leave him alone."

Riley gives Ember a nasty look and then brings her attention to me again. "You'll have to see for yourself, I guess. Just know that I tried to warn you," she sings.

"Riley, first of all, I appreciate your concern, but I think this is more of a private matter between Alder and me. Second, if that's true, you don't know that he still thinks that way. Now that he has been with me for a little while, I'm sure some of his wants and opinions have changed," I reply.

Riley purses her lips together into a tight line. "That's a cute assumption, Jaemes. You see, I just saw him the other day, and we had a little chat. I brought up the subject again to see if he had a new outlook on his life now that he is with someone he claims to love. He told me, verbatim, 'It doesn't matter who I am with, you won't ever see a ring on my finger or an asshole kid glued to my hip. Just a lucky lady whom I can call mine with no strings attached.'" Riley gets up from our table and starts to leave, but that doesn't stop Ember.

"You've got to be fucking kidding me. After everything she has gone through lately, you lay this shit on her?" Ember shouts as Riley walks out the door and down the sidewalk. "Jae, she's a total asshole, and she knows what she's doing. It's obvious she still has the hots for your man, and she will say and do anything to ruin what you two have together."

"She said she has a boyfriend," I remind her.

"No, she said she is *seeing* someone. That could mean anything. Hell, I see that guy over there. And that woman walking in."

"You're being ridiculous. Even if her motive is to still get with Alder, I'm pretty positive he would never entertain the idea." Although I say that with confidence, I can't ignore the pit in my stomach caused by Riley's words.

Couples who are serious about each other should discuss

marriage and kids at some point. It just hasn't occurred to me that it should be brought up now. Was Riley really telling the truth or just trying to throw a wrench in our relationship by getting in my head? Would it hurt to bring it up to him? There is only one way of knowing the truth behind Riley's words, and also only one way to ease my mind.

I PULL INTO Alder's driveway and scan the entire house, analyzing every part of the logs, the stones on the chimney, the windows, and the doors. I take in every inch of its beauty and admire my connection to it. There's a chill to the autumn air, and it grows colder as the day grows older. There is still a hefty woodpile over by the trees, and I believe the lighter fluid is in the garage. I set the matches and lighter fluid by the fire pit and retrieved a few wood logs.

I gaze over where Alder and I stood when we first met at the end of his driveway. And then over to the barn, where we had our first legitimate conversation during his housewarming bonfire. The sight of this log house hits differently now. My body feels like a machine that has gone haywire from every event and conversation I've participated in since I returned home, causing a part of me to want to drop everything and run back to Las Vegas. That twenty-two-year-old coming home from college back in June would have never believed it if someone had told her this is where she would be now with the man who lives here. I moved back home with one thing on my mind and one thing only: to start my new adult life, free of romantic relationships, and focus on bettering myself and my career. When did I go off the rails on that plan? And how did my focus become so blurry so fast?

Then I think about the butterfly effect.

Would everything that has happened still happen if I had not returned home?

Would I eventually meet and fall in love with Alder, or would he be involved with someone else? Would I find my perfect first home, or would someone else be holding up that sold sign? Would I be offered the same job position, or would a different applicant accept that offer? Would Rian still die if I hadn't returned home, or would that plane crash happen to someone else?

Someone else.

I stare at the flames for what feels like hours. It's getting close to the time Alder said he'd be home. I watch the fire slowly fizzle out and go inside before my mind wanders to a dark place with even worse thoughts. The only thing that will help shut my messed-up machine down is sleep. The dogs happily follow me to the bedroom to join me. As my head hits the pillow, I continue to think about more memories I have gained here. The morning after the bonfire when I woke up in Alder's bed, the time we watched the sunset in his beautiful backyard, the time Alder and I shared a romantic evening in front of the fireplace after getting caught in a storm the night of his birthday, and all the nights I've spent with Alder in between those memories.

Unfortunately, all those memories would only remain as memories if he really doesn't want the same future as me. My heart can't take another heartbreak. My machine will completely break down, and there will be no one I can go to for repairs.

Chapter Sixteen

I TRY MY hardest to open my eyes, but it's nearly impossible with how exhausted I feel. However, it doesn't stop me from trying again because I know who awaits me on the other side of my eyelids. I blink a few times and finally notice Alder sitting on the edge of the bed, trying to wake me up. He looks like he just got out of the shower. Soon enough, he will realize that he will have to do more than just a gentle touch and a soft voice to get me in more of an alert state.

My hand searches for his. Once I reach it, I grab it and hold onto him as if it's the last time I'll be able to. My mind tells me to stop acting like what Riley said is true, but my heart overpowers my brain and gives me a gut feeling that we might not work out after all.

"Hi," I whisper.

He leans over and kisses my lips. He means for an innocent kiss, but I want more out of it. Just as he starts to pull away, I grab his shirt and pull him back to me. He doesn't resist and meets me back at my lips. This kiss is different. It feels more despairing. I sit myself up without breaking apart from him. I throw my leg over him to straddle his lap, but I can't continue. I can't do this right now. I end our kiss and rest my head on his shoulder. He doesn't question anything. He wraps his arms around me as I squeeze mine around him. I need to be in his arms for as long as possible because I'm unsure how our next conversation will pan out.

"Can we talk?" I ask him without moving an inch of my

body.

He rubs my back with both of his hands and then lets me go. I remove myself from his lap, and we leave the bedroom. Walking past the window, I notice the fire isn't smoldering anymore. There are fresh logs and big bright flames in the firepit. Alder must have reignited it when he got home. We both find ourselves leaning against the kitchen counter next to the living room. I'm not relaxed enough for a couch conversation.

"What's going on, Jaemes? I understand you still need to recover after what just happened with your family, but I can tell something else is eating at you. You need to talk to me."

"Where do you see yourself in ten years?" I ask him flatly. His facial expression turns confused and maybe caught a little off guard.

"I guess I just take things day by day. I don't think about the future like that," he says.

"Where do you see yourself in ten years, Alder?" I ask again. His facial expression now turns more serious to match mine. "This is an important question, and I need it answered. There is a reason why I am asking it."

"And what's that reason?" he asks, crossing his arms.

I inhale and exhale slowly while still observing his face. I'm not answering his question until he answers mine. He looks downward and shakes his head slowly at the floor.

"I don't know," he continues. "Hopefully, I'll be running my own business by then." I remain silent, wanting him to say more, but he doesn't. "Why? Where is this coming from?" he asks, joining my gaze again.

"Because, in ten years, I see myself married with two kids and maybe one on the way. I want to sit comfortably at my desk in my office as a family therapist, knowing I have fulfilled my career goals and dreams. I hope to travel a lot with my husband and kids. I want to find our favorite vacation spot where the kids beg to go every year. Do you see *any* of this in your future?"

"Honestly, no, I don't."

"So, all you can come up with is work goals? Care to explain?" I ask desperately.

"I don't see the point in marriage. In my eyes, a wedding is a money pit that families contribute to. Marriage is a piece of paper and two pieces of jewelry. In ten years, I want to be able to say that worked my ass off enough to own my own business and go through life with someone I love by my side every day. That's it, plain and simple."

"What if our wants in life don't match up? Then what? You don't want an asshole kid glued to your hip? All you want is a woman who agrees to a 'no strings attached' *fling*?"

He lets out a frustrated laugh. "I see you have been talking with Riley."

"So, is what she said true?" I ask him warily. "Or do you *really* want to go through life with someone you love? Because, at this point, I don't know who to believe anymore."

"I might have said something like that to her a long time ago. Jaemes, you just have to trust me."

"Does a long time ago mean just the other day?" I ask, irritated. None of this is lining up. "Do you truly want us to work?"

"Yeah, I really fucking do," he says with some worry in his voice. "I mean it when I tell you I love you, Jaemes. I just... I have never been a kid person. I don't know how to interact with kids. So, no, I don't want any of my own. Like you, I have big career goals and dreams, too. I don't, and won't, have the time to be a dad. Regarding a relationship, I never once said that I wanted a 'no strings attached' fling. That's Riley fucking with you. I think it's better if you stay away from her. She has gone after every girl I've been with."

That's a hard pill to swallow. The more he explains himself, the more my stomach feels like it's getting punched.

"Then what are we doing, Alder?" I ask him quietly.

"What do you mean?" he asks.

"*What are we doing?* Why are we in a relationship when you don't want anything to come of it?" My voice grows louder this time, hoping he gives me some optimism, but he doesn't answer immediately.

"Jaemes, I want you. I want *you* out of it. Me and you doing life together."

"I can't go through life with someone who doesn't wish to at least compromise with me on huge life wants like marriage and kids, Alder."

"So, what are you saying? You want to end us?"

I look down at my fidgeting fingers and continue to answer him quietly. "No. Maybe? I don't know."

He pushes off the counter and says, "It looks like you have some thinking to do. Let me know when you *do* know." He walks over to the stairs and heads down to the basement. When I hear the TV turn on, I assume he is in the living room and most likely won't come back up for a while. I take the hint and let myself out.

This isn't how I wanted today to go, but it was a conversation that had to happen. Knowing all this now versus finding out after years of being in a committed relationship is helpful, but it doesn't make it any less painful. I throw my phone on the passenger seat, deciding against texting him. What would I even say at this point? It's probably best that we remove ourselves from each other for a good minute and let what we talked about fester in our thoughts before coming back together again. The hardest thing to ponder is that nothing has been resolved, and another worrisome unknown has entered my life.

Chapter Seventeen

I DON'T MIND spending most of my time with my mom. Instead of always going to her and continuing to entertain the idea of her being a hermit, I invited her to stay at my place since I had been off work for the last couple of days. It's nice to finally spend some time at my house and have some company. I haven't had any chance to enjoy it with everything put away and decorated. Since my house has a loud cabin feel, the décor is pretty mild.

"I know something is up with you, Jaemes," my mom says while she chews on her sandwich. We are sitting at my kitchen table eating lunch. I knew she would say something like this at some point. I can only fake it for so long, and then, unfortunately, my body shows its true feelings loud and proud. I look up from the table to acknowledge her. "You've been taking little mouse bites from your chips and haven't even touched your favorite sandwich," she adds.

"Everything is fine, Mom," I tell her with little reassurance.

"I know you all too well, Jae. Now tell me what's going on," she demands.

I keep my line of sight down at my food. I'm focusing intensely on keeping my shit together. Everything has been falling apart all too easily lately, and quite frankly, I'm getting fucking sick of it. I know I have to tell her something; it might as well be the truth.

"I have realized that sometimes life can throw us some pretty shitty curve balls, and we have to work hard to get through them. Sometimes, there are bumps in the road, and we have to try to navigate around them. No matter our paths, something will always try to jackhammer it to small and miserable pieces when we least expect it. I'm sure you are aware, given everything you've gone through in this lifetime."

"Mhm," my mom replies. Her demeanor is laser-focused on what I'm trying to say and concentrating on where I might be going with this. "So, what is this curve ball and bump in the road you are referring to exactly? Is something going on with you and Ember? You and Alder? *Oh God,* are you pregnant?" she asks.

"No, I'm not pregnant, Mom," I clarify. "Apparently, that would be the worst thing to ever happen," I mumble. I attempt to tear open the wrapping around my sandwich, but it's giving me a hard time. I throw it to the side angrily. I look up to the ceiling as my vision blurs, hoping my eyes widen enough to dry the tears. In the meantime, I nibble on another chip while the corners of my mouth twitch into a frown.

"I see," she says calmly. "I have gathered that your friendship with Ember isn't the problem. But it might be your relationship with Alder."

I let out a small, petty laugh as I grab my sandwich. "No, not at all," I say sarcastically. "I just want my damn sandwich opened." I viciously tear open part of the wrapping of my sandwich. "I want my sandwich *unwrapped,* but does everyone want their sandwich unwrapped? No!" I rip the wrapping off, causing pieces of my sandwich to fly everywhere. "*Some* people want to go through life with an unwrapped sandwich because they aren't an *unwrapped kind of guy,*" I say mockingly. The stress forces the tears out of my eyes and down my cheeks. I will never win when I'm up against my own tears.

"I'm assuming Alder might be the sandwich you're referring to," my mom says.

"Mom, could you be with someone who never wanted to

get married *and* didn't want to have any kids? Alder could have his dream girl standing right before him, but he would sacrifice a happy and healthy relationship with her if that meant he would have to get married and have kids. How can I stay with him if I know that wouldn't be in the cards for me? For *us?*"

She ponders that for a minute as if trying to put herself in my position.

"I know I couldn't," she says. "I couldn't go through life knowing that I'm fully capable of having a healthy baby and not having at least one of my own with someone who isn't afraid to commit." She reaches over and grabs the top of my hand. "Jaemes, these are huge parts of life; you only get one life to live. So, please make sure you proceed with caution with whatever you do. Although, you never know. He could change his mind, too."

"What am I supposed to do? Am I supposed to stay with him and pray I can talk him into having a long and happy marriage with a kid or two? There's that scenario, or I could stay with him and not be one hundred percent happy as a childless, single person who is only a mom to a bunch of dogs. If I stay with him and he ends up giving me a petty proposal and then, down the road, we accidentally become pregnant, I'd feel so guilty knowing he didn't want any of it. I want a man who wants to call me his wife. I want a husband who gets so excited he can't help but shed one tear when I tell him we're finally pregnant. I won't have any chance of that if I stay with Alder. But I love him. I love him a lot, and that's the problem. If we stay together, either I'm happy or he is. There *is* no compromising when it comes to these things."

"Honey, it's still pretty early in the relationship, and it's important to have these hard conversations. In a healthy relationship, both people must be willing to tackle everything, even when it's difficult. It says a lot about who you are as a couple, whether it can be discussed maturely or if it gets ignored. If you really love each other, you two will figure it out."

"I know there is nothing wrong with wanting what you want. I can't fault him for that, and he can't fault me for wanting what I want. It just sucks knowing that Alder might not be my person after all." I cry a little harder at that possibility.

"And that's okay," she reassures me. "It might not feel okay at this moment or a month from now if things don't work out between you two, but it will be eventually because you will find someone who will beg to be your husband and the father of your child or children. I mean, look at you," she says with a smile and a goofy wink. She makes me crack a small smile, which feels weird given that I haven't been able to smile in days.

"Thanks, Mom," I tell her through sobs.

"So, what do you think?" she asks. "Dry those tears, clean up this mess, and maybe invite Ember over for a little girl time tonight? I'm sure you already filled her in on everything."

"Actually, no," I confess. "Alder and I just had this conversation a couple of days ago, right after I met her for coffee."

"Well, perfect. I can't wait to hear her advice for you," she laughs.

I text Ember and help my mom clean up the sandwich mess in the kitchen. I don't know what I would do without her. She listens carefully to every word I speak and knows the right things to say. I only hope that I'll be able to do the same for my kids one day.

Chapter Eighteen

I START MY drive to Alder's house, thinking about my night with Ember and my mom. Girl time was what I needed. We all sat in the living room and cuddled up in our blankets. The TV stayed off, and our hot chocolates stayed warm throughout the evening. It didn't stop there because Ember had a little surprise for all of us before I could start filling her in on my situation with Alder.

She whipped out a bottle of peppermint schnapps from her bag and took it to the kitchen with our hot chocolates. She claimed it wouldn't be proper girl time if our cocoas weren't spiked. She was right, however. You can never underestimate Ember when it comes to a good time, especially when it's desired.

After Ember was finally caught up on what had been going on, I asked her what she would do if she were in this situation. I regretted asking after she said the most Ember thing ever. She told us that she would legally change her last name to his and wear a ring. Then, she would poke holes in the condoms. She went on to explain that men are scared right away because they don't know how to be a dad, but after they look at *their* baby for the first time, it all goes away. It's hard to prove until it happens. She told me that Alder and I need to have a baby, and if he realizes that fatherhood is genuinely astonishing, then great, and if he still doesn't want kids after seeing his own for the first time, then good riddance.

Ember's words started to sound too close to home. My

biological dad didn't want to be a dad, and he ran. If I were to become pregnant, I don't know if I would be as strong as my mom if Alder left us. I'm not sure if my mom was oblivious to what Ember was saying or if she just knew how to ignore it. I decided what to do in this circumstance. Ultimately, the decision was mine, but my mom and Ember helped me go through the steps to figure out what I truly needed. I know what I must do, and now all I have to do is act upon it. I texted Alder asking if now would be a good time to stop over.

Alder: *You know you can come over any time you want.*

I'm unsure how I will feel after seeing him again, especially after our last conversation. It was difficult to discuss, but it was only one tough conversation. I'm going to show him that I won't give up on our relationship without a fight. I'll do everything I can to try and make it work, and if that's not enough, then at least I know I tried the best I could.

I'm now sitting in his driveway, rethinking everything in my head. Rehearsing what to say based on his possible responses isn't going to work this time. I have to let the conversation flow naturally and say whatever I feel.

It feels good walking into his house on this cold and gloomy day. It smells like the fireplace must have been on earlier this morning; but otherwise, everything looks and sounds exactly how it was the last time I was here. The main floor is empty, and the TV is on downstairs. The closer I get to the staircase, the more nervous I become. Going to the basement makes my stomach drop a little more with each step. And then I see him, and he sees me.

"There she is," he says from the couch facing the TV. "How are you, beautiful?"

So far, he's off to a good start by making me smile, but I can't get too distracted and downplay why I am here. "I'm okay. You sure look comfy," I point out.

"It's the only way to be on Football Sunday," he says, then takes a sip of his beer.

I take a seat on the sectional couch sitting to his right. His legs rest on the coffee table beside a few empty beer cans.

"How are the Broncos doing?" I ask, legitimately interested.

"Not great," he clears his throat. "They already played on Thursday and lost to the damn Browns. I'm watching the Raiders game, hoping they lose."

"Go, Philly," I say, glancing at the TV.

"Want something to drink? I just stocked the bar," he says, gesturing behind him.

"No, I'm good for right now. Thanks."

We are both quiet for a moment, watching the football game. I watch him as he takes sip after sip of his beer, and then I count the empties on the coffee table. *There are ten empty cans.* He doesn't seem drunk. I know that if I am nervous or anxious about something, I turn to a cocktail or two to help me return to a more normal and calmer state before actually getting into a buzzed state. That was how my mom was while waiting for the God-awful news about Rian. Maybe that's what he's doing? They might not all be from today, either. Or all from him. Alder turns to me after the commercial break starts.

"Something tells me we have something to discuss," he says.

With pressed lips, I nod my head. "Yeah, I would say you're right, given how we left things the other day."

"How about *you* tell *me* what's on your mind?" He takes another swig of his beer.

"Alder, we need to figure something out. I don't want to waste your time, and I'm sure you don't want to waste mine either."

"And how are we wasting each other's time?" he says and side-eyes me with raised eyebrows.

"By being in a relationship that has no future," I clarify.

"I see," he says, and another gulp of beer goes down. "However, I believe that we *can* have a future by just being together. People don't have to get married to have a happy and healthy relationship, Jaemes."

"If you can't see yourself even considering getting married one day or having kids…I don't think I can continue being in a relationship with you."

Oof, that was a hard one to admit.

His gaze is on the coffee table. The game is back on, but he seems caught off guard or deep in thought. Whatever it is, he doesn't say anything back.

"There isn't any way I can change your mind? On any of it?" I ask him. He stays in the same position and remains silent. His absence in this conversation breaks my heart, knowing he can't even try to help our relationship survive. "Not even if your person is me?" I ask through stinging tears that are now drowning my eyes.

He finally looks at me with no emotion connected to his face. "I already told you, Jaemes. I won't change my mind, just like I'm sure you won't change yours either. It is what it is. If you can't accept that a life with me will be different than the one you envisioned for yourself, then maybe we do need to end things between us."

His words pierce through my chest and into my heart. Any hope I had going into this conversation has fled the scene in a hurry. I now know neither of us will back down on what we want. "So that's it then," I whisper.

He has already returned his attention to the football game and is finishing the rest of his beer. I stand up and take the house key he gave me out of my back pocket and place it on the coffee table next to him. I see him glance at it, but he says nothing. I go to leave with my tear-soaked face but turn around one more time to try and savor any last chances of him stopping me. I only see a man sitting on the couch, his eyes watery and redder than when I arrived. He is as still as a statue and as quiet as a mute. So, I continue up the stairs and don't look back. If I let my heart control my brain this time, I'll run back into his arms. As much as I want to so badly, I fight it and walk out the door. I proceed to my car, and then I drive down the driveway. I leave the log house on the right for the last time.

PART TWO
LEDGER YEARWOOD

Chapter Nineteen

GOING THROUGH THE holidays this year was brutal. Without Rian, there wasn't any Halloween fun, no Christmas cheer, and there seemed to be nothing to be thankful for this Thanksgiving. We took the year off from decorating for each season and the holiday that correlated to each month. My mom and I could not wait to ring in the new year and start over.

It has also been a couple of months since Alder and I called it quits on our relationship. It doesn't matter if we lasted four months or four years; it still hurts the same. He was there with me through the most challenging situations anyone could go through. It's what made our bond so tight in such a short time. But in reality, Alder and I would never work out, and that's okay. It's for the best, and I will thank myself one day. I've shied away from going out, minimizing my chances of seeing him. It would be too hard on my soul to be in his presence again. As long as I continue with my job and internship, I should be able to keep myself busy enough to keep him off my mind. The grief of losing someone you loved, whether that be due to a breakup or death, is hard, and it takes a long time to return to your normal self again.

As my alarm sounds off, I can't help but dread going back to work. Today is the first day back from winter break. I'm not ready to be around my coworkers while they ask me how my break was and then proceed to tell me how fun their family vacation was. Or how much time they were able to spend with their parents and in-laws. Quite frankly, I don't give a damn about any of that. The only thing that gets me through every single day is my best friend.

Coffee.

After struggling to get out of bed, I go to the bathroom and turn on the shower so the water can warm up. Knowing that it's going to be difficult getting back into my routine again, I decide to make a few extra cups of coffee than I would typically make. However, I am deeply let down when I notice that I barely have enough coffee grounds for even one cup.

"Fuck me," I say in complete disappointment.

I'm hoping my shower wakes me up. This better not be a sign of how things will go today. Now, I have to leave the house early to grab a coffee somewhere before going to work. I can't function with aggravatedly stressed-out kids if I don't have an ounce of caffeine in my system.

When I get out of the shower, I notice a text message on my phone from my coworker, Jessica.

> **Jessica:** Hey, I won't be in the office today. My daughter is still sick, and I am trying to find an open appointment with a doctor. Can you keep an eye on my kiddos for me, please? Jordan is in Mrs. Nelson's second-grade class, and Kyle is in Mr. Kenzington's fifth-grade class. I can foresee one or both of them needing extra care today with their routines being readjusted and returning to school after an extended break. Thank you!

I love how she expects me to look after her students when she knows I have my hands full with my own group. This is going to be a long and busy Monday. When I start to text her back, I notice a howling sound outside my living room window. I flip on my front porch light and see the wind intensely blowing snow that's falling from the sky. Yet another thing to add to my wonderful morning. Unless they call school off, which would turn my day around for the better.

I dress for work and return to the living room to turn the news on my TV. While I wait for the list to get to my school, I grab my laptop and go on the school's website. If they decide to close, either of these places will have the announcement first. With no such luck, I slam my laptop shut, turn off my TV, and head into the frozen tundra to get some coffee and continue my awful day.

I stop by a coffee shop between my house and my school. To my surprise, it's busier than I thought it would be on a day like today. A snowy Monday won't stop anyone from their coffee, I guess. When it's my turn, I tell the barista I want to order a black dark roast coffee in their largest size.

"Name on the order?" the barista asks me.

"Jaemes. J-a-e-m-e-s," I tell her as she writes it on my cup.

"I never pictured you for a dark roast kind of girl," a deep, familiar voice says behind me. When I turn around, I observe the entirety of him. He hasn't changed since the last time I saw him. It's been months since I spoke with this man, and just locking my eyes with him makes me smile. It reminds me of all the times we have run into each other in the past.

"Oh, wow. Hi, Ledger," I finally say. He smiles back at me and orders the same thing.

"L-e-d-g-e-r," he tells the barista. "Somehow, they always mess my name up, too. Do you come here for coffee often? I don't think I have seen you here before."

"Unfortunately, I chose today out of all days to be out of coffee. This is my first time here," I say back as we scoot ourselves over to the pick-up area of the counter.

"I was going to say, I think I would have noticed you if you've been here before. I sit and have coffee before work every day. I try to, anyway. How have you been? I haven't seen you around in a while."

"Yeah, I'm hanging in there. It has been a pretty rough few months for me, but I'm doing my best to stay sane and get through it one day at a time. How about you? How have you been?" I ask him.

"I'm doing great, but I'm sorry to hear you're going through some shit."

"Jamie," the barista calls out from behind the counter. I know she is referring to me since she is holding what I ordered and is looking right at me.

"It's *Jaemes*," I correct her and pick up my coffee.

"So, *Jamie*, how are you spending the rest of your time on this beautiful day?" Ledger asks me.

I sigh. "Working, unfortunately."

"Ledger," the barista calls out. Sure, they get his name right when he spells it out. He grabs his coffee, and I take out my phone. I have a missed call, a voicemail, an email, and a text message from the school district stating that school is canceled for today and tomorrow due to forecasted severe weather conditions. "Fuck yeah!" I say a little too loudly.

Oops.

No other adult knows how exciting that feeling is when you see that school is canceled and you don't have to go to work. It's like being a kid again.

"Well, enjoy your coffee," I say, raising my cup and then leaving to return home.

"Hey, wait," he says, stopping me. "Would you want to join me? I'm not sure how much time you have before you need to leave for work, but I'd enjoy your company."

"I'm heading back home, actually. I was just notified that I don't have to go in today or tomorrow due to the weather." His offer is tempting, but the weather worsens every time I look out the window. Do I risk getting home safely by staying here with Ledger, or do I play it safe and go home, not knowing when I'll see him next? "I'd love to, but I should really get going before the roads get any worse," I tell him.

His facial expression grows disappointed. "What if I drove

you home before I went to work?"

"Then my car would be stranded here."

"True. Okay, I'll tell you what. You agree to have coffee with me, and I'll follow you home to make sure you get there okay, and *then* I'll head into work."

"You just don't give up, do you?" I say with a smile.

He smiles back and says, "What can I say? I know what I want, and I fight for it."

"Okay, fine, but only if you promise to follow me home and get to work safely. I'll join you in a minute." I pull up my and Jessica's text message conversation and finally reply to her.

> **Me:** *It looks like we are both off the hook for a few more days. I hope your daughter feels better soon.*

Ledger is sitting at a small table next to the window. I happily sit across from him and take off my lid so my coffee can cool.

"I'd love to get to know you better. Whenever we've seen each other, it's only been for a brief time. Are you married? Have any kids? Married *with* kids?" he asks.

"No to all the above. What about you? I know you have a son."

He takes a sip of his coffee and glances out the window. "Yeah, Archie just turned six last week. I was engaged to his mom a little over a year ago."

"Was? Can I ask what happened?"

"We just didn't see eye to eye on many things regarding our relationship, parenting views, and life itself at times. We were only together for about six months before discovering we were expecting a child. Eventually, we fell in love, but mainly with Archie. I proposed when he was three. He is what kept us together for the most part. As he got older, Gretchen and I became more distant. She took him to and from school, attended conferences, and was significantly involved with his academics. I did more sports and extracurricular activities with him.

"We never really did anything as a family. We almost liked it better that way. We'd fight and bicker about everything if we did anything as a family. One day, we sat down and figured there was no reason to stay together if we weren't happy. To this day, we remain cordial and still have one happy kid who loves to hang out with his mom on her days and with me on my days."

"That's incredibly mature of you two," I tell him. "It makes my heart happy that there are people out there who don't run when times get tough and know how to work well enough together to co-parent a happy and healthy child. That's very selfless of you."

We glance outside, and the wind gusts increase. The snow has turned into blustering white globs, making it difficult to see anything. We are quietly sipping on our coffee and watching the snowstorm. The staff at the coffee shop are talking amongst each other as more people fade outside into the colorless world.

"Tell me more about yourself," Ledger says, breaking the silence.

"Oh boy, where do I even start?" I ask myself more than I'm asking him.

"Are you originally from here?" he asks, trying to help me start.

"No, I was born in Nevada," I tell him.

"Oh, Nevada? Where about in Nevada?"

"Las Vegas. That's where I'm from originally," I state.

"Wow. What was it like growing up in Vegas?"

"I only lived there for the first eight years of my life, so I don't remember much. We moved to Los Angeles in 2007 and then moved here in 2008. I've remained here ever since."

"Until you moved back to Las Vegas to attend the University of Nevada after high school."

"Excuse me?" I ask, thrown off guard. He barely knows me, and suddenly, he blurts that out. "How did you know that?" I ask, a little worrisome.

"Lucky guess," he says.

"Am I that easy to read?"

"A little," he smiles. "What brought you and your family to Montana then?"

"My mom met my stepdad when we lived in Los Angeles. He was from Montana, so they moved us here before they got married."

"Do you come from a close family?" he asks.

"For years, it was just me and my mom, and after Rian came into the picture, the three of us became really close. And now it's back to just me and my mom," I say with a melancholy sigh.

"What do you mean? What happened?"

"Rian passed away a few months ago," I choke down another sip of coffee.

"Oh, wow. I'm sorry to hear that," he says sympathetically.

"He was a part of that plane crash a few months back. I'm surprised you didn't hear about that. It was all over the local news."

"I don't watch the news," he says flatly. "It's too depressing."

"That's fair. He was a commercial airline pilot. He flew private planes for tourists for a side job and then one day…" I trail off, not wanting to talk about this anymore. "What about you? Tell me about the family that you come from."

"Well, I have a brother who is two years older than me, and twin sisters who are about two and a half years younger than me. We are all pretty close-knit as well. However, we all have our own lives now, and getting together is harder."

"Let me guess. You've got to be around thirty years old?" I ask.

"Close," he says, taking a sip of his coffee. "Thirty-one."

"Your parents must love that their kids are so close. That's something I'll never get to experience being an only child."

"My parents died when I was three. After my sisters were born, they went to Florida for vacation. They got into a car accident, and neither of them survived their injuries. My siblings and I were staying with my grandparents at the time. The last thing we expected was that we would be living with them permanently."

"I'm so sorry to hear that, Ledger. I guess we both have somewhat messed up lives."

"Luckily, my grandparents play mom and dad very well. My sisters and I don't remember my parents much, but I know it was tough on my brother. I think that's why we are all so close. With my grandparents' age, us kids had to stick together."

Hearing Ledger's story oddly gives me a happy feeling. I don't feel happy regarding the situation God put him through, but I am delighted that there is someone I can relate to. I can connect with him on a level that I can't with anyone else. He gives me a sense of comfort and security when I talk with him.

"So, you're not married and don't have kids," he clarifies.

"That's correct. Hopefully someday, but I am single and kid-less right now," I laugh.

"I don't get that. How can a girl like you be single?" He shakes his head ever so slightly while his blue eyes stare at me. His look alone makes me feel warm and causes my face to blush. "You're beautiful, you seem to have a good head on your shoulders, you're fun and easy to talk to, personable…I could go on and on," he says with a grin.

"You're very sweet, Ledg—"

"No, not sweet. Just my open and honest opinion. I think you deserve to be told these things. I automatically feel ecstatic whenever I run into you at a bar or a coffee shop. After we talk,

I can't wait until the next time we run into each other again."

I can't help but smile at him. I don't know how to reciprocate that I feel the same way. So, I don't. Instead, I continue my explanation.

"I'm twenty-three years old. I'm a young woman, so most guys assume I'm still in my college partying phase who is willing to sleep with anyone who has a dick. I've already grown up and out of that stage in my life. It wasn't long until I knew that lifestyle wasn't for me. I'm looking for a mature relationship that has potential. I have a great job, bought a house last summer, and can't wait to marry my soul mate and have kids someday. In the meantime, I am working toward my career goals and hoping to save as much money as possible. I want to be able to travel the world and make memories so I have stories I can tell my grandchildren in the future."

"Huh," he starts, "thanks for adding to my list. Sounds like any man would be lucky to have you."

I shrug. I don't necessarily think that's true, but hearing that from a handsome, successful man like himself is nice.

"So, tell me about him," he says, looking at me with furrowed eyebrows as if he's trying to figure more of me out.

"I'm sorry?"

"Tell me about the guy who broke your heart. I can see it all over your face, especially when you talk about marriage, kids, and your overall life goals. You are trying to prove yourself when you don't have to."

He's good. Almost too good. We've only been at this coffee shop for about forty-five minutes, and we've already discussed almost everything about each other and then some. That's how easy it is to talk with him. I'm not afraid to hold back on anything about me. However, I'm unsure how to answer his question because it involves two men in back-to-back relationships.

"Um, it's complicated."

"Try me," he says with a challenging expression.

"Let's just say I can't be with someone who doesn't put me first *or* foresees a future that includes marriage and kids. It was a challenge navigating life after ending a relationship with someone I considered to be the love of my life. Fast forward to a few months back, and the same thing happened with someone else. It's becoming increasingly difficult for me to trust someone after experiencing so much heartbreak. How hard is it to tell someone exactly how you feel with honest words?" I explain my thoughts in a quiet tone while looking out the window.

"You can trust me," he says sincerely, bringing my attention away from the outdoors and back to him.

It's hard to talk about this subject, as it's the first time I've spoken about my recent relationship with Alder. We remain quiet to see if there will be more to this conversation, but there's nothing left to say. I stand up to throw my empty coffee cup in the garbage and then return to the table to grab my jacket and purse. "I should probably head out," I tell him.

"I'll follow you to make sure you get home okay, as promised," he says, throwing his coffee cup in the garbage on our way to the door. I can't get in my car fast enough. This winter storm doesn't seem to want to quit. I turn on my heated seats and hit the defrost button so my car can thaw. I watch Ledger get into his vehicle. He gets in a red and older-looking vintage truck that's parked across the lot.

On my way home, I can't help but think about my conversation with Ledger. He seems like a genuine and down-to-earth man. He certainly checks a lot of boxes, and he seems interested in me. At least, that's the feeling I'm getting from him. He's good-looking, has a stable job, makes a good living, has a happy and healthy child, seems like a good dad, and is an overall mature man.

When I pull into my driveway, Ledger continues down the

road so he doesn't get stuck. I take my phone out of my purse when I get inside and text him. He texted me before leaving the coffee shop, so his information is already saved on my phone.

> **Me:** Thank you for following me home. It was nice to see you again. I really enjoyed our cute little coffee date. Hopefully, we can do it again sometime.

> **Ledger:** You're very welcome. I can't wait for the next time I run into you.

I set my phone down on the coffee table in the living room so I can put my belongings away. I bring up my Netflix profile on the TV and search for a movie. I'm curled up on the couch with a fuzzy blanket so that the outside of my body matches the feeling on the inside.

Chapter Twenty

TODAY IS DAY two of the winter storm and the second snow day for me. As I look out my window in the living room, I see the storm lighting up a bit. This gives the snowplows a chance to finally clear the roads, allowing the buses to start operating again tomorrow morning. Since I still don't have any coffee at my house, I'm sipping on the hot chocolate Ember left here a few months ago. I'm hoping I can get on a sugar high since I can't commence a caffeine high. My attention turns to my phone when it vibrates the rhythm I set for it.

> **Ledger:** *Hey, Jaemes. Do you want me to stop by and clear out your driveway?*
>
> **Ledger:** *I'm out and about anyway. My grandparents need clearing out as well. Just let me know.*

Not only am I excited he texted me, but I'm also thrilled that I don't have to do my driveway.

> **Me:** *That would be amazing. Thank you so much!*
>
> **Ledger:** *Not a problem. Give me an hour or so.*

It's time to make myself look presentable. I showered before bed last night, so my hair requires some dry shampoo to give it some life. I apply it to my roots and massage it in. Afterward, I throw my hair up in a messy bun on top of my head. I slip on black leggings and a black crop top sweatshirt to look cute and comfy. Now that I'm ready, I go through my house to ensure everything is neat and clean.

All the dishes are out of the sink and in the dishwasher; *check*.

The laundry is off the floor and in the laundry room hampers; *check*.

Blankets in the living room are folded nicely and put in the basket; *check*.

Candles are lit on the coffee table in the living room; *check*.

Now, it's finally time to sit and wait. I turn on my TV and start watching my Netflix show to kill some time. I keep checking the time on my phone periodically and looking out my living room window. In the distance, a red color stands out against the white air. As the red color gets closer, I recognize it a little more.

Ledger's truck.

He has a plow attachment on the front of his truck for easy snow removal. I turn the TV off and watch him through the window. It only takes him a few times to go up and down my driveway until it's completely cleared. He finally parks and exits his truck with two coffee cups in his hands. I'm hoping one of them is for me. When he's close to the window I'm standing by, he sees me watching him, making him smile. I go to the front door to eagerly let him in. He steps inside and brings the cold Montana air with him.

"I brought you some coffee. I figured you'd still be out," he says, handing me one of the large cups.

"You're a blessing from above. Thank you," I say back. "I had to settle for the sugar content in my hot chocolate this morning to wake me up. Turns out, sugar is not as good as caffeine." I take a sip of the coffee. The temperature is perfect. I'm assuming it has been sitting for a little while. "Dark roast. Just how I like it."

"See, I pay attention," he smiles.

"Come in and stay a while if you want," I tell him, stepping aside. "We can resume our coffee date if that's something you're up for?"

"You're hard to say no to, you know that?" he grins.

He takes his boots off and hangs his coat on the hanger next to the front door before continuing to his coffee and taking a seat on my couch. He smells of a mixture of cedarwood cologne and winter sweat. I wonder if he had to shovel a little at his grandparents' house earlier.

"Thank you again for clearing out my driveway. You saved my body from the aches and pains that come with shoveling," I say, joining him on the couch.

"I was happy to do it, Jaemes."

"Are you like this with every girl you meet? A down-to-earth and generous gentleman?" I ask him.

"Only the ones I like," he replies. "With that being said, I have nine more driveways to clear out and eighteen more cups of coffee sitting in my truck, so I'll need to make this visit quick," he teases.

I laugh at his comment and nudge his leg with my foot playfully. "You're going to have one hell of a caffeine high by the end of the day," I tell him. "No work for you either?"

"I have Tuesdays off every week."

"Well, aren't you lucky," I say, then take another blissful sip of my coffee.

"I'm sorry, but don't you have three months off in the summer?" he smirks.

"Fair enough," I reply.

His phone lights up on the coffee table with an email notification. There is a photo of a boy set as his background. He picks up his phone to dismiss the notification and then sets it back down.

"I'm out of the office. That can wait," he says.

"Is that your son on your phone?" I ask him.

"Yeah, that's Archie." He goes through his phone and

shows me more photos of him. He looks identical to Ledger. Archie has a few more distinct blonde curls, and his eyes are brighter blue. As he scrolls on his phone for more pictures, I see an older family photo of him, Archie, and his ex-fiancé, Gretchen. She is gorgeous. She has a darker olive skin tone with curly chocolate brown hair. Her eyes are a soft light brown, and her smile is magnificent. I don't compare to a woman like her.

"Do you see him often?" I ask.

"We share fifty-fifty custody, so I get to see my little man for a week every other week. It's the same for holidays as well. We switch off every major holiday, so it works out."

"The fact that you and Gretchen can get along so well, especially when it comes to equal and fair share for your son, says a lot about what kind of people you are."

"And what kind of people do you think we are?" he asks.

"Great parents," I tell him.

He half smiles and looks down at his coffee while swirling the last of it around in a circle. "Thank you. It means a lot coming from you. You know, as a behavioral… something or another. Future family therapist," he says.

"He must be in kindergarten?" I ask.

"Yes, and he enjoys it. He always comes home with silly stories and shows me everything he has learned."

"Awe, he sounds fun. I love working with kids his age. Since I don't have any of my own and I don't have siblings, my job is so enjoyable. What does Gretchen do for a living?"

"She is also a medical doctor; however, she specializes in Obstetrics and Gynecology. She has her own practice in Bozeman."

"That's awesome. Good for her," I say, not knowing what else to bring to the conversation. We fill the silence in the room with a few sips of our coffees. Ledger stands up and walks over to the same window I was looking out when he cleared my driveway.

"You must see a lot of wildlife living out here," he says, looking outside.

"Honestly, I don't ever see much. Which is odd," I tell him.

"Really?" he asks. "Because a moose is standing right outside your house."

I jolt up and quickly join him near the window. Sure enough, a vast and beautiful moose is just a few yards away. Not only am I surprised to see this kind of superb wildlife not too far away from my front door, but I feel a sense of shock when the sensation of Ledger's hand gently lands on the small of my back. Gradually, he glides his hand to my side and pulls me closer to him. Now that the whole right side of my body is touching him, I feel a sense of comfort when I rest my head against his chest. We quietly watch the moose for a moment. "He's so majestic looking," I say.

"Thanks for noticing. I try," Ledger jokes.

I push him away as we both laugh at his comment. "You're something else, you know that?"

He pulls me back in, so we are face to face now. His smile fades, and his eyes gaze down to my lips. His hands hold a gentle grip on each side of my hips, and he pulls me closer to him once again. I study his face and attempt to figure him out in this moment.

"Why do I want to kiss you so bad?" he asks me in a whisper. I feel myself get closer to his face with every breath I breathe because I, too, feel the same need as him. Just as I am about to lift onto the balls of my feet, throw my arms around his neck, and force myself to search for the right amount of courage to touch my lips to his, his phone starts to ring. I close my eyes, thinking this moment is over between us. But he doesn't move. He doesn't flinch as if he is contemplating answering it. Instead, he stays still with me until his lips gracefully meet mine. Our first kiss lasts until his phone stops ringing. When the silence starts, our kiss fades apart. But not for long. Ledger pushes my body back with his lips reattached to mine. Neither of us can see where we are going, which causes us to bump into the coffee table and knock over both cups of coffee. His hands hold me as he gradually lays me on the couch behind us. He is holding himself up by his arms and hovering over me. Our lips never break from each other. I feel a sense of desperation run through me as we continue. I can't get enough of what he is giving me. My legs wrap around his waist, and my arms wrap around his neck, driving his body to lay on top of mine. Our tongues eventually meet, and it sends a sensation of chills down my spine.

In the past, I could always feel the sexual tension between Ledger and me, but I never knew that he felt the same way. I lift my hips against him, and his hand caresses my cheek as our tongues deepen and our kiss strengthens. I tangle my fingers in his soft blonde hair, and we stay together for what seems like hours. Unfortunately, his phone rings a second time, which causes him to break free from me. He holds my gaze for a moment and apologizes without saying a word.

"It's okay," I whisper.

He lifts off of me without breaking eye contact. When he grabs a hold of his phone, he wipes it free of the coffee that was spilled and answers the call. "Doctor Yearwood," he answers as he walks into the kitchen for privacy. I pull myself together and get a few towels from the bathroom to clean up the coffee spills. Luckily, my coffee table and hardwood floors are easy to clean. I can hear Ledger's conversation but cannot make out every word he says. I'm assuming it's a work phone call, given how he answered it. I'm dreading the moment he tells me he needs to leave, but I may be in luck if today is his day off.

I make my way to the laundry room to switch out clothes so I can put the towels in the washing machine. The conversation becomes clearer as Ledger paces closer to the laundry room.

"I'll go ahead and refill it this time, but please let him know that he needs to make a follow-up appointment with me to re-evaluate his condition before I approve any more refills after this." He hangs up the phone, and I quickly finish what I'm doing in the laundry room. When I return to the living room, he is seated on the couch, waiting for me.

"I'm sorry, that was my nurse. One of our tougher patients showed up today," he explains.

"Doctor Yearwood has a good ring to it," I tell him.

"Don't make me blush," he smiles. "I'm sorry about the coffee mess."

"No, don't be sorry. I'm also to blame," I say, sitting beside him on the couch. He leans over and connects our lips, only this time, it's soft and gentle. "Something tells me that's a goodbye kiss," I say as we separate.

"I have a few work things to take care of before tomorrow. If you're up for it, I'd love to see you again."

"I just may make coffee trips before work a daily thing," I tell him.

"I'd like that," he says as he casually removes himself from the couch and walks to the front door to get his winter gear back on. I remain on the couch and watch him leave.

Chapter Twenty-One

EVERY MORNING FOR the last few weeks, I have entered the same coffee shop hoping to see Ledger. And every day for the last few weeks, he hasn't let me down. We talk about every little thing that's on our minds, including how our days are going at work, whether that be venting sessions or laughing at something ridiculous that happened. I must say, he has some pretty crazy doctor stories. But I try to compete with the wild stories of my students. I swear, I could write a book.

For some reason, Wednesdays are quieter than the other days of the week. Walking through the doors, I see two people sitting at a table to my right. To my left, I see the same lock screen of an open laptop, but no Ledger.

"Jamie," the barista calls out. Again, I know she means me since no one else is here waiting for coffee, and my name constantly confuses people. I sigh and roll my eyes as I walk up to the counter to grab my coffee.

"It's Jaemes," I hear Ledger tell the barista as he walks by. His correction doesn't faze her, but he sure fazes me. His lips form a slight grin, and he gestures to the seat across from him with his coffee. As always, he's dressed for work, but this time, he has glasses on. "Look who finally decided to show up," he says, taking his glasses off and setting them down next to his laptop.

"Sorry, I was running a little late this morning," I tell him as I sit at the table. "Are you still busy at work?" I ask, pointing to his laptop.

"Extremely. Some of the providers I work with thought it would be a great idea to all take their vacations at the same time. I'm covering for them while they're gone, and last week was also my time with Archie, so I wanted to spend all my free time with him. I don't get much of that when I'm caught up with my patients along with other providers' patients, who always seem extra needy."

"I bet. I understand how that can take up all of your time. I'm in love with the fact that you keep your son number one, though."

"Always." He smiles and takes a sip of his coffee.

I look at the time on my phone, and it's ten minutes past the time I should have left for work. I gather my belongings and coffee and get up to leave. "I need to run, but I'll see you tomorrow?"

"I'll be here."

I take off toward the door until he stops me and says, "Jaemes, you forgot something." I look around the table, not noticing what he is talking about. I hurry back so he can give me what I forgot. He stands up to meet me when I approach. It isn't an item he returns, but a long-overdue kiss.

"You make it difficult to leave you," I tell him.

"That's the point," he says back.

Knowing how late I am, I have no choice but to rush out without looking back. The way he always kisses me before I leave him tells me that this connection between us is genuine. The spark that binds us every time we are together shows how real this relationship can become. But then again, our reality and story have yet to validate whether this is fate. I'm still struggling with my promise to not get involved with anyone, but Ledger seems different as he's helped me get through the darkness from the last few months. I'm eager to know if Ledger will be my story's beginning or end.

Chapter Twenty-Two

I CAN ALWAYS tell when something horrible is going to happen. The night before Rian's plane crash, my body woke me up in a panic with no explanation at the time. Deep in my gut, I could feel that it would be the end of my relationship with Alder when I last saw him. I also had a feeling that the reason my biological father wasn't in my life wasn't a good one based on how I read my mom's face when I would bring him up throughout the years.

When we lived in Los Angeles, my mom gifted me a pet hamster for my ninth birthday. I loved him dearly, and we enjoyed a great friendship together. I had no siblings to grow up with, and all my friends were back in Las Vegas. My mom didn't want large animals around, so we settled on the hamster. One day, I felt like I needed to be with him every minute of the day. I didn't know why at the time. I would cry when I had to put him in his cage. Again, I didn't know why. He had everything every hamster dreamed of. Colorful tunnels, small slides, comfy straw, a sipper water bottle full of water, his favorite food, and a hamster wheel he would run on every night. The sound of the turning wheel helped put me to sleep most nights. It soothed me.

The following day, I found him dead in his cage. The reason I felt like I had to be with him constantly the day prior was because I knew something terrible was going to happen to him. I never understood why I could sense these things, why my body would warn me every time. It's comical how the bad events always seem to outweigh anything pleasant in life. We notice it more. We feel it more.

Just like now.

I have never had a random panic attack during the day hours. It has only awakened me from my slumber and not while I'm busy throughout my typical day. Yesterday, when I got home from work, I started feeling nervous and out of breath for no reason. I started vomiting and didn't think I would be able to calm my own body down. This went on for a good half hour. At the time, it felt like several hours. I know how to manage these attacks and how to soothe my body from what I've learned through my schooling and experiences through my job and internship. I drank a few sips of water, practiced deep breathing, brought myself to my bed to create a safe space, and named a few objects around the room. As I calmed down, I could hear my heart beating like crazy. Since I was already in bed, I did my best to drift off to sleep regardless of the time of day. I would much rather wake up early on a Saturday morning than feel like this all Friday afternoon.

I'm awakened at two thirty in the morning to my body now realizing why I experienced a panic attack just hours earlier. I'm drenched in sweat, and there is excruciating pain residing in my abdomen. I can hardly move with the pain, but I know I have to get help. I pick up my phone and dial 9-1-1. Then, my vision, along with my memory, becomes dark.

I'M NOT SHOCKED when I slowly wake up drowsy in a hospital bed wearing a hospital gown. The pain I was experiencing before has now turned into a dull sensation. My mom is in my assigned room with me. She is sitting on her phone, and the TV is on quietly in the background. Once she hears me shifting in my bed, she drops her phone and joins me at my bedside.

"How are you feeling?" she asks me.

"Nauseous," I tell her.

"The doctor said you might feel that way after waking up from the anesthesia. Here, take this just in case." She hands me a blue emesis basin. I take it and set it next to me. "Your appendix burst. The surgeon had to do an emergency appendectomy procedure."

I nod, acknowledging her. I'm glad someone called her so she could be here with me. She's the person I want to have next to me while going through something like this.

"The doctor will be in shortly to check in on you. He wanted you to get your rest. All you need to do is press this call button when you're ready," she explains while showing me the red button she is referring to. She holds my hand as I remain in the hospital bed, feeling uncomfortable from the nausea. After a few minutes, there is a knock on the door, and I see him enter the room. Why is he here? Who told him?

Once again, he is dressed in work attire, but with a stethoscope around his neck, as if he's on the clock. "Wow, there is never a time you *don't* look gorgeous," Ledger tells me entering my room.

"You know how to flatter a woman, don't you?" I drowsily say to him.

"Only the ones I care deeply about," he says as he walks closer to my bed. He sits on the edge of my bed and observes my vitals on the monitor.

"How did you know I was here?" I ask him.

"This week was my on-call week, remember? I normally make a few rounds during the weekend and before seeing patients during the week."

I should remember, but my memory is a little foggy at the moment.

"When the ambulance brought you in, I had the receptionist call your mom to let her know that you were here."

"Thank you," I tell him and grab his hand. He grabs mine back and gently rubs around the IV that is administered in my hand.

"Do you two know each other?" my mom asks.

We both look her way. I nod, and he explains more details to her since I don't have the energy to. "We met at a bar back in June. I believe it was Sassy Stacy's on your birthday?" he asks, turning to me. I nod again to confirm that he is correct. "Ever since then, we have been bumping into each other here and there. Now, we have coffee together just about every morning."

"I see," my mom starts. "Jaemes, I wish you would keep me more in the loop about your love life." She oddly seems disappointed.

"Mom, you act like I go through guys left and right." I look at Ledger. "Which I don't."

He laughs softly and says, "I know," before moving a strand of hair away from my face. "I have to go check on a few other patients. I want you to get more rest before you get discharged."

"Will you be back?" I squeeze his hand, letting him know that I hope he does.

"Of course, I will." He smiles. "Nice to meet you, ma'am," he says to my mom before heading to the door.

"It was a pleasure to meet you as well, doctor…" My mom trails off, not knowing his name.

"Yearwood. But you can call me Ledger," he tells her.

Suddenly, my mom's face turns ghostly white, and she looks like she might get sick.

"Ledger, can you get me something for my stomach, please? And maybe for my mom, too?" I say, glancing at her.

"Oh, no, I'm okay. I just haven't eaten anything yet today. I'll go to the cafeteria to grab something. I'll be fine," she says.

"Of course. I'll get the nurse on that right away," he tells me. "Are you sure you're okay, ma'am?" My mom nods and walks toward the door. "The elevator to the cafeteria is down the hall and to the left," he says to her as she walks past him. She replies with a smile and goes on her way.

Before Ledger exits my room, he flashes me a flirty smile and a sexy wink. He looks incredible in his work environment. How he manages to make me like him more after every encounter is beyond me. The way he treats me, regardless of the situation, makes me feel unbelievably special in every way possible.

After a few hours, Ember visits me in the hospital. I'm feeling much better than I was earlier. The nurse gave me anti-nausea medication, and after another nap, I feel close to one hundred percent, minus the feeling of my insides being tussled around. As the astounding best friend she is, Ember arrives with flowers and a get-well-soon balloon. Our schedules haven't lined up lately, so I'm glad this happened on her off time. Being surrounded by family and friends through a scary time like this is the greatest thing I could ask for.

"So, did *you* know about this new guy Jae is seeing? Or is it just me?" my mom asks Ember. Disappointed and probably with a bit of confusion mixed in, Ember looks at me.

"Ex-fucking-scuse me, bitch? You have a new man and didn't bother to tell me? Who is he? Do I know him?"

I roll my eyes at their absurdity. "Calm down, you two. There is no confirmation that we are a legitimate couple. It's just a casual friendship for right now. We will see where it takes us in time, but it's nothing to gush over for now."

"Mhm, sure," Ember replies. "I need to know details, but first, I need food."

Ember goes to the vending machine that's down the hall, and my mom accompanies her to get some coffee. In the meantime, I continue to rest before being bombarded with questions about my personal life. But that's what moms and best friends are for, I guess.

"It doesn't take a doctor to know that this isn't merely a friendship, Jaemes." I turn to Ledger as he stands in the doorway of my hospital room. "When I look at you, I can see it all over your face. The way you smile when you look into my eyes and gasp when I'm close to you. I wouldn't get an accurate reading of your heart rhythm because I'm certain your heartbeat is racing now that I'm back in your presence. I know this because I feel the same way about you."

I'm dead silent and speechless after knowing he could overhear our conversation about him, and that those words just came out of his mouth.

Awesome.

"Ledger?!" Ember gasps in shock, realizing he's the new man we were referring to, once she returns to the room with my mom.

"You know Ledger, too?" my mom asks her.

"Yeah, I met him at Sassy Stacy's the night of her birthday. I knew I saw a spark between the two of you. It's undeniable that there has always been a connection there. Like how you watched him walk away the night of Alder's birthday..." She stops talking abruptly, like she regrets bringing that part up.

What the fuck, Ember...

"I'm sorry, I didn't mean to say that. I was just trying to make my point," she says.

"And you did, Ember. Thank you. Please stop talking now...," I beg.

"I was thinking," my mom starts, doing her best to change the subject for my sake, "why don't you come home with me so I can take care of you during your recovery? I don't think you should be by yourself at home so soon after surgery. I would hate for something to happen again while you're alone."

"Thanks for the offer, Mom, but this was only a minor

procedure. I'll be fine," I reassure her.

After a while, my surgeon gives me the okay to go home and discharges me later in the afternoon. I change out of my hospital gown and grab my things to take with me. My mom is taking her car to the front hospital entrance, and Ember left about half an hour ago.

"Why don't I stay with you?" Ledger asks me as we wait for the nurse to wheel me out to my mom. "That way, you won't be alone. I can keep an eye on your recovery and make sure you get what you need. Nothing will happen to you while your care is in my hands."

"I'd like that. Thank you," I blush.

"I'll stop over after my rounds, okay?"

I try to grasp how lucky I am to finally have a man in my life who is willing to do anything for me. A man who puts me first to ensure I'm cared for and makes me feel appreciated and worthy. I'm starting to wonder if this is too good to be true or if I truly deserve this. Only time will tell.

Chapter Twenty-Three

IT'S ALMOST FIVE o'clock in the afternoon, which means Ledger will be back at my house any minute now. I have been off from work for the past week to ensure I fully recover before working with kids again. Ledger has been by my side at every point possible, and I'm incredibly thankful for him and everything he has done for me. I get excited to see him and miss him when he's at work. This health scare and recovery have strengthened our relationship even more, and I feel like I can't get enough of him.

I'm comfortably on the couch, wearing my favorite over-sized t-shirt and short cotton shorts, when he walks through the front door. It's impossible to hide my smile when I see him. It's embarrassing to admit how happy he makes me when doing the little things. He takes his coat and shoes off and sets his laptop case on the floor before leaning over and meeting my lips with his.

"How are you feeling?" he asks me. It's the first thing he asks when I wake up and when he returns to me at the end of his day. It's mindboggling how much he cares for me, and I'm enjoying it. I could easily get used to this feeling.

"I'm good as always when I get to see you. I'm glad I took this week off from work. I feel ready to go back on Monday," I tell him. He smiles at me and then kisses me again.

"I have to pick up Archie from his mom's place soon. It's my week to be with him," he says.

"I understand. I appreciate you taking care of me when

you didn't have to."

"Always," he says, rubbing my cheek with the back of his hand. He had brought a few things from home, like his bathroom items and clothes. He packs up his belongings and sets them by the door next to his laptop case. I didn't think I'd be so sad to see him leave.

"Archie has a friend's birthday party next Friday. I'm supposed to take him there, and then his mom will pick him up afterward for her week with him. I was wondering..." He trails off and looks around as if trying to gain the confidence to say what he wants to say next. He takes my legs and places them on his lap. He takes a deep breath and then continues. "I was wondering if you'd like to join me. Well, join *us*."

"Are you saying you want me to meet your son?" I ask.

"If you want to. I don't want to push things too far or too fast. I completely understand if you don't want to yet," he reassures me.

"Ledger, I would love to meet Archie...." I smile at him mainly because I can never control my facial muscles while in his presence. It feels comforting that he wants to take another step forward in this relationship. He sees something in me and us as a couple. It's heartwarming knowing that I mean that much to him. Enough to meet his son. "But I think it may be too soon."

"I respect that, Jaemes. I appreciate your honesty. I'm sorry, sometimes I get a little too ahead of myself."

"Don't be. Doesn't mean I like you any less."

He tosses my legs off of him and hovers over me, which makes me giggle. He silences me with his lips, and I tighten my arms around him. As content and relaxed as I am with him, I'm a little hesitant about meeting his son. He is the one person who means more to him than anything. It's worrisome to think Archie might not care for me since I'm not his mom. What will he think about his dad being with another woman? From the sounds of it, all Archie is familiar with is his parents being together and his parents separately. I wonder if Gretchen has introduced Archie to any new men in her life. I gather my thoughts and worries and set them aside for now. I want to cherish this moment with Ledger before he leaves. It's crazy to think about how close we have gotten in such a rapid timeframe. It feels as if I've known him for years, ever since I first laid eyes on him. When he took the initiative to give me his phone number at the party downtown, I never thought it would lead to us becoming a couple. It's turning into the perfect relationship that I didn't know my heart was searching for.

I expect him to stop kissing me, but a part of me won't let him. The more appropriate action for me to take right now is to let him leave to be with his son. Another part of me is being selfish and won't let go of him. He isn't letting go of me either, so I take full advantage of this opportunity and keep my lips locked with his.

"Are you sure you're feeling alright?" he asks without separating his lips from mine. I nod against him, and we continue. His hand trails down my body and grips my waist. I lift myself off the couch so we are both sitting upright. I'm kneeling, so I am slightly higher than he is. Our lips never release from each other. He wraps both of his arms around my hips and is now grasping both sides of my ass.

"Are you sure?" he asks me again.

"Yes," I answer him, slightly breathless. He takes that as a go-ahead and gracefully whips my shirt over my head. The butterflies in my stomach intensify, and my level of nervousness starts to rise. Ledger is now the man I want to impress the most, and I'm terrified of failing him.

It doesn't take long until he whisks me to the bedroom and lays me on my bed. He watches the movements of my chest as I continue to breathe hard. He slips his shirt off and then joins me. Lying on his side, he holds his head up with his hand, looking down at me while I remain on my back, looking up at his blue eyes. Breaking eye contact, his eyes travel down to my chest and stomach. His fingers carefully graze around my surgery stitches and continue downward. He places one finger underneath the hem of my shorts—then two, and then three. Soon his whole hand disappears underneath, but then he pulls it back out again.

He shoots me a teasing smile and whispers, "It's too soon."

Touché.

As disappointed as I may be right now, it still doesn't make me like him any less.

"I want you to heal more before we do anything too rough." He goes to retrieve our shirts and tells me goodbye with another passionate kiss, followed by a few playful pecks on my cheek.

"Alright, get out of here," I laugh.

I watch him grab all of his stuff and place it in his old, red truck. After he starts it up, I leave the window and bring up my show on Netflix. I lie back down on the couch and listen to him back out of the driveway and drive down the road until I can no longer hear him.

I'm unsure if his reasoning for stopping is mainly because I still need to recover from my surgery entirely or if he honestly thinks it's too early to take our intimacy to the next level. I mean, I did tell him it's too soon to meet his son.

Did that secretly alter his feelings?

Chapter Twenty-Four

MY MOM AND I turn Valentine's Day into a Galentine's Day evening. We order pizza for supper at her house from a local pizzeria. Every Valentine's Day, they shape their pizzas and cheese bread into heart shapes. Their pasta and wing containers are shaped like hearts, and they cut their sandwiches in half, placing them in a heart formation as well. We go for the classic half-and-half pizza. My mom gets pepperoni and pineapple on her half, which I hate, and I get Canadian bacon and extra mushrooms on my half, which she can't stand.

"How are you and Ledger?" my mom asks, turning on a movie for us to watch while we enjoy our pizza.

"Fine, I guess. Why do you ask?"

"I'm just wondering why you are spending this romantic holiday with your mom and not him."

"He has his son right now, so he's spending it with him, as he should be. There's no rule that you have to be with someone romantically on Valentine's Day. That's why there's a *Galentine's* Day."

"Oh, he has a son? I didn't know that." She presses play on the movie and sits down next to me, grabbing her pizza along the way.

"Besides, Ember is with Bennett, and I wouldn't want to be the third wheel on their date."

My mom laughs. "Oh, come on. You mean you wouldn't want Bennett to be the third wheel on yours and Ember's Galentine's Day date?"

I chuckle at that, nearly choking on the big bite of pizza I have in my mouth.

"You're exactly right," I say in between coughs.

We are about halfway through our movie when my phone vibrates on the coffee table.

Ledger: *Would you mind if I stopped over to see you before bringing Archie to his party tomorrow? I'm getting out of work early and should have some time before I need to pick up Archie from his after-school activities.*

Me: *I never mind if you come over, Ledger. You're welcome any time. There isn't a time that I don't want to see you.*

"Awe, that's sweet," my mom says, startling me away from my text conversation.

"Mom, privacy, please."

The doorbell suddenly dings out of nowhere, causing us both to jump. She pauses the movie and gets up to see who could possibly be at her house at this time. Neither of us was expecting anyone. I listen carefully to see who it is.

"Uh, Jaemes? You might want to come see this," she says, cautioning me.

Utterly confused and a little concerned, I get up to join her at the door. Not who, but *what* causes me to gasp, losing all the air in my lungs. Sitting before me is an unnervingly familiar bouquet of what looks to be two dozen roses along with a note that reads the lyrics of my favorite song and signed with just the letter "A".

What the fuck...

IT'S FIVE-THIRTY P.M. the next day, and I'm still awaiting Ledger's arrival. I was expecting him hours ago. He isn't responding to any of my texts, so I'm assuming he became busy at work and ended up working a full day.

I'm just about to text Ember to see if she wants to go somewhere for a few drinks when suddenly, there is a knock on the door.

Ledger?

"Come in!" I call out toward the door.

"I would, but my arms are a little full," he says behind the front door.

Once I open the door, I immediately notice the reason why he couldn't open the door for himself. He is holding Archie. The look on his face is apologetic.

"I'm really sorry, but I didn't have a choice," he explains.

I sigh in frustration, but I know I can't completely show or express my true feelings right now. I open the door wider so he can walk through, and then I close the door behind him. What else am I supposed to do? Shut the door in his face and send him away?

No, I would never.

"Don't be rude, buddy. Say hi," Ledger tells the shy little boy who is resting his head on his dad's shoulder.

"Hi," Archie says quietly.

"Hi, Archie," I say, still taken aback that he brought his son to my house.

"I'm sorry, he had a little bit of an off day today, so I picked him up right after school. I didn't think it would have been a good idea for him to participate in any activities," Ledger explains further and then sets Archie down to stand on his own.

"We all have those days," I reply. "What about the birthday party?"

"We'll see how he does leading up to that," he says, looking down at Archie and softly patting the top of his head.

Archie clings to his dad's leg. I kneel to his level so that I am no taller than he is.

"Hey, you," I begin in a kind and soft voice. "My name is Jaemes. You must be the famous Archie I have been hearing so much about. Can I ask you what your favorite thing to do is?" I have no choice but to accept that I'm officially meeting Ledger's son, so I should probably start by trying to make a good impression on him.

"Legos," Archie says to me softly.

I'll take it. I wasn't anticipating an answer in the first place.

"Well, thank goodness I have some leftover Legos from work that you can play with. I've wanted someone to build me something cool for *so* long," I tell him.

Archie smiles at me and starts to let go of Ledger's leg. I reach out for his hand, and he readily takes it. I lead him to my closet and dig out a bin full of Legos for him to play with. He takes it to the living room rug and dumps everything out of the bin. As Ledger and I watch him start to build his masterpiece, Ledger takes my hand and leads me to the kitchen, away from Archie.

"Let me explain myself, please," he starts. "I'm sorry."

"A little heads up would have been great, but instead, all I got was radio silence. I thought I said I wasn't ready to meet him yet," I remind him.

"I know, I know. I wanted to see you, but I also had to be there for Archie. I'm still trying to navigate fatherhood and a relationship together for the first time. Maybe I'm being selfish. I should have told you, but I didn't, and I'm deeply sorry."

I'm standing before him, quiet, with my arms crossed. Of course, I believe him, but I feel like I can't forgive him just yet. He broke a boundary and never considered how I felt about the subject.

He gently grasps each side of my head, with his palms on my cheeks and his fingers tangled in my hair. "I promise I'm not trying to do anything to scare you off. Because I feel like

I'm already falling for you," he admits.

Before his words can even register in my head, Archie calls out, "Hey, Jaemes! Come look at what I built!" from the living room. Ledger lets go of me, and I head toward the living room. Ledger stops me with his hand, forcing me to turn back and face him again.

"Wait a minute. Did he just call for *you* and not his dad?" Ledger asks me with a shocked expression written on his face. "That says a lot coming from a shy boy like Archie. I'm impressed."

"What can I say? I have a way with kids." I join Archie to examine his masterpiece. I look back at Ledger, who is still in the kitchen watching me interact with his son. We exchange smiles, and then I return my attention to Archie as he rambles about his Lego creation.

"Hey, bud, we have to get going. You don't want to be late to the party," Ledger tells Archie as he walks closer to us. "Why don't you clean up the Legos for Jaemes, and then we can head out?"

"I can still go to the birthday party?" Archie asks with great enthusiasm.

"You've been good since I picked you up. As long as you promise to be good in school from now on, I'll let you go."

"Yes!" he cheers, then starts destroying his Lego creation into small pieces and placing them in the bin. He's so fast, I can hardly help him. "Is Jaemes coming with us? Can she? Please? With like, eight hundred thousand million trillion cherries on top?"

I turn to Ledger just as he turns to me.

Now what do I do?

Chapter Twenty-Five

"ARE YOU EXCITED for the birthday party?" I ask Archie, who is sitting in the back seat of Ledger's 1970's classic Ford pickup truck. I would imagine we are almost at the party, since we have been on the road for a while now.

"Yeah!" he cheers, playing with his little race cars.

"Is everyone in your class going to be there?" Ledger asks him.

"I think so," Archie replies.

"He is absolutely adorable," I tell Ledger.

He looks over at me and places his hand on the after market central console of his truck. His palm is facing upwards, and he gestures with his two fingers for my hand. I lay my hand in his, and he holds it with a firm grip. I love the feeling of his hand holding mine, but I'm still uneasy about the sudden meet and greet he laid on me.

"I'm sorry, I totally forgot to thank you for the roses," I tell him, hoping the letter "A" at the end doesn't mean what I think it does.

"What roses?" he asks, genuinely confused.

"You didn't send me a bouquet of roses to my mom's house on Valentine's Day?"

He shakes his head no and chuckles. "It sounds like you have a secret admirer."

I was very afraid of this.

"Are we there yet, Dad?" Archie asks.

"Just down the road, bud," Ledger tells him.

When we approach the property where the party is, I can't help but notice the spectacular house the birthday kid lives in. Whoever these people are must have some money. The home sits two stories from the ground and shows off different tones of gray in the bricks that spread across the entire front side. The rest of the house is covered in a darker shade of harbor blue siding. There are cars lined up everywhere.

All of this for a six-year-old? I'm eager to see more of the party. If the outside of the house looks this nice, I can't imagine what the inside looks like. As we walk down the road, I feel a hand cling to mine, but it's not Ledger's because he is walking behind me. Looking down, I see Archie holding my hand as we walk. In his other hand, he swings the birthday gift he brought. I look behind me at Ledger as he watches Archie and me continue our special interaction. He half smiles while nonchalantly moving his head slightly from side to side. He seems to be in awe of how quickly Archie and I have formed a bond. This little boy seems to melt my heart more and more as the afternoon goes on.

We can instantly hear the laughter and shouting from both kids and adults inside the house as we get closer to the front door. A lady opens the door after we ring the doorbell, and I find her to look semi-familiar, but I can't figure out how I know her. I let that thought go as soon as Archie runs inside.

"Archie, the party is downstairs, honey!" she informs him. "Welcome," she says to us with a friendly smile. "I take it you're Archie's parents?" she asks.

"No," I answer without hesitation. "Ledger is Archie's dad, and I'm just a friend tagging along."

"Nice to meet you, Ledger," she says to him as they shake hands. "I'm Saydee, the birthday girl's mom. If you want to stay for a little while, you're more than welcome to. Some parents drop off and leave, and others stay. Feel free to do whatever you'd like."

She steps aside to let us enter the house. The entryway is big and open. The main floor is even more open, featuring a modern kitchen on the left and a living room to the right, with no walls separating the two.

"The bouncy houses are downstairs for the kids, and we have adult beverages in the fridge if you'd like to stay for one or two. Let me know if you need anything," Saydee tells us before heading downstairs. The more I walk forward and to the right, the more decorations I see. A banner on the right wall, above the fireplace, reads, "Happy Birthday, Annie!"

I look out at the backyard. Due to the time of year, an out-of-commission pool sits outside the bay window. "Jaemes," Ledger says from the kitchen. "You want one?" he asks, holding up a can of beer.

"Sure," I say back to him. Based on the number of vehicles outside, I assume their entire family, friends, and other parents are here.

I hear people walking up the stairs from the level below. When I look over, I do a double-take when my eye catches someone I didn't ever expect to be here, talking with Saydee. I quickly turn back around to look out the window again.

No, it can't be.

My stomach is in a bundle of knots, and I start to shake with nervous tension. I know why Saydee looks familiar. And the birthday girl's name on the banner is short for her actual name.

Anniston.

It all makes sense now.

Saydee is Anniston's mom.

Saydee is his cousin.

Anniston is his second cousin.

I turned back to look at him again, and only this time, he has spotted me too. My entire body goes numb, and I become lightheaded. The background noise fades away, and I can only hear my amplified heartbeat. A flood of past emotions re-enters my brain, and I can't seem to look away from him.

Does he recognize me? *That's absurd; of course, he does.*

How can I know for sure? *Uh, I don't know, maybe because you were in a serious relationship with the man not even a year ago?*

What do I do? *Nothing. Just feel it out and don't be weird about it. Obviously.*

More back-and-forth conversations within myself. I can't say they're ever the most helpful. *Hey, thanks a lot.*

He starts moving away from Saydee as she continues to talk his ear off—his slow movements away from her turn into walking strides toward me.

Suddenly, I am startled by Ledger when he approaches from the other side of me and hands over my beer. I take it with a trembling hand. "Are you okay?" he asks me. "I didn't mean to scare you."

"No, um, I'm fine." I take a swig of my beer. "Thank you." I look back again, but Alder isn't there anymore. Where did he go?

From downstairs, I faintly hear a little girl shout, "Get my gruncle!" The same girl I met the evening of July Fourth.

Gruncle. That goofy older man is his Uncle Dave.

I remember him telling me about that guy. *Great Uncle. Since she was born, my uncle Dave has referred to himself as 'Gruncle.' Now, that's all she ever calls him. He's the nicest and goofiest guy you'll ever meet.*

His parents are probably here, too. His whole family is probably here. *I* can't be here. This is all too much. I'm starting to feel extremely hot, and I wipe sweat off my forehead. My nervous breathing increases.

"Jaemes, are you okay? Is something wrong?" Ledger asks. I'm trying not to make it evident that something *is*, in fact, incredibly wrong. The last thing I want to do is ruin any part of this party. I need to leave this house before anyone else starts to put two and two together and recognizes me. I chug my beer as fast as I can.

"Do you think we could leave soon? I'm starting not to feel so great," I tell Ledger, wiping more sweat off my face.

"You do look pale," Ledger tells me.

"I'm going to use the bathroom while you finish your beer." I head to the bathroom near the kitchen and the house entrance. I throw my empty beer can in the bathroom garbage bin and then lock the door. There is a window facing the front yard. I open it for fresh air and then turn the cold water on. I soak a washcloth in water and dab my face and neck to cool off. Luckily, I have a hair tie on my wrist. I use that to throw my long, bronze hair up into a high ponytail. After five minutes of trying to recoup myself, I bravely open the bathroom door and return to the party. It looks like the party is officially starting since many people who were previously downstairs with the kids are now on the main floor of the house.

I see Ledger near the front door waiting for me.

"Hey, let me say bye to Archie and remind him that his mom will be here to pick him up," he says.

"Okay," I acknowledge him and sit on the bench next to the front door.

"Jaemes!" I hear Archie call out from the other side of the house. I anxiously look up as he runs toward me. I begin to walk his way, hoping he won't yell my name again. I can't have any attention on me. We meet in the middle of the crowd, and I kneel at his level again. He hugs me and tells me he wishes I didn't have to leave. I hug him right back, feeling the special connection between me and the little boy who belongs to the man I care a great deal for.

"Don't worry. I'll tell your dad that we can hang out any time you want," I say to Archie before he smiles at me and runs off to the group of kids sitting near a heaping pile of birthday gifts. I immediately meet Ledger's gaze since he was standing behind Archie during our farewell hug. He grabs my hand, and we walk toward the front door to leave. Ledger leads the way as we shift through the crowd of people. I glance over to the kitchen and see him watching me. Saydee is standing near him, still chatting his ear off, all while his focus remains on me.

Fuck. Fuck. Fuck. Hurry.

It seems like it's taking forever to get to the front door. Once we exit the house and close the door behind us, I instantly feel a sense of relief and can finally breathe again. "That's much better," I say to myself quietly, and we take our time walking to Ledger's truck.

"Your color is coming back. You must be feeling better?" Ledger asks me as he climbs into the driver's side. I nod. "He was there, wasn't he?"

I feel my eyes widen, unsure of what to say back. Was it that obvious, or does Ledger pay great attention to detail? I guess it's true that I can be read so easily. My quietness and lack of words give away the answer to his question.

"Want to talk about it?" he asks. I look down and shake my head. The last thing I want to do is talk about my past and the feelings related to it with Ledger, the only one I've been wanting to focus all my time and energy on. "Jaemes, I'm seriously so fucking sorry about earlier. I should have told you I had to bring Archie along with me. The reality is that I have never been with someone who makes me feel the way I feel about you. I feel more strongly for you than I ever did with Gretchen. You overwhelm me in the most fantastic way, and I just knew that Archie would like you as much as I do." I close my eyes and let his words sink in.

I grab his hand to let him know he has nothing to worry about. "Archie is a wonderful little boy, Ledger. And you are a great dad. You *should* always put your son first. As long as we don't throw our whole relationship at him all at once, I think we should be okay. But we need to communicate better next time. Please."

He squeezes my hand and smiles at me. "Absolutely."

I smile back, and we continue to drive to wherever we are going. At this point, I don't care where we are headed. As long as I'm with him, I will be okay.

MOMENTS LATER, WE pull into a driveway. It's a long driveway surrounded by a large patch of tall trees. The white snow on the bare branches sparkle when the sun strikes them. I continuously look at my phone, wondering if he will text me. Why should I care? The chapter of my life that he was a part of has come to an end. There shouldn't be any hope or wish for him to return. He doesn't compare to the man I want to be with now. A successful doctor, a great dad, a wonderful person, and most importantly, a man who wants nothing more than to be with me. Someone who cares so deeply for me. Someone I could spend the rest of my life with. But how can someone possibly tell this early in a relationship? Maybe it was love at first sight with Ledger and me, but I didn't know that then because my love for someone else was blinding me. Everything happens for a reason. My past relationships have led me down a path to lasting happiness.

"Since I have been to your house many times, I thought we could spend some time at my place since Archie won't be home. I hope that's okay with you." Ledger parks his truck at the center of his horseshoe driveway.

"This is your place? *This* house is all yours?" I ask. It's magnificent. No wonder Ledger didn't seem as impressed with the birthday house as I was. I leave the truck to admire the beauty and elegance of a house like this. It's comparable to a mansion-like cottage in the middle of the woods straight out of a fairytale. The different tones of brown in the bricks that make up this castle-like home are dazzling. Certain parts of the house have peaks like a subtle palace in disguise. When I look at this house, I see a prince and princess living here.

"The landscaping is incredible without all the snow, trust me. In the summer and even parts of the fall months, it feels like I'm living in a full-blown fairy garden," he tells me, rounding the corner of his truck. He takes my hand and guides me along the stone path that leads to the French-style front door. Looking around the house, I analyze the main floor's layout. The living room takes up the entire right side of the house, and the kitchen is immediately to the left with a dining room behind it. A large staircase in the middle of the house leads to the second floor, where the bedrooms must be, and an indoor balcony overlooking the entire main floor.

"Ledger, this…this is breathtaking," I tell him while looking around in amazement.

"I want you to feel comfortable here. Just like how I feel while in your home. I want this, Jaemes." He sits down on the loveseat located near the entryway and front window. He pulls me over so that I am standing between his legs and looking down at him. His arms wrap around the back of my thighs, pulling me closer and eventually down onto his lap. I sit on half of his lap while my legs remain between his. He leans closer to my face, and when his lips gently touch my ear, he whispers, "I want you," which causes a slight breeze in my ear and those chills to resurface on my skin. "All of you," he adds.

I don't waste any more time and lunge myself at him. Our mouths are vicious and eager to finish what we started at my house previously. There is no way I am letting him stop this time. Although I don't think he could stop himself even if he wanted to.

Until he does.

"Wait, wait, wait," he says, pulling away from me slightly. I think to myself, *no, not again....* I lift myself back up in a seated position next to him. He better not be teasing me again.

"What's wrong?" I ask, annoyed that I'm not getting the chance to show him how much I like him physically. In certain moments, it's easier to show someone you're falling for them rather than vocalizing it.

"Let me show you around first."

"Really? You want to give me a tour of your home? Right now?" There is disappointment lingering in my tone of voice. A little more than I want to admit. He stands up from the loveseat and holds out his hand. I take it and follow him to the staircase that leads up to the second level of the house.

He looks back at me with a smirk. "Don't worry, you'll like where we're starting."

I'm still trailing slightly behind him once we reach the top of the stairs. With my hand still connected with his, we take a left turn down the open balcony. The windows on the front of the house go up to the ceiling. From this level, I can see the treetops.

We enter a room on the right. It's bright from the floor-to-ceiling windows that line the exterior walls. The bright white walls glow from the snow, shimmering in the sun outside. There isn't much in here for a room this large. A bed with two nightstands on each side, a dresser, a walk-in closet, and a bathroom to the left.

"This is my room. It's one of the most open rooms in the house," he says, pacing around the room. I walk to the bathroom so I can picture Ledger going through his daily routine. The bathroom is just as big and white as his room. Walking through the doorway, I see a two-sink vanity to my right and a mirror the same size as the vanity. The shower is adjacent to the left, and a closet follows behind it. Everything looks so clean and organized. You wouldn't think a single man, who is also a father to a six-year-old boy, would have a home this tidy. I give him props for keeping everything so well put together. Ledger joins me in the bathroom.

"What's through that door?" I ask, gesturing to the door opposite his bedroom. Another bedroom, maybe? It's sort of what it looks like. Two bedrooms connected to the same bathroom. "Is it Archie's room?"

He looks toward the door and stares at it for a moment before answering me.

"That…is the room I've wanted to show you." His arm reaches out, and his hand slowly grips the door handle. The door swings open, and I am in amazement. This is undoubtedly not Archie's room. This isn't just any *room*. All of the walls are glass. To my right, left, and straight ahead, there is nothing but trees and the nature surrounding them, not to mention the glass ceiling that connects all these walls. "One hundred percent privacy with the tree line," he says as I continue to be impressed. It's unlike anything I have ever seen before.

"Is that a hot tub?" I ask, pointing to the other side of the room.

He grins and turns it on. "I was thinking…maybe we could try it out?"

"You know, I would, but I don't have a bathing suit," I respond. He chuckles at my response and walks over to me. His hand goes under my shirt and rests on my bare skin, which causes me to flinch. His gaze stares down at my chest while my eyes remain locked on his face. I feel his hand rub up my side while the other hand meets the other side of me. The more his hands trail upward, the more my top starts to lift.

"One hundred percent privacy," he repeats quietly. "We don't need bathing suits." I inhale the sophisticated cologne that's on his neck. His hands are just under my arms, next to my breasts. My stomach is completely exposed, and I lift my arms over my head as he takes my top completely off. I don't waste any time reaching behind my back and unclipping my bra. After my bra slides off my arms, I instantly wrap them around Ledger's neck, drawing his body even closer to mine, and our lips meet. I feel his hands undo his pants, and he shimmies them off one leg at a time without separating from me.

Impressive.

He pushes his hips against me, making me feel what I am doing to him. I mimic his pants removal strategy, and after several seconds of struggling, he quickly separates from my mouth and viciously whips them down to the floor. I gladly step out of them and rejoin him. In one swift movement, he picks me up and sets me on the edge of the hot tub. Our breaths are heavy now that our lips are no longer touching. He rests his forehead on mine.

"What do you like?" he whispers.

"I like it wet," I tease, then immediately pull him into the water with me as I fall backward into the hot tub. Luckily, the water isn't yet at the set temperature. It feels incredibly comforting to be able to fully submerge yourself without feeling the sting of cold water or the burn of hot water.

It's perfect.

We laugh once our heads are above water and our faces are free of water drops. Ledger stands up and cups underneath each side of my ass and pulls me onto his lap as he sits on one of the seats in the water. For a brief moment, all we do is stare into the colors of each other's eyes. I slick back his wet blond hair, and he brushes away a few random drops of water that slide down my cheeks. "You are out of this world, beautiful," he whispers. He glances down at my chest as my exposed breasts play peek-a-boo with the water. His arm reaches over to a knob on the hot tub, and the jets power on.

I scoot up closer on his lap, closing all gaps between us. When I lower, I make sure to lower *on* him. "Take your shirt off, Dr. Yearwood," I whisper. He groans with a sexy smirk on his face and then quickly removes his soaked shirt. He suddenly stands up while I am still wrapped around him. I study his defined pecs and shoulder muscles and trace around them with my finger. He lifts my chin so that my gaze finds his. He sets me down on the opposite side of the hot tub and then stands back up, looking down at me. His bulge is more prominent in his sopping-wet boxers, and right now, I want nothing more than to rip him free of them.

My thong and his boxers are the only items in the way of going further. "I'll take mine off if you take yours off," he states. I sink myself into the water and then back up again, showing that I am ready for him by revealing my thong, which is now wrapped around my finger. He quickly snatches it from me and flings it across the room.

Slowly, inch by inch, he slithers his boxers downward and keeps his eyes on my face. I'm not sure what it is about guys and getting off on the reactions they get when women see how big their erections are. I suppose it would be a significant turn-off to men if women didn't have much of a reaction or none at all. However, it's not as if they have to work that hard for it.

When he finally displays what will soon be inside me, I can't help but give him that inviting look. He discards his boxers entirely, and now we are two people begging for each other with only silence.

"Come here," he tells me before lowering back down on the other side of the hot tub where we were initially. When I reach him, I suddenly become nervous. We haven't gone this far yet. I've had experience with everything leading up to this point with Ledger before, but now that it's *the* moment we show each other our feelings through sex, I all of a sudden don't know what to do. What if I don't live up to his expectations? I've been flirty and horny for him all this time, so he might expect some dirty, kinky shit that I'm not used to. I start slowly with my movements, being slightly reserved. I place myself back onto his lap, but by his knees, as far away as possible.

"Hey, don't be shy, baby," he says quietly, drawing me closer. "We can take it slow." Our kiss is calm, so I can relax and enjoy being in the moment with him. We have both been waiting for this, and I want it to be outstanding.

I have to get into the mindset—*no, no mindset.*

I must turn my brain off and let my heart do all the work. I sit up and scoot forward until I feel the top of him between my legs. And then I sit back down, causing us both to gasp in pleasure. Now that Ledger is entirely a part of me, I adjust my legs so I can continue to satisfy our urges. It's different in water, but the warmth and the jets add to my arousal.

I pick up speed on him, causing waves to crash over the side of the hot tub. Ledger moans, and his head tilts back. My heavy breathing increases as I watch him enjoy this. When I slow down, Ledger wraps his arms around my waist and places his hands on my back. His mouth meets my breast while I tangle my fingers in his hair. I whimper next to his ear so he can hear what he is doing to me. Before I realize it, he has us both hopping out of the water and is guiding me to his bedroom. He lays me down on his bed with water dripping everywhere. In the drawer of his nightstand, he fishes out a condom and applies it. As he gets back on top of me, he smiles at the sight of my shivering goosebumps and flings the comforter over us to clear them away.

"That's better," I tell him. He inserts himself back inside me, thrusting hard and then pausing before repeating. He does this a few times until I beg for more. "Faster," I command breathlessly. He smirks and shakes his head. He stops but remains inside of me. He takes both of my arms and places them straight above my head. With one hand, he pins my wrists together on top of the pillow and then continues thrusting in me a little faster. The sensation of him pinning me down turns on another side of me.

"Oh my God, Ledger," I cry out.

At this point, I'm about to climax, but I don't tell him. He releases his hold on me, which gives me the freedom to flip him onto his back so I can climb on top of him. Trying to get us both to the finish line, I bounce hard and fast on him until I lose control and fall forward. One of my hands accidentally lands on his neck while the other hand catches my fall on the pillow next to him.

"Sorry!" I tell him, removing my hand.

"No, put it back," he says. "I like that."

Unnaturally, I place my hand back on his neck. His fetish of pinning and getting pinned creates a new desire within me. I put more pressure on the sides of his neck with my fingers and thumb so I don't cut off his breathing. He's going to need air with this kind of physical activity.

The more tension I put on his neck, the faster he thrusts into me, and the harder I try to match his speed. I scream his name as I reach the destination my body is striving toward. Once I stop trembling, he seems to want to keep going. I get off of him and stay on my knees. He places himself behind me, also on his knees. He wraps his arms under mine and grabs both of my breasts. I bring my arm up and place it around his neck as he kisses mine. I can feel him poking me from behind, and I arch my back. Once he stops kissing me, he holds me by my hips and tilts me down with one hand, causing me to rest on my forearms with my ass in the air toward him. He reinserts himself in me while grabbing both sides of my hips. It doesn't take long until he finishes with, "*Oh, fuck,*" and then tightens his grip on me. I turn over onto my back, and he lies next to me. We both remain on the bed and attempt to slow our breathing to a normal state.

Ledger rolls onto his right side, facing me. I look up at

him, and he kisses me one more time. And then another. We don't exchange any words because we don't have to. My smile and the way Ledger looks at me says it all.

I don't think I'm falling in love with him anymore. I'm afraid that I am completely in love with this man.

Chapter Twenty-Six

I WOKE UP in Ledger's bed the following day feeling mentally refreshed. Overnight, everything became dry, except the trail of puddles on the floor. Smelling like sweat and chlorine, we ended up showering together. We haven't been able to keep our hands off each other since last night, and I am okay with that.

When we finally get out of the shower, I check my phone on one of the nightstands and see that Ember texted me a few minutes ago.

> **Ember:** *Hey, can you meet me later today? I have something to talk to you about!*

I secretly want to tell her that I am busy today. I contemplate telling her that, but I haven't seen her in a while, and it might be a good idea to take a break from the sex sessions.

> **Me:** *Sure! When and where?*
>
> **Ember:** *I'll be at Sassy Stacy's with a few coworkers at 5:00 pm.*

Ledger meets me in his bedroom with only a towel wrapped around himself. He stands behind me, wraps his arms around my waist, and gently kisses my neck. He makes my stomach flutter and my heart so happy. I now know what it's like to be on cloud nine.

"Can I make you something to eat?" he asks between

kisses.

I set my phone back on his nightstand and face him so he can lay his lips on mine. "I'd love that," I reply. "I'm going to go grab my clothes from the glass room. I'm freezing."

Ledger heads to his dresser and puts on a pair of boxers, socks, and jeans. He then makes his way to the closet for a shirt. When I get to the glass room, I'm forced to step over the puddles of hot tub water we created last night to get to my clothes.

"I'll meet you downstairs, Jaemes," Ledger calls out from the bedroom. "I'm going to start breakfast."

"Okay, I'll be right down."

I locate my shirt, pants, bra, and thong and put everything on except the thong because it is still drenched in chlorine water.

I go back into the bedroom to grab my phone off the nightstand. I notice that the drawer is still cracked open from Ledger retrieving a condom last night. I go to shut it, but as I do, I see a few envelopes inside that catch my attention. I know it's none of my business, but I'm curious why the return addresses are from a prison. I open the drawer a little more to grab one.

"What are you doing?" Ledger asks from the bedroom doorway, scaring the shit out of me.

"Um…nothing. I was just grabbing my phone and noticed this drawer wasn't shut all the way, so I was going to close it."

He smiles at me. "Well, thank you. I checked to see what I had for breakfast. I have everything for pancakes if you're okay with that?"

I nod and walk his way. My mind is racing with wonder after witnessing those prison letters. Does he have a family member in there? A secret lover? Was *he* in prison? No, that can't be. He's a family doctor and a father with fifty-fifty custody of his son. He wouldn't have the job or that kind of custody agreement if that were the case. I want to ask him about it, but it shouldn't be my concern. I'm sure he will tell me about them eventually. He has to.

Once we're downstairs, I see a few photos on an etagere nearby. I stop and glance at them while Ledger gets breakfast started. They are mostly of him and Archie—one is of Archie in his baseball uniform and Ledger as his coach. There is a photo of them hunting together. And another photo of them together at Archie's school. Looking at these photos, I envision myself in them as well. As possibly another mother figure in his life, like a stepmom. My heart grows heavy when I picture us three as a family. It makes me think of my mom, Rian, and myself. There are so many similarities between my family and Ledger's. Everything happens for a reason, and I believe God sent me Ledger and Archie. I want to be the Rian to this family someday. Tears pool in my eyes at the thought of that. I can hear Ledger dishing up food on plates, so I quickly dry my eyes and join him at the table.

"I'm meeting Ember this evening. I guess she has something to tell me," I mention to Ledger after taking a bite of my pancakes. He's also made a side of scrambled eggs and bacon. I have to take a minute to appreciate my surroundings. Tasty food is placed in front of me, coffee is next to it, and an incredible man is to my right. These last fifteen hours have been purely amazing, and I love where I'm currently at in life. I don't remember ever being this happy. "Do you want to join?"

He shakes his head and waits to give a verbal answer until he's finished swallowing his bite of eggs. "I don't want to impose. I'll let you spend some time with your friends."

"You wouldn't be imposing, Ledger. Besides, it might be nice to introduce you to a few people as my…boyfriend?" I question cautiously.

He looks at me with a grin. "Boyfriend, huh?" His grin gets a little bigger and becomes a full smile as his gaze goes down to his plate. "I like hearing you say that," he says, then takes a sip of his coffee, his eyes peeking over at me.

Me, too.

LEDGER AND I don't arrive at Sassy Stacy's until around six thirty. That way, Ember could have time to visit with her coworkers. It's getting dark outside, which means the neon sign is lit bright green. It's bright enough to light up most of the front porch. Ledger holds my hand the whole time we walk from his truck to inside the building. Mostly because I don't want him to let go and leave my side. I look to my left in an attempt to find Ember, but instantly remember the night of my birthday when Ledger and I spoke, and how he wanted me to stay after I thanked him for paying my bar tab.

I hear a voice call out for Ledger from across the bar just as I spot Ember seated in the opposite direction. We both start moving away from each other but are stopped because I won't let go of his hand. We look at each other, and Ledger lets out a small laugh. "I'll be right back, baby. I'm just going to say hi to Brandt."

I still don't let go of his hand.

He smiles, pulls me in toward him, and kisses me.

"Go talk with Ember," he says against my lips. "I won't be long, I promise." His hand rests on the side of my head, stroking my cheek with his thumb.

"Okay, fine," I pout.

Ember is with three other coworkers at a table to the far right. She is deep in conversation until she finally sees me approaching the table.

"There she is!" she yells out and stands up to give me one of her Ember hugs. I hold on to her longer than usual because I have missed her so much. Every girl needs her best friend, and it has been a while since we have done anything together. The last time I saw her was after my surgery, but that wasn't for very long. I'm just glad I got to see her for at least a little bit that day. As a travel nurse and a good one at that, she is gone a lot, making it almost impossible for her to hang out regularly.

"How's it going?" I ask her eagerly.

She looks at me pointedly. "Girl, don't act like we didn't just see you walk in with Dr. Hottie, hand in hand, and lips to lips." They all giggle while I feel myself blush. "Ladies," Ember says, looking at the two females at the table. "Jeremy," she says, looking at the one male sitting beside them. "My best friend is fooling around with a *doctor*," she squeals.

I roll my eyes at her excitement.

"Relax," I laugh.

Ledger joins our table eventually, and everyone's eyes are now on him. I clear my throat as he sits down next to me.

"Ledger, you remember Ember," I say, reintroducing them. Ember smiles at him, and he acknowledges her with a head nod. "It's good to see you again," Ledger tells her.

"Likewise," she says back.

"Everyone," I say, gesturing to Ember's coworkers, "this is Ledger, my boyfriend."

"Nice to meet you all," he says to them.

Ledger is sitting to my right. My back is slightly turned to him. That way, I can catch up with Ember sitting to my left. She is sitting across from one of her female coworkers, I'm across from the other female coworker, and Ledger is across from Jeremy. Ledger scoots his chair to touch mine, and his arm rests on the back of my chair. He is so close; I can smell his masculine scent, which makes me melt back and relax against him. His arm moves from the back of my chair to around me.

"Well, look at this—just a bunch of medical professionals and one Jaemes," Ember jokes. There's subtle laughter from everyone, and then we break into different side conversations. The two female coworkers converse with each other, chiming in on Ledger and Jeremy's conversation from time to time. It works out great because Ember and I can have a second to chat, just the two of us.

"So," Ember starts ecstatically, "I have to fly down to Florida in a few weeks to—"

"Again?" I interrupt sadly.

"Let me finish!" she roars. "I'm going down there on Friday and will be there for a few weeks. I will be working some of the time, and the rest of the time will be a vacation."

"Spring break?" I ask.

"Spring break, bitch! And I want you to come with!"

I think about that for a moment. I'll already be off work. I could spend my entire spring break in Florida and depart for home early to return to work when the break is over.

"You have to come!" one of her coworkers tells me from across the table. "The three of us will be there, too. That's sort of why we are here. To celebrate how our staffing agency is, cluelessly sending us four crazies to work in Florida over spring break *together*."

I laugh and feel inclined to attend. Her coworkers seem like a good time, and I could use a little vacation. Ledger suddenly kisses my head softly, and my smile gets bigger.

"He can come, too!" Ember shrieks. I love how her enormous energy and outgoing personality have remained unchanged. Some people are easily changed as they get older and are around new people in their lives. Some more than others, but I love how Ember stays true to herself, as I also try to be.

I look at Ledger behind me to grasp his reaction to Ember's invitation.

"I'd love to join, but I won't be able to take that much time off work." He looks down at me. "You should go and have fun. I'll be here waiting for you when you get back."

I'm still unsure about what I want to do. A trip to Florida sounds fun, especially over spring break. I should go while I'm still young enough to enjoy it. But I feel sad when I think about being away from Ledger. I miss him when we are only at work during the day. I can't imagine how I'd feel without him for over a week.

"You have a little time to think about it, Jae. But know, I'll be pissed if my best friend doesn't join the fun with me," Ember says and then takes a drink of her…cocktail?

"Since when did you switch from beer?" I ask her.

"Since I tried gin for the first time. Have you had a gin and tonic before? It's fucking great."

"I'm proud of you for finally trying something new," I tell her. "Does this mean I can get you to try a whiskey cocktail now?"

"Baby steps, honey. Baby steps."

"Whereabout in Florida?" Ledger asks Ember.

"We are working in Tampa, but I found a cute Airbnb in Clearwater, only thirty to forty minutes away. We have a company card, so we can choose our rental car and where we stay," she smirks.

Ledger turns his attention back to me. "You should go, babe. It sounds fun, and you deserve a good time." He kisses me on the top of my head once more. I love it when he does that. Being in his arms, touching him, and those random kisses melt my heart. It's what makes it hard to be away from him.

But this is an excellent opportunity to make new memories with my best friend. I have to take some time to think about what to do before giving Ember a definite answer. I discreetly place my hand on Leger's thigh, indicating he's the reason why I don't want to go to Florida. He acknowledges this by giving me another one of those kisses that I love so much, and brushing my arm with his fingers as his arm stays draped around me. I look up at him in awe as he continues talking with Jeremy.

Ember gets up to play another song on TouchTunes. Once the music starts playing and she returns to her chair, I sit up from Ledger's hold and glare at her.

Two Dozen Roses.

"What the hell are you doing?" I ask through clenched teeth. "Why the need to play *this* specific song, Ember?" I lean in closer to her so Ledger won't ask about the significance of this song.

"Because," she starts quietly and leans in closer to me, "there might be a certain someone who is also going, and I didn't know exactly how to tell you."

"What? Why is *he* going?"

"Bennett and a group of guys are coming along, too, and *he* happens to be a part of that group. You can't blame me for wanting to include my boyfriend, Jae."

"I'm not blaming you for—I just—ugh, I can't think right now." I have an intense feeling in my gut.

I'm afraid I just made my decision.

Chapter Twenty-Seven

Day One

MY NEON YELLOW hardshell suitcase is packed with shorts, tanks, sundresses, and a few "going out" outfits suitable for a fun night out with the girls—and Jeremy, of course. I also have a variety of shoes, including heels, sandals, sneakers, and wedges.

Ledger spent the night at my house since it's our last night together until I return. The plane departs from Bozeman Yellowstone International Airport at ten o'clock this morning. There are no nonstop flights from Bozeman, Montana, to Tampa, Florida, so we have a layover in Minneapolis, Minnesota, which isn't too bad. I've been to Minnesota before. Shoutout to the Mall of America, Paul Bunion and Babe, the North Shore, the Minnesota Vikings, and the founding location of the fantastic Juicy Lucy burger.

Ledger drives me to the airport and plans to pick me up when I return. After a ten-minute goodbye and a make-out session that follows, I entered the airport to look for Ember. I know he will be right here when I get back.

We go through the motions of checking our bags, going through security, finding our gate, and then, most importantly, finding a bar while we wait to board the plane.

Once I'm a few cocktails deep and Ember and her coworkers practically dry out one of the beer kegs, it's finally time to find our way to our assigned seats in our section of the plane.

Flight attendant, shots, please!

WHAT A DAY. We've been flying for over five hours and on the go for a total of over seven hours. It's almost seven thirty in the evening, Florida time, by the time we finally get settled into our phenomenal Airbnb. I text Ledger when I have nothing left to unpack in my room.

Me: *Hey, babe, we made it. We just got settled in.*

Ledger: *Good. I miss you already. What's the plan for tonight?*

Me: *God, who knows…luckily, I'm prepared for anything.*

Ledger: *Good for you. Have a great time. Don't be afraid to check in every once in a while, okay? I can't stand the thought of losing you to a handsome college man.*

He's teasing.

Me: *You never have to worry. I miss you already, too. It's going to be hard not to think about you.*

Ledger: *So, don't.*

Me: *Don't what?*

Ledger: *Don't stop thinking about me. God knows you'll be constantly on my mind until you come home.*

Me: *I'll keep in touch, don't you worry. Talk soon.*

It takes every ounce of me not to type the words "I love you" at the end of my last message to Ledger. Because with all my heart, I do. He is the man I want to spend eternity with. I can see him being the father of my child or children, and I can see myself helping raise Archie. I only hope he feels the same way.

"Earth to Jaemes!" Ember says, clicking her fingers in my direction. "Where'd you go? Since we arrived, you've been lost in thought and on your phone."

"I'm sorry, I was just letting Ledger know we arrived."

"Girl-friend," she says in two separate syllables. "This is a trip we've all been waiting for. A trip that deserves our utmost attention. Let's not get distracted by our home lives. We need to be distracted by the beautiful waters and sandy beaches Florida has to offer."

"You're right. But remember, you have your boyfriend here. I don't. Let me be on my phone."

"Fine, but I'll be making damn sure you aren't nose deep in that thing the whole time. Are you about ready to go eat? I'm mega starving."

"Let me freshen up a bit and I'll meet you outside," I inform her.

Ember's coworkers are having Thai food for supper, which I loathe. Ember knows that, so we are going to a seafood place instead. However, we turn around when the hostess informs us that the wait is ninety minutes. Disappointed that we didn't make any reservations, we search for another restaurant that's not too far away. There aren't many options since we are on foot, as Ember's coworkers are using the rental car. We soon encounter a restaurant called Tino's Italiano and Mexicana—an Italian and Mexican joint.

It's busy, but not as busy as the previous place. The waiters and waitresses are all wearing red shirts with black dress pants. The hostess leads the way to our booth, and we look over the menu. Surprisingly, there is a *wide* variety of Italian and Mexican dishes.

"Hi there, how are we doing this evening?" asks a beautiful, petite blonde waitress as she approaches our booth. Her smile is gorgeous, and her bright white teeth sparkle in our direction. We tell her we are doing well, and she introduces herself.

"My name is Livvy, and I will be helping you out today. Can I get you two anything to drink right away?"

We give her our drink orders, and she proceeds to ask if we have any questions about the menu. After she leaves us, she cleans up the booth behind us and gathers the receipts from the people who were there before.

"What the fuck, Larry," we hear her say to herself. "Linda," she calls out to another waitress who looks to be around our parents' age. She has bright red lipstick on her lips, and her strawberry blonde curly hair is pulled back into a hair clip. She puts on her glasses, which are hanging around her neck, when Livvy shows her the two-dollar tip that was left on the table.

"You've gotta be shitting me," Linda reacts.

"A ninety-three-dollar bill, and this is the tip I get? He does this every time!" Livvy exclaims through clenched teeth.

"Well, you know he just wants to make the total end in either a five or zero," Linda states.

"This is why I never want his table, but somehow I'm always stuck with him." Larry must be a regular here if he does this often. They walk to the bar area where Linda continues working, and Livvy grabs our drinks.

"What brings you two lovely ladies to Clearwater? A little spring break fun?" Livvy asks us.

She seems sweet and sincere. She makes you feel like she genuinely cares about you and wants to ensure you have the best experience here. I don't understand how anyone would feel right about giving such a lousy tip when she clearly works so hard and deserves an appropriate amount.

I gesture to Ember and say, "She is here for work in Tampa, and I'm here along for the ride. We will be in Clearwater for the vacation portion of our Florida trip."

"I couldn't come to Florida for work and not make it into a spring break extravaganza without my best friend," Ember chimes in.

"How fun, you guys! Let me know if you need any fun recommendations. I was born and raised here and know all the spectacular places to visit."

I look at Ember, and she looks at me.

"That would be so awesome!" Ember tells her.

"This is Ember, and I'm Jaemes," I say, introducing us to Livvy.

"It's *so* nice to meet you two! We can swap phone numbers before you leave. Now, what can I get you two to eat?" Livvy asks us with a twinkle in her eye.

This trip is going to be a lot more enjoyable than I thought. Now that we know a Floridian who has spent her whole life here, she can give us the ultimate Florida experience we've been itching for. Plus, she seems like a lot of fun.

But will she be able to keep up with us? No, I think the more accurate question here is, will we be able to keep up with *her?*

Chapter Twenty-Eight

Day 2

I 'VE BEEN PREPARING for our first official full day in Florida for most of the morning. It's already eleven o'clock, and I'm ready to get the day started. My bright-colored bikini is on underneath my jean shorts and my loose, lightweight white top. I'm leaving my hair down, but there's a hair clip in my purse, just in case. I decide to wear my plain sandals instead of wedges. If I eventually want to go to the beach, sandals seem like a better idea.

Ember and her coworkers are meeting with the nurse supervisor at the hospital where they will be working. The four of them start work on Monday. Luckily, they won't be gone for too long. But that leaves me alone for a few hours. I look up places to grab a drink and lunch, preferably somewhere near the beach.

"Ah, here we go," I say out loud. The search on my phone led me to a perfect place.

It's a tiki place just down the road called The Tropical Lagoon. It's right on the beach and only a few miles from here, which is within walking distance. I grab my phone, sunglasses, and small purse, and head that way.

Walking up to the entrance, I notice it's part of a paradise-looking resort. The sign at the entrance states that the pool hours are from eleven o'clock in the morning to four o'clock in the afternoon and open to the public. Otherwise, the pool is strictly for hotel guests outside of that time frame.

Well, that's perfect.

There's a beach entrance located just beyond the pool. I may have to venture in that direction at some point, but first, I walk along the path to the bar. On one side of the bar, it's a standard setup that anyone can sit at. The other side is a pool bar where people can swim and sit in the water while enjoying a drink. Given that I could technically go on either side since I have a swimsuit on, I decide to keep my clothes on and sit at the side of the bar that's not in the water. Being alone, I don't have anyone trustworthy enough to watch my stuff. I also want to continue my text conversation with Ledger. I don't get to hear from him much when he's working, so I want to keep my phone close for when he replies.

"Hola, señorita, I'll be right with you," a cute Hispanic man behind the bar tells me as he walks by. I take a seat and wait for him to come back. The weather is perfect; it's not too humid, the sun is shining, a light breeze is coming off the ocean, and clouds are absent in the sky. There isn't one thing that could ruin this moment for me here in Clearwater, Florida.

Until I'm proved wrong.

I'd know those hazel eyes anywhere. His hair is wet and glistening in the sun. I was warned that he would be here, but out of all the places he could be, he's at this resort, currently seated in the pool section of the bar and looking in my direction.

Alder Daughtler.

"What can I get for you, Hermosa?" the bartender asks, startling me away from that man sitting across the bar from me.

"Oh, um, surprise me," I tell him. I can barely think right now.

"You got it," he says back with a smile.

In a panic, I send Ember a text.

Me: *Do you have any idea when you'll be back? I'm at The Tropical Lagoon and Alder is here…*

Ember: *Shit. We should be wrapping up soon. I'll be there as soon as I can.*

I look up again to see if he is still sitting over on the other side of the bar, but I'm blocked by the bartender setting my drink down in front of me.

"There you go, Hermosa. This is one of our most popular signature drinks. It's called the Tiki Torch. It's a combination of a Miami Vice and a Rum Runner cocktail."

This frozen signature drink has a dark red Daiquiri color to it and a white Pina Colada color in the middle. It sits in a hurricane glass topped with an umbrella and garnished with an assortment of tropical fruits. There's also a test tube shot glass that's filled with rum and tipped upside down on top, slowly releasing more rum as you sip.

"Thank you," I tell him.

Once the bartender leaves to attend to another customer, I notice that Alder is no longer sitting across the bar. A trace of worry starts to ignite through me. He could easily approach me; the last thing I want on this vacation is just that. I scan the area, trying not to be too obvious, but he is nowhere to be found.

Still a little cautious, I suck down my drink and focus on the bar TV that is currently showing NFL football highlights from this past season on ESPN while listening to the music blaring from the DJ booth near the pool.

"I'll take another when you get a chance," I hear Alder say to the bartender as he sets his cup on the bar top to my left.

My body tenses up. He's right next to me. What do I say? Should I just leave and avoid him altogether? No, that would be stupid.

Grow up, Jaemes. Get over it and show him you're not both-ered by him.

"You don't get views like this in Montana," he says to me.

"You don't get drinks like these in Montana either," I reply, holding mine up before taking another delicious sip.

Alder lets out a soft laugh before taking a seat next to me. "How've you been?" he asks.

"Good—great, actually. Yourself?" I stutter.

"I'm alright," he replies with a sigh. "Can't complain, I guess."

There's a booming silence between us as he awaits his refill. I'll eventually have to accept that I'll never be able to avoid these awkward moments.

When I see Ember walking up the path to the tiki bar, it's just past one thirty in the afternoon. My nerves are getting the best of me, and I can't tell if it's my brain or heart that is ignoring my hunger and gravitating toward the sweet alcohol. Regardless, I'm feeling a little tipsy at this point. Ember is in her sexy black one-piece swimsuit with a sheer black skirt cover-up. Her bright red, curly hair is thrown up in a messy bun, and she has on black square sunglasses. Seemingly in an eager rush, she plants herself in the bar chair next to me on my right.

"Well, well, well," I start, "fancy seeing you here."

"Bartender, I need a raspberry mojito and two shots of your finest tequila *STAT*," she says.

"No, no. Try the Tiki Torch," I tell her. "It's so good," I whisper, leaning closer to her.

"And another Tiki Torch for this beautiful soul," she adds.

The bartender sets our drinks in front of us, and Ember lays out a couple of one-dollar bills for his tip. She takes a large gulp of her mojito and then muddles the mint leaves with her straw. She eyes me and then eyes Alder, who is still seated beside me. She does it a few times as no one says anything.

"Well, this is fun…" Ember says sarcastically.

We clink our tequila shots together and down them like it's our last day on earth.

"Hey there, ladies," Bennett says, approaching us. He's in his swim trunks and is dripping wet from the pool. He has a large plastic cup of beer in his hand that's half gone.

"Hey, baby," Ember tells him and greets him with a kiss.

"Oh, Alder, those girls over there were asking where you went." He gestures to a group of three good-looking women by the poolside. "Hey, look who's here," Bennett says with a shit eating grin, now gesturing to me to make sure everyone knows whom he is referring to.

I feel myself slowly shrink down in my chair. Can't we have a nice vacation without the discomfort of my and Alder's new relationship status?

Current relationship status: Non-existent.

I'm well aware Alder can see whomever he wants. It shouldn't make me uncomfortable knowing other women are asking about him. But it does.

Alder tells us that he'll catch up with us later and then walks away with his freshly filled beer. Great, our first civil conversation turned into an awkward "see you later."

Bennett's demeanor aggravates my frustration. "You think this is fucking funny?" I ask him pointedly.

"Relax, princess. If it makes you feel any better, he only agreed to come because he knew you would be here."

"No! No, it doesn't make me feel better, Bennett! You clearly don't understand." I can't seem to dumb it down enough for this blockhead.

"Okay, okay, guys. Let's just calm down. Everything will be fine," Ember chimes in. Bennett must also be a little tipsy because nothing else would explain why he can't shrug off that permanent shit-eating grin plastered on his face during this whole conversation. I no longer give him the time of day and turn all my attention to this Tiki Torch in front of me. Rum seems to be the only friend I can count on at this moment in time.

"Jae, let's order some lunch. I think some food would be good for you," Ember tells me, and then turns to Bennett. "Babe, we will catch up with you a little later."

Although Ember is utterly right about food, I don't think anyone has the right to tell me what is *good* for me right now. I'm not in the mood for people to continue to tell me what they think I need. Because I know deep down that I never needed Alder to make an appearance here. However, I feel increasingly frustrated by my potential excitement over his presence, which causes me to become annoyed with myself more than anything.

AFTER EMBER AND I devour an order of Boom Boom shrimp and boneless chicken wings, her coworkers join us for the rest of the afternoon. We all make our way over to the side of the bar located in the pool. We cool off in the water and enjoy the music being played by the DJ. Of course, Bennett and his friends are with us; however, I can't help but notice Alder isn't here anymore. It's a relief that lets me relax and enjoy myself. After my four rum drinks and the shot of tequila earlier, I turn to water for a while. With food in my stomach and a mix of water, my goal is to sober up so I'm not a puddle so early on our first full day here.

"Where did Alder run off to?" Ember asks Bennett. I pretend not to hear.

"He went to his room to shower," he tells her.

The day is approaching dusk quickly, and a few pink, purple, and dark blue clouds appear above us. The sun is a yellow glowing ball, and orange surrounds the horizon. It's six o'clock in the evening, and there are quite a few people still in the pool. The DJ continues to roar out ongoing pool party hits. I have been out drying off for the last half hour before I decide that I could probably have another Tiki Torch. After the bartender hands me my frozen drink, I take a towel down to the beach and watch the sun continue to set. Hearing the waves crash onto the sandy beach is peaceful, and the slight breeze is still trying to dry my hair. This is the closest I can get my hair to a natural beachy wave look.

"Hey," a soft voice says behind me. I don't feel the need to look back because I know exactly who it is.

"Hey," I say back.

He takes another seat next to me. This time, he sits a little too close for comfort, but I don't let that show.

"You okay?" he asks.

"Of course, I am. Why?"

"Jaemes, even though it's been a while, I can still tell when something is up with you."

There are many things I could say, as they are associated with a wide range of complex emotions. But I won't let him know that. He doesn't have to be there for me anymore.

"Alder, you don't have to worry about me. I'm better than okay. But I should probably find Ember. She wanted to head back to our place soon." I stand up from the soft white sand and brush myself off before walking away.

"Would you want to get together at some point and catch up?" he asks me.

"Maybe," I say with a small smile. "I'm sure we will run into each other again."

"I'm hoping so."

In opposite directions, Alder walks toward the resort, and I head toward the pool to relocate Ember. It's tough to ignore how he makes my heart skip a beat. I pray I don't see him again, but I realize that might not be feasible given the circumstances. It's been months since I've spoken to him, and I almost forgot what it felt like to hear his voice. The energy between us is immense, and I'm already feeling a strong attraction to him again. My want for him is painful, and I only hope I'm strong enough to steer away from him like I know I should. This is where my heart laughs at my brain because it's larger and more powerful.

This will be an interesting Florida adventure.

Chapter Twenty-Nine

Day 3

Livvy: Hi girls! Meet me at The Tiki Jungle tonight at 9:00 pm. It's our go-to beach club, and I know you'll love it!

After reading the text Livvy sends Ember and me, I instantly chug some water and a bottle of Pedialyte for extra electrolytes. I have a hunch that this night out could get wild. Ember loves clubs. It's her idea of a perfect evening, so she is already getting herself prettied up for the festivities.

We invited Livvy to supper with us before going to The Tiki Jungle. We are all dressed to the nines and excited to get to know each other better. Everyone here connects on some level and gets along so well. Livvy invited Linda, the other waitress we saw at Tino's, and we're all enjoying her spunky personality. We are seated outside at the seafood joint we tried to eat at the night before. This time, we made sure to make reservations. The outdoor seating is on the water, and the area is lit with string lights. We can only hear the ocean at this time now that it is finally dark.

"My parents own Tino's. The restaurant is named after our last name, Valentino. My dad is Italian, and my mom is half-Hispanic. That's why it's an Italian and Mexican joint," Livvy informs us.

"Do you work at Tino's full-time?" I ask her.

"No, only part-time, but I tend to be there often to help out my parents. I'm a full-time veterinary technologist.

Between my career and the restaurant, I feel like I have two full-time jobs."

"Not to mention she is a former Buccaneers cheerleader," Linda chimes in. "This fricken Barbie doll would manage all three jobs and still have enough energy to have some fun in her free time."

"Impressive!" I voice.

"Do you have a good man who supports you?" Ember asks.

Livvy gushes with a slight chuckle. "No, I've been single for a while, but I recently started talking to someone, so we'll see where it goes. I'm hoping for a potential relationship with this guy. He's great," she blushes.

"You *need* to invite him out with us! Send him an invite to The Tiki Jungle right now," Ember commands.

"Eek, okay, fine," Livvy says while taking out her phone to text him. She is sitting between Ember and me, so we lean over and watch her text her man. It must be a newer fling, since there isn't a name associated with the message conversation, just a phone number. "There," Livvy says, burying her red face in her hands as if she can't believe she just invited him out with us. She seems smitten. It reminds me of myself with Ledger.

"What about you gals? Any good men in your lives?" Linda asks us.

Ember and I start talking about our relationships. I mentioned that Ledger and I have been seeing each other for several months now and that he's a doctor and a great father to his six-year-old son, Archie. Ember discusses Bennett and their relationship, including how long they have been together. Ember also mentions that Bennett is here in Florida.

"He better be coming out with us, too," Livvy says.

"Girl, you best believe he's coming. He knows I'd kick his ass if he didn't," Ember tells her. "He's with a few of his closest friends, so I'm sure they will also join."

I look at Ember, hoping she doesn't mention how one of

them is my ex-boyfriend. I need that reminder to stay where it is.

Under wraps.

However, she doesn't get the hint. "One of the guys is Jae's ex. I know she's itching to have a good conversation with him. I've been trying to push her to talk with him."

"That's because there is nothing to talk about, Ember. I'm fine with just being acquaintances," I assure her.

"Oh, my goodness, honey, you're blushing! You should see your face," Linda announces.

"Can we please change the subject?" I beg.

"Oh my God, you guys, this will be such a fun night!" Livvy squeals.

After we eat, we head straight to the beach club. It's only a ten-minute Uber ride, which we share amongst the six of us: me, Ember, Livvy, and Ember's three coworkers. Linda declined our invitation to join us. Before we parted ways with Linda, she stated, "A beach club is no place for a fifty-year-old woman." It's understandable, I guess, but you should still live your life to the fullest, no matter how old you are.

It's low tide right now, so the beach is open as an option to dance and hang out. There is a rope cut-off around the club property and security stationed on each side, so the people who paid to get in are the only ones with access to the beach, music, and bar. The rope also stops anyone from venturing out into the water. Naturally, we veer outside to the beach, where many other people are dancing. With drinks already in our hands, I help Ember locate Bennett. Luckily, Ember's coworkers get along flawlessly with Livvy as well. The four of them hit the dance floor like magnets to the music.

"There he is," Ember tells me, pointing to Bennett. She waves him down away from the group of guys.

"Don't worry, those girls are here for Tate and Owen. They sniffed them out the second they walked through the door," Bennett laughs.

"Shocker," Ember sarcastically replies.

It shouldn't surprise me that Alder is here, too, but this place is, without a doubt, not his scene. His eyes haven't left mine since he saw us wave Bennett over. We are a good ten or so yards away from each other. I slurp down my first glass of whiskey and head to the bar for another. Ember asked if I could get her another drink, and that the next round would be on her. After agreeing to her deal, I find a spot at the bar that isn't as crowded and wait for my turn.

"Hey, whiskey girl," Tate says next to me.

"Oh, hey, there's my whiskey boy," I laugh. "Taint, is it?"

"Ha ha. Very funny," he says.

The bartender gazes at me with serious eyes that say, *Hurry up and tell me what you need. I have a thousand other people to get to, and you're decreasing my tips.*

"I need a Jack Daniels and Coke and a gin and tonic, please."

"Make that *two* Jack Daniels and Cokes," Tate says to the bartender and places money on the bar, "on me."

Tate and I take our drinks and return to the group outside. As we shift through the waves of people, I accidentally bump into someone who is trying to get to the bar. With my drink covering most of my hand and Ember's drink covering more of the other, I look up to apologize.

"I'm so sorry!" I yell over the loud music. Of course, the person I bump into is none other than Alder himself. He gives me a smirk and keeps moving toward the bar. Something tells me he did that on purpose.

Ember thanks me after I hand her the cocktail.

"Thank him," I point to Tate. "He bought this round."

When Alder and Bennett return with their drinks, he hands me what looks like another whiskey cocktail. I give him a bewildered expression.

"Hopefully, this will hold you off from going to the bar so often and prevent you from bumping into anyone else," he jokes.

"I'm sorry," I tell him again, but with a glare.

"I see you haven't changed much," he laughs.

"What's that supposed to mean?"

"You still apologize for everything."

I roll my eyes at his observation. "Thanks for pointing that out."

The more drinks I have, the more confidence I gain. When Ember pulls me out to the dance floor on the beach, I don't hesitate. A rush of nerves and butterflies appear inside my stomach as I constantly catch Alder watching me. I try to dance toward the middle of the crowd so that more people block the view, but that doesn't stop Alder from repeatedly finding my gaze. Those familiar feelings continue to intrude into my heart. As much as I don't want them to, it's impossible to avoid.

I don't know what Ember's evil plan is, but I'm terrified it might be working as she catches Alder and me reconnecting with a satisfied smirk on her face.

Chapter Thirty

Day 5

LAST NIGHT WAS pretty low-key for us. With seventy-five percent of us at work all day and one hundred percent of us hungover, we ordered supper and watched movies. I stayed in bed and slept most of the day while I was the only one at the Airbnb. Alder texted me yesterday morning asking if he could take me out for breakfast since everyone in my group was gone, but I told him that I felt worse than the time I stayed at his place for the first time and wasn't in the mood for crawling out of bed. At one point, he threatened to retrieve our Airbnb address from Bennett, but I didn't care. I wouldn't have answered the door if he showed up.

Or would I?

What would he have done if he had shown up and I let him in? Would he have made me food and ensured that my water bottle was filled? Would he have crawled into bed with me?

No, stop thinking that way, Jaemes. You have a boyfriend, *for Christ's sake.*

Today, Ember and Jeremy have the day off. The other two coworkers are scheduled to work. Their schedules are so random, but I guess that's hospital work at its finest. Unlike most people, you have a wide range of hours, especially as a travel nurse. You work when they need you and where they need you.

"Get your suit on, girlfriend. We are going on a boat cruise today," Ember informs me. "And it's 'bring your own booze,' so we have to stop at the liquor store before we head to the boat landing."

Following her orders, I put on my bikini and gather the rest of my belongings for the day. "Who's all going?" I ask her.

"Everyone," she says.

With too much excitement overpowering me, I put more effort into my appearance than most would during a cruise like this. Ember's brochure states that we can play music on the boat, snorkel, tiki bar hop, and even hang out at a sandbar. Oh, and *much, much more.*

When we arrive at the boat landing via Uber, the captain puts everyone's beer and booze in the cooler. Ember, Jeremy, and I are the last ones to arrive.

"It's about time you divas showed up," Tate says as we climb onto the private boat with the captain's help.

"Shut up, dickwad. We aren't late. You guys were just early," Ember snaps back playfully.

"Please take your shoes off and put them in this box," the captain tells us. We do so and then crack open our first beer.

"Hey, Jaemes, there's plenty of room up here," Bennett smirks devilishly and gestures to the only available seat, which is right next to Alder.

Goddamn it, Bennett.

I take a subtle, deep breath and make my way over to my supposed assigned seat.

"Hello, everyone. My name is Captain Chad. You all have a few hours with me today, and I promise to make sure you all have a great time." We all cheer. "Now, if one of you *isn't* having a good time at any point, you best let me know. First, we will stop at a nearby sandbar. I have snorkeling equipment if you'd like to use any of it. Then, we will stop at a few tiki bars along the coast. Later on, we might be able to see a few dolphins as well. Before we take off, who's in charge of the music?" Ember jolts out of her seat and hooks up her phone to the boat's auxiliary cord. When the music starts, Captain Chad turns the volume up and maneuvers to the open ocean.

The Gulf breeze is whipping through my hair, and the sun feels warmer today. When we arrive at the sandbar a half hour later, we see plenty of other people here with their boats in addition to ours. Captain Chad keeps our boat anchored a short distance away, making us swim to the sandbar. Multiple genres of music are playing from different boats. It's a unique party scene here, but I like it.

Ember, Bennett, Tate, and Owen decide to snorkel while Jeremy, Alder, and I relax with a beverage at the sandbar. Alder and Jeremy make small talk, and it's a tad awkward since Jeremy has no idea he has spoken with my current *and* ex-boyfriends. I wander over to the side of the sandbar where everyone is snorkeling and observe them for a while. Jeremy swims out to the boat and grabs snorkeling equipment so he can join.

"Want to go snorkeling?" Alder asks, walking through the water toward me. I shake my head no. "Yeah, me either. I did it once many years ago and didn't think it was anything spectacular. Would I go again? Sure. Would I go searching for it? No."

I turn my head in his direction while he watches everyone do their thing in the ocean. He is wearing the same white hat and black sunglasses he had on the day we met in his driveway. His swim trunks are burnt orange, which does a great job of illuminating his tan skin. I feel my lips turn into a half-smile.

"What?" he asks, looking back at me with the same smile.

I shake my empty beer can, trying to divert away from why I'm smiling.

"Need another?" he asks with a light chuckle.

I nod my head yes.

"A woman of many words," he says before chugging the rest of his beer and grabbing my empty can. I watch him as he gets deeper into the water and eventually swims with one arm out to the boat with the cans in hand. His body is dripping wet when he climbs up the boat ladder; his sun-kissed skin glows in the sun, and his muscles enlarge with every movement he makes. Once he fishes two more beers from the cooler, he dives into the water and swims back to me.

"Thank you," I tell him after he hands me a beer. I crack it open and take a sip that tastes of beer and salt water. "How long are you here for?"

"Until Monday. You?"

"Sunday. I have to go back to work on Monday," I tell him, still attempting to make minimal eye contact.

He lowers to meet my eyes. It's still hard for me to talk with him, let alone look at him while I speak. "There you are," he says, forcing me to look at him, but I turn to look away. He takes my chin and turns my face toward his.

"Everything okay? You can barely look at me."

This time, I look right into his eyes with confidence. "No, Alder. Everything is not okay. How is this so easy for you? It pains me to be this close to someone I once considered to be the love of my life at one point. After months of not seeing you, talking with you, being near you...I—"

"And you really believe I don't feel the exact same way?" His face is just inches away from mine, and I can tell he's serious. "It took every ounce of my willpower to approach you at the bar when I first saw you here. I don't know how to operate normally when I'm around you. Because all I can think about is holding you in my arms and never letting go. But I know I can't, and because of that, I feel myself malfunctioning. Do you think it's *easy* for me to have a normal conversation with you? Huh?" His hold on the sides of my head gently tightens with his frustration. "After seeing you, I went back to my room to look for flights home. There was no way I could stay here without continuing where we left off. I didn't want to be here if it meant we had to stay cordial. I have never stopped loving you, Jaemes. To me, you still are the love of my life. The one that got away."

What he does to me is unlike any other feeling I have ever felt, and I only feel this way with him. I don't know how he does it. My eyes swell with tears, and my brain is so foggy that it's unclear if they are happy or sad tears. My heart is on overload, and the only thing I can do is soak in all of his words, hoping they are true.

"I'm sorry," I whisper.

"Still apologizing, I see." He tries to fight away a smile and wipes a fallen tear from my cheek.

I sink myself into the sand and sit cross-legged. The water is barely to my knees. Alder sits and joins me.

"I don't know how to process any of this," I tell him.

Alder takes a deep breath. "Yeah, me either." His legs are stretched out in front of him, crossed at the ankles, and he is leaning back on his hands. I can't help but notice that we have been mimicking our positions from the time we watched the Fourth of July fireworks from the top of the hill at his family's ski resort.

Once everyone gets back onto the boat and gets rid of their snorkeling gear, we take that as a sign that we are about to head out. Alder stands up and reaches his hand out to help me up. We walk into the water with our hands remaining connected until I tear mine from his. As difficult as that was to do, we can't be touching like that. I can still feel that magnetic pull toward him, and I'm afraid we'll take things too far if I let our actions continue the way they're going.

"Next stop, Sunset Paradise. It's the nearest tiki bar from here," Captain Chad announces. We all grab towels to sit with before taking off. As we find our seats, Alder and I are on opposite ends of the boat this time.

SUNSET PARADISE IS a massive bar with a loud tiki atmosphere. This Polynesian-inspired hut didn't fail to express the palm-thatched roof of the bamboo-like structure accurately. As impressive and out of this world as this place might be, I find it hard to enjoy any of it. Ember, Bennett, Tate, Owen, and Jeremy don't hesitate to hop off the boat once it docks. Needing to use the restroom, the captain follows the crew, leaving Alder, the last one aboard. He stops when he notices I'm still seated.

"Coming?" he asks me.

"No, I think I'm going to sit this one out. Go ahead, enjoy yourself," I tell him with a forced smile. Unfortunately for me, he can still read me like a book. He makes his way over to the cooler and grabs two beers. He hands me one and then places himself beside me. We're facing the tiki bar where the music blares and the colorful lights shine against the darkening day. We still have an hour before sunset, but the sun is low enough to recognize that this cruise is nearing its end.

I'm tempted to tell him that I've never stopped loving him, too, but then Ledger enters my mind. As badly as I want to jump into Alder's arms and lock my lips with his, I need to remember who I get to go home to at the end of this—Ledger, Archie, my family, and so many more. Alder shouldn't define my happiness because there will always be an end when it comes to me and him. But why do I naturally feel like Alder is the only one who brings me happiness? He occupies my thoughts effortlessly, and I allow it to happen.

"Come here," Alder tells me. His arm is extended, resting on the ledge of the boat, and leaning back as if he wants me to sit closer so he can wrap his arm around me.

"I don't think that's a good idea, Alder. I don't want to end up doing something I regret."

"What, you don't trust me?"

"No, I don't trust myself. We're playing with dangerous fire here."

He has a look of sadness and disappointment on his face, but he has to know that I didn't come here for him, even though he ultimately was my deciding factor for joining the trip, and I may be the only reason why he is here as well.

With a much-needed interruption, we hear the sounds of our drunk friends laughing and stumbling on the dock back to the boat. I scooch over a tad to my left. Captain Chad follows, watching as everyone puts their shoes in the box as they should.

"Awe, look at these two love birds," Ember sings. I cringe at the sound of her words as Jeremy's facial expression turns to confusion. It wasn't too long ago that he was meeting me and my *boyfriend*. "Please tell me you are back together. Ugh, I would totally cry right now if I learned that you were," Ember continues with her drunken escapade.

"No, Ember. Why don't you come sit by me?" I ask her. I need her, whether she is sober or not. She, too, brings a sort of comfort to my well-being. It makes me feel less...shitty knowing she can understand my situation even without having to confirm it.

On the way back to the boat landing, I grow tired as the sun sets and the breeze tickles my face. I haven't felt this kind of emotional pull for a long time, and I don't necessarily like it. My head rummages through the relationship I once had with Alder and everything we went through together. Some happy, some sad.

While we unload our items from the boat, Ember tips Captain Chad, and I thank him for the joyous outing. I put on my sandals, grab my things, and walk down the dock without looking back.

Chapter Thirty-One

Day 6

W HEN WE RETURNED to our Airbnb after the boat cruise yesterday evening, I mentioned that I wasn't feeling well and turned in early. Ember continued her fun with her other two coworkers as they tried catching up to her tipsy level when they got off work. Jeremy also turned in early after nearly vomiting in the Uber ride back.

This morning, I'm mainly keeping to myself since everyone had to go to work. I'm not hungover, but I do need time to myself. I haven't heard from Alder since the boat cruise, but I wasn't expecting to. I'm sure he also needed a brain break from what happened between us.

Today, Ember is the only one scheduled to work, so I'll be accompanied by everyone else. This afternoon, we are meeting Livvy at the beach for some sun and relaxation. It won't be much of an eventful day, but we plan on going out tonight to have more nightlife entertainment as soon as Ember can rejoin us. Livvy has other plans, so she won't be able to attend our outing this time. But seeing her again will be fun.

Ember: Bennett is taking me out on a little romantic dinner date when I get off work. We will all go out afterward, but make sure you are ready by 7:00 pm. All the guys are meeting us at our Airbnb.

"Talking to your man?" Livvy asks me as we all set up our

chairs in the sand near the water.

"No, he's working, so he can't talk much until he gets off. He's been swamped lately. I guess this was the perfect time to be on vacation."

"Oh gosh, for sure! I bet a lot of families take their kids in for check-ups during school breaks." Livvy lays out her towel on her chair and lies on her stomach, letting the sun rays soak into her backside. I sit in my sun chair and admire her perfectly toned and slender physique. I'd kill for a body like that.

"Yeah," I reply.

"Something wrong? You seem different today," she asks.

I shake my head. "Just my damn ex getting in my head."

"That's right," she says, sitting up on her knees and facing me. "I forgot that he's here too! Which one is he?"

"Alder. He's the taller man with short brown hair."

"Oh…"

"Oh, what?"

"Oh…nothing," she nervously laughs. "I just didn't know that's who your ex was. He's cute! What happened between you two?"

"I don't really want to talk about it."

"Well, you brought him up, girly," she reminds me as she lies back down on her stomach to return to the sun. Why was her reaction to Alder so weird?

I guess I did bring him up, but she asked me what was wrong. I *want* to talk about him, but the more I do, the more I can't keep my mind off of him. Ugh, is this all this vacation is going to be about? All about Alder? I thought that I'd come here for a fun and exciting time with Ember, but all it's turning out to be is me trying not to fall back in love with Alder.

I need to call Ledger. I need to get my mind and emotions back in order, and he's the perfect person for just that.

IT'S FOUR-THIRTY IN the afternoon, and we are walking back from the beach after a casual day of sitting in the sun while the crystal blue water crashes its waves into us as we station ourselves in the sand. I could definitely get used to this.

After I shower, I put on cotton shorts and a loose T-shirt to be comfy while I get ready. My outfit for tonight is lying on my bed, prepared to be put on afterward. Jeremy is in the shower now, and the other two girls are fighting for the other bathroom at the other end of the house.

There is a knock on the front door, and when I look at the clock, the time reads only six fifteen in the evening. When I open the door, I see Alder standing in front of me.

"Sorry, I'm late. The rest of the guys will be here later. They're picking up a case of beer to pregame before we head out, but they should be here shortly."

"What do you mean by *late*?" I ask. "Ember said everyone was coming at seven."

His lips turn into a roguish smirk as he says, "Ember told me six."

Of course, she did. I wish I had known Alder was going to be here early. I'm not quite done with my makeup yet, and my hair is still wet from the shower. I open the door and let him in.

"This is a nice place," he says, looking around.

"It's not bad for a three-bedroom house. Ember and I share a room; the two girls share a room, and with Jeremy being the only guy, he gets a room to himself. Between the five of us, we battle over the two bathrooms."

"I'd love to see that," he laughs.

"We have a few drinks left in the fridge if you want one."

Alder grabs two bottles of beer and then goes toward the patio door, where a fire pit and outdoor games are set up. He looks over at me and gestures with his head to join him.

"I should probably finish getting ready," I tell him, standing halfway out the sliding patio door.

"Come on, have one drink with me. Besides, you look fine."

After hesitating, I give in and join him on the cushioned bench on his right. Since everyone else is busy getting ready, I suppose this would be an excellent time to discuss...*us?* Pretending he's not affecting my time here isn't going to work for me.

"Alder, I think it's for the best that we stay away from each other. There are plenty of other people in our group that we can be around, but for me, I can't be around you. I'm sorry."

"Alright..." he says before taking a drink. "So, I take it you don't have any feelings for me?"

"I'm trying not to let any feelings I have for you resurface. I'm sort of seeing someone," I admit to him. He stays silent and continues to drink his beer.

"Okay," he says eventually.

Why does it kill me to admit this to him?

"So, I won't be near you anymore. Problem solved," he states.

"Yes, no touching or talking..."

"Oh, talking even? This guy must be something else if you aren't supposed to be talking to other guys," he says in a more severe tone.

"He doesn't care who I talk to. But I know that he wouldn't like me talking to you," I clarify.

"Why me?" he asks before bringing his can of beer to his mouth again.

"Alder...why do you think?"

"Enlighten me," he says, looking straight into my eyes.

"I don't think I need to," I say with defense.

"Well," he clears his throat, "if I do anything off-limits to you, just tell me to stop."

"I will," I say flatly.

He then slides closer to me so that his leg touches mine, and we are shoulder to shoulder. His right hand slowly slides on top of my left thigh and then toward the inside with a tauter grip. "Just tell me to stop," he says again.

But I can't. My actions completely contradict everything I just told him.

I remain silent, wanting to know how far he'll go if I don't tell him to stop. But what would that say about me as a person? As Ledger's girlfriend?

He pushes me down by the shoulders so I'm lying on the bench. Hovering over me, he brings his face close to mine. "Just say the word any time, and I'll stop."

I'm at a loss for words. The angel on my shoulder is non-existent, and all I can hear is the shouting of the devil telling me to keep him going, knowing deep down that I want him to. His face gets closer and closer to mine. I'm having trouble keeping my breath at a calm and even rhythm. I'm sure he can feel my heart beating out of my chest. It's the only thing I can hear.

Suddenly, we hear the front door open and then shut. All the guys' voices are muffled as only one wall separates us from them.

"Stop," Alder whispers for me, against my lips. His eyes scan my face, and it looks as if, for the first time, he can't read me. We were definitely sitting too close to the fire this time. The last thing I want is to be burned with a reigniting kiss. He bites his bottom lip and then gets up to walk inside. Disappointed in myself for not stopping in the first place, I follow not too far behind him. As he walks into the kitchen to join the guys, I head straight for the bathroom, knowing everyone can see me since this house has an open layout. I text Ember immediately and ask when she will be here since it's past seven o'clock.

Ember: *Almost to the Airbnb.*

I finish up my makeup and style my hair, which is nearly dry now. I'm hoping that enough time has passed, and no one comments on the fact that Alder and I were just sitting outside in private. I didn't help the situation by rushing to the bathroom immediately afterward.

I'm sure that wasn't suspicious.

I exit the bathroom to go to my room and change my clothes. Everyone, including Alder, is staring at me.

"Maybe she'll tell us," I hear someone say.

"What?" I ask.

"What were you two doing alone out there?" Tate asks me. "Alder won't break." My eyes wander over to Alder as he rolls his eyes and finishes his beer.

"Oh, please. You're kidding me, right?" I laugh softly. "Alder was told to be here at six for some reason."

"Oh yeah? Says who?" Tate asks, challenging me.

"Ember. And who the fuck are you to worry about what *we* do? Huh?" I ask him, getting more defensive. This guy is starting to piss me off. It could be that I'm more pissed at myself for putting myself in this situation after I knew Alder would be here when I agreed to go on this trip, and I'm taking it out on Tate, but he makes it easy as he puts himself in these positions as well.

"Easy! I'm just teasing. Relax," Tate replies.

I raise my eyebrows and give him a look, letting him know he shouldn't start what he can't finish.

"Hasn't anyone ever told you that you should never tell a woman to 'relax'?" I ask him, genuinely wondering what the answer is.

"No," he says softly, "no one's ever loved me enough," he teasingly pouts with his bottom lip pushed out.

"Okay, fuck off, Tate. Leave it alone," Alder chimes in. I lock eyes with Alder before going into my room.

Ember and Bennett walk through the door and immediately mention something about a glow-in-the-dark pool party that's going on tonight at the guys' resort. We all change out of our nightlife attire and into swimwear. The guys change once we arrive at the resort. The tiki bar and DJ booth are both decked out with glowing lights. People everywhere are wearing glow sticks as bracelets and necklaces. It's a cool concept, but I wish my mind weren't elsewhere. I'm finding it difficult to enjoy my time here.

Ember and her coworkers have been great, and we get along so well, but I can't shake off this feeling with Alder. We haven't said anything to each other, mainly because our looks say it all. I know I'm not the only one who is feeling this way. Whenever I look at him, he seems absent from the conversations around him. I can sense something is off ever since I told him I'm with someone else. It's like he thought that there would be a chance that this trip could bring us closer together, if not back into a relationship. But we both know that's not feasible.

"I'm going to get an Uber back. I'll see you in the morning," I tell Ember, hoping she can hear me over the music and conversations around us. Alder overhears me tell Ember that I'm leaving. As I walk down the path from The Tropical Lagoon, he stops me by grabbing my hand and turning me around. "Why don't you go up to my room? You know…in case you change your mind and want to come back down. Then you don't have to deal with another Uber back or lie in bed wishing you were here."

"Alder, please. You know damn well that I can't do that."

"I'll stay with one of the guys tonight. I won't be near you. I just thought I'd be nice and offer my room if you'd like it, since you're here."

I don't know what to say to him. He fights for what he wants, but I can't give him what he wants, even though I'd love to, deep down.

After standing in silence and thinking about his offer, I end up taking it, and he brings me to his room. What exactly am I thinking? This is the exact reason why Harrison and I didn't work out. He failed to be truthful with his feelings regarding his ex...*current* girlfriend. And I'm doing the same thing with Ledger and Alder. So, do I blame Harrison after all? Feelings for someone are hard to get over, and sometimes, they never go away. It's a punch in the gut to realize I could hurt either of these men the way I've hurt for so long.

After we walk into his hotel room, he pulls out one of his t-shirts and a pair of athletic shorts for me to change into.

"Where are you going?" he asks me.

"To the bathroom so I can change," I inform him.

He laughs and shakes his head.

"What?" I ask.

"It's not like I haven't seen all of you before," he says.

"Alder, I'm not all yours to see anymore," I tell him before going into the bathroom and locking the door behind me. I unfold the articles of clothing Alder gave me and notice the t-shirt is the gray Coors Lite shirt that I love. I'm positive he gave me this one on purpose.

Once I'm finished changing into his clothes, I drape my suit over the bathtub to dry. I see Alder sitting in one of the chairs on the balcony, watching the pool party continue as I exit the bathroom.

"Not going back down?" I ask as I sit in the other chair beside him.

"Is he the one?" he asks me, still gazing at the party below us.

I let out a sigh. "He's a really great man, Alder," I say quietly. I'm not enthused about having this conversation with him, but it could be what we need right now. "He's been nothing but perfection and—"

"I just need to know one thing, Jaemes," he says sternly.

"Is he the one?" he asks again.

"I think so."

"So, you love him?" he asks, looking at me this time.

I nod.

He looks away with pained eyes and nods back with pursed lips. He gets up from his chair and leans against the railing with his back toward me. He rubs his face with both hands and takes a deep breath. "Who is this guy?" he asks. His hands muffle his voice.

"Alder, please…can we just—"

"Who is this dream guy of yours?" he asks with his hands away from his face this time.

"His name is Ledger Yearwood."

He turns around to face me. "Ledger Yearwood? As in the doctor?" he questions.

"Yeah." It's hard to have a conversation with a knot in your stomach.

"That explains why you were at Annie's party. He has a son that's in her class, yeah?"

I nod.

"*Fuck!*" he shouts and kicks his chair as if he's now starting to feel like he is losing this battle. I jump at his reaction and freeze as I watch him stand there with his hands on his hips and looking downward. He is trying to compose himself the best he can. He rubs both eyes with his hands and then rubs his face again before leaving the balcony. I no longer watch him, but I hear the door to his hotel room open. I turn around to face the inside after I listen to it close.

I couldn't lie to him. I can't fall in love with someone and then fall back in love with Alder, even if that's what he expected. I watch him walk back over to our group at the pool party, and then I head inside to lie down. A part of me wants to leave and get an Uber back to the Airbnb, but I find myself crawling into his bed and crying myself to sleep. Because no matter how much I try to convince myself that I don't love Alder, I can't ignore the fact that I could never *not* love him.

JUST LIKE THE fairytale of a Cinderella story, I wake up at midnight sharp with another panic attack. I can't shake this bad feeling of something happening out of my control yet again. I'm scared shitless as I hyperventilate in this dark room, by myself, with no idea where anyone is. I call Ledger, but he doesn't answer. I know it's late at night, but I could really use him right now. I call him a few more times, but I'm still unsuccessful.

Me: *Help!*

I drop my phone as uncontrollable tears stream down my face. My whole body starts to shake, and I'm gasping for air. Ten minutes pass until I hear someone fiddle with the keycard to the hotel room door and then burst inside. Alder rushes over to me on the bed, sitting beside me.

"I got your text. What's wrong?" he asks, concerned, but I'm too far gone to speak. He analyzes my panic attack and gathers me in his arms. I'm on his lap, and my head sinks into his shoulder as I weep. I start to scare myself even more by how hard I start crying. I don't think I have ever cried this severely. "Jaemes, you need to breathe. Take a deep breath with me." My breathing is shaky as I inhale deeply with him and then exhale.

Alder doesn't say anymore. He tightens his hold on me and rubs my back with his hands. He lets me ride this out as my trembling body tries its best to relax against him.

Chapter Thirty-Two

Day 7

THE SUN IS shining its way through the shades. I wake up not remembering ever calming down enough to fall asleep. Alder is still holding me in his arms as we lay in his bed in his hotel room. He may never want any kids or to get married, but he sure knows how to take care of me. And he knows exactly how to love me even when he knows he shouldn't.

Maybe that's all I need. Someone to be there for me and love me unconditionally. Someone who can put their entire heart and soul into just *me*. I have never wondered why getting married and having kids was so important to me. Is it because that's just how life is for most people? Am I afraid of being judged for being a childless single forever? It would be nice to share a last name with the man I devote myself to, though. To signify that I am his and he is mine.

Do I really need a wedding ring? I don't ever wear jewelry anyway. And kids are a lot of work, and they're expensive. We could put our money toward other things, right? We wouldn't be house-broke; we could get brand-new vehicles and still have money left over to do whatever we want without being held back by kids.

As I lie here, trying to convince myself that a life with Alder would be all I need, I also consider the extraordinary life I could have with Ledger. Ledger can offer me so much more. A second mom to his son, a potential child of our own, a dream wedding that would be the start of a beautiful marriage to a perfect partner. Given our careers, we'd have plenty of money to travel, go on family vacations, and still be well off in our bank accounts.

But can Ledger love me the way Alder can? Do I love Ledger as much as I love Alder? The deciding factor ultimately comes down to love. I want to be happy, but I won't be satisfied if the love I share with someone isn't present or authentic. I don't want to sit around wishing I were with someone else or constantly wondering about the other guy. That's not fair to anyone.

So, what do I do?

I feel Alder shift his body away and loosen his hold on me as he stretches out his body. "Good morning," he whispers.

I turn onto my other side and face him. "Good morning," I whisper back.

"Are you feeling alright?" he asks, lightly dragging his fingertips up and down my arm.

I nod with a small smile.

"Good," he says. "You had me scared. I knew exactly what was going on when I read your text. I couldn't get up here fast enough." He then stops stroking my arm and places his hand on my cheek.

"I appreciate you coming to help me. I didn't know what else to do," I say back to him.

"No matter what happens between us, I will always be by your side whenever you need me. Forever. Remember that."

"Thank you, Alder."

"Don't thank me. It's what people do when they love someone." He gets out of bed and heads to the bathroom, leaving me to ponder the last thing he said.

He must have dressed in the bathroom after showering and brushing his teeth because he left the room right after. I know this isn't easy for him. I couldn't imagine Alder holding another woman the same way he holds me. But that shouldn't bother me. I should be more bothered by the thought of Ledger holding anyone else besides me.

I make my way to the coffee maker next to the TV. I make a cup of dark roast coffee and then take a blanket to the balcony. It's a gorgeous morning, and the sun is just above the ocean on the horizon. The sound of seagulls and waves fill the quiet morning air. The smell of the ocean water and my coffee bring a sense of calmness that I need.

After my last sip of morning bliss, I head to the bathroom to change out of Alder's clothes and make myself presentable enough to get back to the Airbnb. I have no idea who is supposed to be working today, but I also don't care. I guess whoever is home is who I come home to.

When I turn on the bathroom light, the hotel notepad and pen are lying next to the sink. As I get closer, I see there's writing on it.

Jaemes,
"If I could cry a little harder and get a little less sleep
at night,
If I had two dozen roses, would it change your mind?
Baby, could you change your mind?"
—Alder

Those aren't just song lyrics. Those are words that mean so much more. They have a great deal of meaning behind them because they represent us, but in the past. I rip the page off the notepad and fold it into my pocket. When I leave the resort, I don't request an Uber for a ride. Instead, I pass the pool and go down to the beach entrance. I sit in the sand under the orange rising sun and think about everything. Everything about Alder and everything about Ledger. So, what does the heart do when it's being pulled in two different directions?

It does what it wants.

PART THREE

THE SECRETS

Chapter Thirty-Three

The Last Day

I CAN'T HELP but notice the pit in my stomach still making me ache as I sit in my assigned seat on the plane waiting to land in Bozeman, Montana. I wish my time in Florida wasn't so caught up in Alder, but I decided to go in the first place with only him in mind. I have no one to blame but myself.

It always seems to take forever for the luggage to arrive at baggage claim. One by one, the suitcases fall onto the conveyor belt circling the carousel. I'm waiting for my bright neon yellow hardshell suitcase, but all that seems to show up are dull-colored ones. I head to the bathroom to throw my bronze hair in a ponytail. I'm hot and can't stand my lengthy hair plastered against my neck. Looking in the mirror, I notice bags under my blue-gray eyes due to my lack of sleep last night.

My phone vibrates inside my pants pocket, letting me know Ledger texted me. He is waiting for me at the airport pick-up area outside.

I grab my suitcase when it finally lands on the carousel and head out the door. I'm a little nervous to see him, as I know he will want to hear all about my trip. I don't know how to tell him anything without expressing my true emotions. I've never been a good liar.

When I see him standing by his parked red truck, he doesn't wait for me to approach him. He starts walking toward me and picks me up, squeezing me tight. He sets me down and kisses me long and hard. I almost lost the sense of our connection while I was intensely distracted during my trip. But again, that's no one's fault but my own.

"I can't wait to hear all about Florida," he says, looking at me with those gorgeous blue eyes.

"It was a good time," I say, trying to sound truthful.

He places my suitcase next to Archie's booster seat in the backseat of his truck. Once we are comfortably seated in the front, he immediately takes my hand and drives us back home.

"You okay?" he asks, sounding slightly concerned. "You seemed a little off when we spoke last night."

"I'm just drained. It was a long day of traveling, having gotten little sleep. I think a nap is in my future."

That isn't a lie. I'm having trouble focusing on anything right now. I'm finding myself wondering what Alder is doing, and if his mind is filled with thoughts of me, like mine is with him. It's obvious I'm not myself. If I were, I'd be much happier to see Ledger.

"Well, make yourself comfortable. Sleep all the way home if you need to."

I don't hesitate to close my eyes and drift off to sleep. Mainly because I can't help myself. My body is begging me to turn off my brain and get the rest I so desperately need. Maybe when I awaken, I'll finally be back to normal again.

LEDGER NUDGES ME gently to wake me up once we get into town. I can hardly pry my eyes open after waking up from such a short slumber. I take no time to get out of his truck and into the house just to fall back asleep again. I'm not doing anything else until I get more rest. What I don't realize is that I'm crawling into Ledger's bed instead of mine. I could have sworn that he was taking me home. But at this point, I don't care where I'm at. My belongings can stay in his truck, and he can occupy himself for a while.

After a four-hour nap, I can finally say I'm well rested. But does the pit in my stomach still remind me of Alder and my Florida trip? Absolutely. It's hard to ignore. I head downstairs to find Ledger and hear a small voice coming from the living room.

"Jaemes!" the little boy calls out as he runs my way and hugs me with his tiny arms.

"Hi, Archie. It's so good to see you," I tell him.

"I didn't know you were here," he tells me.

"I didn't know I was going to be here either," I smile at him. "But I'm glad I am so that I could see you."

"I have to get back to my game. Do you want to watch me? It's so cool!"

"Maybe later, buddy. I need to find your dad first. Do you know where he is?"

"Um…" Archie looks around and thinks for a minute. "Oh, I think he is in the garage."

I smile and ruffle his curly, blond hair before he runs back to his video game in the living room.

Ledger's truck is parked in the garage with the hood up. He is dressed in jeans and a casual t-shirt with grease stains. He has a ball cap on backward, and his hands look rough and dirty. When I look at him this way, he reminds me of Alder. The man I can't stop thinking about. I'm used to Ledger being a clean-cut man—the sophisticated doctor who dresses in classy clothing. But instead, at this moment, he's helping my thoughts remain on Alder.

"Look who's up. Feeling better?" he asks me while wiping one of his tools free of grime.

I nod. "Much better," I lie.

"Good. Archie is inside somewhere, if you'd like to see him. I'm sure he'd love that you're here."

"Oh, he already greeted me," I tell him with a smile. "It was quick since he had to return to his game."

Ledger lets out a small chuckle. "Yeah, that boy and his video games. I'm surprised he could tear himself away for even a second."

He steps away from under the hood of his truck when he realizes I'm silent.

"Are you sure you're okay? You still seem a little off," he says with furrowed eyebrows.

"Everything is fine. I'm just trying to wake up fully, that's all," I lie again.

He stares at me as if he's trying to believe me before finally nodding and returning to his truck. However, everything is not okay. I'm constantly being reminded of Alder and not resuming my relationship with Ledger. Perhaps I should speak with Alder one more time when he returns from Florida tomorrow. Who knows, maybe being in Florida only altered the ambience between Alder and me. Could just a few days away really cause me to reconsider being with him, even after knowing the whole reason why we ended things in the first place? I need to feel things out with Ledger first to make sure I'm making the right choice for my well-being, with a clear mind and a refreshed focus. I'm sure I'll be reminded of why I'm with *him* and all the happiness he brings me.

Chapter Thirty-Four

"JAEMES, CAN I see you in my office, please?"

I slowly lift my head off my arm, which is lying on my desk. It was a long and difficult day at work today, and I'm exhausted. Jerry and Dr. Wimer have been patient with me, but I assume it has run out, as Jerry is calling me into his office.

Jerry gestures to one of his chairs across from his desk, and I take a seat.

"Jaemes, we've noticed you've been late the last few days. I wanted to check in and make sure you aren't being overworked. Our primary goal is for you to learn and gain knowledge about your career path. Perhaps we need to take a step back and regain focus on why you're here in the first place."

"I have to apologize to you and Dr. Wimer. I've been a bit distracted with my personal life, and I'm doing my best to keep it from affecting my day-to-day job duties. I promise I'll do better."

Jerry has his hands folded and is resting them on his desk. His glasses are loosely sitting on the bridge of his nose.

He takes a pen and paper and sets them in front of him.

"Would you like to talk about what's been bugging you?" he asks me.

"No, sir. I'll be fine. I just have to focus more on separating my personal life from my professional life. That's all."

Jerry forms a smile and sets his pen down next to his pad of paper.

"Jaemes, it's my job to notice when someone is feeling 'off'. And it's also my job to help people navigate through tough feelings and situations. I'm offering you my services to help you better manage both your work and personal life. It's part of the perks of interning here. It will also give you a sense of how clients feel when you'll be working with them someday in the future."

If I want to improve my life in general, I need to take action and make positive changes. That includes taking care of my mental health so I can live a happier life both personally and professionally. How can I be successful in any way if I can't learn and grow from my work and life experiences? Here goes nothing.

I give Jerry the lowdown on what's been going on with me lately. And it's not all about Ledger and Alder. I'm reliving my relationship with Harrison all over again, but this time, in a different role. I promised myself I would never hurt anyone the way he once hurt me. I'm still grieving Rian and trying to get used to my mom in her new life without him. I don't see my mom the same anymore, and that's hard to accept. She and Rian were always a package deal, and I miss how my family used to look—my mom, Rian, and me.

My biological dad has always been in the back of my mind as well. Ever since my mom lit that fire with the scrapbook she made me. Sure, it was a grand gesture for her to finally take that step and teach me about my dad after all this time. It makes me wonder about him even though I don't want to. He doesn't deserve to be in my thoughts. But it certainly looked as if he had made my mom happy once upon a time.

"Being with Ledger has been challenging, to say the least. I'm trying my best to give him a fair shot. Give *us* a fair shot. Before my Florida trip, I wanted no one more than Ledger. I don't know how those strong feelings vanished unless they were only being masked in the first place. It's been difficult to decipher what my heart wants versus what my brain *thinks* I want."

Both can play mean tricks on you.

"I've spent a month making sure my decision was the right one. I've been spending a lot of time with Ledger since I returned from my trip. At this point, I'm either convincing myself that Ledger should be my person or completely ignoring the fact that I'm not with the right man. Ledger has continued to catch me acting differently, but I'm unsure if it's me acting or just being my genuine, stupid self."

Jerry finishes what he's writing down and takes his glasses off his face.

"Jaemes, I'd like for you to listen to me closely. You've been through a lot of trauma for a young adult. It's going to take some time for all those burdens to calm down. What are you doing to manage all of this?"

"Um, honestly…nothing," I admit.

"I think it would be beneficial for you to attend an emotional support group. Both you and your mom, but perhaps not at the same meeting, since you two have experienced traumas, but not of the same scope. If this is something you'd be interested in, I can send you the information. Maybe working through these tough emotions will give you a new perspective on your relationships and help you better understand what and who influences your purpose."

"If you think that's something that will help, I'll give it some thought," I tell him.

He provides me with the information for the meeting times and locations.

"Please let me know if you need anything else. But I hope this helps you. You are a tremendous person, and you deserve to live the life you want and with *whom* you want to live it. Don't let anyone else determine what your happiness looks like. You, and only you, can do that. Good luck, kiddo."

THERE'S A MEETING down the street at one of the local churches in town. After I enter the main doors, I see a room to my right with chairs lined up. It's similar to what you'd see in a movie or a TV show. There are more people here than I expected. I never thought I'd need to attend an emotional support group, but if Jerry saw something in me that I didn't, maybe it's worth giving it a shot. If it helps me in any way, I'll have to be sure to let my mom know about these meetings. She likes to deal with things on her own, so there's no promise of her agreeing to go.

"You must be Jaemes," a lady says to me just after I take a seat in the back.

"Yes, Jaemes Dovaughn. Jerry Shaw recommended that I attend one of these meetings."

"Yes, of course. If you find that today has benefited you, please be sure to come back as many times as you need. We are all here for each other." She smiles. "I wanted to introduce myself and welcome you. I like to do it personally rather than in front of everyone. It can be a little intimidating for some people."

"I appreciate that," I tell her.

"My name is Lisa Beckett."

"Nice to meet you, Lisa."

She smiles at me and walks to the front of the group to begin the meeting. Everyone is of all different ages with a range of issues. A middle-aged man is going through a brutal divorce. A teenage girl is suffering repercussions after learning she became pregnant. An elderly woman is having a difficult time dealing with the loss of her husband of over fifty years, and so many others in between—everyone who wanted to talk about their experiences and how they are doing, share, including myself. I mean, I'm here. I might as well do what I'm here for.

Lisa concludes the meeting with a mental exercise.

"I want everyone to close their eyes and take a few long and deep breaths. Inhale for five, hold for five, and exhale for five. Repeat this a few times until you feel as relaxed as possible. Then, I want you to think of the first place that comes to mind that makes you feel the happiest. A place where you can easily be your truest self."

The log house.

"What does this place look like? Who is there with you? What does it smell like? What do you hear?" she continues.

Alder.

"Stay there for a minute. Let these feelings and thoughts take root deeply in your mind. Think about why this place makes you feel the most comfortable. And when you're ready, open your eyes. How do you feel? I want you to think about this every time your trauma memories and experiences creep up on you. I want you to remind yourself that there is a happy place that you can always go to. There are people you can go to when times get more challenging than ever. Our experiences will never go away. That's a fact. The way we manage ourselves when the memories flood back in is essential. The aftermath of our traumas and what happens next can be controlled."

Lisa made my first meeting calming and reassuring. She gave me great mechanisms to help me slow down my thoughts and take things one step at a time. This isn't just a chapter in my life, it's a whole, never-ending story that I'll be living forever. And it's up to me on how I manage the hard times whenever they may pop up.

I DIDN'T PLAN on just showing up out of nowhere, but I've come this far; I'm not turning around now. I feel disappointed when his truck isn't in his driveway. Without thinking about what to do, I exit my car and sit on one of the chairs on his front porch while I wait.

I end up waiting for about twenty minutes until my stomach flutters with nerves as I watch his truck pull into the driveway. Alder parks near the barn shed and slams his truck door shut. He seems heated and distraught. He leans against his truck with his hands and arms extended and his head hanging down. I see his shoulders rise and then come back down as he takes a deep breath. Slowly, he walks over to the stone path leading to the house's front porch, where I'm seated. It seems like he doesn't realize I'm here waiting for him. Something must be wrong if he didn't even notice that my car was parked just a few yards away.

"Holy shit. Jaemes," he says, finally seeing me when he gets to the top of the porch stairs.

"I'm sorry. I should have told you I was coming," I tell him, standing up from the chair. He looks pale and frozen, as if seeing me was equivalent to seeing a ghost. Something doesn't seem right with him. "Everything okay?" I ask cautiously.

He shakes his head. "What are you doing here?" he asks.

You're my happy place.

"Can we talk?" I ask.

"Now isn't a good time, Jae." He walks toward the front door and unlocks it.

"And why not?" I ask him, surprised by his response. Based on how he was toward me in Florida, I was sure he'd want to talk to me again. Maybe I was right when I thought Montana would remind me why we aren't together anymore, while Florida only gave us a fictional paradise.

He's quiet and still until he unleashes whatever is causing him to act this way. "God fucking damn it!" he yells while punching the door. I step back, not knowing what to do, so I let him be. He doesn't continue into the house after the door is unlocked. Instead, he sits in the other chair. I sit beside him while remaining silent, waiting for him to talk when he is ready. If he really didn't want to talk to me, he would have gone inside by now and shut the door in my face.

He doesn't say anything for a while. He doesn't try to look at me. He just stares at the floor of the porch. I grab his hand and hold it in mine. He tightens his grip on my hand while a tear falls down his face. He wipes it away angrily.

"Alder, talk to me, please," I plead. It's his turn to be vulnerable, and my turn to be there for him like he always has been for me. He continues to stare endlessly at the porch floor. I take his face in my hands and make him look at me. There's a lot of hurt in his eyes, and it's incredibly sad to see him like this. Because this isn't him. I've never seen him in this state before. Now, I'm afraid to find out what happened to make a man like Alder feel this way.

"Jaemes," he whispers as he closes his eyes. "I can't…" he says with more forceful, falling tears. He hides his face with his hands, not wanting to show his emotions. All I want to do is comfort him and help ease his pain as much as I can. As much as he'll let me.

"Let's go inside. I can make you something to eat while you shower," I tell him.

We slowly stand up, but he's still unable to look at me. Alder has gone from a confident and motivated man willing to do anything to be with me to a man who seems to have given up on everything he has worked so hard for. Did I hurt him that much in Florida? A part of me feels like I'm to blame. However, there seems to be more to this than just finding out that I have a new man in my life.

Alder starts his shower, and I inspect his kitchen, which looks bare. I can't make anything with a bottle of ketchup, moldy bread, and milk that has expired two weeks ago. His dishes are piled up in the sink, the dishwasher is filled with clean dishes that still need to be put away, and his garbage is overflowing. As I throw out all the old food, I notice several empty beer cans accompanied by a large empty bottle of Jameson. There are piles of clothes in his room. Possibly some dirty mixed in with some clean, but it's hard to tell.

What happened to him?

A nice meal with no alcohol will be good for him once he emerges from his room. Although he's now cleaned up, he still looks like a mess.

"I can order some food if you want. You literally have nothing in your kitchen, Alder."

"I'm not hungry," he states.

"You need to eat actual food. It looks like the only meal you've had lately has been solely alcohol. I won't sit here and watch you dig yourself into an early grave."

"Then leave."

"Do you seriously want me to leave? What the hell is going on with you?" I ask while carrying a basket full of dirty clothes toward the stairs.

After a response of only silence, I drop the basket at the top of the stairs and join him on the couch in his living room. "This is enough, Alder. Why won't you talk to me? What has changed since the Florida trip? You need to help me understand why you're acting this way so I can help you. Did I make you feel this way?"

"Why aren't you with Ledger? The man you claim to love. Why are you *here*?" he asks me with a sense of despair. Even throughout this conversation, he still can't look at me.

Do I tell him about how he makes me feel versus how Ledger makes me feel? Do I say to him that even though Ledger may check every single one of my boxes, it's not him who makes me the happiest? I should say *something* to him.

"I got someone pregnant," he blurts out. "She just told me a few days ago. The baby is due mid-December. It's one of the biggest mistakes I've ever made, but I can't undo it. I'm sorry."

My brain is having a hard time comprehending the words that were just spoken to me. The look on his face confirms that what he just said is really the truth. Because no one makes a face like that when they're lying, unless they're that good at it. Not Alder, though. This is a scared face that's full of brokenness and regret and not knowing what's going to come next.

"Please…say something, Jae."

"Congratulations," I say flatly before leaving the house with him alone.

What else was I supposed to say to that? I should have known something big was going to come out of his mouth after seeing him in such rough shape, but I never, ever expected *that*. I'm in utter disbelief and can't grasp the reality of this news. Am I being pranked? Either this is a prank, or everything he said in Florida was a complete joke. It doesn't matter. Both would be just as cruel. You can't go from wanting someone so badly to impregnating someone else all within such a short timeframe. But maybe Alder can, and that doesn't sit right with me.

What hurts the most is feeling like my happy place and my person were merely a disguise. Alder has broken my heart one too many times, but why can't I just stop loving him? I don't know who I'm more upset with…Alder or myself.

Chapter Thirty-Five

I T'S FUNNY HOW life can reveal what you truly need by putting you in the worst predicaments. How could I even think for a second that Ledger wasn't the right person for me? I feel so stupid, like I've been brainwashed by a man who says he loves me more than anything in this world.

What was I thinking?

I'm en route to Ledger's house when I get a text from Livvy in our group message with Ember.

> **Livvy:** *Guess who just landed in Montana to see her girls?!*
>
> **Ember:** *Shut up! Are you seriously here?*
>
> **Livvy:** *Yup! My brother is attending college here, and I'm visiting for a few days. We have to meet up!*
>
> **Ember:** *How do I not remember you telling us your brother goes to college in Montana? Good lord, I need to stop drinking so much…*

I ignore the conversation at this time. I have bigger things to worry about than having a girl's night with Ember and Livvy. Although maybe that's exactly what I need at a time like this. No, everything is too fresh, and all I need right now is the man who makes me feel seen and wanted—my boyfriend.

I arrive at Ledger's house and let myself in. He is in the kitchen when he sees me walk through the front door.

"Hey, beautiful. Where have you been?" Ledger asks as he stirs a pot on the stove.

I frantically think of what to say. Telling him I was recently at Alder's house might not go over so well.

"Just visiting my mom," I end up telling him.

"I thought she was working this weekend," he says, glancing over at me as I remain standing in the entryway.

Fuck.

"She is, but she doesn't leave until later tonight," I say, trying to save myself.

"Hi, Jaemes!" Archie says from the dining room. He is seated at the table, waiting for Ledger to finish making supper. "Are you going to eat with us?"

"No, buddy, I'm not very hungry. But I can join you at the table and keep you company. How does that sound?" Archie doesn't have the chance to answer me. Ledger places the wooden spoon he was stirring with on the counter and pulls me toward the living room.

"Can we talk in private, please? Away from Archie," he says quietly, so Archie doesn't hear.

"What's going on?" I ask him.

"How about you tell me what's going on? You haven't been yourself since the day you returned from your trip. What happened down in Florida? I know *something* happened because you left being the person I fell in love with and came back a different person. Where'd you go, Jaemes? *Talk to me.*"

Did he just tell me he loved me for the first time? Before Ember invited me on the trip, I wouldn't have thought twice about saying it back, but now I only feel numb. The man I thought I loved recently told me he was expecting to be a dad after voicing how much he hated the idea of that. Some woman will be the mother of his child instead of me, the person he said was the love of his life. It's impossible to wrap my head around the shock of that news.

"Is there someone else?" he asks with a distressed look.

"No," I answer. Because there isn't anymore. "Can I just please have a hug?" I ask him quietly through stinging tears. It takes him no time to gather me up in his arms while I weep. I know I must tell him everything that happened, but not now. I need time. I can't move on in this relationship with Ledger when lies are flying all around us. I owe him the truth, just like I would expect him to be truthful with me in return.

"Will you tell me eventually?" he asks me in a gentler tone this time.

Still comfortably in his arms, I respond with, "I will." I know deep down that I *do* love Ledger. I hope that as more time goes on, I'll be able to say it to him.

Archie and Ledger are eating supper at the dining room table when my phone continues to ding with multiple text messages. A few are from the group message.

Ember: *Jaemes, are you in for a get-together?*

Livvy: *Come on, Jaemes!*

And one is from Alder.

Alder: *Don't throw me out of your life yet. I'll let you have your space, but please come back to me when you're ready.*

I reply to the group message and leave Alder in the dust.

Me: *I'm in. Just tell me when and where.*

I MEET EMBER and Livvy in Bozeman later in the evening. We plan to have dinner, and then who knows what we will do afterward. Livvy is staying with her brother at the house he and two friends are renting together. Ember called me, and we talked the whole way to Bozeman since we drove separately. She is still deciding if she wants to stay with Livvy tonight or if she is going to go home. As for me, I'm fully dedicated to going home afterward. I have too much going on as it is. I'm certain Ember can't tell anything is wrong since I couldn't get a word in. She talked my ear off during the whole thirty-five-minute commute. But it's better that way.

Ember and I spot Livvy sitting at a table waiting for us. We approach her, and she hugs us both. It's nice to have more friendly faces around. I can't wait until my mom returns from work. She would be the best person to talk to about what's happening in my life. Ember is too close to Alder, and I'm not close enough to Livvy yet, but I'm optimistic our friendship will evolve. If anything, Ember and Livvy seem much closer, which makes sense since they have spent more time together. The three of us catch up on typical boring everyday stuff. It has only been a month since the Florida trip, so not much has changed.

"What should we do after we eat?" Ember asks us. I shrug, not wanting to think. I'm just here for a good distraction.

"Well," Livvy starts with a smirk, "I would much rather chill tonight. Maybe watch some movies versus going out and drinking."

"What? Seriously?" Ember asks with furrowed eyebrows. "You are on a little vacation to Montana and don't want *us* to show *you* the ropes this time? We, without doubt, owe you for helping us have the time of our lives in Florida."

"Yeah, why do you want to relax? We can do that anytime. Let's go out and have some fun. I'll buy the first round of drinks," I tell them.

"I don't know how fun I'll be..." Livvy says. "I haven't been feeling well..." Ember and I look at each other and then back to Livvy since she is still smirking. "Because I'm *pregnant!*"

"Oh my God!" Ember and I say in unison.

"Congratulations!" Ember says while standing up to hug her.

"Yeah, wow, that's exciting!" I tell her before hugging her myself. "I didn't know you and your boyfriend were that serious."

"We are working on it," Livvy says with a smile. We haven't been together for very long, and it just happened, so I think we are both a little nervous."

"When are you due? How are you feeling?" Ember squeals with excitement.

Livvy wipes her face with her napkin, trying to hide her smile. "I'm due December sixteenth. I've felt slightly nauseous, which is common in the first trimester. Luckily, I've felt pretty good other than that."

"Awe, I hope it's a girl," Ember says. However, I can't help but notice the disturbing coincidence with her due date.

"Hey, Liv…" I start, "how exactly did you meet this guy?"

"Oh, through a dating app. At first, it wasn't anything serious. It was just a way to connect with other guys and put myself out there in the dating world. Now look at me!"

"I see," I say flatly. "And does this guy live in Florida, too?" There's worry lingering in my tone of voice versus an exciting curiosity, as there should be during a conversation like this. But I can't seem to control that. Livvy quickly looks at Ember before answering me, and her smile fades.

"No, he lives in a different state," she says vigilantly. "Why do you ask?"

I lean in a little closer to her. "Which state does he reside in, Liv?"

"I don't know. He never told me. He finally flew down to hang out with me in person for the first time a little over a month ago, and we just kind of…hit it off."

"What's going on, Jaemes?" Ember asks me with legitimate concern.

I lean back in my chair and cross my arms. I don't want to see the look on my face right now, as I can't control the glare

I'm throwing in Livvy's direction. I can feel my supper start to invade my throat.

"Tell me more about this guy," I demand. I don't ask what his name is because I would rather figure it out for myself than hear his name come out of her mouth. "What does he look like? What does he do for a living? How long have you two been talking on this dating app?"

"Um… well… he has short brown hair, hazel eyes, he's very charming. He works in construction, and we have been talking for about six months now."

That's all I needed to hear before darting out of the restaurant. Before getting in my car, I vomit as if I'm trying to get rid of the sensation of heartbreak. It doesn't take much to put two and two together.

This can't be happening.

I RETURN TO Ledger's house, hysterical, and tell him everything. And I mean *everything.* I told him about my past with Alder, including our interactions in Florida and the recent news I had been given. However, I leave out that I went to Alder's house, and that *he* had told me the news first.

"Wow. That's, um, a lot to take in," Ledger finally says. "So, let me get this straight…the guy you were most recently in a relationship with pretty much ended things because he doesn't want a wife and kids, but then goes and gets a random woman pregnant?"

Hearing the summary coming from Ledger is hard to listen to. It sounds worse coming from someone else than thinking about it in my own head.

We are both sitting on the couch in his living room. Archie is in bed for the night, which gives us the time and space to have this difficult conversation.

"Why are you so upset about it? You're with me, now. Are you not entirely over him?"

"It's just the fact that we ended things so abruptly, and then he went off and did something that contradicted everything he ever told me. I can't help but think that there is something wrong with me."

"There is absolutely nothing wrong with you, Jaemes. You made me fall in love with you, and I don't fall easily."

I lean into him, and he holds me tightly. His hand gently rubs my back in a soothing motion.

"Thank you for never lying to me. I appreciate the man you are," I tell him genuinely.

"Let's go to bed and try to sleep all of this off. We'll wake up refreshed in the morning."

I like the idea of starting over. It feels good to get everything out in the open to the point where Ledger knows all of my past, and I know all of his. There are no secrets between us, and it is helping us get even closer.

Of course, I can't fall asleep easily. My mind keeps reminding me that Alder and Livvy are having a baby together. The man I once considered my forever person and "Ember's friend" slept together right before my eyes. That's why his name wasn't attached to the messages on Livvy's phone when Ember and I watched her text him that one night in Florida. Their fling was so new that she hadn't even saved his name in her phone. This all makes perfect sense now. It explains why I had my recent panic attack in Alder's hotel room. I could feel something horrible happening as it occurred on our trip.

Alder and Livvy were never in the same place when I was around. It makes me wonder if anyone else knew what happened between them. I feel like a complete fool. While all this continues to flood my mind, I quietly cry myself to sleep in Ledger's arms.

Chapter Thirty-Six

I QUICKLY REACH for my phone as soon as I wake up. The time reads just after nine in the morning. Ledger isn't lying next to me anymore, and that oddly doesn't affect me. I'm sure Archie gets up pretty early, so that means he has to as well. I expect to have a bunch of messages waiting for me, but the only notification on my screen is from Ember.

> **Ember:** Hey. I tried catching up after you left the restaurant, but you were too far gone. Livvy gave me the name of the guy she was talking about, and I can't believe I didn't realize it then. I now know why you are so upset. I'm so sorry, Jaemes. I had no idea that was happening in the slightest. Talk about the most fucked up coincidence…If you need a friend to talk to or a shoulder to cry on, please let me know, and I'll be there. I love you, Jae Jae!

I took a mental day off from work and went to Ember's house because that's exactly what I need from her. Someone to talk to without judgment and a shoulder to cry on.

"I left after I paid our bill. I wasn't up for hanging out after you left," Ember tells me. We are on the old playset in her parents' backyard. It's the same one we played on when we were kids. Now, it's all rusted out and squeaky sounding. We are seated on the swings, gently rocking back and forth.

"Yeah, I owe you for that meal. I'll pay you back, I promise," I tell her.

"Don't sweat it. It sounds like you've been through enough. Does Ledger know about all of this?"

"Yes."

"No, like, *all* of it?" she asks again to make sure.

"Yes. Every single thing and every little detail."

"Yikes. How is he taking it?" she asks, pushing off the ground with her feet to make herself sway more in her swing.

I shrug. "As good as he possibly can, I guess. It was a lot to put on him all at once, but I can tell he is trying to process it the best he can. I'm lucky he feels so strongly for me."

"As you do for him," she adds.

I don't say anything to confirm or deny.

"Right?" she asks for possible confirmation, but I remain wordless.

Neither one of us could have predicted this happening. Ember would have been the first person to stop these unfortunate events, since she was the one person who wanted Alder and me together the most. Being a close outsider and the one person who knows me best, she could easily see that what Alder and I had was special and unlike anything else. It's too bad nothing has worked out in our favor.

"I think you should go talk with him," Ember tells me, breaking the silence.

"I already talked to Ledger last night. I want to give him time and space to—"

"Space for him, or more so for you?" she interrupts. "And I wasn't talking about Ledger."

"Who then?" I lean my head against one of the chains of the swing, and she gives me a pointed look. "I'm not going to talk to him, Ember."

"I think you should," she says in a slight singing tone.

"And say what? That I'm pissed off and hurt that he could do something like this? After everything we've been through, he gets someone pregnant. And not just someone, but *Livvy* out of all people."

"Yes, exactly. It would be best if you told him all of that

and more. Get it all off your chest and out in the open. You need to talk with him if you two want to start moving forward and get past this. Let him have it!"

I hate when Ember makes valid points. All I want her to do is let me vent and agree with me. My mom doesn't come home from work until tomorrow. As much as I need her right now, I wouldn't be able to talk to her even if I tried my hardest. It's tricky when your office is thousands of miles above sea level.

"Ember, the thought of having any more conversations with Alder terrifies me. Who knows what he will admit to me next, and who knows what will come out of it," I tell her.

"That's my point. No one knows what will come out of it. It could be something positive. You know, Jaemes... he's probably hurting just as much as you. And as much as you don't think so, you both need each other more than ever right now."

"That's bullshit, Em. He fucked up and ruined everything. Why should I give him the gratification of comfort and support when it's the last thing he deserves from me?"

"Because you love him."

Alder once told me that he would be there for me whenever I needed him, no matter what. I know that to be true, but I can't find it in myself to do the same for him. It will be the last time I decide to talk with him again. My patience for Alder is thinning out, and I don't know if I can continue to put myself through any more despair because I know that I deserve better.

My phone dings as I walk back to my car in Ember's driveway.

Ledger: *What are you up to?*

Me: *I'm visiting Ember. You don't have to worry. I'm no longer giving Alder the time of day.*

My mind feels just as screwed up as my heart, and they

both constantly bicker back and forth. It's like I don't have any control over what I do or how I feel.

Before I realize it, I'm back in Alder's driveway. It's two-thirty on a Monday afternoon, and his truck is parked near the shed again. This can't be good. One of the things he values most in life is his career and the goals surrounding it. It would take a lot for him to miss a day of work. Ember's words replaying in my head were enough for me to pull into his driveway, get out of my car, and walk to his front door. As nervous and scared as I am, I am unsure if I should walk in, knock, or turn around and head in the other direction.

I find that the door is unlocked, and after I step inside, I notice his house is exactly how it was before I helped clean it out a few days ago. Alder isn't in the living room or his bedroom. I quietly head downstairs, where I can faintly hear the TV. When I reach the basement, I see beer cans overflowing the coffee and end tables. He's sound asleep on the couch, and his appearance looks scruffier. His five o'clock shadow has grown longer on his face, and his hair needs a haircut.

Why am I here, letting myself into his house? More importantly, why does my heart break for him?

I walk toward the couch and sit beside him. I take the half-empty beer can from his hand and place it on the floor. I don't know how much sleep he has gotten lately. It can't be much since he is passed out and didn't move a muscle when I took his beer out of his hand. I place a blanket over him and decide to leave. I think I finally came to my senses.

But then he opens his eyes, and I'm the first thing he sees.

"Hey," I say first.

"Hey," he says back in the same forlorn tone. He reaches for my hand and pulls me down to sit with him. Still tired, he closes his eyes again and places his arm over my lap.

"We should talk," I tell him.

He nods in agreement.

"You know," I start, "I don't think you getting someone else pregnant is what hurts the most. It's the fact that you got someone pregnant after telling me you loved me, with the firm belief of never wanting to get married or have kids with me. Even after you say I am the most important person to you. I was willing to give up *everything* just to be with you. Because you're *my* person, Alder. How could you be so careful when it came to me, yet could easily be so careless when it came to someone else? Someone you barely know. *That's* what hurts the most. It's like you took my feelings and any future chances of us being together and threw it all away like it was nothing.

I tell him, "Livvy, Alder? Fucking *Livvy*? You stood there and watched me fall right back in love with you in Florida, all while hooking up with Livvy. Not only did you hook up with her, but you got her pregnant! What the hell is wrong with you?" At this point, I'm so deep in this moment that I don't notice all of the tears streaming down my face.

"I understand if you hate me—"

"No, Alder, I don't hate you. I love you, and *that's* the problem!" I correct him and throw his arm off of me. "When did it happen? Was it just once? More than once?"

"Jaemes…"

"No, I need to know."

"It happened twice. Once, when I arrived, and again during the pool party at the resort."

Okay, maybe I didn't want to know that.

"Jaemes, I was broken inside when you weren't in my life anymore. I couldn't stand living my life without you. The only thing I could do was try to get involved with someone else, hoping it could distract me from those unfamiliar feelings."

"Oh, so wait…I told you I was dating someone else, and that made you go sleep with someone and then have no problem coming back to me when I was suffering from a panic attack that you caused in the first place?"

"Do you know how hard it is to hear the person you love the most say that they found their forever person?" he asks, trying to defend himself.

"No, Alder. I had it worse. The person that *I* love the most told me he impregnated some random chick after telling me, *the love of his life*, that there was no chance of that ever happening between us!" I'm yelling at this point. I don't know how much clearer I can make this for him. How hurt do I need to be for him to realize that we will never be able to recover from something like this?

"I understand," he says, defeated.

"Do you, though?" I ask with furrowed eyebrows.

"Yes, Jaemes. Trust me, I've thought long and hard about how I made the mistake of a lifetime. Not only did I go against everything I believed in, but I also lost the love of my life along the way. Forever. And I realize that."

"Excuse me? What do you mean by '*everything* you believed in'? What else did you do?" I ask cautiously.

He takes a deep breath before continuing. "When we ended our relationship, I thought there might be a way to get you back." He gets up from the couch and walks upstairs. I hear his footsteps go into his bedroom. There's a sound of a drawer opening and then closing. When he returns to me on the couch downstairs, I see him holding a small black box.

"When you said you were willing to give up everything for me, well, I was too." He opens the box, and a gorgeous engagement ring is lying inside.

"And you think by showing me this will get me back?"

"I used to. But not anymore."

"I can't do this. I need to leave," I tell him, getting off the couch and making my way to the front door.

"Please don't leave me again, Jaemes," he says, doing his best to stop me. His voice sounds pained and sorrowful. "I can't take living without you. I have to watch you leave repeatedly, and I can't take it anymore. I'm going crazy!"

"Good," I say to him before slamming the door behind me.

Chapter Thirty-Seven

ALTHOUGH GOOGLE CAN give you all of the various definitions of the word "love," it can't tell you the actual human experience that it attaches itself to. All of the definitions resonate with me in one way or another. Just like they should with everyone else. Love can sometimes be vague, as it encompasses many different meanings. Love is also a very powerful word. To play around with it like it's nothing is like throwing around knives and hoping it won't hurt someone. I can honestly say I'm not guilty of that. For years, I was taught to know what love is. I can recognize when love isn't true and visualize it clearly. My mom gave me the ability to see the difference between love and lust, but somehow, I'm finding it to become a blur, and I hate myself for that. I've been caught up in too many relationships that I can personally handle. Who do I say I love, and who do I genuinely love? Do I only feel the sense of lust when it comes to Ledger? I can't tell anymore. I thought I had it all figured out until Alder reinserted himself in my life. How I feel about Alder is utterly different than how I feel about Ledger. With many different kinds of love, how do I know which one is true? It's all quite complicated, to say the least.

"You haven't been yourself lately," my mom says, sitting across from me on her patio. The sun is setting for the day, and I'm elated that it's finally time to start another weekend. One week closer to the end of the school year. Everyone, including students and staff, feels burnt out and ready to head into summer break.

"There's a reason for that, I guess," I tell her while playing with a piece of my hair and staring at the ground.

"Well, talk to me. I haven't seen you in a while and want to know what's happening. I still haven't heard how your trip to Florida went. Did you guys have fun?"

I nod. "Yeah, it was fun."

"And?" she asks, wanting me to elaborate more. Based on what happened during and after I returned, I want to skip to the part that affected me the most.

"Alder got someone pregnant," I blurt out, making my mom spit out her drink. I wait for her to stop coughing before I continue. "He was included in the trip, and I didn't know the girl Ember and I befriended in Florida would eventually become pregnant with Alder's baby. *Alder*. The man who couldn't fathom ever being a dad is now going to be a parent with someone he barely knows. Can you believe that?" I snicker while shaking my head from side to side in disbelief.

"Jaemes...I don't know what to say. I have no words."

"But yet, I'm still drawn to him, and I hate myself for that. I feel more upset about my emotions toward him than his actions. Maybe I was never meant to have kids. I'm either meant to be with Alder and be a stepmom to his baby or I'm meant to be with Ledger and be a stepmom to his son. The universe is trying to tell me something, Mom, and I'm trying to figure out why I'm being led down this path. *Maybe* what we are meant to have in life isn't what we necessarily want."

"Jaemes, your future is whatever you want it to be. And no one can get in the way of that. Not even God. The only person who can stop you is you. Don't do that to yourself." My mom leans forward and places her hand softly on my lap. "You are a good person. You deserve the world and more," she reassures.

"Thanks, Mom," I say while trying to force a smile.

"Sweetheart, you also need to remember that you are *so*

young yet," she starts.

"Mom…" I try to interrupt before she goes on.

"No, just hear me out. You're almost twenty-four years old. These two men are in their thirties. Ledger seems to have life figured out, and Alder is just starting to move forward with huge life responsibilities. He will be forced to grow up whether he likes it or not. You, on the other hand, are still trying to plan your life out. You can't base your wants and needs on someone else's life situations, Jaemes. Maybe you need a little 'you' time before continuing with a relationship. Use that time to figure out *Jaemes*."

That was supposed to be the plan when I moved back to Montana. However, I have my own house, a great job, an internship in my field of work, and I have a good head on my shoulders. Have I already figured out who I am? Maybe in general, but not in the sense of relationships. Sometimes we lose track of what's most important, and these occasional reminders are essential to help us get back on track because it's easy to get lost in love.

"Mom, what if you stopped talking to me as my mom and started talking to me more like a friend or a stranger asking for advice? What would you say to me?" I ask her.

She thinks about that for a moment before answering me. "If I'm going to be honest with you, I would probably tell you the same thing. And when you're ready to move on with a relationship after allowing yourself to be taken care of, then follow your heart and listen to what it tells you. If you have any inkling of a bad feeling, then you know that's not the right decision. Remember, you can't give another person one hundred percent if you aren't taking care of yourself first."

AFTER MY TALK with my mom, I realized that what I *want* to

do with my future and what I *should* do are on two different ends of the spectrum. Ledger has his life together. He already has a family and a stable job. But on the other hand, Alder still feels like the love of my life. Despite my true feelings, the thought of a stable life draws me to Ledger. So, I let myself give in to this urge and head for his house.

I pull into his driveway just before six o'clock in the evening. He always has the garage door open when he's home, so the fact that it's currently closed tells me he isn't here. I've been losing track of which weeks Archie is with him. He is either dropping him off at Gretchen's or picking him up. I decide to wait for him inside. I feel like we've reached that point in our relationship where it wouldn't be unusual if he came home and found that I'd let myself in.

Again, I'm exhausted. My mind has been doing nothing but racing as I juggle my career, my relationships, and all the stress that comes with it all. I have lost almost ten pounds since I returned from Florida. I look great but feel terrible.

I plop my tired body on Ledger's living room couch and lie on my back. I take a deep breath and stare at the sparkly popcorn ceiling. When I turn to the right to look toward the big bay window, a familiar white envelope on the coffee table catches my eye. It's similar to the ones I once saw in Ledger's nightstand drawer. I take full advantage of being the only one here and look at it closer.

It's addressed to Ledger in handwriting, making me believe whoever is writing him is likely a male. The return address is a premade red stamp that says *Union Correctional Institution* in Raiford, Florida. I googled this place before looking in the ripped-open envelope to better understand who might be writing Ledger from here.

This place is a mixed-security prison that houses male inmates who are typically on death row. It opened in 1961 and is one of the largest prisons in Florida, holding over 1,400 inmates.

What the fuck…

My curiosity intensifies. Do I look at what is inside? I have to. This is not the first time I have seen envelopes like this in his house. Now, it lies here for anyone to see. He hasn't mentioned anything about them, making me think he has something to hide.

Here goes nothing.

Ledger—

My daughter will be getting ready to graduate college soon if she hasn't already done so. I need your expertise and skills to help me find her. I need to know everything there is to know about her. Khrystal has cut off all ties with me. It's killing me knowing that my daughter is out there somewhere all grown up, and I don't know who the hell she is. I don't care what you have to do to get the information I'm craving. I received a different piece of information from another source stating that Khrystal has a man in her life. I'll be damned if I let some asshole think he can be the father to my child. Rumor has it on the outside that he's already been in the picture for several years. If they are going to have any man in their lives, it's going to be me and only me…I don't know who he thinks he is, but claiming my family is the last thing I'll allow that son of a bitch to do. I will go over the logistics with Marky and let you know when it's time for you to step in. In the meantime, you also need to get your ass in gear and get closer to Jaemes, but keep it casual. The last thing I want is for her to get caught up in the Horsemen's shit, as you already know. This will be your final warning before I give you up to the Horsemen. If you want to keep yourself in good standing, you might want to step it up. This is what you've signed up for. As for the man who claims—

sorry—claimed *to be the man of* my *family, let's just say it's a matter of time before news breaks of his disappearance. That poor fucker won't see it coming. I'll keep you updated as long as you keep your end of the deal. If you take care of what I want, I'll keep you and your son safe. Your dad was a legend. Your whole family was legendary. I would never let them down.*

Unless I have to.

—*Jason Kellen*

The name rings a bell.

Of course, it does.

That's my biological dad. This letter makes no sense. I have so many questions going through my mind. How does Ledger know Jason? What does he mean by Khrystal cutting off all ties? Has my mom also been lying to me about my dad? This has to be a joke, an awful and cruel joke that's making me feel sick.

With the letter still in my hands, I glance up at the window, making sure Ledger isn't home yet. I read the letter over and over again. I place my hand over my mouth in disbelief when I realize that he is talking about Rian. My heart sinks, and I start to sob uncontrollably. Is he saying that *they* killed Rian? Was this all just an act? Did Ledger pretend to be interested in me for the sole purpose of spilling information about me to this guy in prison?

I'm frozen. I don't move. I can't even if I try my hardest. I can't believe Rian, the guy who was the best dad, is gone because of these assholes. Jason sounds absolutely crazy. And who the hell are these "Horsemen," and why could Ledger be in trouble with them?

As I wonder how many letters there could be, I recall seeing more in the drawer of his nightstand in his bedroom. I run upstairs and go through every drawer I see. However, there are no other letters to be found.

What did he do with them?

I'm starting not to feel safe. I'm in utter shock at everything I just found out. It's all racing through my head when the sound of a vehicle door closing jolts me back to life, and I shove the letter into my purse. I need to dart out of Ledger's house before he notices it's gone. I make a beeline for the door and run past him to my car.

"Hey, what a surprise seeing—" He stops abruptly once he notices my tears and the look of fear that spreads widely across my face. I don't stop until I reach my car. He's looking at me with concern. But what he doesn't do is chase after me. Instead, he sprints inside his house for something more important as I speed down the road in fury and sorrow. Sorrow for Rian and now for Ledger.

Chapter Thirty-Eight

M Y SPEED GAUGE shows eighty-five miles an hour, but it feels like twenty. I have no idea where I'm going, but I know I have to find a safe space and quickly. I can't go home by myself, and I can't lead anyone to my mom's house. Who knows what Ledger's next move will be? Once he sees that this letter is missing, I, too, may be in trouble with these *Horsemen*. Whoever they may be.

My immediate instinct leads me to the log house. My safe space happens to be with the man who lives there. As much as I don't want to admit that, I'd be lying to myself if I said I didn't need him right this second. When something exciting happens in my life, I want to turn to Alder. When something terrifying happens, I want him to hold me and tell me he'll make everything okay again because that's precisely what he does.

My face is still soaked with tears when I pull into his driveway. I feel lightheaded from hyperventilating the whole way here. I can't get to him fast enough as I run to his door. By now, the sun has dipped behind the mountains, and lightning can be seen on the opposite end of the sky. It won't be long until the twinkling stars disappear and the thunder rolls its way in.

I bang on Alder's front door as my other fist grips my purse. In between loud knocks, I look behind me to make sure I haven't been followed. Growing more impatient, I continue to pound on the door several more times, but still no answer.

The wind starts whipping, drying my face as tears continue to fall. I frantically take out my phone and call Alder, praying to God that he will answer his phone.

Ring…ring…ring… Nothing.

I try again.

Just as I start to believe I'm going to get his voicemail again, he finally answers my call.

"Hello?"

"Alder! Where are you?" I say manically.

"I'm over at Bennett's place. What's wrong?" he asks.

"I'm at your house. I need you to come home. Please!" I beg.

"Are you okay? Are you hurt?" he asks me, concerned.

"No, I'm not okay, and I'm not hurt…yet. I'm scared and need your help," I tell him breathlessly.

"I'm on my way. Hang tight," he says before hanging up.

It takes him fifteen minutes before speeding into the driveway. Another truck follows behind him, and I'm relieved when I realize it's Bennett. They both run up to the front door where I've been waiting. It looks like Alder was able to fix himself up with a much-needed haircut, and his beard is trimmed down to a length slightly longer than a five o'clock shadow again. Their clothes are damp from the rain that's starting to pour. Alder doesn't stop his rush to me until the front side of his body is practically touching mine. Both of his hands land on each side of my face, holding up my weak head. He is looking hard into my eyes, examining anything and everything he can to read me, but I start to cry harder. I can still feel his love for me even after everything we've been through. All the ups and so many downs. His fast breathing hits my face, and his scent gives my heart the hug it's needed for a long time. Bennett stands beside us, his hands resting on his hips, as he listens intently.

"What did he do?" Alder asks me. "I'll fucking kill him if

he laid a finger on you."

The sound of the thunder increases in volume, and the lightning bolts now hover over the log house. The wind is thrashing the rain closer to us, and I shiver. I shiver from the frightening storm and the general feeling of fear itself.

I shake my head no. "I need to show you something."

Alder opens the door, and we rush inside. He grabs a blanket for me and tells Bennett to lock the door behind him. I sit on the couch and cross my legs as I drape the blanket over my lap. I'm sitting on the end of the couch, closer to the patio doors to my left. I ask Alder to close the blinds because I'm far from feeling safe. I now feel like I have a bunch of lurking eyes on me.

"You're scaring me, Jaemes," Alder says as he closes the blinds to the patio doors.

"Yeah, you got me a little riled up too, not gonna lie," Bennett says, sitting on one of the kitchen stools. I wait for Alder to return to me on the couch before I reach for my purse. I fiddle around the inside of it to get the letter. Alder and Bennett keep their eyes locked on my actions, anxiously waiting for me to explain what's going on.

"I have reason to believe that my dad has people watching me." I feel uneasy, knowing that I'll always have to be looking over my shoulder wherever I go. Alder and Bennett's facial expressions turn from concerned to confused.

"Wait, isn't your dad…you know…dead?" Bennett cautiously asks.

Alder's eyes never leave mine. He doesn't scan the room or look back at Bennett. He keeps his eyes locked on me.

"Let her finish," Alder says.

"Yes, Bennett, my *stepdad* is, in fact, dead. I'm talking about my biological dad. He left my mom when she was pregnant with me, and he has never been seen or contacted since. But I know he is in prison and is communicating back and forth with Ledger about me." I take out the letter and hand it to Alder. I watch him closely as he opens it. His hand rests over his mouth and then slides down to his chin, resting his head as he starts to read it.

"This Jason guy is your dad?" he asks with his eyes on the letter.

"Yes."

Alder finishes reading the letter, and he hands it to Bennett.

"Is this the only letter?" Bennett asks me.

"As far as I know. Some were in his nightstand, but I can't find those," I tell him. "I think Rian was murdered, and Jason and Ledger had something to do with it," I add quietly. Alder stands up, places his hands on his hips, and paces the living room with his head tilted downward.

"What are we gonna do, man?" Bennett asks Alder, who is still deep in thought. "Call the police?"

He stops pacing and says, "They won't get here in time if he was following her. I'm going to make sure all the windows and doors in this house are locked and all the blinds are closed. Bennett, can you move her car to the shed? We need to make it look like she isn't here."

"On it," Bennett replies as he walks toward the door. I throw him my keys before he disappears outside. I stay put on the couch as Alder goes around the house, ensuring everything that separates us from the outside is locked and secure. While I wait for them to return, I read the letter once more.

Why am I doing this to myself? My heart can't take reading it, but on the other hand, I must try to understand what everything in this letter means. The more I know, the better I have a handle on this insane situation. Teardrops stain the letter in my hands. There is not a chance in hell I'd ever think about meeting that man. I have never encountered something this impractical, nor did I think I ever would. I hear Alder cocking one of his guns downstairs as he puts ammunition in it. He returns to the living room just as Bennett walks back inside the house.

"Did you shut the shed door?" Alder asks Bennett.

"That's a silly question. You know I did," he replies.

Alder looks at him pointedly. "I'm not risking Jaemes' safety because of assumptions, Bennett."

Alder sees the letter sitting next to me and picks it up to analyze it again. "Who the hell is this guy and what is he doing?" he asks more to himself.

"Hey, Ember is expecting me to meet her at my place soon. Are you okay if I fill her in on what's going on?" Bennett asks me.

"Yeah, I don't feel like reliving this any more than I have to. Thanks, Bennett," I tell him.

Bennett leaves to join Ember. It's probably the best idea, given no one knows what will happen next. Now that Ledger knows I took this letter, we must be careful with our actions. He could easily figure out that I'm with Alder. I call my mom to make sure she is okay, but I don't tell her what's going on. She is on her way to work and will be out of the state again for a while. That makes me feel better in the meantime. I'll sit down with her when she gets home and tell her what I found.

Alder places the loaded gun on the kitchen counter, pointing away from us. He sits beside me on the couch, and we stay silent. There is a big elephant in the room, and I know it has to be brought up at some point.

"You can stay here tonight. I don't feel comfortable with you going to your place," he tells me.

"No, I have to take this to the police," I tell him as I get up to gather everything I have and head toward the door.

Alder rushes to my side before I can reach for the door handle. "You can do that tomorrow. My phone is going crazy with severe thunderstorm and flash flooding alerts. It's not safe for anyone to go anywhere right now."

"Alder, I have to go." I try again to open the door to leave.

"And do what?" he asks with a tightening grip on me. "Get stuck in high running waters? Hydroplane and go into the ditch? Do you want Ledger to find you in this shit?"

"Fine. I'll stay in a bedroom downstairs," I say, finally comprehending what he's trying to get through my head.

He shakes his head. "No, you should sleep in my room. It's the farthest from any entrance to the house, and I want to make sure you're in my sight at all times." He looks me in the eyes. "I'm not going to make a move on you, I promise. I just want to make sure you're safe."

"Are you being this nice to me because of what you did?" I ask. "Because you really don't have to do any of this."

"I already told you, Jae. You have to listen when I tell you I'll always be here for you. I'd do anything for you, no matter what. These people sound pretty fucked up, and if they're capable of killing Rian…" he trails off.

"Then they're capable of killing me or anyone close to me," I add. He nods, and there's a look of rage in his eyes. I slowly take his hands off me and move away from the door.

"I do listen, Alder."

He finally brings his gaze toward me again. "Then, believe me."

"What am I supposed to do? Everything has been tough to deal with ever since you told me…well, you know. I don't have to say it, nor do I have the slightest *want* to say it. And I'm not going to say things like 'I forgive you' or 'let's make this work' or 'I love you, and I want to be with you so God damn badly.'"

"Then don't. You don't have to, and I don't blame you."

"But I *do* love you, and I *do* want to be with you. I just don't know how to forgive you or know how we can make any of this work."

"Telling you what happened in Florida was one of the

worst things I ever had to do, alongside letting you leave your key to my house and watching you walk out that door. I will never forgive myself for the way we ended things between us, and I will never forgive myself for what I did in Florida. You deserve the world and more, and I fell extremely short of giving you that. I want to spend the rest of my life trying to make it up to you."

"No, you need to spend the rest of your life raising a child and making damn sure you're always going to be there when they need you. I can't be the most important person in your life anymore, Alder."

I know he knows that. But I wanted him to know that I know that as well. I'm not sure where we go from here. I'm not sure if we can go anywhere. But that's the last thing I should be worrying about right now. Ledger is out there somewhere, probably looking for me and wondering where I've taken this insane letter. All I can do is wait out this storm and go to the police first thing in the morning. Until then, I'm going to be a nervous wreck.

Chapter Thirty-Nine

I T'S TWO-THIRTY IN the morning, and I wake up to someone knocking on Alder's door. I went to sleep immediately last night, while Alder stayed up for a while and watched TV in the living room. I assumed he would sleep on the couch, but the knock on the door wasn't the only surprise I woke up to. Next to me, I feel Alder get out of bed, revealing his bare chest and gray sweatpants. All three dogs lift their heads in alert. I don't have a good feeling about this, and based on the look on Alder's face, he doesn't either. I can honestly say that I was relieved when I realized he had been sleeping by my side this whole time.

"Please don't answer it," I plead. "You don't know who or what is on the other side of that door."

"It'll be fine. No one besides Bennett knows you're here," he says before leaving the bedroom and closing the door behind him. I get out of bed and sit on the floor, leaning my ear up against the door. I can't make out much of what's being said, but I can tell who he's talking to.

"I don't know where she is, man," Alder says, "but this is the last place she'd be. She can't stand me right now. Out of all places, I thought she'd be with you." I can only hear what Alder is saying. "I'll let you know if I see or hear from her if you want."

When I hear Alder close the door, I sink with relief, knowing Ledger is leaving.

He's actively looking for me.

I quietly climb back into bed as Alder returns to the bedroom. After he closes the door, he does the same.

"What did he say?" I ask.

He takes a breath before answering. "He asked if I had seen you recently or knew where you might be. He looked behind me quite a bit, and I could tell he had seen the gun lying on the counter. His demeanor changed after that, and then he left."

"His demeanor changed how?"

"I don't know. He seemed genuinely worried about your whereabouts at first and then tensed up a little after spotting the gun. I don't know if I intimate him or..."

"Or what?"

"Or if he wants me to be next."

"Alder, don't say that," I say with tears burning my eyes.

He brings me closer to him and holds me in his arms. I will always be thankful for the way Alder makes me feel safe. Not only that, but he *keeps* me safe, too. He'd take a bullet for me, and that's more than what I would expect from any man who enters my life. He holds me the rest of the night, and I cling to him like there is no tomorrow. Because who knows if there will be. And if there is, who knows what tomorrow will bring. I know I'll be okay as long as I have Alder by my side.

A FEW HOURS later and after some restless sleep, I'm rushing to get ready so that I can head to the police station. Saying I'm nervous is a complete understatement. My busy brain gets interrupted by an incoming text from none other than Livvy. This is the last thing I need right now. I contemplate opening the message for a while. I could very easily delete it and pretend she never sent me anything. But my curiosity sparks, and before I know it, I'm starting to read her message.

Livvy: Hey...I know I'm the last person you want to talk to right now, but I want you to know how bad I feel. I feel terrible, Jae...I had no idea you and Alder were connected in any way. The outcome of what happened between us was something we definitely didn't plan or expect. I hope you know that I would never intentionally hurt you like that. And I know for a fact that Alder feels the same way. I can honestly say that I cherished the new friendship between you and me. My wish is that you find it in your heart to forgive us. I understand you might need some time, and I fully support that. I just wanted to send this message so you know that I still care about our friendship and respect what you and Alder have together, whatever that may look like. Take care of yourself, Jaemes...I hope we talk soon.

I notice her sincere bravery behind the message. It takes a lot of courage to step forward and express one's feelings, especially given the situation she found herself in. I don't respond right away because I know I shouldn't. I'll either regret the words I type or forgive too quickly. I'm already feeling like I'm starting to forgive Alder, knowing it's too soon for that.

"Your girlfriend just texted me," I tell Alder, who is standing at the kitchen counter with his laptop open. I'm unaware of what he's doing exactly, but it's not my place to know.

He looks up at me with just his eyes and glares. "Jaemes, she's not my girlfriend, nor has she ever been."

"Yeah, like that makes it any better," I mumble. "What are you up to over there?" I ask, unable to control my curiosity once again.

"I'm looking into these Horsemen."

"And?" I ask right before walking out the door.

"They're a motorcycle club called the Horizon Horsemen. They are most known for being successful hitmen who travel throughout the United States. They don't stay in one place for very long. They do what they get paid for and then flee."

"Unless they are in prison," I add.

Alder sighs. "I guess now we know what your dad is in prison for."

"He's not my dad. Call him by his name. I don't know who that guy is," I say sternly. "I need to take this information to the police. I'm not letting them get away with organizing Rian's murder." Paranoid, I check my purse for the hundredth time to ensure the letter is still inside.

"Let me drive you. You shouldn't be driving your car right now or be alone," Alder tells me, closing his laptop shut.

I let him come with me. I'm already nervous about being in my current situation. Bringing what I know to the police could put me in an even worse predicament. I feel more at ease being with Alder and knowing he's safe too.

As he pulls up to the door of the police station to drop me off, the bundle of nerves in my stomach increases substantially, and all I do is stare at the people and officers going in and out.

"Hey," Alder says to get my attention. "Everything will be okay. I'll be right here waiting for you when you're done. And when this is all over."

"Will you come in with me?" I ask him. Without saying a word, he moves his truck to a parking spot and grabs my hand as we walk toward the entrance.

Chapter Forty

"JAEMES, ARE YOU okay if we record this meeting?" a woman in a navy-blue pantsuit asks me as she enters the small conference room where I'm seated. I'm in here alone since Alder wasn't allowed to join me at this time. They plan to meet with him separately, as I got him involved in this mess. As much as I wish we could be here together, I also understand that this is protocol, and if I want my voice to be heard, I need to follow suit. This woman is tall and skinny and looks to be in her late forties. She has blond hair that reaches just below her shoulders and wears enough makeup to conceal her facial flaws, yet still presents herself professionally.

I nod to let her know that she has my permission to record our meeting. Seconds later, a man enters the room wearing black dress pants, a cream-colored button-up shirt, and a white tie. He appears to be in his mid-to-late thirties, bald, and has a darker skin tone. Both the man and woman have badges buckled onto their belts.

As the two of them sit across from me at the small rectangular table, the woman places a recording device in the center of it. After she turns it on, the red recording light blinks, and then she begins to speak. "Today's date is Saturday, May fourteenth, 2022. The time is currently eight thirty-three in the morning. Can you please state your full name before we begin?"

"Jaemes Dovaughn," I say with a shaky voice. Both the man and woman open their notepads.

"Ms. Dovaughn, my name is Detective Shawna Fox, and this is my partner, Detective Vince Nolan. Moments earlier, you permitted us to record this meeting. Please say 'yes' if it's true that you agreed to this."

"Yes," I state.

"Great. Can we get you anything to drink? Water? Coffee?" Detective Fox asks me.

I shake my head. "No thanks. I'm okay."

"We were told that you have some information regarding Rian Barlowe's death," Detective Nolan starts. "Can I ask what information you are referring to?"

I clear my throat. "I came across a letter from an inmate who resides in the Raiford Florida State Prison. It was addressed to someone I know."

"Ms. Dovaughn, you know that opening another person's mail is illegal, right?" Detective Nolan asks before I can continue.

"It was already ripped open and sitting on his coffee table in the living room. I let myself into his house because we were a couple," I clarify. They both continue to jot down their notes as the recorder continues to flash its taunting red light.

"When you found this letter, was it accompanied by others or just this one?" Detective Fox asks.

"I had seen others before, located in the drawer of his nightstand, but never looked at them. When I tried to relocate them, they seemed to have disappeared."

"What did the letter say when you read it?" Detective Fox asks, probing for more information.

"As far as I know, an inmate named Jason Kellen has been in contact with my ex-boyfriend. Jason mentioned he wanted information about me. I don't know how they know each other, but I know from this letter that Jason is close with Ledger's dad."

"And Ledger is the ex-boyfriend you are referring to?"

Detective Fox asks.

I nod, trying to come to terms with our new relationship status.

"Can you give us Ledger's last name?"

My stomach drops. Ledger went from someone whom I genuinely cared about to a probable suspect in my stepdad's death. It's something that I don't think will ever fully sink in for me. Of course, I still feel love for him, as all of this happened so fast and unexpectedly. Should I have given Ledger a chance to explain? A part of me feels guilty for going to the police before talking with him, but given what was in the letter, I wouldn't have felt safe or myself in the slightest.

"Yearwood," I gulp. More notes are being etched on their notepads.

"Do you know who Jason Kellen is? Or why he would want to seek information about you?" Detective Nolan asks.

"Jason is my biological dad. I don't know much about him. I have never met him, and my mom rarely talks about him. I have a few photos from when my mom was in a relationship with him before I was born, but that's it. The only information she ever gave me about Jason was that he vanished right after my mom told him that she was pregnant with me. The letter mentioned that he wanted to get to know his daughter, and Ledger was the way to go about it."

"What's your mom's name?" Detective Fox asks without looking up as she scribbles more words on her notepad.

"Khrystal Barlowe," I reply. "K-H-R-Y-S-T-A-L." They take a moment to finish what they are writing and observe what information they already have.

Detective Nolan starts to ask me another question without looking up from his notes. "Do you know if your mom, Khrystal, has had any recent contact with your biological dad, Jason?"

"I honestly don't know for certain, but I've always assumed

she hasn't since she hates talking about him so much," I say. "She told me she hadn't heard from him since the night he left her. She never knew where he ran off to and could never find him."

"What else did the letter say?" Detective Nolan asks me. "Anything pertaining to Rian Barlowe's death?"

"There were a few things mentioned. Jason hated that my mom was married to someone other than him. He said a few things about wanting him 'gone' and 'out of the picture.'" I pause a moment. My eyes blur with tears as I have to relive this over again. "There was something about mentioning the confirmation of Rian being 'history' and of his disappearance. It's obvious that they are talking about Rian."

Detective Fox hands me a few tissues. "Do you want to take a five-minute break?"

"No, I'm okay. I don't have much more information left," I tell her.

"Continue when you're ready," she says.

I wipe my eyes free of tears and clean up my nose. I gather the rest of my thoughts and take a few deep breaths. "There was something about *Horsemen*...Alder looked them up online and found out they are a motorcycle club called the Horizon Horsemen. Apparently, they are known for traveling the country as hired hitmen. I can't imagine they are friendly acquaintances."

Both detectives slowly look up at each other. Detective Fox points to a few of her notes, and Detective Nolan nods while breathing in a significant inhale and then exhaling.

I don't have a good feeling about this.

"Ms. Dovaughn, the Horizon Horsemen are, in fact, hired to kill. They are infamous hitmen and are very hard to catch due to their frequent running. Law enforcement agencies nationwide have tried various tactics and setups to catch these men in the act but have been unsuccessful every time. Their skills are unlike any other, making them very dangerous," Detective Nolan informs me. "Mr. Yearwood's dad was one of the Horsemen's top men before he passed back in the early 2000s. Did you know that piece of information?"

I shake my head no.

It's all coming together now. That's how Ledger and Jason know each other. We basically came from the same background and didn't even know it. But he sure did.

Detective Nolan clears his throat. "We need a verbal 'yes' or 'no,' Ms. Dovaughn."

"Oh, sorry. No, I didn't know that. All Ledger told me about his dad was that he died alongside his mom while on vacation. Now I'm starting to believe that isn't true."

"It is to an extent," Detective Nolan says, but doesn't elaborate any further on the subject. "Okay, so here is what we know thus far. You, Jaemes Dovaughn, found an already opened letter from the Raiford Florida State Prison at your boyfriend's place of residence, Ledger Yearwood—"

"*Ex*-boyfriend," I interrupt him.

Detective Nolan continues with the synopsis of what we already discussed. "You, Jaemes Dovaughn, were *formally* involved with Ledger Yearwood romantically when you found an already opened letter from the Raiford Florida State Prison, sitting on the coffee table in his living room." He stops to look at me to ensure he stated that correctly this time. I confirm that he is correct, and then he continues.

"When you read the letter, you saw that the sender from the Raiford Florida State Prison was an inmate by the name of Jason Kellen, your biological dad, whom you have never met before. Also written in this letter from Jason, you learned he is a member of the infamous motorcycle club, the Horizon Horsemen."

"Yes, that is correct," I tell him.

"Do you think there is a possibility that Ledger was hoping

you'd find this specific letter?" Detective Fox asks me.

"I don't think so. Honestly, I don't think he was ever going to tell me our relationship was all a ruse."

"And where is the letter currently?" Detective Fox asks.

"I have it with me," I tell them. I take the letter and set it in the middle of the table. They take the envelope and analyze what's said on it before placing it in a large Ziplock bag. After sealing the bag, Detective Nolan writes something on it with a black marker.

"We will look this over in the evidence room with forensics. There's a good possibility that we'll have enough information and proof to reopen Rian Barlowe's case. Is there anything else you want to mention before we send you on your way?" Detective Fox asks me.

"No, that's all I know."

"We will give you our cards in case you think of anything else. In the meantime, I think it would be in your best interest to lie low until we get everything sorted out. We will be sure to update you as we move along," Detective Nolan adds.

I receive both of their cards, which includes their contact information. They remain seated as they look over their notes one last time. Just as Detective Nolan reaches for the recorder to turn it off, Detective Fox stops him. "Wait. You briefly mentioned someone named Alder. Is that the man who is here with you?"

"Yes, that's correct."

"Who is he to you? Friend? Relative?" she asks for more clarification.

To my surprise, I no longer have to think hard about that question. It's obvious, isn't it? I confidently let the words slip right out of my mouth. And once they are wholly said, it feels... *right.*

"My fiancé."

Chapter Forty-One

WE PULLED MY car out from Alder's shed, and he followed me to my house. He still refuses to leave me by myself, but I don't mind Alder's company. In fact, I love it. I keep thinking back to what I told the detectives at the end of our interview. At some point, I have to tell Alder what I said. I'm not sure how he will react to me saying something like that, and I'd be lying if I said I wasn't nervous about his response. We've been through the highest of highs and the lowest of lows together. Everything about our relationship has been unpredictable. We even surprise ourselves by the things we do and the words we speak to each other.

We are sitting on my porch swing outside my front door. It's abnormally warm for this time of year. Low sixties, no wind, and a clear sky to show off a beautiful blanket of stars. All we need is warm clothes and the soft quilt my Grandma Jeanie bought me just after I was born. She told me she isn't like the typical grandmas who knit their own quilts. She doesn't have the talent or the time. So, she claims, anyway.

"What are you thinking about?" Alder asks me.

Neither one of us said much after leaving the police station. I'm sure he's trying to give me my space while constantly feeling the urge to be in my presence.

"How God can create something so outrageous and stunning, like the stars and the moon, and yet, he can still create something as little as me and you. Just two normal people walking around on this giant planet. It baffles me."

I can feel him watching me as I gaze at the night sky. His right hand drifts toward me and doesn't hesitate to grip the top of my left hand firmly. "You know," he starts, "if you're going to tell people I'm your fiancé, you really should be wearing a ring."

My eyes widen while my gaze falls from the sky, and a lump in my throat forms. I slowly turn my head to look at him, and a slight smirk appears on his lips. His thumb starts to graze the top of my ring finger gently. My face heats up as I begin to blush.

"I don't know what you're talking about," I lie.

"When I went in to talk to the detectives, they mentioned something along the lines of, 'Your fiancé seems to be going through a lot.' When I asked them what they were talking about, they told me you had said your relationship to me was '*My fiancé.*'"

Uh, oh...

His smirk grows into a grin, and I have to look away. "I'm really sorry. I don't know what I was thinking. When you showed me the ring you bought, I couldn't stop thinking about it. I didn't want to accept that you had changed your mind about marriage. I mostly wanted to think that this was all just a petty act. We don't always get what we want, but I certainly know I want you. Regardless of a ring or marriage or...kids."

"Jaemes, I just want you to be happy. Don't change for me."

"I never changed my happiness. My happiness left along with you. It always does when we go our separate ways," I say in almost a whisper. "Alder, I never loved him the way I love you. And he could never love me the way you love me. I deserve someone who will unconditionally love me through all the difficult situations life throws at us. You are my person."

He lets go of my hand and leans in to finally do what I've wanted him to do for a very long time now. I've missed the way he kisses me. And I can tell by this kiss he feels the same way. When he separates himself from me, I lean into him and rest against him. He wraps his arm around me, and we slightly sway in the porch swing while watching the stars appear and occasionally shoot across the sky.

"I want you to take this," he says while digging in his pocket, "and accept it, only if you want to." He takes out the same engagement ring he had recently shown me.

"And what changed your mind about getting married?" I ask him.

"Nothing. I still dislike the idea of ever getting married," he says. "But I'm willing to do it if it means I get to make you happy. Baby steps."

We slowly lean into each other, and just before our lips can meet again, we are stopped by bright headlights approaching my driveway. The red truck becomes more apparent and recognizable as it eventually comes to a stop in front of us.

Shit.

"Alder, what do I do?" I ask nervously.

Before he has time to answer me, Ledger hops out of the driver's side and approaches us on the porch.

"Jaemes, you can't be serious…I've been looking everywhere for you. Don't you think I deserve to know that you're okay at least? You should have given me the chance to explain things. But instead, you gravitated to him? Why, Jaemes? This makes no sense," Ledger expresses.

"I think it was blatantly obvious when she saw that letter, asshole. Which you, by the way, hid very well, I must add," Alder tells him sarcastically.

Ledger glares at Alder. "I'm pretty sure I was talking to her. Not you."

Alder jolts up from the porch swing and gets inches from Ledger's face. "No, but *I'm* talking to *you*. Does it look like she wants to fucking talk to you? I don't think so. So, why don't you get back into your truck and get the fuck out of here?"

I can tell Alder has been building up anger ever since I told him I was with Ledger, and with everything that has led up to where we are now, he's about to unleash.

Ledger takes both of his hands and shoves Alder away by his chest. Alder turns away from him and lets out a frustrated chuckle before punching in Ledger's direction. As Alder's fist meets Ledger's face, I gasp.

"I said, get the fuck out of here!" Alder shouts at him.

Ledger gathers his bearings and readjusts his jaw. "Look, I just need to talk to Jaemes—"

"Fuck that. You don't need to say shit to her," Alder barks back.

Ledger holds up both hands, letting Alder know he surrenders. He looks my way, and my stomach turns. My hands cover my mouth, and most of my body hides under the blanket.

"Looks like the man that broke your heart finally came to his senses," Ledger says, gesturing at the ring on my finger. My eyes widen again as I slowly look down at the sparkling rock.

The only feelings I have at this moment are fear and anger. I look over at Alder, who keeps his eyes rigid on Ledger. Eventually, Alder's eyes meet mine, allowing me to answer for myself.

"There is nothing to explain, Ledger. I need you to leave and stay out of my life," I tell him with tears slowly welling in my eyes. Ledger starts to walk closer to me to continue his begging and pleading for a chance to explain. However, Alder doesn't let him get too far. He takes him by the back of his sweatshirt and drags him to his truck. Alder throws him to the ground near the driver's side door.

"You heard her. Now, get lost before I have to reiterate what she just told you. And if I find out that you try getting near her again, I won't be so pleasant." Alder flashes what appears to be a gun toward Ledger.

Before I fully comprehend everything happening, Ledger jumps back into his truck and speeds down the road. He vanishes in a cloud of dust, leaving a trail of his tire tracks in the gravel behind him. Alder stays in the driveway and doesn't move. I walk toward him, and I can still feel his anger radiating throughout his body. He continues to watch Ledger drive off until he is no longer visible. He grabs me and holds me tight against him. His touch is warm, and his heart is beating like crazy. It's all a reminder of how intense his feelings truly are for me.

Chapter Forty-Two

M Y MOM IS finally home from all of her work excursions, and I anxiously make my way to her house to talk to her about everything I have discovered. I could never tell her something like this over the phone or FaceTime. I have been spending every minute of my free time with Alder. We've been going back and forth, staying at each other's houses. The idea of me being alone still makes him nervous. He keeps telling me that he would never forgive himself if something were to happen to me.

Alder is giving me a ride to my mom's house. He said he would stay in the truck so I could have space and privacy with my mom. However, he wouldn't be far away if I needed him. We are just down the road when Alder gets a text message notification on his phone.

"Can you see who that is for me?" he asks.

I pick up his phone and examine the notification. "It's Bennett."

"What does he want?"

"He wants to know what you are doing this weekend for Memorial Day," I tell him. "Want me to say anything back?"

Alder shakes his head no. "He can wait. I'm busy." He takes my hand and holds on to it, letting me know that his time is all mine.

When I close out of his text messages, I'm left with his home screen. I can't make out his background, so I move the screen pages until it's free of apps. I'm taken aback when I notice it's the picture he snapped of me near the neon-colored flowers at his parents' ski resort last Fourth of July.

"Since when has this been set as your background?" I ask while showing him what I am referring to.

He looks at his phone and smirks. "Since July fifth."

"You've had this as the background of your phone for almost a year? And months after we broke up?"

He nods. "Yeah, I guess you just meant a lot to me, and it never occurred to me that I should change it after we broke up. Now that I think about it, I don't think I ever really wanted to change it."

I stare at the photo a little longer. I looked so happy. Back when Alder and I had our first kiss. Everything between us was new, and our feelings were robust. All before Ledger was even considered an option. Alder *was* my everything. And he is proving to me all over again that he still is.

He squeezes my hand and rubs his thumb across mine. He then brings my hand to his lips and plants a gentle kiss on the back of it. Butterflies start to swarm in my stomach, sending chills down my arms. It reminds me that the initial feelings I had are still steady within my heart.

There's an unfamiliar vehicle in the driveway when we approach my mom's house. I look at Alder because I'm not sure this is the right time to talk to her about any of this with company present. Alder gestures toward the door with a slight head tilt. "Go ahead. Everything will be fine. I'll be right here if you need me."

I squeeze his hand back and then let go of it. My mom's front door opens as my fingertips graze his truck's door handle, and two people step outside. My mom remains in the doorway as they walk down the sidewalk to their car.

Oh, fuck.

Unlike the vehicle, these two people look very familiar to Alder and me. The tall, blond-haired woman and the bald, dark-skinned man casually get into their car as if they don't realize Alder and I are parked on the side of the road. I wait until the two detectives are out of sight before reaching for the door handle again. My mom is still standing in the doorway. She waits for me to approach her before saying anything.

I'm about three yards away before I stop in front of her. We stand the same, our arms crossed, waiting for one another to speak. I can't tell if she is upset with me or with herself. What I *can* tell is that she knows she screwed up. She knows she lied to me. Now, I need to understand why.

"Mom…" I start. Her expression doesn't flinch. She can't be mad at me. All I was doing was living my life when everything started crumbling before my eyes. If only she had told me the truth beforehand, none of this would have reached the police. At least, I don't think it would have. It depends on what she knows now and what she knew before her conversation with Fox and Nolan.

She sighs heavily and then steps aside so I can enter the house. I slowly do so, but I'm unable to make myself comfortable. I find myself pacing in the living room.

"You need to start talking. I don't know what the hell is going on, Jaemes."

Her comment stops me dead in my tracks. "Excuse me?" I ask with fury. "You tell *me!*"

"What are you talking about?" she snaps back. Her face is red due to either anger or embarrassment. She never wanted me to know any of her truths, and now that they are all out in the open, she is flustered and doesn't know whether to keep playing an act or give up and lay everything out on the table.

"Please don't play this game with me anymore. I am not a child. Treat me like an adult already," I beg of her. She lets out another vast sigh. "If you knew what I knew, Mom, you wouldn't blame me for going to the police. The lack of knowledge you gave me about my past got us into this situation. It's time you told me everything. Otherwise, I don't know if I can ever trust you again." And for the first time, my mom looks defeated. "Are you also affiliated with the Horizon Horsemen? Have you been in contact with my dad? I need all my questions answered *now,* and this time, I need pure honesty."

"Fine. You're right," she surrenders. "You deserve to know the truth." She takes a deep breath before explaining. "Your dad and I met when he was fifteen and I was fourteen. He was a friend of a friend, and eventually, we became regular acquaintances. When he was seventeen, he was invited to be a prospect in the Horizon Horsemen Motorcycle Club in California. We ran off together and started a serious relation-ship. Right before I found out I was pregnant with you, he was officially patched in as a Horseman. That meant I became property of the Horizon Horsemen as his 'old lady.' At this time, I was pretty familiar with the club president, Jack Yearwood. Jack and his old lady, Nova, had a little boy.

"Ledger," I say out loud to her so that she knows I'm following.

"A few years went by, and your dad started treating me terribly. I'll spare you the details on that. I'd rather not talk about that part anyway. I knew I had to get out of the relationship and my affiliation with the club. It was dangerous, to say the least. When I found out I was pregnant with Jason's baby…I ran. In the middle of the night, I moved back to Las Vegas and restarted my life as a single mom."

"Where did his note come from then? The 'I'm sorry' note?" I ask her.

"He sent his favorite bandana to my parents' house with that note attached. I'm sure he knew what I was doing and hoped I'd get what he sent. I knew we'd be okay there. The Horsemen travel together, and only if they need to. They would never waste their time or risk exposing themselves trying to find a member's old lady. Las Vegas is a big city, and we would be harder to find. Ledger grew up in the Horizon Horsemen Motorcycle Club. Everyone became very close to that little boy. His parents, Jack and Nova, were killed in a bike crash while trying to run from police after causing some trouble in Arizona somewhere. After that, no one felt able to take care of him full-time, so they left him with his grandparents."

"What about his siblings?" I ask.

"As far as I know, he doesn't have any siblings." I let out a chuckle after more lies surface. "We wrote letters back and forth for a while. I was still madly in love with him and leaving that love in California was tough. Let alone the father of my child. When we moved back to Los Angeles when you were a young child, I found myself chasing that love all over again, but I made sure to be very careful. However, before I could even think about bringing you into a life that I initially tried so hard to keep you out of, Rian came into our lives and changed everything for the better. When we moved to Montana, I never looked back and never wrote your dad a single letter after that. I only told him your name and birthday after you were born. That's most likely why he asked Ledger for more information about you after he was sentenced to prison. He couldn't find out for himself, and he knew damn well I wasn't going to reveal anything else about you. Ledger, I guess, was willing to do it."

"I can't believe you lied to me about all of this. You had every chance to tell me when you gave me that scrapbook," I tell her.

"I went back and forth in my mind constantly. I ultimately wanted you to feel like you didn't come from such an intense background. I also tried to keep you safe. The story I told you seemed like a wise decision at the time. I'm sorry for leaving you in the dark about it all. I had no idea Ledger and Jason were still communicating.

"Until you found out about the letter I came across?" I ask.

She nods, and tears start to fall down her cheeks. "When those two detectives knocked on my door and started talking to me about Rian…" she trails off.

"Mom, I'm sorry I didn't tell you right away. It didn't feel right to talk about this over the phone. You've been gone so much for work, and this was the first time I've been able to *see* you."

"I know. I understand."

"Do you think it was the Horizon Horsemen who killed Rian?" I ask quietly.

"I wouldn't put it past them," she admits. "I knew *something* might happen since I left Jason twice. I was hoping that moving to Montana would be safe enough. He turned into a very possessive man. He couldn't have me, and I wouldn't let him have you either. So, I'm sure when he found out I moved on with another man, it sent him over the edge. All of the members of the Horizon Horsemen would do anything for each other. Their brotherhood bond is strong, and they would kill for any one of their men."

"Does this mean Ledger is a member of the Horizon Horsemen?" I ask her.

She shrugs her shoulders and wipes her tears. "I mean, maybe? The letter stated that he had to do this to be in good standing with the Horsemen. He could be prospecting. They have to do everything they're asked before getting patched in. It shows their loyalty," she explains.

"So, the detectives showed you the letter?"

She nods her head. "The police are the last people anyone should go to with Horsemen information. They will seek you out and kill you, Jaemes."

"I had no idea about any of this, Mom. You can't blame me for feeling unsafe with the little knowledge you gave me."

"I get it, Jaemes!" she cries. "I didn't know how to protect you and include you at the same time. You can't blame me for that either."

We sit silent for a minute as my life reveals its true story. My past was nothing I've always thought it was, and my mom did a spectacular job keeping it from me. However, it ended up blowing up in her face anyway.

"Now what? Where do we go from here?" I ask.

"At this point, as long as we don't showcase that we are helping out the police, we should be safe. If we get involved with the Horsemen, there's no saying what will happen in the end. Until this is all over, please lay low. I will try my hardest to get us out of this mess."

"Okay," I tell her as I stand up to walk for the door.

"Oh, my God, Jaemes Dovaughn…" My mom stops me as I walk by her. She grabs my hand. "*Please* don't tell me this is from Ledger." She looks concerned when I look into her red eyes. I feel the worry and sense of unease when she touches the ring on my finger with a trembling hand.

"Of course, it's not, Mom. I would never give my life to a Horseman." I walk out of the front door, and as soon as I hit the lawn, I collapse. I can't catch my breath, and my chest is heavy. My mom lied to me my entire life about the past. I don't know who Ledger truly is, and it's apparent that the Horizon Horsemen murdered Rian. It's all becoming clear, but I feel so cloudy inside. At least Alder could tell me to my face what he did. He was brave enough to say that he fucked up. Ledger had the chance to do so, but what he did behind my back was too personal to forgive, and I won't give him the satisfaction of explaining himself. I have no need or want to hear him out. He can take his excuses and reasonings to the grave.

Chapter Forty-Three

I'VE BEEN OFF work for the summer for a couple of weeks now, and things have been pretty quiet. Alder and I have spent every day of the summer together so far. We don't leave his house unless he has to for work. We've been making up for lost time by never leaving each other's side. It's like quarantining our relationship and trying to heal the big dent that was created. I'm still not over the fact that I won't be the mother of Alder's child. I'd be lying if I said that it didn't kill me, knowing he did what he did. I'm holding on to the slight chance he might change his mind about wanting a small family with me in the future. After all, he did end up changing his mind about getting married.

I only hope we don't have to go through any hardships to get there like we did before he gave me a ring. But does any of that matter? Ultimately, our love for each other is vibrant, and *that's* what truly matters.

For my birthday, Alder mentioned something about having a surprise for me. I laugh at that because he knows how I feel about surprises. He came home from work about an hour ago and has just finished showering.

"You ready to go soon?" he asks me.

"Go where?"

"To see your surprise," he clarifies.

"How far away is it?" I whine.

"*Really* fucking far away," he says in a sarcastic tone and a sexy smirk on his face. It's one of my favorite flirty looks of his.

"I'm not going, and you can't make me," I say flirtatiously back to him.

"Don't be a little bitch," he laughs while grabbing me by the waist and pulling me down on top of him on the couch in the living room.

"I love you," I whisper to him.

"I love you too. Forever remember that," he whispers back, followed by a long, sensual kiss.

We are stopped by the sound of knocking on the door. "Who's that?" I ask.

"Your surprise," he says against my lips.

"Ugh, does that mean we have to stop?" I whine again.

"It absolutely does. I don't need everyone looking at my pants, Jaemes."

"Everyone?" I ask, confused.

Alder guides me to the door and opens it for me. The evening sky is dimming into a purple shade as the bright sun starts to hide behind the mountains. Stars are visibly twinkling around the fluffy clouds. The trees sway lightly in the breeze, and a giant fire is lit. Surrounding the fire pit is a crowd of people quietly chatting among themselves.

"What's going on, Alder?" I ask.

"We first met during my housewarming party. Little did I know that would be the best day of my life, as it led to forever with you. I'm recreating that night for your birthday. And I also want to ask if you'll accept this as an invitation to move in with me officially?" He takes out the spare key that used to be mine. The key to the log house he just finished renovating a year ago. "Maybe we can make this *our* housewarming party this time?"

I take the key from him and jump into his arms. I'm tightly wrapped around him when I say, "Of course I will," against his ear. "I will always choose you. Forever remember that."

Epilogue

ALDER AND I arrived in Tampa, Florida, a few hours ago. This trip has to be one of the strangest ones we've ever been on. We are meeting his daughter for the first time. Lucy was born a few months ago, and she looks just like Livvy. It's weird seeing Alder with a child. Parenthood doesn't come naturally to him. It also feels odd being in the same room as your fiancé's daughter's mother, who was once a great friend. But we are all civil, and that's the most important thing. Alder's daughter is number one in all of our hearts.

Livvy had made it very clear that she wanted both Alder and me to be a close part of Lucy's life. We agreed to visit her in Florida once a year, and Livvy would bring her to Montana once a year. I'm very proud that Alder will be a part of his daughter's life. It's a small part, but it's a start. Seeing her a couple of times a year will help fill that parenting void for me, and Alder can resume his everyday life, as he always wanted it to be in the first place.

Alder and I are still happily engaged. Alder is maneuvering through being a first-time dad, and I'm okay with waiting for a few years. Who knows, maybe Lucy will be old enough to walk down the aisle as our flower girl at some point.

Detective Fox and Detective Nolan did their jobs and kept us informed on the outcome of Rian's death. It took months until Ledger was eventually convicted of assisting with Rian's murder. He was ultimately charged with accessory to murder and has joined a similar prison as Jason. Shortly after Ledger was sentenced, I coincidentally ran into Gretchen and Archie at a local farmers' market. I'd never met her before, so I didn't know how this interaction would pan out, but I couldn't ignore Archie's excitement when he spotted me. I learned quickly that Gretchen is a lovely woman. She has a great head on her shoulders, and we had a substantial conversation over coffee that morning while Archie played on a nearby playground with other kids.

Gretchen had known about Ledger and his affiliation with the Horizon Horsemen. They ended their relationship because of Ledger's involvement with the motorcycle club. Gretchen told me that she agreed to a fifty-fifty custody arrangement, as long as Archie stayed away from the Horizon Horsemen and never knew anything about the club. As long as that remained true, Ledger could be with Archie half the time. Unfortunately, Ledger broke that promise once he was convicted.

As for me, I'm currently working on obtaining my master's degree in marriage and family therapy. I feel motivated and determined to succeed in this field of work. I can draw on the hardships Alder and I went through, being on opposite sides of marriage and children, and apply that to other couples and families facing similar challenges. We can relate to this and know that no one is alone. It's a chance to remind people that many others face the same bumps in the road. It doesn't have to be an end-all, be-all. For couples, it's an opportunity to learn from each other and grow together, rather than apart. We all need to be reminded of that occasionally, and that's okay.

It will *all* be okay. Because, in the end, love will always win.

THE END

Acknowledgments

When I sat down to write *this* part of my first book, I was overwhelmed by the support and encouragement I received. I don't know where to begin with my acknowledgments. A lot goes into writing a novel; although it's a fun process, it's also hard work.

My first thank you goes out to my husband, Cole. You helped boost my confidence and cheered me on from the sidelines. Your daily encouragement made this dream of mine come true. I'm so grateful to have you by my side daily. Thank you for being my rock! And to my daughter for being my lovely assistant, especially over summer break. When my fingers became tired, you were more than happy to help with the typing! Thank you for being my number-one fan, little lady!

Thank you to my coworker, Stacy (or should I say Sassy Stacy…), not only for being the best coworker any nurse could ask for, but also for constantly letting me bounce ideas off you. Your assistance helped me improve my work when times were tough. I appreciate your honest opinions and being among the first to read my work!

I want to thank everyone who read my book in manuscript form and gave me their *honest* feedback: my mom (who also printed my manuscripts many times for me!), my mother-in-law, and my sister-in-law. Thank you from the bottom of my heart. You guys rock!

I also want to thank my best friend, Savannah, for being

my biggest cheerleader. Thank you for allowing me to share my excitement with you and for providing further inspiration. Your support does not go unnoticed. I appreciate you for always being there for me!

Thank you to INK Book Designs on Etsy.com for creating my original book cover. You made my vision come to life, and I couldn't be happier with how it turned out. A huge thank you to Evgeniya G on Reedsy.com for perfecting my book cover and adding the final details. You exceeded my expectations, and I cannot wait to collaborate again. Without the perfect cover, there is no story. Thank you for going above and beyond for mine!

Another big thank-you goes to Images 4 Life Photography and Silver Lining Marketing for all my author photos. They turned out amazing, and I'm excited to showcase them. Thank you for capturing my genuine self and encouraging me to follow my dreams! Silver Lining Marketing was and still is a huge part of my writing journey. I was provided with amazing social media posts to help with my hard launch. I can't wait to collaborate with SLM again for my next book!

Thank you to all the middle school students who checked to see how my book was coming along. You know who you are! Your daily support in the health office motivated me to keep going. I loved the excitement you all brought every time I saw you.

Thank you to all my ARC readers who read my book early and gave me permission to put their reviews on my website. Because of you, my website was able to grow! I appreciate you taking the time to read my finished masterpiece and for giving me honest feedback on the story.

Last but certainly not least, THANK YOU to my Reedsy team! My editor, Jennifer Rees, provided amazing developmental edits and proofreading services for my debut novel. I have learned so much from you, and collaborating with you was the most spectacular experience! Thank you to Ben Galley for the much-needed support with self-publishing. You've taught me how to market and advertise my book and my journey. Evgeniya G. saved my book cover! When I needed someone to edit my existing cover, she was more than ready to save the day and make the final version readers see today. Also, a big shout-out to Alyssa Matesic for guiding me through edits on my query letter, synopsis, and literary agent list. You were more than happy to answer any of my questions and provide amazing suggestions.

The amount of encouragement, support, and motivation that poured out from everyone who knew I was writing a book was nothing I ever expected. No matter what happens with my novels, I know I have already succeeded with my family and friends. Thank you for taking the time to read my writing. It means the world to me!

And thank YOU for taking the time to read my book, which is so special to me. I couldn't thank you enough!

About the Author

Holly Jo is a contemporary romance novelist inspired by real-life relationships and the emotional complexities of everyday life. Drawing from her experiences and observations, she writes stories that highlight the power of human connection, love, and resilience.

She made her debut with *The Log House on the Right*, fulfilling a long-held dream she began pursuing in February 2024. Before turning to writing, Holly Jo worked as a school nurse in her hometown in southern Minnesota.

When she isn't writing, Holly Jo loves to travel with her husband and daughter, often finding moments of inspiration in unexpected places. Whether she's on the road or at home with their two dogs, she's always dreaming up her next story about the beauty and strength of love.

More books coming soon!
Let's stay connected.

Website: www.hollyjoradtke.com
Facebook: Holly Jo – Author
Instagram: @hollyjoauthor
X (Twitter): @hollyjoauthor
TikTok: @hollyjoauthor
Snapchat: hollyjo-author